BY THE GODS BELOVED

BY THE GODS BELOVED

By BARONESS ORCZY

WHITE LION PUBLISHERS LIMITED
London, Sydney and Toronto

First published in Great Britain
by Hodder and Stoughton Ltd.

White Lion edition 1977

ISBN 0 7274 0271 4

Made and printed in Great Britain
for White Lion Publishers Limited,
138 Park Lane, London W1Y 3DD
by Hendington Limited,
Lion House, North Town, Aldershot, Hampshire

CONTENTS

PART I

THE DESERT

PART II

MEN-NE-FER

PART IV

TANIS

PART I
THE DESERT

CHAPTER I

TANKERVILLE'S HOBBY

It is a curious fact that, although Hugh Tankerville was destined to play such an all-absorbing part in the strange and mystic drama which filled both our lives, I have no distinct recollection of my first meeting with him.

We were at St. Paul's School together, and I, a boisterous schoolboy of the usual pattern, have but a vague memory of the silent, dark-eyed lad, who hated football, and was generally voted to be a " bookworm," called " Sawnie Girlie," and was, without exception, the most unpopular boy in the school.

The masters must have thought a great deal of him, for, in recreation time, we often saw him go to one of their rooms and emerge thence, when the bell rang, in close conversation with old Foster, or Crabtree, the Greek or History master. This, together with the fact that he carried off every prize and scholarship with utmost ease, did not tend to make him more popular. I, for one, who was captain of our football team and the champion boxer of the school, held the taciturn bookworm in withering contempt, until one day—and this is my first distinct recollection of him—he and I had . . . well! a few words;—I forget what about. I think that I wanted him to join in a tug-of-war and he wouldn't; anyway, I indulged in the words—grand, sound, British schoolboy vocabulary it was, too—and he indulged in contemptuous silence for fully five minutes, while the floods of my eloquence were poured over his dark, unresisting head. Yes, contemptuous, if you please, towards *me!* the captain of the football team, the champion boxer of the school. I could hear that ass, Snipey, and Bathroom Slippers sniggering behind me like a pair of apes; and contempt in the front, derision in the rear, soon became more than schoolboy nature could bear.

Well, I don't know exactly how it happened. Did my language wax more forcibly eloquent still, or did my champion fist actually come in aid to my words? I cannot say; certain it is that there was a shout, a draught that sent my cap flying to the other end of the schoolroom, a whirlwind which caught both sides of my head at once, and Sawnie Girlie was all over me in a minute. Where I was during that minute I would not venture to state definitely. I was vaguely conscious of a pair of dark eyes blazing down at me like the hall gas, and of a husky voice hissing at intervals, "How dare you? how dare you?" whilst I, blinded, breathless, bruised and sore, contrived to wonder how, indeed, I had dared.

When the whirlwind had at last subsided, I found myself in an unaccustomed position on the floor, underneath one of the forms; those blithering cowards, Snipey and Bathroom Slippers, were disappearing through the door, and Sawnie Girlie was quietly knocking the dust off his nether garments.

Well! after that interesting downfall of the champion boxer of St. Paul's, nobody who knows anything of schoolboy nature will wonder that Sawnie Girlie and I became the closest of chums, and that, with that well-deserved licking, Hugh Tankerville laid the foundations of that friendship and admiration which has lasted throughout my life.

Silent and taciturn he remained towards the others, but from the moment that I—having struggled to my feet, after my ignominious downfall—went up to him and offered him my hand, in token of my admiration for his prowess, he and I were practically inseparable.

Gradually the strange influence, which savoured of the mystical, and which he seemed to exercise over all those with whom he came in contact, asserted itself over me, and I began to find pleasure in other things besides football and boxing. It was he who kindled in me a spark of that enthusiasm for the great past which was so overwhelming in him, and after a few months of our friendship I had one or two fairly stiff tussles with him for a top place in Classics or History. I will do myself the justice to say that never once did I succeed in getting that top place, but it certainly was not for want of trying.

Never shall I forget the memorable day when Sawnie

Girlie—for so I still continued to call him—asked me to go home with him to afternoon tea one Saturday.

He lived in Hammersmith, he told me, and I, whose parents lived in Kensington, vaguely wondered what sort of mud-hut or hovel could be situated in such an out-of-the-way suburb as Hammersmith. I had never been down King Street, and as we two boys picked our way through the barrows on the edge of the kerb, and among the dense, not altogether sober crowd, I marvelled more and more how any civilised being could live in this extraordinary neighbourhood, when suddenly, having left King Street behind us, Sawnie Girlie stopped before a large, old-fashioned iron gate, behind which tall chestnuts and oak trees threw a delightfully mysterious shadow on the ground.

"Here we are!" he said, as he pushed open the gate, and I followed, astonished at this quaint bit of old-world garden in the midst of the turmoil and tawdriness of suburban London. Beyond those gates everything seemed cool, peaceful, silent; only a few birds twittered in the great trees. The ground was covered with the first fallen leaves of autumn, and they made a curious, sweet-sounding "Hush-sh-sh" as we walked. Obviously the place had been, from a strictly landscape-gardening point of view, sadly neglected, but I did not notice this. I only saw the great, tall trees, smelt the delicious aroma of the damp, fallen leaves, and stopped a moment, anxious and awed, expecting to see down the cool alley some cavalier with plume and sword walking arm-in-arm with his lady, in great hooped skirt and farthingale.

Hugh Tankerville had taken no notice of me. He walked on ahead towards the house, which must have lain far back from the road, for it was not discernible from the gates. The scene was, of course, familiar to him, and he knew that no plumes or farthingales were left anywhere about, but from the moment that he had pushed those great gates open his whole being seemed to have changed. He walked more erect, he threw back his head, opened wide his nostrils and seemed, as it were, to breathe freedom in at every pore.

I was but a mere raw school lad at the time, and no doubt my impression of the old-fashioned house and garden was exaggerated in my mind, through its very unexpectedness after the picture of sordid Saturday afternoon Hammersmith. The house itself was as picturesque as the garden, with a quaint terrace and stone stairs leading up to a glass door. Sawnie Girlie led me through this and across a hall, and presently I found myself in the most wonderful spot which up to that moment it had been my happy lot to see.

The room into which I followed Hugh Tankerville was low and square, with a great bow window that looked out on to another bit of tangled, old-fashioned garden; but to my delighted fancy it was crammed with everything that could fill a boy's soul with delight.

There were great cases filled with all sorts of strange arms and shields, spears with flint heads, axes and quivers of arrows; there were great slabs of stone, covered with curious writing and adorned with weird and wonderful images; there were strange little figures of men and women in funny garbs, some with heads of beasts on their shoulders, others with human heads on fantastic bodies; but what seemed to me more strange than all, and made me stop awestruck at the door, was that the whole length of two walls there stood a row of mummies, such as I had once seen in the British Museum, some in their coffins, but others showing their human shape distinctly through the linen bandages—dark and discoloured with age—that covered them.

Hugh's voice roused me from my stupor. " Father, this is Mark," he said, and at the further end of the room, from behind a huge desk, littered with ponderous books and pyramids of papers, there emerged a head which I, in my excited imagination, fancied to be one of those mummies come temporarily to life. It was yellow and wrinkled all over, and a reading-lamp which, in spite of the daylight, stood burning on the table, threw a weird blue light on the thin, sharp features. The eyes, however, bright and small, looked across very kindly at us both and a voice said—

" Well ! you two boys had better go and get your tea, and after that you may come up and Mark shall see the museum."

I was delighted; I had no idea that this was the treat my newly-found friend had prepared for me. Even with me he had been strangely reserved about his home and about his father. I knew nothing of either.

We had a delicious tea, and were waited on by a dear old thing, who evidently was more a friend than a servant, for she hugged and kissed Hugh as if he were her greatest treasure; and though she did not kiss me, she shook hands and said how anxious she had been to see me, having heard so much about me from "the young master." I blushed and wondered if Sawnie Girlie had also told of that memorable whirlwind episode, and did not enjoy my first slice of Sally Lunn in consequence.

But it was a glorious tea, and I, no doubt, in true schoolboy fashion, would have contrived to stow most of the delicious cakes and muffins away had I had time to do so; but I remembered that after tea we were to go up and see the museum, so after my third cup and seventh slice of cake I stopped.

Oh, the delights of that museum! A real museum all to yourself, where there is no horrid attendant behind you to tell you not to touch, but where every piece is actually put into your hands and you are allowed to turn it over, and look at every one of its sides, just as you please. I shall never forget the feeling of delicious horror that crept over me when first I absolutely touched one of the mummies with my hand. Mr. Tankerville was more than kind. He answered every one of my schoolboy questions with cheerful patience, explained everything, showed everything. It was—I think I may safely say—the happiest day of my life.

From that eventful afternoon I became—for as long as we were schoolfellows together—a constant visitor at The Chestnuts. Mr. Tankerville, who was one of the greatest archæologists and Egyptologists of his generation, took a keen delight in initiating us boys into the half-veiled mysteries of ancient Egyptian history. We were never tired of hearing about Ra and Horus, about the building of the great Pyramids, about the tombs and the wonders of Thebes and Memphis. But above all did he delight our ears with tales of that mysterious period which immediately followed the death of Queen Neitakrit and the close of the Sixth Dynasty. This, so far as the scientific world is concerned, also marks the close of the old Empire. Strangers appear to have over-run the country, and for over 400 years the history of ancient Egypt is a blank; neither tombs nor temples mark the changes and vicissitudes which befel that wonderful nation, only a few royal names appear on scarabs, or tablets, but of the great people themselves, and of their ancient civilisation, the people who built the great Pyramids and carved the immortal Sphinx, of them there is not a trace.

When once more the veil is lifted from Egyptian history the whole aspect of the land is changed; we see a new Empire, and it is a new people that dwells along the banks of the sacred Nile.

What had happened to the old? This blank page in Egyptian history Mr. Tankerville had reconstructed on a theory all his own, and his fancy had filled it with warriors and conquests, with downfalls and regeneration. Open-eyed, open-mouthed, we listened to him for hours, while, sitting round the huge, old-fashioned grate, with the light of the great log fire illumining his shrivelled features, he told us of Neit-akrit and of the strangers who overran the land, and of the great Egyptian people, the old, original builders of the most ancient monuments, they who disappeared, no one knew whither, to make way for the new Empire, with its new art, its new architecture, its new religion.

This point in history was his hobby, and I learnt long afterwards with what derision the scientific world looked upon it; but we boys listened to these tales as if to the words of a prophet preaching the Gospel. Hugh's eyes would then begin to glow, his hands would be tightly clenched, he would hang on every word his father uttered; and I too listened, awed and amazed, while before my eyes Cheops and Khefren and the mysterious Neit-akrit wandered in gorgeous and ghost-like procession.

Then, as we both grew older, gradually Mr. Tankerville extended our knowledge of that most ancient of all histories. His erudition was perfectly amazing, but his hobby—at least, I looked upon it as a hobby then—was the language of ancient Kamt. Upon Dr. Young's and Champollion's methods he had constructed a complete, though somewhat complicated grammar, and this, with marvellous patience, he began slowly and thoroughly to teach to us, together with the hieroglyphic and cuneiform writings practised by the ancient Egyptians.

In the literal sense of the word, he put new life into the dead language; no word in it, no construction of sentence was a mystery to him. He read it all as easily as he did his Latin and Greek. Hugh, naturally, was a most apt pupil. He worshipped his father, and was passionately enthusiastic about the mystic science. I tried to follow Hugh in his ardour and aptitude, and I don't think that I was often left far behind.

I remember that my uncle, who had charge of my education since I had lost both my parents, shrugged his shoulders very contemptuously when I spoke to him of Mr. Tankerville. "That old fool," was my Aunt Charlotte's more forcible comment; "I hope to goodness you are not wasting your time cramming *his* nonsense into your head." After that I never mentioned my friend's name to either of them, but spent more and more time at The Chestnuts, imbibing that fascinating and semi-mystic lore of the great people of the past.

Such as Mr. Tankerville had reconstructed it, ancient Egyptian was not a difficult language, not nearly so difficult as Greek, for instance, and, certainly to me, in no sense as complicated as German. By the time that we were lads of about sixteen we could read almost any inscription on steles or potteries of old Egypt, more readily than we could have read a French poem, and Hugh was not quite seventeen when he translated parts of the Gospel of St. John into ancient Egyptian.

No wonder then that after some five years of that happy time my heart well-nigh broke when the exigencies of my future demanded that I should go to college. I was destined for the medical profession and was to spend three years at Oxford, while Hugh meant to remain as an active help to his father in scientific researches. With many protestations of eternal friendship I bade good-bye to the museum, the mummies and the phantom of Queen Neit-akrit.

When at the first vacation my eager thought was to go and see my kind friends at once, I learnt with much sorrow that Mr. Tankerville was seriously ill. Hugh came to the door to speak to me for a moment. He looked pale and worn from long-continued night watches.

During the weary period of his father's terrible illness, through which he nursed him with heroic patience and devotion, I saw practically nothing of Hugh. While I was at college I frequently wrote him long letters, to which he barely sent a short reply. Then I read of Mr. Tankerville's death, and to my horror and amazement read also in various papers satirical and seldom kind comments on the scientific visionary who had just passed away. It seemed to me as if profane hands had dared to touch at my most cherished illusions. I had imagined that the whole of the scientific world would go into mourning for the illustrious antiquarian gone to where all nations, young and old, mingle in the vast mansions; and lo and behold! a shrug of the shoulders was the only tribute paid to his memory. I sincerely hoped that Hugh would be too busy to read the obituary notices about his father. I longed for the vacation so that I might go and see him. I knew he would preserve intact the old chestnut trees, the old-world garden, the museum and the mummies, and I looked forward to once more watching in imagination by the fitful light of the great log fire the shade of Queen Neit-akrit wandering before my enraptured gaze.

CHAPTER II

THE SHADE OF NEIT-AKRIT

My uncle died soon after my return from college. After that I was supposed to be busy laying the foundations of a good consulting practice in Harley Street, but in reality was enjoying life and the newly-acquired delights of a substantial fortune left to me by a distant relative.

My Aunt Charlotte kept house for me and tyrannised over me to her heart's content. To her I had not yet begun to grow up; I was still the raw schoolboy, prone to mischief and to catching cold, who was in need of sound advice since he no longer had the inestimable boon of the birch-rod vigorously applied by loving hands.

Dear Aunt Charlotte!—she really was a very worthy soul, but she held most uncomfortable views on the subject of duty, which, according to her code, chiefly consisted in making oneself disagreeable to other people "for their own good." She had those twin characteristics peculiar to Englishwomen of a certain stamp and an uncertain age—self-righteousness and a narrow mind.

She ruled my servants, my household, my one or two patients and me with a rod of iron, and it never seriously entered my head to dispute her rule. I was born with a temperament which always preferred to follow rather than to lead. Had I ever married I should have been hopelessly henpecked; as it was, my Aunt Charlotte decided how many servants I should keep, and what entertainments I should give. She said the final word on the subject of my suggested holidays and on the price of my new pyjamas.

Still, with all her faults, she was a good sort, and as she took all household cares from off my shoulders, I was duly grateful to her for that.

I saw less and less of Hugh Tankerville during all this time. At first, whenever I could, I found my way to the silent and cool Chestnuts, but as often as not Hugh seemed absorbed in thoughts or in work; his mind, evidently, while I chatted and we smoked, seemed so far removed from his surroundings that by-and-by I began to wonder whether my visits were as welcome as they used to be, and I took to spacing them out at longer intervals. Once—I remember I had not been to see him for over two months—I was bidding him good-bye after a very short and silent visit; he placed his hand on my shoulder, and said, with some of his old wonted cordiality—

"I am not as inhospitable as I seem, old chap, and soon, very soon now, you will see me quite myself again. It is always delightful to see you, but the work I am doing now is so great, so absorbing, that I must appear hideously unresponsive to your kindness to me."

"I guessed, Old Girlie," I said, with a laugh, "that you must be busy over something terribly scientific. But," I added, noting suddenly how hot his hand felt, and how feverishly his eyes seemed to glow, "it strikes me that you are overworking yourself, and that as a fully qualified medical man I have the right to advise you . . ."

"Advise nothing just now, old chap," he said, very seriously, "I should not follow it. Give me two years more, and my work will be done. Then . . ."

"Two years, at this sort of work? Girlie, you'll be a dead man before then at this rate."

He shook his head.

"Ah! but it's no use shaking your head, old man! The dinners you do not eat, the bed you don't sleep in, the fresh air you do not breathe, all will have their revenge upon you for your studied neglect. Look here! you say you want to do another two years' work; I say your health will not stand the strain if you do. Will you pander to our old friendship to the extent of listening to me for once, and coming away with me for one month to the sea—preferably Margate—and after that I promise you I shall not say a word about your health for the next half-year at least."

Again he shook his head.

"I could not live if you parted me from my work now."

And he looked so determined, his eyes glowed with such a strange inward fire, while there was such indomitable will expressed in his whole being, that I was not fool enough to pursue my point.

"Look here, Hugh," I said, "I don't want, of course, to interfere in your secrets. You have never thought fit to tell me what this all-absorbing work is that you pursue at risk of physical damage to yourself. But I want you to remember, Girlie, that I have independent means, that my time is my own, and that your father often used to tell me, when I was a great many years younger, of some of his labours, and of his work; once I helped him—do you remember?—over some . . ."

"My father was too fond of talking about his work," he interrupted. "I don't mean to offend you by saying this, old chap, but you must remember the purport of most of the obituary notices written about one of the most scientific men that ever lived. He toiled all his life, contracted the illness of which he died, wore himself out, body and soul, in pursuit of one great object: when he died, with that great object unattained, the world shrugged its shoulders and called him a fool for his pains. But I am here now. I am still young. What he could not complete I have already almost accomplished. Give me two years, old chap, and the world will stand gaping round in speechless amazement at the tearing asunder of its own veil of ignorance, torn by me from before its eyes, by me, and by my father: 'mad Tankerville' they called him! Then it will bow and fawn at my feet, place laurel wreaths on my father's tomb, and confer all the honours it can upon his memory; and I . . ."

"You will be sadly in need of laurel wreaths too, Girlie, by then," I said half crossly, half in grudging admiration at his enthusiasm, "for you will have worked yourself into your grave long before that halcyon time."

He pulled himself together as if he were half-ashamed of his outburst, and said, with a mirthless laugh—

"You are talking just like your Aunt Charlotte, Old Mark."

I suppose my flippancy had jarred on him in his present highly nervous state. Before I finally went, I said to him—

"Promise me one thing, Girlie."

"What is it?"

"How cautious you are! Will you promise? It is for your good and for mine."

"In that case I will promise."

"Promise me that, if you want any kind of help in your work, you will send for me."

"I promise."

I did not see him for the whole of those two years. I wrote: he did not reply. I called: he would not leave his study to see me. It was useless being offended with him. I waited.

Then one day I had a telegram—

"Come at once if you can."

I jumped into a hansom, and half an hour later was seated in the dear old museum once more, beside the great log fire, which burned cheerfully in the grate. I had said nothing when first I saw Hugh. I was too much shocked at his altered, emaciated appearance: he looked like his own ghost, wandering about among the mummies. I could see that he was terribly excited: he was pacing about the room, muttering strange and incoherent words. For a moment I had feared that his reason had begun to give way under the terrible strain of absorbing brain work.

"It was good of you to come, Mark."

"I was only too happy that you sent for me, Old Girlie," I said sadly.

"I have done the work."

"Thank God for that!"

" And now I must have your help."

" Thank God again, Girlie ! What is it ? "

Silently he took my hand and led me across the room, behind the ponderous desk which I remembered so well in his father's lifetime.

" Here is the work, it took forty years—my father's whole life and my own youth—to complete."

He pointed to a large flat case, placed slanting on the desk, so as to receive the full light from the window. The top of the case was a sheet of clear plate-glass, beneath which I saw, what I at first took to be a piece of brown rag, frayed and irregular at the edges and full of holes. Again the terrible thought flashed across my mind that Hugh Tankerville had suffered from nerve tension and that his reason had given way under the strain.

" You don't see what this is ? " he asked in reproachful amazement.

I looked again while he turned the strong light of the reading-lamp on the case, and then I realised that I had before me a piece of parchment rendered brown with age, made up of an infinity of fragments, some too minute even to see with the naked eye, and covered with those strange Egyptian hieroglyphics with which dear old Mr. Tankerville had originally rendered me familiar. Inquiringly I looked up at Hugh.

" When my father first found this parchment," he said, while strong excitement seemed to choke the words as they rose in his throat, " it was little else than a handful of dust, with a few larger pieces among it, interesting enough to encourage his desire to know its contents and to whet his enthusiasm. At first, for he was then but a young man, though already considered a distinguished Egyptologist, he amused himself by placing the larger fragments together, just as a child would be amused by piecing a Chinese puzzle; but gradually the secrets that these fragments revealed were so wonderful, and yet so incomplete, that, restlessly, by day and by night, with the help of the strongest magnifying glasses money could procure, he continued the task of evolving from that handful of dust, a page of history which for thousands of years has remained an impenetrable mystery."

He paused a moment as his hand, which was trembling

with inward fever, wandered lovingly over the glass that covered the precious parchment.

"Illness and death overtook him in the midst of a task but half accomplished, but before he died he initiated me into the secrets of his work; it was not necessary that he should request me to continue it. One glance at the parchment, then still in a very fragmentary condition, was sufficient to kindle in me the same mad enthusiasm for the secrets it revealed which had animated, then exhausted, him. I was young, my sight was at its prime, my patience unbounded. He had all his life helped me to a knowledge of hieroglyphics as great as his own. The sneer of the scientific Press at what it called 'mad Tankerville's hobby,' his visions, acted but as a spur to my enthusiasm. It is six years since my father died, and to-day I fitted the last fragment of the parchment into its proper place."

Amazed, I listened to this wonderful tale of toil and patience, extending over the greater part of half a century, and amazed, I looked down at the result of this labour of Sisyphus, the fragments of brown dust—they could have been little else—which now, after thousands of years, had revealed secrets which Hugh said would set the world gaping. My knowledge of Egyptology and hieroglyphics had become somewhat rusty since the happy days when, sitting in the room in the fitful light of the fire, I used to hear from the dear old man's lips the wonders of Khefren and the mysteries of Queen Neit-akrit, but, as I looked, suddenly the old familiar cartouche, the name of the Queen, caught my eye. There it was

Neit-akrit, Child of the Sun, my queen as I called her then; and as Hugh was silent and the shades of evening began to draw in, I thought I saw, as I did in my schoolboy days, the glorious procession of Pharaohs, priests and gods pass before my eyes again.

Then Hugh began to tell me of the contents of the parchment. His voice sounded distant and muffled, as if the very shades that peopled this dear old museum were themselves telling me their history. It was the same old theme, so familiar and yet so mysterious still, with which Mr. Tankerville used to rejoice our schoolboy hearts; the blank page in Egyptian history when, after the reign of Queen Neit-akrit and the close of the Sixth Dynasty, the grand old people, who built the great Pyramid and carved the mystic Sphinx, disappeared from the scene, gone—no one knows whither—to make way some hundreds of years later for a new people with new ideas, new kings, new art, new gods.

To me it seemed, as Hugh was speaking, that it was the shade of Neit-akrit herself who was telling me in that soft, sing-song Egyptian tongue, how her Empire had been run over by the stranger. How she was weak, being a woman, and how she allowed herself to be dominated by him, for he was handsome, brave and masterful. Then I seemed to hear the voice of the high-priest of Ra, bewailing the influence of the stranger and his hordes over the great people of Egypt, whose origin was lost in the rolling billows of primæval chaos: and I saw the uprising of the multitude, the bloody battles, I saw the ultimate triumph of the stranger, as he spread his conquest from Net-amen to Men-ne-fer, from Tanis to Assuan; and at last I saw the people, the owners of that land which had once been so great, which they had covered with monuments that stood towering skywards, defying the rolling ages, that same people I saw, as Hugh still spoke, wandering off in one dense horde, driven onwards by the remorseless hand of the usurping stranger—homeless, on, ever on, across the vast wilderness, to be heard of no more.

"No more until this day," now sounded Hugh's voice, clear and distinct in my ears, "until I, and my father before me, have lifted the veil which hid this strange and mysterious past, and are prepared to show the world once more this great people whose work, whose art, whose science has set it agape since hundreds of years."

He seemed like a prophet inspired, whilst I, having forcibly aroused myself from my stupor and my visions, was gradually returning to the prosy realities of life. It seemed suddenly absurd that two sane Englishmen—at least I could vouch for the sanity of one of them—should get into a state of excitement over the fact, as to whether a certain people five thousand years ago had had a war, been licked and had wandered across the desert or not.

I even caught myself wondering in what light Aunt Charlotte—as being a good typical example of the narrow and sane-minded, unimaginative Englishwoman—in what light she would regard the disappearance of the most ancient, civilised people of this world, and what importance she would attach to their problematical wanderings across the desert.

Personally, though the subject had had a weird and unaccountable fascination for me, I soon felt that I did not care much whether Mr. Tankerville or other historians were correct about the Seventh, Eighth or Tenth Dynasty or not, and I asked, with a last semblance of interest—

"Then this parchment sets forth all these historical facts, no doubt; they are invaluable to the scientific world, but personally I, as one of the vulgar, do not consider that they were worth either your father or you wearing yourselves into your coffins about them."

He looked at me in complete amazement, and passed his hand across his forehead once or twice, as if to collect his thoughts.

"Ah, yes! I see, of course, you do not understand. How could you? You have not spent years in this work, till it has become a part and parcel of your very life."

"Well, I certainly do not understand, old man, why you should work yourself into a brain fever for the sake of a people, however interesting, who have disappeared from this world for the last five thousand years."

"Disappeared?" he almost shrieked. "I see now why you did not understand. But come, old chap, sit here by the fire. Have a pipe, I'll have one too. . . . I'll tell you all about it, quite calmly. Of course, you thought me mad—a maniac . . . Matches? Here you are. Shall we have the lamps?"

He rang the bell. Old Janet, more wrinkled and pleasant than ever, brought in the lamp. She threw a log on the fire and left a delicious atmosphere of prosy cheerfulness behind her as she left. We were now both comfortably installed by the fire, smoking. Hugh seemed quite calm, only his eyes stared, large and glowing, into the fire.

CHAPTER III

THE TOMB OF THE GREEK PRIEST

" I DON'T wonder that you think me mad, Mark, old chap," began Hugh very calmly after a little while; " the work has been so close, that no doubt it did get on to my nerves a bit. When I actually put the finishing touches on it to-day, my only other thought, besides that of exultant triumph, was that of sharing my delights with you. Then you came, so ready to help me since I had called to you, and I, like a foolish enthusiast, never reflected on the all-important necessity of putting the facts clearly and coherently before you."

He pointed to one of the mummies that stood upright in a glass case at the further end of the museum. The human outline was clear and distinct under the few linen wrappings, painted all over with designs and devices and the portrait of the deceased, after the fashion introduced into Egypt by the Greeks.

" When you and I were schoolboys together all those mummies were our friends, and our imaginations ran riot when my father, in his picturesque way, explained to us the meaning of the various inscriptions which recorded their lives. We knew in those days that this particular mummy had once been a Greek priest and scribe of Assuan, who had expressed a desire to be buried in a peculiarly lonely spot in the desert land opposite what is now Wady-Halfa. A pious friend or relative had evidently carried out this wish, for it was in that desolate spot that my father found this mummy in its solitary tomb. I remember how, for my part, I loved to think of that pious friend sailing down the silent Nile, with the body of the dead scribe lying at rest in the prow of his dahabijeh, while the great goddess Isis smiled down approvingly at the reverent deed, and the sacred crocodiles watched curiously the silent craft, flitting ghostlike amidst the lotus leaves. More than two thousand years later my father visited this lonely desert tomb. It was before the days that a strict surveillance was kept over tourists and amateur explorers, and he was alone, save for an old and faithful fellah—dead now—who was his constant attendant in his scientific researches. Beside the mummy of the dead scribe stood the four canopic jars, dedicated to the children of Horus and containing the heart and other entrails of the deceased; my father, with less reverence than scientific enthusiasm, had with his penknife loosened the top of one of the jars, when, to his astonishment, he saw that it contained in addition to the embalmed heart a papyrus closely written in Greek."

"In Greek? Not this one then?"

"No, another, equally priceless, equally valuable, but only as a solution, a complement of the first."

He went up to the desk, and from one of the drawers took out a papyrus, faded and yellow with age, and placed it before me.

"I have made a translation of it, old fellow," he said, with a smile, seeing my look of perplexity; "you were a pretty good classic scholar though at one time, you will be able to verify that mine is a correct rendering of the original."

He took a paper out of his pocket-book and began to read, whilst I listened more and more amazed and bewildered, still wondering why Hugh Tankerville had worked himself to such a pitch of excitement for the sake of a dead and vanished past.

"I pray to Osiris and to Isis that I may be buried on the spot where my footsteps led me that day, when I was still young. Oh, mother Isis! what was thy sacred wish when thou didst guide mine eyes to read the mysteries of thy people? I pray to be buried within that same tomb where I found the papyrus, that guided my way to the land of wheat and barley of ancient Kamt, that lies beyond the wilderness of the sand from the east to the west. I stood upon the spot and I, too, shot my arrow into the heart of Osiris as he disappears behind Manou, into the valley of perpetual night, on the first day that Hapi gives forth goodness to the land. I, too, crossed the sands from the east to the west, and I, too, rejoiced when I saw the Rock of Anubis, and found the way no longer barred to me, to that land of plenty, wherein dwell the chosen people of Ra, secure from all enemies—great, solitary and eternal. But, alas! it was not for me to dwell in their midst! Enough! They are! and Ra and his children have surrounded them with a barrier, which no child of man can traverse."

I had to confess that after hearing the contents of this so-called explanatory papyrus I was more perplexed than before.

"You don't understand this, do you, Old Mark?" resumed Hugh, "any more than my father did; but the whole thing seemed so enigmatical to him, and yet so real, so strange, that he looked round him eagerly for a solution. One by one he opened each of the other three canopic jars, and it was in the last one that he found the priceless papyrus, of a date some three thousand years previous to the existence of the scribe in whose tomb it rested. Here was obviously the key to the puzzle propounded in the Greek priest's writing, and the explanation of his mysterious statements; but alas! the moment the outer air reached the ancient treasure, it fell before my father's very eyes into more than a thousand minute fragments."

He paused, then added, as if he wished every one of his words to impress itself indelibly on my mind—

"It has taken forty years of ceaseless toil to solve that great and glorious mystery, but now at last it is done, and I, Hugh Tankerville, am ready, with your help, to prove to the world that those great people, who were driven off by the stranger across the desert, did not perish in the wilderness: that they found a land which lies beyond the rolling billows of sand and shingle, where they formed an empire more great and vast, more wonderful and glorious, than aught we have dreamed of in our so-called science."

"This is a theory," I said, with a smile.

"It is a fact," he replied earnestly, "at least it was a fact two thousand years ago, when that same Greek priest wandered across the wilderness in search of the vanished hordes of Egypt: when he with simple conviction, perhaps with his dying breath, pronounced, 'Enough! They are!'"

"Then do you mean to tell me? . . ." I began.

"I tell you, Mark, that beyond those inaccessible sand dunes that surround the Lybian desert, in that so-called arid wilderness, there live at the present moment the descendants of those same people who built the Pyramid of Ghizeh and carved the mysterious majesty of the Sphinx."

"Let them live in peace," I said flippantly, "since no one

can get at, or to, them. You have said it yourself, they are—if they are at all—beyond the inaccessible dunes."

"Inaccessible only to the ignorant, but not to those who know. They were not inaccessible to the scribe who wrote this parchment over three thousand years after the great emigration into the wilderness."

"Do you maintain then," I said still incredulously, "that the writer of parchment No. 2 actually set out on a desert journey and verified the truth, as set forth in parchment No. 1?"

"How he came possessed of the original papyrus he does not very clearly say, but, as soon as he had deciphered it, he started forth across the Lybian desert, and crossed those inaccessible dunes, using those landmarks which are clearly explained on the old Egyptian document, and which proved, in every instance, to be absolutely correct in indicating a way across the impassable wilderness."

"Well! but he never got there."

"That we do not know. . . . His MS. ends abruptly, and . . ."

"Like Poe's *Arthur Gordon Pym*, eh, Old Girlie? It is a way narrators of adventure have."

"His is not a narration; he set out to verify certain facts He verified them. We do not know what caused him to turn back in sight of goal."

"Hm! that turning back in sight of goal does not carry conviction to the mind of an obstinate Britisher."

"No! . . . Nothing would deter us, Mark, old chap, would it?" he said calmly. "*We* will not turn back."

"*We?*"

I jumped up in bewildered amazement, the object of Hugh's excitement, of his patient explanations to my dull intellect, suddenly dawning on me. I gave a long whistle, buried my hands in my pockets, fixed Hugh with my most professional eye, and said—

"You are absolutely and unmistakably cracked, Girlie!"

He came up to me, put his hand on my shoulder, and looked at me. I have said it before, he was a man of boundless influence over his fellow-creatures, whenever he chose to exert it.

"Come and look at the papyrus," he said.

"D—— the papyrus. The whole thing is too preposterous for words."

He said very simply, "Why?"

"Because. . . . Because. . . . Damn it, Hugh," I said very crossly . . . and . . . I went to have a look at the papyrus.

It was still very fragmentary, of course, as in places quite large pieces were missing, but certain passages were peculiarly clear; for instance, the part which described the way the wandering hordes of Egypt took when in search of a home.

"You see, they wandered down the Nile," explained Hugh eagerly, showing me the drawing of the river and of the multitude following its course; "and then it was that from the lonely spot where the Greek scribe lay buried they went forth towards the west."

"That is a mere surmise," I objected.

"The scribe says, '*Let me be buried there where I found the papyrus!*' and later, '*I stood upon the spot, and I too shot my arrow into the heart of Osiris,*' etc. Osiris is the sun, and a figure shooting an arrow is one of the simplest hieroglyphics known, meaning a perfectly straight course."

"Yes! and here," I exclaimed suddenly, "is the figure shooting an arrow at the setting sun."

In spite of myself a very little of Hugh's enthusiasm was beginning to filtrate into my mind. The whole thing was preposterous, of course, but the old fascination which ancient Egypt, with its gorgeousness, its mysteries, its glorious art had ever excited, even in my raw schoolboy mind, began to hold me enthralled.

"Remember, Mark, too, that due west, line for line with Wady-Halfa, a couple of thousand miles away, lies the high peak of Uj-en-ari, and that almost at its very base Rholfs found traces of an ancient way which he took to have once led to, and therefore from, Egypt."

"And the arrow which the hieroglyphic person is shooting, is depicted in the next sign as being stuck in a high and precipitous mountain, which might easily be Uj-en-ari," I added excitedly.

There was no doubt that my common sense was lulling itself to rest.

Hugh took hold of my coat sleeve and made me turn to where a large map of Egypt and the Lybian desert hung against the wall.

" There lies the land," he said, running his fingers round the vast blank space on the map, " and that is where I mean to go."

And common sense gave another dying gasp.

" Rholfs and Caillaud both found that inaccessible, and shifting dunes running from north to south, barred any way across the Lybian desert," I objected.

" If we go due west from that one spot I feel convinced that we shall find a way through those inaccessible sand dunes," replied Hugh emphatically.

He was so sure, so convinced, there was so much power in his whole personality, that the conviction very soon dawned upon me that, if I did not choose to accompany him in his wild search after his Egyptians, he would risk the dangerous desert journey alone.

With an impatient sigh I turned to the papyrus.

" See how clear are the directions," resumed Hugh. " Having started from the spot, we evidently have many day's march before us, due west, across the desert, for we see the multitudes wandering, and one or two dead on the way, but soon we come to this figure, a man rejoicing—can you see it? it is very clear—look at the arms ! and now the words : '*Then when to be seen is the Rock of Anubis not is barred against him the way, and opened are before him the gates of ground of wheat and barley of the land of Kamt.*' "

" How do you explain that, Girlie ? " I asked.

" The Greek priest saw that rock. I imagine its shape is something like a jackal's head—Anubis, old Mark, was the jackal-headed god of ancient Egypt—or there may actually be a figure of the god carved into the living rock. We shall see when we get there."

It was a fairy tale, of course. My reason stood up confronting me, and telling me that the idea was preposterous beyond what words could say : it told me that, even granting that those Egyptians had found and established themselves, in some distant and fertile oasis, in the heart of the most arid wilderness on the globe, future generations would have heard about or from them, and recorded their existence or extinction. It told me that no people could have lived on any one spot on earth for five thousand years and have been content not to extend their dominions, with their growing population; that they could not have gone there without wanting to come back; that Rholfs, Caillaud, Cat, any of the great desert explorers would have found some traces of the route to this unknown land, if route there was. It told me that, and a hundred other arguments besides, and yet, as Hugh Tankerville talked, explained and argued, I listened more and more eagerly; his influence, which he himself knew to be boundless, and which he was endeavouring to exert to its full, was beginning to pervade me, my objections became more and more feeble.

"You cannot bring forward one single positive argument against my elaborate scaffolding of facts, Mark! You are not going to tell me that two people, one living more than three thousand years before the other, have joined hands across thirty centuries to concoct the same lie. What object would a Greek priest have in corroborating the falsehoods of an Egyptian, whose existence even he would ignore?"

"I cannot make that Greek priest of yours out," I argued. "What made him turn back?"

"He may not have been sufficiently provisioned for any further journey; having ascertained that the landmarks did exist, he may have gone back with a view to make a fresh and more elaborate start. He may . . ."

"He may have been a confounded liar, as most inhabitants—notably the priests—of those countries generally are," I laughed.

Hugh frowned, and said at last, with a trifle less enthusiasm—

"Of course, old chap, I have no desire to persuade you against your will. When I wired to you I was merely fulfilling my promise, and . . ."

"Well?"

"I can always go alone."

What was the use of further argument? I had known all along that I should ultimately give in. After all, I had independent means, was my own master—in spite of Aunt Charlotte; I had nothing to do, and was barely thirty years of age. Is it great wonder that the love of adventure, inherent in every Englishman, had by now completely annihilated my reason. After all, I'd just as soon go and hunt for ancient Egyptians in impossible desert regions with Hugh Tankerville, as wait for problematical patients in Harley Street.

I stretched out my hand to Sawnie Girlie and said—

"No you don't, Girlie. When do we start?"

CHAPTER IV

THE ROCK OF ANUBIS

We started about a week afterwards; personally, I should find it difficult to say exactly how much of Hugh's wild theories I believed. The whole thing fascinated me immensely, and although I never for a moment credited the notion that we should find any living beings, other than wild Bedouins and Tibestis, in that part of the Lybian desert which we meant to traverse, yet I certainly did hope that we might find a few interesting relics of a great and vanished past.

Hugh had made a good photographic reproduction of the two papyri, leaving the originals safely locked up in a ponderous fire-proof safe, which had been screwed to the floor of the museum in the dear old Chestnuts. Old Janet, with her daughter and son-in-law were to take care of the house in the master's absence, and . . . we started.

No one who met us, either at Charing Cross or Paris, or subsequently at Marseilles or Cairo, could have guessed, in our thoroughly matter-of-fact form of procedure, that we were aught but a pair of young, enthusiastic tourists visiting the glorious country for the first time, and with no other object in view save that of our own selfish pleasures. And we were bent on crossing half a continent to find a people who had disappeared from the history of the world since nigh upon five thousand years.

The dragoman from whom we hired the dahabijeh and its crew, which were to take us up the Nile as far as Wady-Halfa, was struck with speechless wonder at the two mad English, who obstinately refused to do more than cursorily glance at the glories of Thebes and Luxor and seemed impelled by some chasing spirit, which forbade them to land or to waste time. I could not, of course, very accurately estimate Hugh's thoughts and feelings, as our little craft slowly and silently flitted up the sacred and historic river. At eventime, when the waters lay dark and peaceful, and the moon shone silvery and radiant on date palms and distant mosques, on sandy shores and majestic ruins, the boatmen, whom we had provided with tambourines and darabukas, would crouch on deck and intone some of their half-melancholy, monotonous tunes. Then I would see Hugh's eyes fixed longingly and searchingly on that distant horizon towards the west, and I myself, quiet, matter-of-fact Britisher as I was, would begin to dream of the great people whom we had set forth to seek. I saw, as the dahabijeh glided noiselessly along, the great procession of the wandering hordes quitting their homes, polluted by the conquering stranger, and seeking a new and glorious resting-place in the west far away.

The great and mysterious immensities of the Lybian desert became peopled in my mind with high priests in flowing robes and leopards' skins, with priestesses in heavy plaited wigs, and priests with shaven crowns, with men and women, angular and gaunt, dark and high cheek-boned, flat-footed and large-eyed, such as we see depicted on ancient tombs and papyri. I seemed to hear the monotonous, sing-song tones of the ancient Egyptian language with which dear old Mr. Tankerville had rendered me familiar; the air became filled with sounds of the sistrum and the drum, and the tall papyrus grass, as we passed, seemed to send forth in the evening air a long-drawn sigh for the glories past and gone.

In the daytime we pored over Champollion's and Mr. Tankerville's Egyptian grammar; and if at times I smiled indulgently at Hugh's patience and ardent study of a language I believed to be dead, yet I tried to emulate him in my eagerness to master its many difficulties. We set each other daily tasks in conversation, and we each kept a diary written in hieroglyphic and cuneiform characters.

Before we reached Wady-Halfa, however, reason, as represented by my humble self, made a final compact with enthusiasm, as personified by Hugh.

"Look here, Girlie," I said to him one evening, as we sat lazily smoking on the deck of the dahabijeh, "I am only too delighted to join you in any mad adventure upon this dark and interesting continent, and the Lybian desert is as good as any other place for me in which to spend six months in your company; at the same time, I am not sufficiently devoted to science, to risk perishing of hunger and thirst in the midst of some terrible wilderness. Now, when Rholfs tried to do the journey which you and I propose to start on, he had to give it up because he found a line of inaccessible and shifting dunes right across his path in the desert."

"He started from Beni-Adin, and Assuan, and . . ."

"I know. We start from a given point—the tomb of the defunct priest, and you are absolutely convinced that in a straight line due west from that tomb, we shall find that the said line of inaccessible dunes is not inaccessible."

"I am absolutely convinced that the Greek priest crossed them."

"Very well; this is my point. If, having started from that tomb and travelled due west, we find that we cannot effect a crossing straight ahead, you must give me your solemn word of honour, that you will not entertain any foolish idea of roaming about the desert in search of imaginary ways, which may after all have vanished, nor risk a miserable and inglorious death in the mazes of the arid immensity."

He looked at me and smiled. I was half ashamed of my eagerness and pompous diction, for I had spoken very solemnly.

"I can safely promise you that, old chap, for I am sure we shall find the way."

Hugh had already given me his views on the subject of taking attendants with us on the desert journey.

"What in the world is the good of them?" he asked. "They do not know the way any better than we do, and they would, of course, terribly increase our responsibilities and anxiety. Their only advantage, as far as I can see, is that they look after the camels. Well, old Mark, will you tell me if there is anything in the world that a set of beastly niggers can do, which two resolute and practical Englishmen cannot do equally well, and a great deal better?"

I must confess that I fully endorsed these views. We both were ready to rough it, both had plenty of gumption, and both hated niggers about our persons. The result of our decision was that we elected to spend a month quietly in Wady-Halfa, where we lodged with an old Arab store-dealer and his family, whose ways of talking and walking, of scraping and shuffling, we set ourselves to study and were soon able to closely imitate. We had, of course, decided to start on our desert journey, dressed in the burnous and general rig-out of Arab small traders, this costume being far more cool and comfortable for our purpose than any European suit of ducks, besides being so much less likely to attract attention.

Hugh spoke Arabic like a native, and by the time that our month's probation at Wady-Halfa was over, we both looked as brown, red and other colours of the rainbow as any actual son of the desert soil.

Our host's eldest son, who was a camel-dealer by occupation and a thief by nature, was of great service to us in the choice of the four beasts we would require for our journey. He looked upon us as the most crack-brained Englishmen he had ever come across. He tried hard to cheat us, but as he did not succeed he conceived a violent admiration for us both, and I believe was genuinely sorry to see us go so cheerfully to certain death.

By his aid, and acting under his guidance, we spent that month practically living in constant companionship with the four camels, which were to bear us and our equipment on the great journey. We learnt their ways, their manners and customs, their wants and requirements, and after the first fortnight could look after a camel better than most Englishmen can look after a horse; and—as we had selected two strong, healthy milchers—we solemnly and conscientiously (oh, shade of Aunt Charlotte!) learnt the gentle art of milking, so as to have the delicious and nourishing commodity on our way.

Our equipment was not complicated: we were not going to make astronomical observations, take altitudes, or catalogue the fauna and flora of the wilderness. Our own supply of provisions was as concentrated as modern scientific grocery could make it—meat lozenges and essences of all kinds constituting its main portion: there was our supply of water in gourds, plenty of tobacco and matches, half-a-dozen bottles of brandy, all to last us sixty clear days, by which time, if we had not found the land of wheat and barley of ancient Kamt, we hoped at least to strike the point where the great caravan route to Wadai crosses the interior of the Lybian desert.

Then, if our expedition had proved to be—well! a wild-goose chase, we could perhaps fall in with a caravan, and in a chastened and humbled spirit attach ourselves to it, and in its train travel southwards or northwards as the case might be. This was, of course, very problematical; caravans do not travel along that route very frequently, and it was just as likely as not that, if we ever reached that point, we could comfortably starve by the wayside before we caught sight of a single human soul. Still, as a concession to common sense, this plan served well enough.

We also provided ourselves with sundry soaps and shaving creams, also with a rather more gorgeous change of attire than the one in which we meant to travel, all with a view of presenting a respectable appearance before the highly-civilised people we meant to visit. A good light folding tent and a magnificent compass completed our simple equipment. Moreover, we each carried a rifle and a revolver and a hundred round of ammunition, and—well!—we started.

Up to the last moment I fancy that our hosts thought that we would give up our mad undertaking, but when they actually saw us depart, and realised that we seriously meant to cross the desert with four camels and no escort, they shrugged their shoulders with true Oriental placidity. "Our lives," they said, "were our own to throw away."

The tomb of the Greek priest, from which we were, in our turn, to shoot the arrow from the east to the west, was about a couple of miles from Wady-Halfa, and faced straight out across the desert towards the setting sun. Mr. Tankerville had explained to Hugh exactly how to get to it, and late one evening we found our way there, ready to start. It was carved out of the living rock, and, of course, was empty, now that the secrets it had guarded for over two thousand years were safely lodged in The Chestnuts. The paintings on the walls recorded that the priest had been a good and pious man who had offered sacrifices to the gods, and who, I concluded, would be above leading his fellow-men astray.

By the time night came we had pitched our tent four miles from Wady-Halfa. Already we seemed in another world: London, civilisation, hansom cabs and top hats, even the dear old Chestnuts and the museum of mummies and papyri had become akin to dreamland. Hugh looked magnificent in his abajah and white burnous: the Eastern clothes seemed to suit his romantic personality. I am afraid I looked somewhat less impressive than he did, and I felt that in the distant and mysterious land which we were about to visit I should be looked upon merely as Hugh's satellite.

At first I enjoyed the journey immensely. The romance of the adventure, the delightful peace of the vast wilderness, the novelty of the whole thing, and above all, Hugh's companionship made day follow day in agreeable monotony.

For it was monotony of the most absolute unvarying order. Day after day the same sky, the same sand and shingle, the same tufts of coarse grass and clumps of seedy palms, the same pools of brackish water, the same glittering pieces of rock, smoothed and polished with the roll of ages, the same, the same, always the same. After a while I got to hate the colour of the sky, the interminable billows of sand, which seemed never to vary in shape or size, but to repeat themselves in weary numbers day after day, week after week. Soon I lost count of time, while we wandered on straight towards the setting sun. Yes, straight! Though sand dunes rose before and round us, steep, rocky tableland, moving shingle, inaccessible heights, yet, straight before us, as the arrow flies, from the tomb of the Greek priest to the heart of Osiris, we always found a mountain pass, a way up or round a boulder—a way, in fact, straight on towards the west.

We went forward in the early mornings and late after noons, and rested during the hot parts of the day and the darker hours of the night. Our worst foe decidedly was *ennui*, at least it was so as far as I was concerned, though Hugh helped me to pass many weary hours by plunging into his endless store of knowledge about the people we had set out to seek. I could see that as we wandered on, his belief and enthusiasm never for a moment flagged, and when I expressed my abhorrence of the interminable expanse of shingle and sand he would rouse my spirits by glowing descriptions of what lay beyond.

After the first week we had ceased to perceive the slightest trace of animal life, and this terrible silence, which hangs over the desert like a pall, was more oppressive than words can say. So oppressive was it, that one almost longed for the weird cries of the hyenas, which had made the nights hideous in the beginning of our journey.

Then the day came when exactly one half of our provisions which we had taken with us had been consumed by us and by the beasts, the day after which the question of turning back would become more and more difficult to answer; and still before us sand and shingle, and rising upland, and monotony, and slowly-creeping mortal *ennui*.

I fought against it honestly as hard as I could. I was ashamed that I, the stronger physically when we started, should be the first to show signs of weakness, but somehow this *ennui*, caused by the ceaseless, terrible, appalling monotony of the wilderness, and of the slow shambling gait of the camels, developed into a malady which robbed me totally of sleep. Still, I said nothing to Hugh, but I could see that he knew what ailed me, for the efforts he made to distract my thoughts became positively touching.

One night, when we crouched as usual under our tents smoking, I asked,—

"Girlie, how long is it since we left Wady-Halfa?"

"Thirty-one days," he replied quietly.

Yes, quietly. He could speak with equanimity of thirty-one times twenty-four hours, of thirty-one times 1440 minutes spent in gazing at the same sand, the same scraps of coarse grass, the same limitless blue sky, the same horizon far away.

"And how many miles do you reckon that we have travelled due west?"

"Nearly six hundred, I should say."

I said nothing more, and he went outside the tent, where I could see him presently gazing out longingly towards the west. I went up to him and put my hand on his shoulder.

"Girlie," I said, "we have wandered thirty-one days in the wilderness. If everything goes at its best, and if we are very economical with our food, we can perhaps wander another thirty and no more."

He did not reply, and I had not the courage or the cowardice to continue with what was going on in my mind. But I knew that he guessed it, for later on in the evening, when we made a fresh start, I saw him examining the various packages on the camels' backs, and, when he thought I was not looking, he hastily passed his hand across his eyes as if he wished to chase away a persistent, unpleasant thought.

Two more days elapsed without any change, save that one of our camels, the one which had given us the best milk, suddenly sickened and died. We left her by the wayside and continued to wander on, but a couple of hours later, when we took our customary midnight rest, Hugh said to me—

"Mark, old fellow, there are three sound camels left. Will you take two and a sufficient amount of provisions and return eastward to-night?"

"And you?"

"I am going on, of course."

"So am I, Girlie."

"I refuse to take you any further, Mark."

"I was not aware that I was being taken, Girlie."

"I was a fool to persuade you to come. I feel morally responsible for your welfare, and . . ."

"And?"

"The game is becoming dangerous."

"So much the better, Girlie, it was getting deuced monotonous."

"Will you turn back, Mark?"

"No! I won't. Not without you, at least."

We laid ourselves down to sleep after that, but I don't think that either of us found much rest. I, for one, never closed an eye, and I could hear Hugh tossing about restlessly in his rug on the ground. Towards early dawn I got up and looked out on the ever-monotonous landscape, when, from afar, towards the west, high over head, I saw three or four tiny black specks approaching—birds, of course. I gazed astonished, for it was over three weeks since we had seen any sign of bird or beast. The specks came nearer, and soon I recognised a flight of vultures, attracted, no doubt, by the dead camel we had left on the way, whilst at the same time, through the oppressive silence around, my ears caught the dismal sound of a pack of hyenas, crying in the wilderness. As I turned I saw that Hugh stood behind me; he too had seen the carrion birds and heard the melancholy cry. His whole face beamed with a sudden re-awakened enthusiasm, and he laid his hand on my shoulder, saying—

"Will you come with me for another five days, Mark, and I promise you that if at the end of that time we have found no further traces that we are on the right track, I will accompany you back to Wady-Halfa? We can be a little more economical with our provisions and make them last out a few days longer than we had intended."

Strangely enough, with the dismal advent of the birds of prey, my enthusiasm seemed to have revived. I think it must have been owing to the sound of other life than ours, through the terrible, unvarying silence. Hugh's promise also comforted me, and for the next three days I delighted him with my re-awakened spirits.

One morning, at break of day, as we were loading the camels, Hugh pointed westward.

"The enemy at last, Mark. It is no use attempting to make a start, he will overtake us before we are well on our way. I have been wondering how it was that he has avoided us all this while."

I had read a great deal about sandstorms, and had, when we first started, spoken about the chances of our meeting with one with perfect equanimity. We made what preparations were necessary to meet the enemy: the camels, poor things, were trembling from head to foot. We spread the canvas of our tent right over them and us, and our heads well protected with cloaks and rugs, we could but wait and trust our lives to a higher keeping.

The experience was a terrible one, one that made me forget my *ennui* and Hugh his visionary dreams. The stunning blows from sand and shingle, the darkness, the fright of the camels, the suffocation, all helped to make me long for that monotony of calm desert sand, which I had railed against for so many days.

I think I must have been hit on the back of the head by some sharp loose stone, for I can remember the sensation of a terrible blow and then nothing more. When I recovered consciousness it was with the sensation of brandy trickling down my throat, of an even blue sky above me, and of Hugh's cheerful voice asking me how I felt.

"Just like one gigantic and collapsed sand dune," I murmured.

Indeed it seemed to me as if it ought to be impossible for any one human being to hold as much sand about their person as I did. It was absolutely everywhere: in my mouth, in my eyes, in the brandy which I drank, at the back of my throat, in my shoes, and under the roots of my hair.

"How are the camels?" I asked.

"Badly, I am afraid. One of them refuses to stir."

"Not our milcher, I hope?"

"Unfortunately, yes!"

This was bad business, for the milk had been very delicious and nourishing, and the water, which had been stored in goats' skins, was but a very unpalatable substitute.

The question of going back the way we came was thus finally settled: we had been on the road since thirty-four days, the last pool of stagnant water we had seen was thirty days ago, and that was undrinkable, and we certainly had not water enough to last us another thirty-four days.

"It is obviously a case of 'Forward does it!' old man," I said, "and the sooner we reach that fertile and elusive land the better I shall be pleased."

We covered another fifteen miles westward that day, and as night drew on, it seemed to me as if I had never breathed such delicious and invigorating air, as reached us through the folds of our tent. The moon had risen and looked down placidly at the unvarying monotony beneath her, and I, in spite of the peace and silence of the night, could not get to sleep, but tossed about restlessly on my rug, with intervals of short, troubled unconsciousness.

Suddenly something roused me and caused me to sit up listening and wide awake; the cry of the vultures perhaps, or of a hyena rendered bold in the night. Hugh, too, had jumped up, and I followed him outside the tent, with an unaccountable feeling of something strange in the air round me.

The wilderness, arid and desolate, looked almost poetic as it lay bathed in the moonlight. The stars shone down bright and mysterious overhead; to the south we could see the summits of a long range of hills dimly outlined against the deep indigo of the sky, and before us the great and immeasurable vastness, with its secrets and its mysteries, its evenness and peace, which we had learnt to know so well, and yet I could not say what it was that seemed so strange, so unaccountable in the air.

"Can you smell it, Mark?" asked Hugh suddenly.

Smell it! Yes, that was it! I realised it now; my nostrils had been so long accustomed to the smell of sand, and rugs, and camels that they did not recognise the strange and penetrating scent which filled the air. It was sweet, yet pungent, like a gigantic bouquet of lotus blossom: the very atmosphere, clear and cool, had become oppressive with this curious scent.

"Where does it come from?" I asked.

We strolled out further and climbed up the low hillock, at the base of which we had pitched our tent.

When we reached the top of the boulder, and our eyes, as usual, searched the horizon longingly towards the west, we both uttered a cry and gazed outwards, not daring to trust to our senses. There, far ahead, outlined clearly against the dark, starlit canopy of the sky, towered, some thousand feet above the surrounding table-land, a white solitary rock, the summit of which, carved by almighty nature in a moment of playful fancy, was a perfect stone image of a jackal's head: the black cloud of the sirocco had hidden it from our view this morning, and even now we stood, wondering whether our excited brain was not playing our wearied eyes a cruel and elusive trick.

"The Rock of Anubis," whispered Hugh.

All around us the same death-like silence reigned; the

shingle and sand glittered in the moonlight like myriads of diamonds, the rugged upland rose in majestic billows, while the midnight air was filled with the strange, pungent odour of a thousand lotus blossoms, and a score of miles ahead, dominating this wilderness with awesome and mysterious majesty, the Rock of Anubis stood before us as the first tangible sign that Hugh's conjectures were no empty dreams. Perforce we had to wait until dawn to start once more upon our way; the night, lovely as it was, seemed interminably long, and the first streak of light found us loading our two remaining camels. We were both keenly excited now that the end of our journey was near. The ground was very rough, rising over precipitous boulders and crags at times, but nevertheless with a decided downward slope towards the valley in which stood the Rock of Anubis. Our camels were tired and weakened with sparse food; at midday we seemed only to have covered half the distance, and the base of the rock was still hidden from our view.

"Do you notice, Girlie, those white specks which lie dotted about on the ground to the south of the rock?" I remarked to Hugh later in the day.

"Yes, I have been wondering what they are."

The sun was just setting when we at last reached the top of the last boulder that divided us from the valley. The Rock of Anubis now stood before us in its entirety, with the jackal's head sharply silhouetted against the ruddy sky not two miles away.

From its base a path led due south towards the distant long range of hills: it was easily traceable by the numerous white specks which glittered on it, clear and distinct, against the yellow sand. As we emerged with our camels over the crest of the hill a great noise suddenly rent the deathlike stillness of the air, and a gigantic black cloud seemed to rise from the ground. It was a flight of vultures which flew with dismal croaking upwards, whilst, terrified, a pack of hyenas fled screeching into the wilderness.

Then we saw that the white specks on the ground were human bones, and that the Rock of Anubis towered over a gigantic graveyard.

CHAPTER V

THE GATES OF KAMT

We were forced to encamp in the very midst of this weird desolation. A thousand conflicting conjectures chased one another in our bewildered minds. What was the explanation of this strange and solitary abode of the dead? who were these whose whitening bones were left to mingle with the sand and shingle of the desert?

"The wandering hordes of Egypt, who found death on this spot after ceaseless roaming in the desert," was my first suggestion; obviously a foolish one, for Hugh quietly pointed to one or two skeletons on which the flesh still hung.

"None of these skeletons have been here more than ten years, I should say," he remarked.

"A battle-field then, where some wild tribes of the desert have lately fought a bloody battle."

But he shook his head.

"There is not a single skeleton of beast among them."

"Anyhow, it is horrible," I said.

"Horrible? Well! perhaps it is. But I feel convinced that it marks the end of our journey."

"Do you think then that we shall add our British bones to this interesting collection?" I asked.

"No, I don't, Mark. But I think that after we have had a night's rest we shall follow this path, which obviously leads southward to that distant range of hills."

"About another twenty miles?"

"Behind it lies the land of wheat and barley of ancient Kamt."

I looked across the horizon, where the crests of those distant hills caught the last rays of the setting sun, and again I could smell the strange and pungent odour of lotus blossoms, which brought back to my memory visions of the great people in gorgeous garments and gems, and of palaces and temples, such as sober, twentieth-century moderns can harldy conceive.

I wanted to start at once, the path seemed so clear.

"Am I to be the cautious one this time, Mark?" said Hugh,

with a smile. " We are not going to jeopardise success, just when it lies so near."

" That's so, old man," I replied with my old flippancy. " I had better occupy myself with brushing up those Egyptian prepositions and personal pronouns. I feel I shall have need of them soon, if I don't want to disgrace myself."

I am afraid that that night we spent a considerable amount of time in foolish vanity. We dared not waste our minute provision of water, but we indulged in a shave with the patent cream, brushed our clothes, and generally endeavoured to assume a respectable appearance. The poor camels were very sick, and we were much afraid that one of them at least might not manage another day's march. However, neither of us felt as if we could leave the poor creature behind, and lightening its load as much as possible, we all four started to walk southward in the early morning. I must say it was not cheerful walking on the road : skulls and skeletons lay in great numbers, and black ravens and vultures, disturbed in their grim meal by our footsteps, hovered over our heads, filling the air with their dismal croaking; but, against that, each step brought us nearer to that range of hills behind which, both our convictions told us, there lived the people who used the wilderness as a burying-place for their dead.

Hugh felt convinced that those people would appear before us in all the glory of ancient Egypt : I, less sanguine, dared hope no more than that they would prove to be a friendly desert tribe, who would give us the means of returning to civilisation once more.

The road, at first, had wound round a number of low and rugged boulders, but now, after a last sharp turn southwards, it lay even and flat, stretching out for many miles before us; and as I looked straight along it, it seemed to me as if I saw an object moving in the distance.

" Can you see it too, Girlie ? " I asked. But there was no need for a reply, for Hugh was staring, with eyes literally blazing with excitement, on that moving object.

" A bird ? " I suggested.

" No, a man ! "

" Yes, a man ! He seems to be gesticulating furiously."

" Now he has started to run."

"It is becoming decidedly exciting, Girlie," I said.

We had paused beside our camels, who, hungry and half dead with thirst, had lain down in the road. We waited, hardly daring to speak.

Already we could see clearly the silhouette of the man, tall and gaunt, with long, thin arms, which he waved frantically in the air, brandishing what I at first took to be a club or axe. Then, through the silence of the air, we suddenly heard his cries, which seemed to me like the dismal howls of the carrion beasts of the desert. His hair, which was long, and looked dark, flew about his head. He was naked save for a tattered loin-cloth around him. A few more minutes of suspense and the next moment the man—or apparition, so gaunt and weird was it—had rushed up towards us, and throwing out his arms had fallen on his knees, uttering hoarse and piercing cries—

"Osiris! Anubis! Mercy! Pardon!"

Without a word Hugh turned towards me with a look it were impossible to describe: *the words the poor wretch uttered were unmistakably ancient Egyptian.* The creature, which seemed hardly human, had crawled at our feet, and his great dark eyes stared upwards at us with a mixture of awe and maniacal terror, and as he crouched before us, to my horror I noticed that what he held in his hand was a human thigh bone, half covered with flesh, which he began to gnaw, while uttering the desolate shrieks of a hyena, mingled with the appealing sounds—

"Osiris! Anubis! Pardon! Mercy!"

I must confess that I felt absolutely paralysed with the horror of the situation and the awful dread, which struck me with the chillness of death. Had we toiled and travelled a thousand miles across the terrible wilderness only to find some half-human creatures who lived on the flesh of their kindred, almost deprived of reason through their brutishness, who had forgotten the glorious civilisation of the past in a present of suffering and scantily-eked-out livelihood? I remembered the golden visions of art and majesty which the name of ancient Egypt always evokes, then I looked down upon the creature who babbled that vanished tongue and wondered if, after five thousand years, its people had come to this.

Some such thoughts must have crossed Hugh's mind too, for it was some time before he brought himself to speak to the thing at his feet.

"Be at peace, my son, thou art pardoned."

No wonder the poor creature, as it looked up, mistook Hugh Tankerville for one of its gods. He looked simply magnificent. His face, worn thin and ascetic through the privations of the past few weeks, appeared strangely impressive and ethereal; his eyes were very large and dark, and his great height and breadth of shoulders were further enhanced by the long white burnous which draped him from head to foot. Still, I thought that it was a decidedly bold thing to do for a born Londoner to suddenly assume the personality of an Egyptian god, and to distribute mercy and pardon with a free hand on the first comer who happened to ask for it.

The poor wretch, somewhat comforted, had turned again to his loathsome meal.

"Whence comest thou?" asked Hugh.

"I was cast out from Kamt," moaned the unfortunate creature, as, evidently overcome by some terrible recollections, he threw himself down once more at our feet and repeated his piteous cry—

"Osiris! Anubis! Mercy! Pardon!"

Thus it was that from this poor dying maniac we first heard with absolute certainty that the papyrus had not lied. Evidently he, like the other unfortunate wretches, whose bones littered the desert sands, had been driven out of the fertile land beyond the hills and left to become a prey to the vultures of the wilderness, and slowly to die in the midst of terrible tortures of hunger, thirst and isolation.

"They don't seem to be very pleasant people to deal with out there," I remarked, "if this is an example of their retributive justice."

Hugh looked down at the man at his feet.

"Why wast thou cast out?" he asked.

The maniac looked up, astonished, perhaps, that a god should have need to ask such questions. I could see in his eyes that he was making a vigorous effort to recollect something in the past, then he said—

"How beautiful is thy temple, oh, all-creating Ra! . . . so beautiful . . . and so dark . . . so jealously guarded . . . no one knows what lies beyond. . . . I tried to know . . . to learn thy secrets. I know now! . . . the valley of death, whence no man returns, the valley of earth and sky, where hunger gnaws the vitals and thirst burns the throat . . . where evil birds croak of eternal darkness, and vile beasts prowl at night. . . ."

He was trembling from head to foot, and his eyes, quite wild with terror, watched a black raven close by, which had alighted on a skull and was picking out some débris of flesh out of the hollow sockets of the eyes.

"Give me sleep, oh, Anubis!" he moaned, "and rest . . . eternal sleep . . . and rest . . . and rest . . ."

"He is dying," I said, kneeling down beside the maniac and supporting his head. "Give me some brandy, Girlie."

"I think it would be kinder to knock him on the head; this prolonged agony is terrible. What fiends, I wonder, invented this awful mode of dealing with criminals?"

"Well! we shall know soon enough. I wish he could manage to tell us how he came across those hills, and how best we can find our way."

I had poured a few drops of brandy down the dying maniac's throat; it revived him momentarily for he gave a gasp and murmured—

"Is this thy fire, oh! Osiris?"

"It is life," said Hugh.

"Life is a curse outside the gates of Kamt."

"Then thou must endeavour to go back to Kamt."

And the dying man whispered, after a pause, while his head rolled from side to side upon his shoulders—

"The gates are closed for ever that cast out the evil-doer. . . . No one can enter Kamt, but thou, oh! Osiris, on thy crested eagle, or thou, Anubis, astride on the winged jackal."

He had begun to wander again in the realms of merciful oblivion; his eyes gradually closed, whilst his lips continued to murmur—

"Take thou my soul, oh! Anubis. . . . Pardon. . . . Mercy. . . . The gates are guarded . . . I cannot return. . . . Oh, great and glorious land of Kamt . . . where eternal streams flow between marble dwellings and gardens of lotus and lilies . . . where at night Isis smiles down on the beautiful daughters of Kamt . . . dark-eyed and slim as the white gazelles of the fields . . . I shall not behold thy loveliness again . . . my soul flies from my body . . . already . . . I feel thy hand . . . oh! Anubis! guiding me to that mysterious land . . . where dwelleth Ra . . . and where thou sittest in judgment, oh, Osiris, the Most High . . ."

Obviously it would have been inhuman to try and drag the flitting soul back to earth and suffering. I even thought that it was cruelty to try and prolong his life with brandy and restoratives. I shuddered as I looked round at the terrible wilderness, and as the conviction was forced upon me that these skeletons and débris of human creatures were the records of thousands of such lonely tragedies as we were now witnessing, since the great hordes of Egypt had found a home in the mysterious oasis of the desert.

For of this fact now there could be no doubt. The dying maniac had, with his last breath, blown away the few remaining clouds of doubt that sat upon my mind.

"I think he is dead," I said after a long pause, whilst I looked round for some hollow where I could put the body in safety from the carrion.

"May God have more mercy on his soul than human justice has had on his body," said Hugh, looking down compassionately on the gaunt form of the dead criminal.

We improvised a grave for him. At least he, who had drawn before us the first picture of the land we had come out to seek, should not become a prey to the vultures. It certainly had not been a cheerful picture: people who would invent so terrible a form of punishment, and carry it out wholesale, were not likely to be very kindly disposed towards strangers.

"I cannot understand our late friend's talk about the gates being closed for ever. Surely an entire country cannot be closed up with gates!" I said, after we had thrown a few handfuls of earth and shingle over the body of the unfortunate wretch.

"I imagine that those hills are very precipitous, probably very difficult of access, save perhaps through some passes or valleys across which the gates may have been built."

"Anyhow, we had better go straight on and trust to the same good luck which has brought us so far."

"Do you wonder that an elderly Greek priest should at such a juncture have retraced his steps homewards?"

"No, I don't. . . . But our late friend drew such a picture of marble halls and dark-eyed girls, that I, for one, am determined to demand admittance into that jealously-guarded land, in my new capacity as one of its gods."

Unfortunately, as already we had feared, one of our camels now absolutely refused to make a move. It meant, therefore, that we should have to make the rest of the journey on foot, with as small a supply of food and water as possible, as our sole surviving beast of burden was too weak to be very heavily loaded, and would also probably break down in a few hours. Distances are terribly elusive in the desert, and the hills, which at one time had appeared but a few miles from us, seemed no nearer after a whole day's march. Darkness overtook us, seemingly without our having made much progress southward. We were tired out, and pitched our tent on the wayside. In the early morning our first look was for the hills beyond; they did not appear more than five miles away, and as the sun rose higher in the east its rays suddenly caught one spot on those distant rocks: a large square patch, some hundred feet from the valley beneath, which glistened like a sheet of gold.

"The gates of Kamt, I am sure," said Hugh.

We started with renewed vigour, and late in the afternoon we reached the foot of the hills. But gradually, as we drew nearer, we realised the truth of the mysterious sayings of the doomed criminal cast out into the desert: "None can enter Kamt, but thou, Osiris, on thy crested eagle, or thou, Anubis, astride on thy winged jackal!"

The range of hills which surrounded the mystic land, an oasis in the midst of the awful wilderness, rose abrupt and precipitous to a height of two and even three hundred feet; they rose side by side in one uninterrupted chain of heights. Like the other rocks of the desert which we had traversed, the incessant action of the sand had polished the stone till every boulder had worn away, leaving a smooth and slippery surface which defied the foot of man.

Immediately facing the road, across the wilderness, there had once been a wide valley between two hills: now it had been built in—by those same hands which had fashioned the pyramid of Ghizeh—with monstrous blocks of granite, placed tier upon tier till they formed a gigantic inverted pyramid sloping out towards the desert from the ground on which its apex rested, while its two sides were encased in the rock right and left.

Some hundred feet above us, in the wall of this mammoth inverted pyramid, there was a huge, solid slab of burnished copper, which glittered with a hundred ruddy colours in the morning sun. As far as our eye could reach, where Nature had failed to make the chain of rocks uninterrupted, where any break in the line of hills, or any valley occurred, the great people, who had been cast forth by the stranger into the wilderness, and had found beyond it a paradise, had blocked it with gigantic slabs of granite, which barred every entrance to the new home they were so jealous to guard.

"Unless we fly, old man, we cannot get in by this gate," I remarked.

"No! and I expect that every entrance to this mysterious land is guarded in the same impenetrable way."

"We must try and get over these hills somehow. Surely there is a valley or mountain pass somewhere."

"I am absolutely convinced that there is none."

"Then what do you propose to do?"

"For the present, nothing . . . wait . . ."

"We have provisions here which, with the strictest economy, will last us six or eight days," I remarked casually.

"Exactly. And that is why we cannot afford to go wandering at random in search of imaginary entrances to the stronghold. This entrance is here, above us; we know it, it stands before us, and that is the way we must try to get in."

"But it seems very hermetically closed."

"But it will open again," said Hugh eagerly. "Listen, Mark. I have reckoned it all out. The poor starving wretch had been cast out say ten or twelve days before we met him, which was two days ago. Ten more days say, during which we can still manage to hold out, making twenty-four days altogether or thereabouts from the time that the copper gate was last opened. Now, assuming that this Elysium has an average of not less than one evil-doer a month, I propose that we wait here until the next unfortunate wretch is hurled out on to the ground where we stand."

"Even granting," I objected, "that everything will happen exactly as you imagine—which, by the way, things never do—the gate when it opens will still be a hundred feet above us, and we can neither of us fly."

"Mark, old chap, reflect a moment. Had our late informant any broken bones?"

"No."

"Therefore he was not dropped from an altitude of a hundred feet, and the same object which lowers the criminal into the valley of death will be the means of our effecting an entrance into the fortress."

Hugh was quite right, of course. Obviously there was nothing else we could do but wait. I had no other suggestion to make, and set to work to revise our commissariat. We found that, by the strictest economy, we could divide our water and food supply into eight equal parts. Eight days we could sit and wait opposite that slab of burnished copper, waiting for admittance to the strange and mysterious land which, now that we were near it, seemed farther off than ever. It was a curious vigil, for we never moved out of sight of the glowing gate, but watched it ceaselessly, never both sleeping at the same time. But day followed day in endless monotony beneath hot noonday sun and cool silvery moon. At times we thought that our ears caught strange sounds of sweet music, and every now and then the air was filled with the penetrating odour of myrrh and lotus blossom.

Day followed day, while we lived, as it were, only through our eyes; we were no longer conscious of heat or cold, of the terrible wilderness around us, the thousands of skeletons which told a tale of inexorable justice and vengeance, of a great people, indomitable and masterful, of the weird cries of the hyenas, and the vultures which hovered over our heads, scenting the coming approach of death. We fought against Nature, who tried to conquer us by hunger and by thirst, by weakened nerves and by drowsiness; we allowed our minds free play, and through that grey and frowning barrier, our eyes rendered far-seeing by suffering and enforced asceticism, we saw the marble halls, the gardens of lotus blossoms, the endless rivers and fragrant glades; we saw the procession of priests and priestesses, heard the sound of the sistrum and the harp, smelt the incense, and gazed at the dark-eyed dwellers of this land of paradise, and in these visions and these dreams forgot the awful doom which, with slow and sure footsteps approached stealthily and threatened to close our eyes for ever in the sight of the opening paradise.

CHAPTER VI

THE TEMPLE OF RA

I HAVE no wish to dwell over that vigil in sight of goal. The sufferings of two men, tortured morally and physically, by anxiety and vanishing hope, by hunger and by thirst, by heat and by cold, are neither pleasant nor interesting reading. Personally, all through those dreadful days I never once lost the belief that we should succeed in the end. As a medical student, my faith in an all-guiding Providence, in the God of our childhood, had necessarily become sadly mauled about by my own dissecting knife, but I had spent now nearly sixty days in the desert between earth and sky, away from civilisation, twentieth century, and modern thought, and, in the wilderness had forgotten how to scoff, and begun once more to learn how to believe and how to pray; and now in the face of coming success I refused to believe that the same hand, which had guided us unerringly so far, would snatch the glorious prize from us, at the moment when our enfeebled arms were stretched out ready to grasp it.

Throughout the long days of suffering, when gnawing hunger and raging thirst made paltry creatures of us both, Hugh's wonderful buoyancy of spirits never forsook him entirely, and many a weary hour did he help to lighten with his picturesque descriptions of the people, whom all the world believed to be dead, but which we knew to be living behind those impenetrable walls.

As I said before, I have no wish to dwell on those ten days

during which we incessantly watched that brilliant copper gate glistening with a myriad golden tints in the rising and the setting sun, but my thoughts love to linger on that memorable dawn when, suddenly, as the first rays of the sun peeped out across the immensity of the desert, our ears caught a sound, soft, and low, and distant, which made our hearts stop beating and made our weakened pulses thrill with a newly-awakened hope.

It was a chant, melancholy and monotonous, which reached us like the noise of a swarm of myriads of bees, whilst at intervals there came the roll of muffled drums far away.

"Can you hear it, Mark?" whispered Hugh.

I nodded.

"It sounds like a funeral dirge."

"Mark! they are bringing a criminal to execution."

I almost caught myself saying, "God grant it!" but felt that such a speech would be doubtful in its morality.

The chant came no nearer, but suddenly it seemed as if a vigorous arm struck a ponderous metal gong. Then there was silence, while we waited and looked. . . .

Looked! and saw that the massive copper door was slowly dropping from out its granite frame, throwing out innumerable sparks of glistening light as it moved; it was gradually being lowered by unseen hands, like a drawbridge in one of our ancient Norman castles, until it remained suspended over our heads like a gigantic and glowing canopy.

The chant died away, the sound of muffled drums had ceased, but from where we stood we became aware of shuffling footsteps on the bridge above, and of something weighty being dragged along; there was also the sound of heavy metal, and presently, over the edge, the body of a man was slowly lowered into space.

He was supported round the waist by a broad metal belt; there was a bandage over his eyes, and his arms and legs hung downwards, rigid and inert, as if he were dead or in a drugged sleep.

Gradually the body was lowered to the ground until the feet touched it, quite close to where we stood watching, breathless and appalled, this silent and inexorable act of vengeful justice. Then one of the ropes was jerked from above: the criminal, still wrapped in unconsciousness, rolled in the sand at our feet.

There was no time to think of aught save of swift and sudden action.

"Ready, Mark?" whispered Hugh.

And I knew what he meant. With one bound we had jumped over the body of the condemned man, had passed our arms through the metal belt, and as it was dragged upwards again, it bore two enterprising and victorious Britishers right into the precincts of the jealously-guarded land.

We had managed to get a foothold on the bridge, and to loosen our grasp of the belt, just before it was vigorously jerked over its edge, and was dragged away into the darkness before us by the same invisible hands which had presided over the execution. Before us there yawned what looked like a dark and gigantic tunnel. There was no time for hesitation, nor any desire on our part to delay. Quickly we walked across the bridge; already it was beginning to be raised upwards. Soon the light from outside became more and more narrow, then disappeared altogether. There was no sound, no clash as the ponderous gate shut to; everything remained as silent as the vast grave behind it, but we were for good or for evil—for ever, probably—prisoners in ancient Kamt!

We could see nothing at first, but we seemed to be in a tunnel or cave, so dark was it, and it was only after a few moments that, our eyes becoming accustomed to the gloom, we saw that we were standing on a platform of granite, whilst before us a flight of steps led downwards. At irregular intervals a thin fillet of light filtrated down from above. The atmosphere was hot and heavy, a faint and penetrating scent, as of some burning aromatic herbs, rendering it peculiarly oppressive. In the far distance we could hear the sound of retreating, shuffling footsteps, those of the executioners, no doubt, who had done the grim work of execution, and as they died away we became aware of a strange, hissing sound, which seemed to come from somewhere below where we stood.

"Welcome to Kamt, old fellow," said Hugh in a whisper; "there is no turning back now. Here we are!"

"Go ahead, Girlie," I rejoined, "the adventure has become decidedly interesting."

"Will you follow me, Mark?"

"To the death, Girlie!" I said.

"Silence then till further orders!"

And cautiously, in the darkness, we began to descend. The hissing sound had become louder. I obeyed and followed Hugh, but my hand was on his arm, ready to drag him back, for I had a presentiment of what was to come. We had gone down some twenty steps or so, when suddenly before us, just beneath the shaft of light, which illumined their sleek and shiny bodies, two cobras rose, hissing and beating the air with their heads. We had instinctively drawn back before the grim and loathsome guardians of the secrets of Kamt, but obviously hesitation was death. Already the reptiles were creeping up the granite steps towards us; in the thin streak of light we could see their forked tongues glistening like tiny darts of silver. Hugh had quickly torn the burnous from off his shoulders; I had done likewise.

"Swiftly does it, Mark," he said.

"I'll tackle the left one, Girlie, you the right," I replied, "and let us hope to God there are no more of them below."

As Hugh had said, it was a case of "Swiftly does it!" Our burnouses were large and heavy, fortunately, and violently we threw them right over the venomous reptiles and smothered their hisses in the ample folds of the draperies: then, without looking behind us, we fled down the steps.

Soon the staircase began to widen, and from below a strange blue light reached upwards. We could distinguish the walls on either side of us, of black, polished granite, like the steps, on which our feet slipped as we flew. We were evidently nearing the bottom, for we could see a wide archway before us, which seemed to frame in a flood of weird, blue light, and presently we found ourselves on a circular landing, supported all round by enormous, massive columns of the same black granite, smooth and funereal-looking, without a trace of carving or ornamentation of any kind.

Each side of the stairway we could dimly distinguish the monstrous feet and legs of some huge figures, the bodies of which were lost above us in the gloom. In the centre stood a massive tripod of bronze, supporting a bowl of the same dark metal from which issued a blue flame, that flickered weird and ghostlike over the polished stone, leaving dark, impenetrable shadows behind the pillars, and making the air oppressive with the penetrating fumes of incense and burning herbs.

At the further end of this hall a curtain made of some dull black stuff hung in heavy folds, and beyond it we could faintly hear the murmur of a distant chant, accompanied by some stringed instruments and drums.

"There is nothing for it, Mark, but to go straight on," said Hugh; "the burning incense and the pillars suggest to me the rear of some temple through which probably the condemned criminals have to pass on their last journey. We must trust to our good luck that we are not discovered in the very place where we have the least right to be.

We crossed the great black hall, and Hugh pushed aside the curtain! . . .

It seemed like the sudden bursting of golden dawn after a dark night. Behind and all round us, black granite, dull bronze, dense shadows, the atmosphere of a threshold to the grave; before us, a glittering radiance of gorgeous colours, a vista of marble columns and golden pillars, a vision of splendours in enamels and gems such as we, in our sober, Western civilisation, have never even dreamed of.

Immediately in front of us, occupying the centre of an inner sanctuary, there towered upon a pedestal of burnished copper and gold a mammoth figure carved in rose-coloured, spotless marble. As we were behind the figure we could only see high above us, half lost in a hovering cloud of incense, the gigantic head crowned with a tiara which literally blazed with gems. A flight of steps covered with sheets of polished copper led up to the statue of the god, and on each step an immense bronze candelabra stood, supporting great bowls from which a flickering blue flame emerged, throwing fantastic and ghostly lights on the dull red of the copper, the purity of the marble, the jewels on the head of the god.

The roof above us was lost in the clouds of incense and burning herbs, but from it somewhere high above our heads there hung on metal chains innumerable lamps of exquisite design and workmanship. A solemn peace reigned in the majestic vastness of the temple, only from somewhere, not very far, a sweet, monotonous chant reached our ears, sung by many young, high-pitched voices, and accompanied by occasional touches on stringed instruments and beating of muffled drums.

Cautiously we advanced round the pedestal of the god and looked straight before us. The inner sanctuary was divided from the main body of the temple by a gossamer veil of silver tissue, which looked almost like a tall cloud of incense, rising up to the invisible roof and floating backwards and forwards with a gentle sighing sound when it was fanned by a sudden current of air. Through it we could only vaguely see row upon row of massive marble pillars of the same rose-hued marble, stretching out before us in seemingly interminable lengths, and here and there great tripods of bronze, with bowls filled with many-coloured lights, which flickered on the granite floor and on the columns, bringing at times into bold relief bits of delicate tracery or quaint designs in bright-coloured enamels. The picture, low in tone, delicately harmonious, in a blending of blue and green and purple, was a perfect feast to the eye.

Hugh had left the protection of the great pedestal and had just stepped forward with a view to exploring further the beautiful building into which Fate had so kindly led us, when the chant we had heard all along suddenly sounded dangerously near, and hastily we both retreated up the copper flight of stairs, and each found shelter immediately behind the huge marble tibias of the presiding god.

In spite of danger and risks of discovery, I could not resist the temptation of craning my neck to try and catch sight at last of the inhabitants of this strange and mystic land, and I could see that Hugh's dark head also emerged out of his safe hiding-place.

Beyond the filmy, gossamer veil something seemed to have detached itself from the gloom and the massive pillars and was slowly coming towards us. I almost held my breath, wondering what my first impression would be of the great people we had come so far to find.

They advanced in single file, and gradually the outline of

the most forward became clearer and more distinct. They were young girls draped in clinging folds of something soft and low-toned in colour; they walked very slowly towards the inner sanctuary—straight towards us, as I thought. Some held quaint, crescent-shaped harps, from which their fingers drew low, monotonous chords. Others beat the sistrum or a small drum, and all were chanting with sweet, young voices the same invocation or prayer, which had been the first sound of life that had greeted us from beyond the gates of Kamt. There were a hundred or more of these fair daughters of the mysterious land, and fascinated, I gazed upon them and listened to their song, heedless of the danger we were running should we be discovered. They looked to me as if they had been carved out of an old piece of ivory; their skins looked matt and smooth, and their eyes—abnormally large and dark —stared straight before them as they approached.

The foremost one I thought must be looking absolutely at me, and I, as if enthralled, did not attempt to move; and then I saw that those eyes, so brilliant and so dark, stared unseeing, sightless before them.

The first songstress had passed and turned, still leaving the gossamer veil between us; the second followed, and then another and another. They all filed past us, walking slowly and beating their instruments, and grouped themselves on the steps of the sanctuary, some crouching, others standing, and each as she turned and passed stared straight before her towards the god, with the same lifeless, sightless gaze.

I shuddered and looked towards Hugh. He too had noticed the vacant look of the young girls; he too stared at them, pale and appalled, and I guessed that he too wondered whether Nature had smitten all these young beings in the same remorseless way, or whether the same hands that cast out their fellow-creatures from their homes and doomed them to slow starvation in the wilderness had taken this terrible precaution to further guard the mysteries of the land of Kamt.

But we had no leisure to dwell for any length of time upon a single train of thought. The picture, full of animation and gorgeousness, changed incessantly before our eyes, like a glittering pageant and ever-moving, brilliant kaleidoscope. Now it was a group of men in flowing yellow robes, tall and gaunt, with sharp features, and heads shorn of every hair, till their crowns looked like a number of ivory balls; now a procession of grotesque masks representing heads of beasts—crocodiles, rams, or cows, with the full moon between their horns; now a number of women with gigantic plaited wigs, which gave their bodies a grotesque and distorted appearance; and now stately figures carrying tall, golden wands headed with sundry devices wrought in enamel and gems. And among them all there towered one great, imposing, central figure, who, after he had stood for awhile with arms stretched upwards facing the mammoth god, now turned towards the multitude of priests and priestesses, and in a loud voice pronounced over them an invocation or a blessing. He was an old man, for his face was a mass of wrinkles, but his eyes, dark and narrow, shone with a wonderful air of mastery and domination. His crown was shaved, as was also his face, but on his chin there was a short tuft of curly hair standing straight out—an emblem of power in ancient Egypt. Over his white flowing robes he wore a leopard's skin, the head of which hung over his chest, with eyes formed of a pair of solitary rubies.

Fortunately the gossamer veil still hung between us and the group of priests. The sanctuary itself was more dimly lighted than the main body of the temple; we therefore had not yet been discovered, and if no one pushed aside the protecting curtain we were evidently safe for the moment.

Suddenly a terrific fanfare of silver trumpets and beating of metal gongs, accompanied by prolonged shouting from thousands of throats, prepared us for another tableau in the picturesque series.

This time it was a litter, which, borne on the shoulders of swarthy, abnormally tall men, detached itself from the distant shadows, and as it approached, suddenly one and all, priests and priestesses, songsters and harpists, prostrated themselves on the ground, touching the granite floor with their foreheads. Only the tall central figure—the high-priest evidently—remained standing with arms outstretched, as if in benediction, towards the approaching litter. On it, in the midst of rose-silk cushions and draperies, which helped to enhance the ghastly pallor of his face, there reclined a man—

little more than a youth, yet with the foreshadowing of death marked in every line of his countenance: in the deep, sunken eyes, the wax-like tone of the skin, the damp, matted hair which clung to the high forehead, polished like a slab of ivory. He looked strangely pathetic as he lay there, surrounded by so much richness and pomp, his head trembling beneath the weight of a gigantic diadem—the double crown of Egypt, in crimson and white enamel chased with gold, with the royal uræus encircling the pallid brow—the crown, in fact, which is so familiar to every reader of Egyptian mysteries, the crown which told us more plainly than any of the wonders we had seen hitherto, that we had penetrated in very truth to the midst of the great people, who gave to the astonished world the first glimpses of a wonderful and vanished civilisation.

Hugh, I could see, was, with sheer excitement, almost as pale as the great Pharaoh who lay upon his gorgeous litter; for Pharaoh he was, ruler of a Lower and Upper Egypt, the same as those of his ancestors, of whom we poor Western folk have known, and as all those of whom we know nothing must have been, since they brought their high civilisation, their gorgeous art, their knowledge and beauty, to this mysterious oasis in the midst of the ocean of wilderness.

Heavily enough did the noble diadem seem to rest upon the head of the present scion of a thousand kings. Half-fainting he lay among the cushions, while his hands, which were covered with rings and gems, toyed listlessly with a pair of tiny apes, who disturbed the solemn majesty of the temple by their shrill and incessant chatter, whilst I felt my very brain reeling when I realised that I, Mark Emmett, M.D. of London, a prosy British medical practitioner, was absolutely gazing with my own eyes at a living, a breathing, a real Pharaoh.

A large retinue of trumpeters and gorgeous attendants, too numerous and wonderful for my poor reeling senses to take in all at once, were standing round the Pharaoh's litter, which was placed a little to the left of the solemn high-priest; then suddenly, once again, all those present beat the ground with their foreheads, and I saw a second litter approach, borne by eight men of almost negro-like complexion. This litter was draped in funereal black, with here and there a glint of gold and jewels, and on it there half crouched, half lay a most beautiful woman. She could not have been very young, for there was an obvious look of maturity about her voluptuous figure and graceful pose, but the black of the draperies set off to perfection the ivory whiteness of her shoulders and arms. (A fact of which I doubt not but that the lady was fully aware, for surely the daughters of this mystic country have some of the charming weaknesses of their more sophisticated sisters of the North.) Her small head looked regal beneath the lovely diadem, in shape like a crouching ibis, which we all know so well, and from the top of her head to her tiny sandalled feet she seemed one gorgeous glittering mass of gems. Her garment—the little of it there was—was clinging soft and silky, and of the same most becoming funereal hue.

Her litter had been placed beside that of the Pharaoh, of whom I vaguely wondered if he were her husband, for he seemed, in spite of his ailing look, to be a great deal younger than she. Round the two central personages I caught sight of a great many people, some with tall wands, others with garments covered with devices and hieroglyphics, of groups of naked slaves, and of musicians with sistrum and harps.

The high-priest and his satellites were standing with their backs towards us, in a dense group facing the Pharaoh and the royal lady. I could not see what they were doing, but heard the high-priest recite one after another a number of short invocations, and presently I heard the bleating of a lamb, while the priestesses again intoned one of their monotonous chants. I was thankful then that I could not see what was going on—a sacrifice, no doubt, to the deity behind whose tibia we crouched. Then the high-priest raised his voice, and even my unscholarly ears caught, clearly and distinctly, the words, which he uttered slowly and solemnly in the language, which the scientific world of Europe has believed to be dead—

"*Oh, arise, Ammoun-Ra! Thou self-creating God!*

"*Isis and Nephthys attend upon Thee!*

"*Ra! Thou, who givest all goodness, Ra! who dost Thyself create!*

"*Thou hast caused the vault of heaven to rejoice, by the greatness of Thy soul!*

" The earth of Kamt doth fear Thee, oh, Sparrow-hawk, that art thrice holy ! oh, Eagle, that art blessed !

" Oh, great lion, who defendest Thyself, and dost ope the way to the ship of Sekti !

" King of Heaven ! Lord of the Earth ! Great image in the two horizons of Heaven !

" Ra ! Creator of the world !

" May the son of Osiris, Pharaoh, the Holy, be reverenced through Thy merits !

" Hail to Thee !

" Descend on the Pharaoh ! Give him thy merits in Heaven, Thy powers upon earth !

" Oh, Ra, Who hast made the heavens rejoice, and made the earth tremble with holy fear ! "

I did not understand every word, but caught the general tone of the invocation, which went on in similar short sentences for some considerable time, whilst a smell of burnt flesh began to fill the air, quickly smothered by a pungent odour of aromatic herbs.

" Behold ! Ra has accepted thy sacrifice, oh ! Maat-kha, and thine, oh ! holy Pharaoh ! He has opened wide the portals of his wisdom to his High-Priest, who stands ready to answer thee, and to advise if thou wilt question him."

Then a woman's voice, deep and musical—that of the Queen—replied—

" Dismiss thy priests and priestesses then, for I would be alone with thee ! "

And as solemnly as they had entered, at a sign from the high-priest, all rose to their feet and slowly filed out of the temple, till there remained in the vast building no one, beside ourselves, save the high-priest, and the Pharaoh and the Queen upon their litters, borne high on the shoulders of their black slaves. (These, I concluded, were deaf or mute, or both, for they stood as rigid as statues, with a vacant, semi-idiotic look on their dark faces.)

When the Queen was fully satisfied that her entire entourage had gone, she raised herself a little on her litter and began eagerly—

" My son is sick unto death, Ur-tasen. Yesterday again a veil like that of death lay over him for nigh upon an hour.

His physicians are ignorant fools. I wish to know if he will live."

"Thy son will live for a year and a day," replied the high-priest solemnly.

I don't know where he had gathered this somewhat enigmatical piece of information. Certainly, if it related to the sick youth before him, it did not need any spiritual powers to gain knowledge of so obvious a fact. The Pharaoh, however, if it was his chance of life which was being so openly discussed, seemed not to trouble himself about it at all. He yawned once or twice very audibly, and amused himself by teasing his hideous little apes, taking no heed whatever of the solemn high-priest, nor of the royal lady, his mother.

"Thou art ever ready with evasive answers, Ur-tasen," said the Queen, with an impatient frown. "It is meet that the Pharaoh, when he attains his twenty-first year, shall take unto himself a princess of royal blood for wife. But if Ra has decreed that the sickness of which he suffers shall ultimately cause his death, then it is *not* meet that he continue ruling over the great people of Kamt, for his hand will soon be too weak to safely guide their destinies."

"Ra has placed thee beside the throne of the holy Pharaoh to guide his hand when it begins to tremble," said the high-priest.

"But when the hand is stiff and cold, Ur-tasen, I have no other son to share the throne of Kamt with me."

"Then thy hour will have come, oh, Queen! A woman cannot rule over Kamt, if there be no husband or son to sit upon the throne beside her. Thy hour will have come, together with that peace which Isis doth give to those she loves, and thou wilt be happy, far from the turmoil of thy court and the glitter of thy crown."

But this charming prospect did not seem to appeal to the royal lady, for she leant forward on her litter, while her small hands nervously clutched at the black silk cushions.

"There would be no peace for me, Ur-tasen; for if the Pharaoh die childless, which I fear is Ra's decree, then my crown and his shall pass on the heads of those whom I abhor."

"If the Pharaoh die childless," repeated the high-priest calmly, "the crown must inevitably fall from thy head, on to that of Neit-akrit of the house of Usem-Ra."

How strange that name sounded in the mouth of the high-priest! Neit-akrit! My Queen, as I used to call her! Neit-akrit, of whom Mr. Tankerville originally spoke! She had a namesake then in this land which was her own; or had her shade come wandering back after the lapse of centuries, to fascinate our senses and our minds with the mystic charm of her personality? Evidently, however, Queen Maat-kha was not under the magic spell of that name as I was, for a look of violent rage and hatred suddenly marred all the beauty of her face.

"Thou liest, Ur-tasen!" she said.

"Woman! Queen though thou be," retorted the high-priest, "hold thy sacrilegious tongue, lest thou see the heavenly thunder crush thee and thy throne before the feet of Ra!"

Humbly Maat-kha bowed her proud head at this severe reprimand, and it was with softened, almost appealing, tones that she said—

"I hate Neit-akrit of the house of Usem-Ra."

"The gods care nought for human loves or hates," pronounced the high-priest coldly.

"Neit-akrit is young. . . ."

"And the gods have made her fair to look upon," said the high-priest, with more enthusiasm, I thought, than his venerable appearance warranted.

"She is vain and frivolous," added the Queen, with unconcern, which was obviously affected, for I could see that she was watching the effect of her words upon the priest's face, "and she seldom gives offerings to the gods and their priests."

"Age will bring wisdom," he replied quietly.

"It will not, Ur-tasen," she began with more vehemence, while she raised herself on her litter and drew closer to the priest. "See! I have brought here rich offerings for Ra; emeralds from my mines beyond Se-veneh, sapphires and rubies from Ta-bu. I have brought ostrich feathers as long as a man's arm, and oil from the sacred tree of Hana, in the garden of my palace. I have brought thee rare pigeons from my aviaries, and an ibis whose plumage is like the opening petals of the lotus blossom. I have brought thee enough gold dust to strew the steps of the altar of the god. Rich gifts and rare, sweet herbs and brilliant gems, that thou mayest pray to Osiris, that he find some other head on which to place the crown of Kamt, than that of hated Neit-akrit."

"But she is thine own sister's child! Thou canst not hate her. Thou wouldst not see the crown of Kamt on the head of a stranger?"

I thought this a very weak speech on the part of the high-priest. Evidently the visions of those emeralds and sweet-scented herbs, or perhaps the pigeons from the royal garden, had shaken his enthusiasm for the absent Neit-akrit.

"I humbled myself before her and asked her to wed my son. She laughed at me and vouchsafed no answer."

At this point, for the first time, the sick youth showed some interest in the conversation; he pushed the chattering apes roughly to one side, and over his pale, wan face there came such a look of acute mental suffering, that, for the first time since I had trodden upon this strange land, my heart felt the presence of a fellow-being and went out to him accordingly.

Then the Queen made a sign to one of the black giants who stood behind her, and he came forward carrying a gold casket, which he placed on the ground before the high-priest. I could not see its contents, but noticed how Ur-tasen made pretence of looking above and beyond it, and concluded that they must have been very tempting.

"Ten white oxen await outside, oh, Ur-tasen," whispered the Queen; "each is laden with two caskets, the contents of which are richer far than these."

"But what dost thou ask of me?"

"Give life to my son!"

"The gods alone can do that. I am but mortal. Death is in my hands, but not life."

"Let me wed again; I am still young, still beautiful; while my son lives, I am still a Queen."

"I cannot forbid thee to do what thou wilt; but the people of Kamt will rise against thee, if thou placest one of thy subjects in the bed of Hortep-ra, the most holy. There are no royal princes old enough to wed with thee."

"They will not rise," she urged, "if thou wilt but tell them that it is the will of Ra that I should wed again."

"Woman, wouldst thou urge me to blaspheme?" he retorted in holy wrath, but she repeated—

"Ten more white oxen await at my palace, and in the caves beneath my chambers, there are bars of gold which I would give to thee."

"And Osiris would smite me for the blasphemy," said the priest. "What good are thy treasures to me if my bones lay whitening in the grave?"

"Ur-tasen!" she pleaded.

But the high-priest turned suddenly towards the mammoth figure behind which we crouched, and holding aside the gossamer veil of silver tissue, which divided the inner sanctuary from the suppliant Queen, he pointed upwards at the gigantic majesty of the god and said—

"I tell thee, woman, that, Queen as thou art, thou canst not change the thread of thy destiny. The crown of Kamt, after hovering on the head of thy ailing son, will descend on that of Princess Neit-akrit. Ra, who sits up there enthroned, guarding the gates of the valley of death, could alone, through some awful and terrible upheaval, change the course of the future of this land by descending himself to sit upon its throne."

The priest had spoken very solemnly and his voice, sonorous and clear, went echoing through the majestic vault of the temple. The Queen who evidently, in spite of her petty hatred and arrogance, was a devout worshipper of the god had looked upwards with awe and reverence, whilst in her eyes I could see that she had realised the crumbling of her last, most cherished, hope. Suddenly, as she looked, I saw a curious change pass over her face; her eyes gradually dilated, her lips were parted as if to utter a cry, her cheeks from ashy pale turned to vivid red, and, stretching forth her jewel-laden arm, she pointed towards the god with trembling hand. The sickly youth, too, was looking in our direction with face as pale as death, while the high-priest appeared to tremble from head to foot, as his hand grasped the gossamer tissue of the veil. Then I saw that Hugh Tankerville, with head bare and erect, had come forward from his hiding-place and was standing facing the temple, on the very pedestal of its god. Each side of him, from the bronze tripods, a blue and a purple light threw a flickering radiance upon his tall, commanding figure and his fine dark head, and I must confess that had I not known that he was my old friend, Hugh Tankerville, I should most willingly have admitted that he might be the personification of a pagan deity.

There was a long and awful pause, during which I almost could hear the anxious beating of five human hearts, then the high-priest murmured—

"Who, and what, art thou?"

"Thou spakest of Ra," replied Hugh. "He sent me."

"Whence comest thou?"

"I come from the land where dwelleth Osiris and his bride, the glorious Isis, where Ra sitteth in judgment, and where Horus intercedes for the dead, whom jackal-headed Anubis has guided to the judgment throne of the Most High."

"And what is thy will, oh, stranger, who hailest from the land where dwelleth Osiris?"

Hugh calmly pointed towards the Queen, who was still looking at him, wrapt in superstitious ecstasy.

"To wed that woman and sit upon the throne of Kamt."

PART II

MEN-NE-FER

CHAPTER VII

THE IDOL OF THE PEOPLE

When I look back, dispassionately now, upon the awful moment when Hugh Tankerville so suddenly thrust himself into the political turmoil of this strange land, I quite see that he then seized, with characteristic presence of mind and boldness, the only opportunity there was of saving both our lives. Knowing the priests of Ra, as I did subsequently, with their almost maniacal hatred and terror of the unknown, their dread of the stranger, whose existence, after five thousand years of isolation, the most learned amongst them only dimly guessed, I feel convinced that, had Hugh then not assumed the daring *rôle*, which he kept up afterwards with such marvellous histrionic powers, our lives would, at that moment, not have been worth two minutes' purchase. But at the time I was literally staggered by the sublime insolence of his proceeding. To have hoodwinked a dying maniac in the wilderness was one thing, but to think of leading an entire population—of the size of which we had not the faintest conception—by the nose, including the somewhat aggressive feminine ruler thereof and a host of priests, was quite another matter.

Breathlessly I waited when Hugh had formulated his modest request. The high-priest, with one trembling hand still holding back the gossamer veil, was staring at the intruder with great, wondering eyes, whilst in the Queen's face a look of superstitious dread and one of slowly-awakening hope struggled for mastery. The Pharaoh's thin sallow face was inscrutable as a waxen image. He too stared at Hugh for a moment, then presently he yawned audibly, as if the advent of any celestial emissary was a matter of complete indifference to him, and turned to the more congenial companionship of his bald-faced chattering apes.

A few minutes—an eternity I thought them then—elapsed in this breathless silence, whilst to my excited fancy it seemed as if I could hear the beating of my own heart; then Hugh, beckoning to me to follow him, walked down the metal steps and stood at the foot of the sanctuary, framed in by the clouds of the gossamer veil, himself the most impressive thing in this strangely impressive place. His great height, his fine erect carriage, his air of indomitable will and masterfulness, his handsome head, rendered almost spiritual-looking by the long fast and enforced asceticism, seemed all to tower over this land, which was still unknown to him, and over its few awe-struck representatives.

He took no heed of the priest, but looked straight at the woman, throwing into his gaze that strange, almost mystic attraction which I myself had so often felt. After a while we heard like a soft sigh, an appealing whisper, a woman's voice repeating—

"Who art thou?"

"The wandering soul of Khefren, come back to Kamt to claim his own again."

"Khefren?"

"Far out, oh, Queen, beyond the valley of death, where flows the sacred river, by whose shores thy ancestors were born and were great, Khefren left a record of his glory and his might, and to-day, after five thousand times the seasons of the year have been and have gone again, Osiris sent his soul back into my body that I too might bring glory and might to the beloved land."

"And this?" she asked, pointing to where I, puzzled, amused and humble, stood waiting to know what my share in this wonderful drama was to be.

"He is my second self," said Hugh, "placed by my side by Ra himself, to love, to counsel and to protect."

The Queen raised herself from her litter, and placing her tiny sandalled feet upon the marble floor she walked slowly but unhesitatingly towards Hugh. She certainly was exceedingly beautiful, tall above the average, with queenly bearing, magnificent eyes, and rich, voluptuous figure: but somehow, as she walked, with the shimmering folds of her black gown clinging tightly round her, she reminded me of the two grim guardians at the gates of Kamt, up there beyond the granite halls, and I did not envy Hugh his luck. Immediately in front of us stood the sacrificial altar, on which the lamb had been offered up to Ra with such astonishing results, and on it was the casket, with which the Queen had tried to win over the high-priest to her views. She skirted the altar, and coming close to Hugh, she knelt down at his feet, and looking up at him, she said—

"The will of Ra be accomplished upon thy servant;" and she added, turning to the high-priest: "The sacrifice thou hast offered for me to the gods has brought me peace and happiness. Command the slaves of the temple to bring forth the oxen, laden with the gifts which I, in my gratitude, do offer thee."

It was impossible to conjecture what the thoughts of the solemn and learned Ur-tasen were during this brief scene. Superstition struggled vigorously with reason, beneath that shaven crown of his; greed too, I thought, played an important part in the workings of his conscience. He certainly was more than puzzled as to how we had got into the inner sanctuary, whilst our fair skins obviously disclaimed any idea that we were natives of his own country. How much he knew of the existence of a great world beyond the wilderness and outside the gates of Kamt, I only found out afterwards; for the moment superstition, after a brief struggle, obtained the upper hand, and after a few seconds of terribly anxious suspense, I saw that the high-priest of Ra was prepared, at any rate outwardly, to accept the stranger as the emissary of the gods, which he had proclaimed himself to be. Silently he dropped the gossamer curtain, which closed in with a soft rustle behind us, making a shimmering background for Hugh's tall figure, with the beautiful woman kneeling at his feet.

Then Ur-tasen walked up to the middle of the temple, where on a tall pedestal there stood a gigantic gong: he took the mighty clapper, and with vigorous arm thrice struck the metal, till the sound went echoing in deafening clamour, like continued claps of thunder, through the vastness of the building. And, as he struck, from everywhere doors were opened, and curtains pushed aside, letting in floods of light into the gloom. The shorn priests, in their robes, and those with marks of beasts, returned, followed by the blind priestesses, who chanted in monotonous tones their invocation to the god. And from everywhere crowds of people poured in, men and women, tall and slenderly built, with dark, almond-shaped eyes, and warm olive complexions. They filed in, in hundreds and thousands, some in gorgeous garments, others with but a loin cloth round their waists, rich and poor, evidently, humble and mighty, but all stood still as they caught sight of Hugh at the foot of the altar of their god, standing erect, while their Queen knelt humbly at his feet.

Then the high-priest, who was on the left of the altar, surrounded by his priests, began to speak in loud and solemn tones—

"Oh, people of Kamt, ye specially citizens of Men-ne-fer, behold the great and glorious mysteries of Ra! Lo! Osiris has given you the great privilege of being the first to set eyes on him who is beloved of the gods! The Most High has not willed that the great house of Memmoun-ra be erased from the face of the earth, and from the foot of his throne Osiris has sent us his well-beloved. Khefren, who ruled over the land when the sacred river, of which your forefathers spoke, flowed from the north to the south, hath come back from the regions where dwelleth Anubis, to sit upon the throne of Kamt once more. It is the will of Osiris, of Ra himself, transmitted to you by my mouth, that you should honour and obey his beloved as you would himself. People of Kamt, behold your future king!"

The blind priestesses intoned a sort of triumphal hymn. The people had prostrated themselves face downwards and kissed the granite floor. I looked across to where, in the midst of rose-tinted draperies, the sick Pharaoh leant back against the cushions toying with his two bald-faced apes. Then, once again in this region of dreamland, among these people who had seemed so strangely unreal, I saw that I had before me a bit of genuine human nature. On the pale face of the invalid, as he looked up at Hugh from under his heavy lids, a look of absolutely deadly hatred and of contempt appeared. He had seemingly taken not the slightest notice or interest in the proceedings, since the first moment of astonishment when we arrived upon the scene; he seemed entirely engrossed in the difficult task of slipping a diamond ring over the foot of one of the little apes. The look had been momentary, and no one, I think, saw it but I. The next instant he had again yawned audibly and laughed his wonted sarcastic, dry laugh, as the ugly little beast bit him savagely in the hand.

A complicated and solemn ritual ensued, with much chanting and beating of the sistrum and drum. The people, I could see, looked at Hugh and at my humble self, with the same superstitious reverence and awe, with which the Queen had accepted our mystical appearance. I wondered what passed in the high-priest's mind. The ten oxen, laden with emeralds, pigeons and other treasures, had evidently outwardly silenced his doubts, for, at a given moment, he and all his priests knelt at Hugh's feet and in turn kissed the ground immediately in front of him. Then two priests led a sweet little lion cub by a chain and put it upon the altar, and to my horror I saw the high-priest place a large dagger-like knife into Hugh's hand. Poor old Hugh! When he was a boy he could not bear to see me crush a beetle, and obviously, in virtue of his self-assumed *rôle*, he was expected to murder that pretty little creature which, playful as a kitten, was running round after its own tail, in the very middle of the sacred altar. I saw he had become very white, and that the sick youth opposite him was viewing him with a malicious and sarcastic look, while the high-priest and all the people waited. It was a very palpitating moment, for I was terrified lest Hugh, who must have been very weak for want of food and the strain of the excitement of the past few hours, should faint ignominiously at the very foot of the throne of the god whose beloved he was. What would ensue was pretty evident. The "casting out" process of the two defrauding evil-doers would be swift and sure.

"Shut your eyes, Girlie, it must be done," I whispered.

And Hugh did shut his eyes and pulled himself together with an almost superhuman effort. I followed him to the altar, and held the little creature for him, ready to guide the knife, so that death might be instantaneous. But though he was as pale as death, Hugh's hand was quite firm, only when the blood flowed freely from the cub's throat on to his hand, he tottered and his lips became livid. Fortunately I was near him, and imperceptibly was able to support him, whilst everyone was engrossed in listening to the solemn invocation, or rather commands, which the high-priest spoke over the accomplished sacrifice.

"People of Kamt, in the name of Osiris, I enjoin you to reverence his beloved!

"In the name of Isis, the goddess whose image illumines the nights of Kamt, and makes them beautiful above all, I enjoin you to look upon him as your future lord and king!

"And in the name of Ra, the great and awesome mystery, who buildeth up every throne and maketh every empire, I enjoin you to swear fealty to him, to his children and to his children's children as the ages roll away!"

Then he raised his hands aloft and pronounced a solemn blessing over the assembled multitude.

"*May the blessing of Ra rest upon your heads.*

"*May Osiris make your land fruitful and rich!*

"*May Isis give you grace and wisdom, and to your daughters beauty above all the children of men!*

"*And at your death may Horus intercede for you before the awesome judgment seat of the forty-two judges!*

"*Whilst the hand of Anubis guides your souls to eternal rest and peace!*"

The blind priestesses swung their golden censers towards us, and very soon Hugh stood enveloped in a sweet-scented cloud, through which his tall figure appeared swathed in the white drapery, and dimly lighted from behind by the sanctuary lamps, which threw flickering blue rays round his head, like some ghostly halo.

After a few moments of absolute silence in the vast and crowded building, the Queen rose to her feet and said to Hugh—

"Will my lord honour the dwelling of his servant by his presence?"

And she led him to her litter, where she invited him to sit beside her. I followed and stood close to Hugh, for he had contrived to whisper, as he brushed past me—

"Keep near me, old chap. Don't let them divide us whatever happens!"

The eight black giants had already raised the Pharaoh's litter aloft, and he was being borne away among a crowd of prostrate figures, across the vast aisle of the temple. He took no notice, however, of his adoring subjects; contemptuously he passed them by, and as his litter disappeared through the wide portals beyond, I could still hear his audible yawns and his loud, sharp, sarcastic laugh.

The Queen and Hugh were also hoisted upon the shoulders of the bearers, and I was allowed to walk by his side, whilst a crowd of gorgeous personages, with wands of office, of attendants and of slaves, closed in behind us and followed in solemn procession.

If the picture of the temple of Ra, with its ante-chamber of black granite, its mysterious vastness, its blind priestesses and solemn priests, had been impressive and majestic, certainly that which lay before us, as we emerged through the open portals, was radiant and bright and beautiful above all: the air was sweet and balmy as an English June, and filled with the penetrating and pungent odour of thousands of mimosa trees and acacia blossoms, and with the sounds of innumerable songs from myriads of bird throats. The sky was cloudless and blue, and from the top of the gigantic marble steps, where we stood, we could see the city nestling at the foot of the range of frowning hills, which divided it from the arid desert waste. The houses were tall and square, with flat roofs supported on massive columns, which glittered with quaint arabesques and devices in tones of exquisite enamel, and between them, forming the streets, broad canals were cut, the waters of which, clear and blue, scintillated as with myriads of gems; on the canals innumerable boats, with tall prow and poop high above the water's edge, in shape like a crescent moon, flitted busily along. Some were laden with piles of orange and scarlet fruit, and mountains of flowers, all of which threw vivid patches of colour on the canvas as they glided swiftly by. The granite of the houses was a soft-toned pink, and over some of the ponderous gateways huge carvings, covered with enamel, towered between clumps of date palms and acacia trees; and far ahead before us, sharply outlined against the dome of the sky, there arose, awesome, mysterious, majestic, the great and wonderful pyramids, the tombs of the kings of Egypt.

Ay! the picture was truly gorgeous, a realisation of all the beauties, the art, the colours of which scientists tell us, in words which, as I recalled them then, seemed hollow and tame. A picture such as dear old Mr. Tankerville alone knew how to paint before our delighted school-boy eyes, when he spoke of the temples of Khefren, the sphinxes of Kheops, of the mysterious Neit-akrit, and the beautiful land over which a pall of oblivion had lain for so long. Here it was new and fresh, alive as ever, and we two prosy Britishers were here to enjoy its beauties. The crescent-shaped boats, with bright-coloured sails, the naked boatmen, whose skins shone beneath the sun like pieces of yellow marble, their scarlet tight-fitting caps, their metal collars, the life, the movement, the beauty, the colour intoxicated me and made me feel as if this were, at last, life and beauty indeed.

I looked at Hugh: he had thrown back his head, and raised on his elbow, was looking out upon the land he had so daringly decided to rule and which he found so fair. As for the Queen, there was in the midst of all this beauty, this gorgeousness, but one sight which to her eyes was worth the seeing, and which gave a singular softness to her fine voluptuous face, and that was the sight of the mystic stranger who had demanded to share her throne with her, the envoy of Osiris and of Ra, the Beloved of the gods.

The invalid Pharaoh had been taken on to one of the boats, and was already being rowed along the canal, followed by his gorgeous retinue; the Queen's litter had also stopped at the foot of the temple steps, and Hugh helped her to alight and to step into her own boat. She seemed very unwilling to part from him, and prolonged her "sweet sorrow" with many whisperings, which my imperfect knowledge of the language prevented me from catching. At last she waved us a last adieu, the eight oarsmen dropped their sculls into the water, and with slow and rhythmic movement the royal craft, draped in the Queen's favourite black hangings, and glittering with ornaments of gold, disappeared down the canal, and I at last was, comparatively speaking, alone with Hugh.

A boat was evidently waiting for us, for, prostrate on the ground, eight swarthy-looking men seemed to be waiting for us and to be requesting us to step into it, which we did. From the temple the stream of people had poured out, and stood in dense and picturesque masses on the tall steps, watching from a respectful distance every movement of the Beloved of the gods.

"Perhaps you will tell me, old man, how all this is going to end," I remarked as soon as we, in our turn, were being rowed down the canal some half a dozen lengths behind the Queen's boat, and I felt that, at last, I was alone with Hugh.

He turned round to me, and the sunniest of smiles drove all the solemnity from his face.

"I don't know, old chap, and I don't care," he said with a merry laugh. "Tell me if this isn't the most glorious, the most beautiful thing mortal man can conceive?"

"It certainly is the most magnificent picture I have ever set eyes on, Girlie; but tell me what on earth you propose to do."

"Do? old chap!" he said, in his quiet, convinced way. "Why! rule over this gorgeous country, with you as my prime minister."

"I know your wants are modest, old man," I laughed, "but I should like to know how you propose to accomplish this laudable object and whether the fund of deception, from which you drew the wondrous history of your origin, is inexhaustible, for you will need plenty of it."

"That was a capital idea of mine, now, wasn't it? old fellow. Another moment and we were bound to be found out, and you can guess as well as I what would have been the summary proceeding, by which we should have made our forcible exit from this beautiful land."

"It was a bold stroke, Girlie; worthy of you. But I want to know where it will all lead to."

"To the most glorious discoveries the world of antiquity has ever dreamed of," he replied enthusiastically, his eyes literally glowing with buoyancy of spirit. "Discoveries of which my dear father used to dream, over which he broke his heart when he realised that they would be made by other eyes, other hands than his. I mean to rule over these people, Mark, study them, know them, love them, conquer them; then, having learnt all their secrets, go back to England and set the world gaping with the treasures which I shall place before its wondering eyes."

"Go back to England, Girlie," I said with a laugh; "that sounds feasible, doesn't it? You forget that Hammersmith lies some considerable distance from this picturesque Elysium, that the last 'bus to the Broadway has gone, and the tramway service is interrupted for the present. There is only one exit from this fairyland, and that is the one through which malefactors are cast out, without food or water, into the desert wilderness; unless you propose to cross those hills over there in a balloon."

"Propose? I propose nothing at present, old Mark, but to enjoy ourselves to our hearts' content. I as king-regent of this land, and you as my guide, philosopher, etc. After that—presently—a long time ahead, I hope, when you and I are tired of this place, and are ready to let the world know some of these wondrous secrets, then . . ."

"Yes? then?" I said, for he had paused awhile letting his gaze roam over the distant pyramids far away.

"Oh, well then, old chap," he said with his sublime self-reliance, "then something will happen, I am sure—something wonderful—stupendous—I don't yet know what. The upheaval of those rocks perhaps—a general chaos somewhere—to allow *me* to pass. What does it matter? Is not the present glorious enough that you want already to think of a future?"

How could I help admiring him, with his grand belief in himself and all the world, his enthusiasm, his faith, ready to kick aside a mountain if it happened to stand in his way, his set purpose, which defied alike earth and sky, atmosphere, sun and universe?

"In any case," I said with a smile, "the present for you has one additional charm: you are already provided with a very beautiful bride."

"Yes, she is beautiful," he said quietly, "though I should say she was somewhat unpleasant at times."

"A genuine Cleopatra, Girlie; in looks at anyrate."

"And probably in character. Think of it, Mark! Cleopatra, alive to-day! The Cleopatra we all read of, all fell in love with, when we were in our teens, actually alive! and the Pharaoh, Kheops! Khefren! Mena himself! and these people still building to-day tombs which rival the pyramids of Ghizeh, and carve sphinxes and mammoth gods, beside which the figures at Abu-Simnel are mere students' work!"

"And think of a real Pharaoh, Girlie, who is a real, direct enemy."

Hugh frowned a little, then he laughed.

"Yes; he is no friend. He was the only one who did not believe the story of my interesting origin."

"He may be scientifically inclined, or perhaps his illness has made him more sharp-witted than his fellow-men. I wonder what the high-priest thought of it all?"

"It is difficult to say. We shall find it out by-and-by; but in any case he has burned his boats, since he solemnly declared at the foot of his own god, to a very large crowd of people, that I was indeed the envoy and Beloved of the gods. He cannot go back on that now without proclaiming himself a liar."

"I wonder what his position is in the government of the country?"

"Paramount, I should say. If you remember he practically forbade Queen Maat-kha to wed one of her own subjects, and she was quite prepared to obey, when I, the Beloved of Osiris, appeared upon the scene."

His eyes twinkled with the humour of the situation, and he added—

"What do you think Aunt Charlotte would say, old Mark, if she saw you in your new character as a defunct Egyptian come to life again, to gladden the hearts of the great people of Kamt? How do you feel, eh?"

"About the same as you do, Girlie, in your character of usurper of someone else's property. Now you can't get away from the fact that by your assumption of a semidivine *rôle* you have helped to defraud a lady of her just rights, and she, to judge from the enthusiastic eulogies of that old rip, the high-priest, is young and beautiful."

"And moreover is called Neit-akrit," added Hugh, musingly, "a name which to you and me is associated with the most cherished memories of childhood, with the dear old Chestnuts, the museum, where the shade of the mysterious queen used to wander before our excited fancy, conjured into life by the picturesque story told by my father, and rendered glowing by the fitful light of the great log fire as it flickered in the old-fashioned hearth. Perhaps, after all, old Mark, this is all a dream; you and I are not really here, and presently I for one shall wake up and find myself sitting beside that hearth, trying to decipher by those dying embers the last few lines of a sneering article, vilifying the memory of mad Tankerville and his hobby."

We had left the temple of Ra far behind us now, and our boat, as Hugh was talking, turned into a wider canal, on each side of which the houses were more imposing, more luxurious than heretofore. Beneath the peristyles of massive columns, and in the gateways, we caught sight of groups of people, richly dressed, who followed our boat with eager gaze as it glided swiftly by. Evidently the great and mystic news had spread throughout the city, and in the houses of rich and poor alike, all were anxious to be among the first to set eyes on the emissary of Ra.

We passed an island, which was evidently a market-place, for gigantic piles of pomegranates, melons and dates stood everywhere, together with mountains of golden mimosa, snow-white acacia, spotted orange and flame-coloured lilies and pink aloes, behind which sat enthroned women in gay draperies, and striped kerchiefs floating over their dark hair; while between this wealth of fruit and blossom busy figures flitted to and fro. But at sight of the royal boats pomegranates and dates, aloes and palms were abandoned and an excited throng rushed to the water's edge. Presently one little maiden, more venturesome than her elders, took up a bunch of mimosa, and, with wonderful dexterity, flung it with all her might towards our boat, where it alighted right on Hugh's shoulder, deluging us both with a sweet-scented shower of golden dust. Then a loud shout of delight rent the air, and in a moment we, the boat and the boatmen, nearly came to grief beneath a veritable avalanche of blossoms—lotus flowers and honeysuckle, branches of papyrus and bouquets of iris, penetrating tuberoses and sprays of orange blossom—till we had much to do to keep up a dignified appearance under this persistent and uncomfortable shower.

"No doubt, Girlie, that this is no dream," I said as soon

as we had left the enthusiastic market-square behind, "and no doubt that you won't find it difficult to exact veneration and obedience from these excitable people. They look upon you already as one of their deity."

"They fascinate me, Mark. They are so intensely picturesque. But it strikes me there is a terrible vein of cold-blooded cruelty in those that rule them."

"Perfect monsters, I should say, remembering the awful doom they mete out to criminals."

"I am going to try my hand at that amount of civilisation, anyhow. Civilising!—" he added, with a laugh. "A strange word indeed to use in connection with people who build such cities and carve such temples. But they have yet one thing to learn."

"Christianity?" I said. "You are bold."

"Christianity?—No, old chap, you and I are not cut out for missionary work. I suppose there is a something wanting in our education for that, something out of tune—perhaps our sense of humour, but we can pave the way for worthier men than we are, whose prosy minds will be above the petty scruples, which I confess would stay my hand from destroying these pagan yet gorgeous temples, these false, yet oh! such picturesque deities. Then, presently, when the world, guided by us, will have revelled long enough in the picturesqueness of this great and unknown land, the Western nations can begin their endless fight as to who shall best desecrate it."

There was no time to prolong our chat, for the boat was slowing towards an island, which lay in the middle of the stream. On it, amidst shady groves of giant fuchsias and drooping clematis, we saw glistening the gilt and copper roofs of a vast palace, half-hidden in the bower of many-coloured blooms. Gradually, as we approached, we saw its noble proportions, its walls and columns of alabaster-like marble, covered with arabesques and tracings of several tones of gold. It stood close to the water's edge, above a flight of marble steps, up and down which there stalked in stately majesty a number of pink flamingoes. In the branches of acacias and palms many apes chattered shrilly, and beneath the shadows of overhanging leaves we caught sight of a herd of snow-white cows with tall slender horns. A crowd of tiny girls, in turquoise blue dresses, lined the long flight of steps, and as the Queen's boat was moored below, they all began to sing a sweet-sounding greeting.

"It seems that we are to be the royal lady's guests," I remarked as our boat also drew to the side. "I don't know what you feel, Old Girlie, but I, for my part, am ready to collapse if I don't get some food within the next hour."

As soon as we had landed the Queen came up to Hugh and said some pretty words of welcome to him; then, at last, she deigned to take notice of me.

"Wilt thou accompany my lord beneath the humble roof which he will honour with his presence?" she asked.

Now I felt that in reply to this invitation it would have been ill-mannered to nod, and again, at that moment, I could not for the life of me recollect a single word of my Egyptian vocabulary. Innate British shyness, when placed face to face with foreign modes of speech, had completely paralysed my tongue and my memory, and all I could do to save appearances was to bow silently and somewhat clumsily before the lady.

"Is thy counsellor dumb?" she asked, turning to Hugh with astonishment.

"He speaks but seldom," he replied with characteristic presence of mind—impudence I called it, "for his words are pearls of wisdom, treasures given to him by Horus, the most learned, and as such most precious."

She seemed satisfied, for she smiled very sweetly at me as we all began to mount the steps to the palace, but she did not address her words directly to me afterwards.

In the inner hall of her palace she parted from us, but not before she had placed herself and her house, her advisers, ministers and slaves unreservedly at Hugh's command. One portion of the palace was evidently to be given over exclusively for us. A gorgeous personage carrying a wand of office, and wearing a belt emblazoned with writing, led us through many rooms, at the threshold of each of which he solemnly knelt down in front of Hugh, and kissing the ground before him, bade him welcome. Not the least attractive among the many grand halls we traversed was one in which the marble floor was sunk some six feet below the level and the basin filled with sweet-smelling, slightly steaming water. It suggested the most delicious vision of a swimming-bath my excited fancy could conceive, and only the sense of my dignity, as chief counsellor of the gods, prevented my giving way to the overwhelming temptation of then and there plunging into that inviting basin. However, the gorgeous official having welcomed us a few times more, and shown us our sleeping-apartments, which led one into the other, where he salaamed again, until I was ready to kick him out of our godly presence, we were at last left in the hands of some dark-complexioned attendants, face to face with the sweet-smelling, steaming water !—and the rest is silence ! save for the splash and the groans of content—silence and infinite bliss !

Then, afterwards, arrayed in wonderful garments, which seemed to have dropped down from heaven, and the fit of which was apparently of no consequence, for they consisted mostly of cloaks, we were solemnly led to another earthly paradise. In the centre of one of the halls, where a number of solemn personages welcomed us in various fantastic ways, there stood a low table covered with everything that could delight nostril and palate of two starving creatures whose last meal, partaken of some eight hours ago, had consisted of a piece of raw vulture's leg. Great baskets of fruit and olives, bread and cakes of different kinds, and above all, occupying the centre of the table—a happiness to the eye, a joy to the heart—a gigantic roast goose, with brown crisp skin, and a delicious odour of aromatic, sweet herb stuffing.

And didn't we enjoy that goose, in spite of the fact that we had to carve it with blunt bronze knives, and to convey the pieces to our mouths with a spoon ? I should not like to have to state how much of it there was left, by the time we really considered that we had finished with it. The gorgeous personages had fortunately most discreetly retired when we began our repast, and our attendants consisted of the sweetest little army of dark-eyed waitresses, I personally have ever known to hand sauces and fruits. They were very picturesquely, but, I blush to say, very scantily attired in a collar of leather studded with turquoise, and a deep blue kerchief held round their tiny heads with a circlet of dull metal; but I am bound to confess that this unconventional uniform by no means took away our appetites—even, I thought that it added a very special, piquant flavouring to that roast goose—and when the pretty maidens poured the wine into our cups, out of great stone jars, I thought that never had juice of grape tasted half so sweet.

CHAPTER VIII

THE MESSENGER OF PRINCESS NEIT-AKRIT

THE next day only exists in my mind as a memory of one long and gorgeous pageant: triumphal processions through the city, shouts of enthusiastic people, messengers sent flying in every direction throughout the land, to announce the great news to the inhabitants of its most outlying corners, with a promise to some of the more important cities that they should soon in their turn be gladdened by the sight of the Beloved of Ra, the son of Osiris, the messenger of the Most High. It was a wearying day to us both, who, occupying a comparatively humble position in our own country, were unaccustomed to the pomp and glitter of courts, and to the worship and salaaming of innumerable picturesque people. I, for one, found my long flowing robes very difficult to manage, and my belt of lapis-lazuli, on which were engraved sundry characters denoting my dignity, exceedingly uncomfortable. Hugh seemed to take a keen delight in wilfully upsetting my gravity at the most solemn moments, by making irreverent remarks about the elderly dignitaries, who looked for all the world like mummies out of the British Museum escaped from their glass cases.

In the precincts of the temple of Osiris, raised aloft upon a golden throne, Hugh Tankerville received the homage of the nobles of the land, the functionaries, the priests, the scribes and servants of the court. The "mob," as the traders and agriculturists were contemptuously called by the more elevated personages, were not admitted to this impressive function. They, however, showed their reverence for the emissary of the gods by making a carpet of themselves on the temple steps, the terraces and embankments, on which the Beloved of the gods and his wise counsellor were expected to tread. (A process which I, for one, found exceedingly uncomfortable, especially when I had to tread on the daintier portions of this novel carpet; the dark eyes which then peered up at me, in half-awed, half-inquisitive fashion were very disconcerting.)

Truly reverential and adoring! Good old Hugh! It amused him, I know, for I could see his eyes twinkling in merriment, but his gravity was unshakable and his dignity superb. The Pharaoh did not appear at these solemn processions—perhaps he felt that his own importance was being put in the shade—but Queen Maat-kha never left Hugh's side throughout that day long. I could not of course hear the sweet whisperings with which she helped to beguile the gorgeous monotony of the festivals, but when I had an opportunity of watching Hugh closely, I could not detect the faintest sign of enthusiasm on his part in response to her blandishments.

There was an official banquet in the latter part of the afternoon, at which the Pharaoh, sarcastic, ailing and silent, presided. I looked at him as often as I could during the interminable repast, beginning to guess the nature of the disease from which he was suffering, and wondering what physicians there were in this strange land, to alleviate his pains and give him relief. He contemptuously ignored the obsequious greetings of his entourage, as each in their turn, having entered the banqueting-hall, knelt down before him and kissed the ground. He seemed to have but one interest in life, and that was in his two apes, which never left his side, and which appeared to cause him endless delight. My still imperfect knowledge of the language prevented me from venturing on an animated conversation with my neighbour, a pompous, abnormally fat old man, who reeked of aromatic pomades, and was fed from a spoon by a young girl, who tasted of every morsel before handing it to him. Hugh sat next to me on the other side, and in one of the few intervals of rest which his interesting bride granted him, we contrived to exchange a few words together.

By this time I had got very tired of my robes and my lapis-lazuli belt. I longed for a clean shirt, a stiff collar, anything firm about my body, in place of all the flapping, swathing garments which always got in my way whenever I tried to cross my legs. Now I always had a habit of tilting my chair back and crossing my legs in good, honest, insular manner, and I had not yet realised that, in a sort of Roman toga and petticoats, this attitude was far from elegant; and when in addition to this I vainly groped for my trousers pockets in which to bury my hands, like the true-born Englishman I was, and found that not only I had no pockets but also no . . . well! I said "Damn!" loudly and emphatically.

No sooner was this useful and impressive portion of the English language out of my mouth, than I perceived that in the vast hall a deathlike silence had succeeded the noise of talk and laughter, and three hundred pairs of ears were straining to catch the strange word I had uttered, whilst the Pharaoh's keen dark eyes were fixed mockingly upon me.

But it certainly would take a great deal more than just one good British "damn!" spoken in an inopportune moment, to ruffle Hugh Tankerville's supreme dignity and composure.

"Ye know not the secrets of the tongue which Osiris teacheth his beloved to speak," he said with perfect impudence, "and my counsellor and I speak many words which it is not meet ye people of Kamt shall hear, unless indeed the gods do grant you leave. Only those who lead a just and blameless life, who pardon their enemies and relieve the oppressed, can hope to understand the veiled mysteries of Osiris's tongue."

I tried not to smile. I tried to imitate Hugh's dignity, and in a measure I succeeded; but the idea that the true understanding of a British swear-word could only be the reward of virtue, nearly upset my utmost endeavours at gravity.

Respectful silence had greeted the wonderful announcement, and three hundred pairs of eyes gazed with awed superstition at the expounder thereof. Only from the head of the table there came a low and sarcastic chuckle. Hugh affected not to notice it, and did not even glance towards the mighty Pharaoh, but from that moment I had a strong suspicion that, however ignorant on the subject of the outer world the people of Kamt might be, their ruler at any rate had but little belief in our divine origin.

What his attitude in the future towards us might be, it was impossible to guess; but weak and ill as he was, he evidently for the present had no intention of breaking into open enmity against the Beloved of the gods, who was also the idol of his people.

However, after this little episode, Hugh and I tacitly decided that it would be best only to speak English when we were alone.

The shades of evening were beginning to draw in, when at last we all rose from the table. Queen Maat-kha led us into the gardens, while the guests followed or still loitered round the tables, drinking wine or nibbling honey cakes. The Pharaoh's litter had disappeared beyond the alleys, and I for one felt much relieved by his absence.

" The evening is young yet, oh, my beloved," said the Queen, clinging affectionately to Hugh. " Isis hath not yet risen beyond the hills, and the hour is still far, when thou must leave me to preside over the court of judgment at Kamt. Wilt stay with me alone and try to find, in that mysterious language which Osiris hath taught thee, words which would convey to me the thought, that thou dost think me fair."

" Fair above all, my Queen," said Hugh, earnestly.

" Yet thou knowest not how much fairer I will be, the day when thou standest by my side at the foot of the throne of Isis, in Tanis, when clouds of incense hover round us, hiding us from the gaping multitude, and the high-priest raises his hand over our heads to give us a supreme benediction."

" Thou couldst not be fairer than thou art," he said, with a certain want of conviction, which no doubt the lady perceived, for she said a little sadly—

" How silent thou art, oh, my beloved ! Already, perchance, the destinies of Kamt sit heavily upon thy shoulders. The Pharaoh is sick, he has no will save for rest and peace, and his enemies have become powerful in the land."

" The ruler of Kamt should have no enemies, oh, Queen ! for his rule should be merciful and just; justice disarmeth an enemy's hand."

" Nay, but there are the jealous, the envious," she said with the sweetest of smiles, " those who stand so near to the Pharaoh, that with a touch of the hand, they might easily reach the crown which sits so lightly upon his head."

" My place, oh, Queen, will be beside the Pharaoh, to protect his crown from the hands of the jealous and the envious."

" Ay ! I know ! and thy protection is great, oh, Beloved of the gods ! But is it not meet," she added pensively, " that someone who is near and dear to him should pray to the gods night and day, that their continued blessing may rest upon his head ? "

I was beginning to wonder why Queen Maat-kha was suddenly showing such unwonted solicitude for her son; her sweet manners, her fascinations exercised to the full, led me to think that she was playing some hidden game.

From the first, the fascinating, exotic queen had deeply interested me. I was always a keen observer and earnest student of human nature, and the one or two incidents, in which Maat-kha had been the central figure, had already shown me that, in spite of the many thousands of miles that lay between them, in spite of barriers of desert waste and inaccessible heights, this radiant product of an ancient civilisation and her Western twentieth-century sister had the same feminine, capricious, un-understandable heart.

That she was even at this moment playing some little game of her own there could be no doubt; that there was some little feminine cruelty hidden behind her solicitude for her son was clearly shown by her almond-shaped eyes, which had gradually narrowed until they were merely two glittering slits, that again brought back to my mind the two grim guardians of the gates of Kamt.

The same thought had evidently struck Hugh, for he said, with a smile—

" Art already tired of thy future lord, oh, my Queen, that thou turnest thy thoughts to daily and nightly prayers ? "

" I ? " she said, astonished. " Nay, I was not thinking of myself. There is truly no one more near or dear to the Pharaoh than his mother, but my mission is greater and more important in the land, than that I should spend my days and nights in prayer. Nay ! there are others."

" I do not understand."

" Is it not meet," she said, speaking rapidly and eagerly, " that one who, besides being kith and kin to the holy Pharaoh, is also young and pure—a maiden—beloved of Isis—should devote that young and still blameless life to the service of the Most High ? Her prayers, like the fragrance of the spotted lily, would rise heavenwards, pure and undefiled by thoughts or memories of the past. Thou, who has dwelt among the gods, thou knowest that Ra loveth the songs and worship of a maid. His priestesses are indeed privileged, for they can sing to him at all times, praise and worship him, and he always grants their prayers."

"Privileged dost thou say? Hast forgotten, oh, Queen! that some cruel and godless decree of this land doth deprive the priestesses of Ra of his most precious gift?"

"What is eyesight beside the purity of the soul? The maids of Kamt vie with each other for the privilege of being among the chosen priestesses of Ra, who, alone among all women, kneel within the inner sanctuary of the god. And now when the Pharaoh is sick, when he hath most need of prayers, there is not one maid of the house of Memmoun-ra who mingles her song with their song, who kneels with them, entreating at the foot of the throne of the Most High."

"Young girls of the royal house, no doubt, have no desire for such a sacrifice."

"Girls are thoughtless and selfish," she said sweetly; "it is for the older and the wise to counsel them."

"Dost propose then to counsel one of thy young kinswomen to give up her life, and what is dearer than life, for the sake of praying for thy sick son?" asked Hugh, who, I think, as well as I, was beginning to perceive the subtle game his bride was playing.

"I cannot counsel, I am but a woman, and the Pharaoh's kinswoman is wilful and proud," she said with a sweet smile.

"The Pharaoh's kinswoman? Art speaking of *one* young maiden then?"

"What other being is there in this fair land more worthy of the honour to be priestess of Ra than my sister's child, the princess Neit-akrit? I cannot counsel her, for, alas! she hath hatred for me, but thou, oh, son of Ra! canst give her the message which emanates from the god himself. Thou canst command, and she will not disobey. Then, when shut off from all temptations, all turmoil and strife of this world, she will soon forget that she was once young and fair, and killed the souls of men by her wiles and her beauty; then she will bless thee for that command, and cherish thy name in her heart as she would a god's."

So that was the hidden game Queen Maat-kha was playing.

She was madly, barbarously jealous of her young kinswoman, and in that passionate, exotic nature love and hate were absolute, simple and paramount.

She had fallen a ready prey to Hugh's mystic personality; his handsome presence, his supposed supernatural origin had invested him with a halo of romance. But she knew that Princess Neit-akrit was young and beautiful, she scented a probable rival, and being a woman, a simple, ardent, semi-barbaric creature of flesh and blood, her instinct was to render that rival helpless, before it was too late.

That her suggestion was cruel and abominable goes without saying; that it would have no effect upon Hugh I felt, of course, quite sure: he turned to her and said, with quiet sarcasm—

"Dost hate thy young kinswoman so deeply, then, that thou dost ask me to formulate so monstrous a command?"

But like a cat who has shown her claws before she is ready to spring, and hides them again under the velvety paw, Queen Maat-kha said, with the sweetest of smiles and a look of childish astonishment—

"Thou makest a mock of thy servant, oh, my beloved! Thy words are but a jest, I know. I hate no one, least of all my sister's child."

"Dost fear her then?"

"Not as long as thou art near me," she said, throwing, with sudden impulse, a pair of very beautiful arms round Hugh's neck. "Wilt tell me that thou dost love me?"

"I claimed thee as my bride before the throne of Ra," he answered quietly.

"Wilt prove thy love for me?"

"It needs no other proof."

"Wilt bind thyself to grant me a request?"

"Command, oh, Queen; I will obey if the gods allow."

"Stay by my side in the palace," she pleaded; "go not forth by night or by day beyond the walls of Men-ne-fer. Men-ne-fer is beautiful and great, it shall be a feast to thine eyes, until the day when our barges will bear us to Tanis, there to be made man and wife."

"Wilt hold me a prisoner of love?" he said, smiling. "I know not if I can thus bind myself to thy feet, beautiful as thou art. My counsellor will tell thee that it is meet I shall visit my people and see the cities wherein dwell my future subjects. Dost begrudge them that, which already messengers have gone forth to announce ? "

" Ay, I begrudge every moment which takes thee away from me. Presently, to-night, when Isis has risen to illumine the night, thou wilt go to sit beside the Pharaoh, in the judgment-hall of Kamt, to pronounce sentence of life and death on all those who have erred or sinned against our laws. That hour will be martyrdom to me. Think of what I should suffer if thou wert absent for a day and a night."

I could see that Hugh, like myself, was much amused by her strange persistence and her sudden change of tactics. She was evidently bent on gaining this point, having apparently lost the other, for she put forth before him all the charms and artifices, which a woman loved or loving, alone knows how to use. It was getting very dark, and in the east a faint streak of greyish light heralded the rise of the moon, but in the semi-darkness I could see the beautiful Queen's eyes fixed with a truly magnetic look upon Hugh, whilst she half-offered, half-pleaded for a kiss. I think it would have required a very adamantine or very worn-out old heart to resist such charming pleading, or refuse so flattering a request, and I doubt not but that in spite of her earlier, decidedly unpleasant, tactics Hugh was ready enough to yield and promise all she asked, but, unfortunately at this moment, the poetic little scene was suddenly interrupted by a fanfare of metal trumpets, and from a distance we heard the cry—

" Make way for the messenger of Princess Neit-akrit ! "

Even in the darkness I could see that Queen Maat-kha had become very pale, and a dark frown appeared between her eyes.

" Thou hast not yet promised," she whispered hurriedly. " Promise, my beloved, promise."

" Make way for the messenger of Princess Neit-akrit ! "

The sound of the trumpets, the repeated cries, drowned the words in Hugh's mouth.

" Promise thou wilt not go," she entreated for the last time ; " promise thou will not leave my side ! "

But it was too late, for the trumpets now sounded quite

close in the garden, and preceded by some of the Queen's servants, a messenger, in shining tunic and silver helmet, with winged sandals on his feet—an emblem of his speed—was rapidly approaching towards us. Impatiently Maat-kha turned to him.

"What dost thou want?" she said imperiously. "Who has given thee leave to intrude on the presence of thy Queen? Thou deservedst a whipping at the hands of my slaves for thy daring impudence."

The messenger, however, seemed well accustomed to this inhospitable greeting, or in any case was very indifferent to it, for he knelt down and kissed the ground, then rising again, he quietly waited, until the flood of the lady's wrath had passed over his head. Then he began, solemnly—

"From the Most High the Princess Neit-akrit, of the house of Memmoun-ra, to the Beloved of the gods, greeting."

And again he knelt and presented Hugh with a dainty tablet, on which a few words had been engraved upon a sheet of wax. I thought for one moment that the Queen would snatch it out of his hand, but evidently, mindful of her own dignity, she thought better of it and stood a little on one side, pale and frowning, while a slave brought a torch close to Hugh and held it over his head to enable him to read.

"From the humblest of thy worshippers, greeting, oh, well-beloved of Ra, envoy of Osiris. This is to apprise thee that the dwelling of thy servant will be ready to receive thee on the day after to-morrow, and Neit-akrit will be waiting to welcome thee when Isis is high in the heavens. Wilt honour her and her house by setting thy foot upon its threshold?"

"Do not go, my beloved," whispered the Queen, excitedly.

"Tell thy mistress, messenger," said Hugh, calmly, "that on the day after to-morrow, when Isis is high is the heavens, I and my counsellor will lay our homage at her feet, according to her will."

The messenger salaamed again. Queen Maat-kha, among her many powers, had evidently not the one of killing with a look, for probably otherwise the unfortunate messenger would have paid dearly for the privilege of bringing Princess Neit-akrit's greeting. As it was, he was allowed to depart in peace, and a few very uncomfortable moments followed—uncomfortable, at least, as far as two of us were concerned, for good old Hugh seemed highly amused at the episode, and even had the heartless impudence to give me a nudge, which fortunately the Queen did not see.

"Wilt thou not bid me farewell, my Queen?" he said, trying to keep up a sentimental tone. "It is time I went to the judgment-hall, for Isis will appear anon."

But without another word she had turned away before Hugh could stop her, and had disappeared among the trees, while we both heard a heavy, almost heart-broken sob, which I think ought to have filled Hugh's heart with remorse.

CHAPTER IX

THE JUDGMENT-HALL OF MEN-NE-FER

Half an hour later we were being rowed down the canal by moonlight on our way to the judgment-hall of Men-ne-fer, and had full leisure to discuss the funny little incident in the garden.

"It was a damnable idea," said Hugh, with true British emphasis. "She must have taken me for a fool to think that I should not see through her artful game."

"Queen Maat-kha seems certainly to have vowed deadly hatred to her royal niece. I wonder why."

"Feminine jealousy, I suppose. All the more serious as the lady seems to have very few scruples hidden about her fine person. It strikes me that I shall have to extend a protecting hand over my defrauded kinswoman."

"My dear Girlie, it strikes me that that young woman will need no protection, and that, for aught you know, she bids fair to be your most dangerous enemy. She is evidently very beautiful, and a beautiful woman deprived of her rights, justly or unjustly, always has a large following."

"A statement worthy of your best college days, oh, Doctor Sagacissime. Well! we will not despise an enemy worthy of our steel. So far we have had nothing but triumph, and easy conquests might begin to pall. But I'll tell you what we can do, old chap," he added with his merry, infectious laugh, "that which shall disarm our bitterest foe, if indeed she be one. *You* shall enter the lists for Princess Neit-akrit's hand, marry her, and when presently I leave this fair land to return to the foot of the throne of Ra, I shall solemnly appoint you and your heirs my successors to the double crown of Kamt."

"I'll tell you what you had better *not* do," I rejoined half crossly, "and that is to fall in love yourself with the fascinating lady. Everyone seems to be doing it about here."

"Oh, I?" he said, suddenly becoming serious, and with a touch of sadness, "I am here with a purpose, altogether beside my own self. I have to prove to the world that neither my father nor I were fools or liars. I must study the life, the government, the art of the men; my heart is crusted over with fragments of papyrus and mummies, it is impervious even to the beauty of these warm-blooded women."

"For shame, Girlie! at your age!"

"I have no age, Mark, only a number of wasted years behind me, and a few on ahead, which I am determined shall be well filled."

It was a beautiful starlit night, and the crescent moon shone wonderfully bright, over the ancient city, with its marble edifices, its water-streets, which wound in and out among mimosa and acacia groves like a bright blue ribbon covered with glistening gems. As they rowed the boatmen sang a sweet, monotonous barcarole, and from east and west, and north and south, at regular intervals, fanfares of trumpets greeted the crescent moon as she rose.

The great judgment-hall of Men-ne-fer stood—a gigantic circular roofless building—high above a flight of dull grey granite steps. Open to the sky above, it was only lighted by the brilliant yet weird rays of the moon, which threw into bold relief the semi-circular rows of seats on which, when we entered were seated a number of solemn-looking Egyptians in long flowing robes. They all rose as Hugh's figure appeared in the massive, square archway, and he and I paused a moment to take in the strange picture which lay before our eyes.

It would be impossible for me to give any definite facts as to the proportions of this vast coliseum. It looked probably larger than it really was, owing to the dense shadows into which one half of it was plunged and which looked almost limitless. There were several tiers of stone seats, placed in semi-circle each side of a tall throne, on which, propped up with cushions, the mighty Pharaoh reclined. On his left, a foot lower than the kingly throne, sat Ur-tasen, the high-priest of Ra, and at the foot of the throne sat three old men, in one of whom I recognised my fat neighbour at the banqueting table. They also rose when Hugh entered, and I noticed that they wore round their waists heavy belts of lapis-lazuli, on which was engraved the device: "Justice. Mercy."

A seat had been placed on the right of the Pharaoh, with a low one close behind it. These were for the Beloved of the gods and his wise counsellor.

No one spoke a word in the vast and crowded building, as we made our way down into the arena first, and then up the gradients to the seats allotted to us. In the shadows behind and all around, my eyes, becoming accustomed to the gloom, distinguished a crowd of moving figures, with here and there a glint of helmet and shield.

The silence was becoming weird and almost oppressive. We were all standing, except the Pharaoh, who looked terribly cadaverous beneath the gorgeous diadem which he wore. At last Ur-tasen, raising his hands up towards the starlit sky, began to recite a long and solemn prayer. It was an invocation to all the gods of Egypt—of whom I noticed there was a goodly number—for righteousness, justice and impartiality. The solemn Egyptians in white robes, who, I concluded, were perhaps the jury, spoke the responses in nasal, sleepy tones.

While Ur-tasen prayed, a number of slaves, who were naked save for a white veil wound tightly round their heads, were going about carrying large trays, from which each member of the jury one by one took something, which I discovered to be a branch of lotus blossom. This each man touched with his forehead as he spoke the responses, and then held solemnly in his right hand.

We were, of course, deeply interested in the proceedings: the mode of administering justice in every country is the surest keynote to the character of its people. Here a decided savour of mysticism accompanied it; the peculiar hour of the night, the weird light of the moon, the white draperies, the hooded slaves even, all spoke of a people whose every thought tended towards the picturesque.

But now Ur-tasen had finished speaking. The last response had been uttered, and silence once again reigned within the mysterious hall. A herald came forth with long silver trumpet, and stood in the centre of the arena, with the light of the moon shining full upon him. He raised his trumpet skywards and blew a deafening blast. Then three times he called a name in a loud voice—" Har-sen-tu ! Har-sen-tu ! Har-sen-tu ! " and every time he called he was answered by a flourish of trumpets from three different ends of the buildings, accompanied by the loud cry—

" Is he there ? Is he there ? Is he there ? "

The herald then added—

" Let him come forthwith with all his sins, before the judgment seat of the holy Pharaoh, and in the immediate presence of him whom Osiris has sent down from heaven, the son of Ra, the Beloved of the gods. Let him come without fear, but let him come covered with remorse."

Evidently Har-sen-tu was the first criminal to be tried in our presence in the great hall of Men-ne-fer. There was a stir among the crowd, and from out the shadows a curious group detached itself and came forward slowly and silently. There were men and women, also two or three children, all dressed in black, and some had their heads entirely swathed in thick dark veils. In the midst of them, carried by four men, was the criminal, he who, covered with sins, was to stand forth before the Pharaoh for judgment, mercy or pardon. *That criminal was the dead body of a man*, swathed in white linen wrappings, through which the sharp features were clearly discernible. The men who had carried it, propped the corpse up in the middle of the building, facing the Pharaoh, until it stood erect, weird and ghostlike, stiff and white, sharply outlined by the brilliant moon, against the dense black of the shadows behind, whilst round, in picturesque groups, a dozen or so men and women knelt and stood, the women weeping, the children crouching awed and still, the men solemn and silent.

And the Pharaoh with his high-priest, the three learned

judges, the numerous jury, sat in solemn judgment upon the dead.

From amidst the group a man came forward, and in quiet, absolutely passionless tones, began recounting the sins of the deceased.

"He owned three houses," he said, "and twenty-five oxen; he had at one time seventy sheep, and his cows gave him milk in plenty. His fields were rich in barley and wheat, and he found gold dust amidst the shingle by the stream close to his house. And yet," continued the accuser, "I, his mother's sister's child, asked him to lend me a few pieces of money, also the loan of his cow since my child was sick and needed the milk, and he refused me, though I asked him thrice; and all the while he loaded Suem-ka, his concubine, with jewels and with gold, although Isis had pronounced no marriage blessing upon their union."

It took this speaker some little time to recount all the misdeeds of the dead man, his hardness of heart, his negligences, and the frauds he had perpetrated: and, above all, his unlawful passion for Suem-ka, who had been his slave and had become his mistress.

When he had finished a woman came forward, and she, in her turn, related how she had vainly begged of the rich man to repent him of his sins and cast the vile slave from him, but he had driven her away, though he was her own brother, roughly from his door. There were several accusers who spoke of the dead man's sins, and each, when they had finished their tale, added solemnly—

"Therefore do I crave of thee, oh, most holy Pharaoh! of thee, who dost deliver judgment in the name of Ra all-creating; of Horus, all-interceding, and of Osiris, bounty-giving, that thou dost decree that Har-sen-tu's body is unfit for preservation, lest it should remain as an abode for his villainous soul, and allow it to rise again in after years to perpetrate further frauds and cruelties."

While the accusers spoke there were no protestations on the part of the mourners, who crowded round their dead. Once or twice a sob, quickly checked, escaped one of the women's throats. Judges and jury listened in solemn silence, and when no more was forthcoming to speak of the sins of

Har-sen-tu, the defenders of the silent criminal had their say.

His friends and relations evidently, those who had benefited by his wealth or had not suffered through his hardness. Those too, perhaps, who had something to gain through the rich man's death. The most interesting witness for this strange defence was undoubtedly Suem-ka, the slave. She was a fine, rather coarse-looking girl, with large dark eyes and full figure. She was entirely wrapped in the folds of a thick black veil, but her arms and hands, as she raised them imploringly towards the Pharaoh, and swore before Isis that she had never been aught but a lowly handmaiden to her dead master, were, I noticed, covered with rings and gems.

The rich man had many friends. They formed a veritable phalanx round his corpse, defying the outraged relatives, confronting his enemies, and entreating for him the right of embalming, of holy sepulture, so that his body might be kept pure and undefiled from decay, ready to once more receive the soul, when it had concluded its wanderings in the shadow-land where dwelleth Anubis and Hor, and Ra, the Most High.

I felt strangely impressed by this curious pleading for one so silent and so still, who seemed to stand there in awesome majesty, hearing accusation and defence with the same contemptuous solemnity, the same dignity of eternal sleep.

When accusers and defenders had had their say, there was a long moment of silence: then the three judges rose and recapitulated the sins and virtues of the dead man. Personally, I must confess that, had I been on the jury, I should have found it very difficult to give any opinion on the case. Suem-ka, the slave, with her arms and hands covered with jewels, was, to my mind, the strongest witness against the master whom she tried to shield. But then it did not transpire that the deceased had had a wife, or had any children. The numerous jury, however, seemed to have made up their minds very quickly. When the last of the judges had finished speaking, they all rose from their seats and some held the lotus flower, which they had in their hand, high over their heads, whilst the others —and I noticed that these were decidedly in the minority— dropped the blossom to the ground.

The judges took count and pronounced a solemn "Ay," and Suem-ka, overcome with emotion, fell sobbing at the feet of the dead man.

After this Ur-tasen rose and delivered judgment upon the dead.

"Har-sen-tu! Har-sen-tu! Har-sen-tu! rejoice! The holy Pharaoh has heard thy sins! But the gods have whispered mercy into the air. Isis smileth down in joy upon thee.

"Har-sen-tu! Har-sen-tu! Har-sen-tu! go forth from the judgment-seat of the holy Pharaoh, to face fearlessly the more majestic, more mysterious throne of Osiris!

"Har-sen-tu! Har-sen-tu! Har-sen-tu! may Anubis, the jackal-headed god, guide thee! may Horus intercede for thee and Osiris receive thee in the glorious vault of heaven, where dwelleth Ra, and where is neither sin nor disease, sorrow nor tears! Har-sen-tu, thou art pure!"

A scribe handed him a document which he placed before the Pharaoh, who with his usual contemptuous listlessness placed his seal upon it. Then I saw the high-priest hesitate one moment, while the scribe waited and the Pharaoh shrugged his shoulders, laughing in his derisive way. Hugh smiled. I think we both guessed the cause of the high-priest's hesitation. Ur-tasen was frowning, and looking now at Hugh, and now at the document in his hand; but Suem-ka, the slave, happy in her triumph, ended the suspense by shouting—

"Thy hand upon the seal, oh, Beloved of the gods."

With a slight frown Ur-tasen ordered the scribe to hand the document across to Hugh, who placed his name beside that of the Pharaoh in bold hieroglyphic characters—

Then the parchment was handed over by one of the judges to the relatives of the deceased, who, as silently as they had come, retired, bearing their dead away with them. The laws of Kamt had granted them leave to perform the last and solemn rites of embalming the body of their kinsman, and making the body a fitting habitation for the soul until such time as it should return once more upon earth from the land of shadows.

And the herald again called thrice upon a name, and again the dead was arraigned before the living, his virtues extolled by his friends, his sins magnified by his enemies; but in this case he was deemed unworthy of embalming; the soul should find no more that dwelling-place which had been the abode of cruelty and of fraud, of lying and of cheating, and it should be left to wander homeless in the dark shadows of death till it had sunk, a lifeless atom, merged in the immeasureable depths of Nu, the liquid chaos which is annihilation. The wailing of the relatives of this condemned corpse was truly pitiable: the law had decreed upon the evil-doer the sentence of eternal death.

Two more cases were dealt with in the same way. Mr. Tankerville had often in his picturesque way related to us this judgment of the dead practised in ancient Egypt, and I remember once having seen a picture representing the circular hall, the judges and the accused; but, as in everything else in this wonderful land, how infinitely more mystic, more poetic was the reality than the imagining. The hour of the night, the crescent moon above, the silent and solemn corpse, the most dignified in still majesty amidst all those who dared to judge him, all this made a picture which has remained one of the most vivid, the most cherished, in my mind.

CHAPTER X

THE TRIAL OF KESH-TA, THE SLAVE

THEN came the turn of the living.

Once more the herald called a name—a woman's—three times—

"Kesh-ta! Kesh-ta! Kesh-ta!" and thrice the cry resounded—

"Is she there? Is she there? Is she there?"

By this time there were no reassuring words about mercy and fearlessness. The living evidently were more harshly dealt with in Kamt than the dead.

Pushed and jostled by a couple of men, her hands tied behind her back, a rope round her neck, a woman suddenly appeared in the circle of light. Her eyes roamed wildly round, half-defiant, half-terrified; her hair hung tangled over her shoulders, and the whole of one side of her face was one ugly gaping wound.

"Who and what art thou?" demanded the judges.

The woman did not reply. She looked to me half a maniac, and wholly irresponsible; but the men behind her prodded her with their spears, till she fell upon her knees. Hugh had frowned, his own special ugly frown. I could see that he would not stand this sort of thing very long, and I held myself ready to restrain him if I could, from doing anything rash, or to lend him a helping hand if he refused to be restrained.

Suddenly his attention and mine was arrested by a name, and wondering, we listened, spell-bound by its strange and unaccountable magic.

The judges had peremptorily repeated—

"Answer! Who and what art thou?"

"I am Kesh-ta," replied the woman, with surly defiance, "and I am a slave of Princess Neit-akrit."

"Why art thou here?"

"Because I hate her," she half hissed, half shouted, as she turned her ghastly wounded face to the moonlight, as if to bear witness to the evil passion in her heart.

"Take care, woman," warned the judge, "lest thy sacrilegious tongue bring upon thee judgment more terrible than thou hast hitherto deserved."

She laughed, a strange, weird, maniacal laugh, and said—

"That cannot be, oh, learned and wisest of the judges of Kamt. Dost think perchance that thy mind can conceive, or thy cruelty devise a more horrible punishment than that which I endured yesterday, when my avenging hands tried to reach her evil form and failed, for want of strength and power?"

"Be silent! and hear from the lips of thy accusers the history of the heinous sin which thou didst commit yesterday, and for which the high-priest of Ra will anon deliver judgment upon thee."

"Nay! I will not be silent, and I will not hear! I will

tell thee and the holy Pharaoh, and him who has come from heaven to live amongst the people of Kamt, I will tell them all of my sin. Let them hate and loathe me, let them punish me if they will; the Pharaoh is mighty and the gods are great, but all the powers of heaven and the might of the throne cannot inflict more suffering on Kesh-ta than she has already endured."

"Be silent!" again thundered the judges; and at a sign from them the two men quickly wound a cloth round the unfortunate woman's mouth and a few yards of rope round her body. Thus forcibly silent, pinioned and helpless, she knelt there before her judges, defiant and, I thought, crazy, while her accuser began slowly to read the indictment.

"Kesh-ta the low-born slave, who has neither father nor mother, nor brother nor sister, for she is the property of the most pure and great, the Princess Neit-akrit of the house of Memmoun-ra.

"The gods gave her a son, who through the kindness of the noble princess became versed in many arts, and being a skilled craftsman was much esteemed by the great Neit-akrit, of the house of Memmoun-ra.

"Yesterday, whilst Sem-no-tha knelt before the great princess, whilst she deigned to speak to her slave, Kesh-ta, his mother, crept close behind him, and slew her son with her own hand before the eyes of Neit-akrit, the young and pure princess, and then with the blood of the abject slave his murderess smeared the garments of Neit-akrit, causing her to turn sick and faint with loathing.

"Therefore I, the public accuser, do hereby demand, in the name of the people of Kamt, both freeborn and slave, that this woman, for this grievous sin she committed, be for ever cast out from the boundaries of the land; that her body be given as a prey to the carrion that dwell in the wilderness of the valley of death, so that the jackals and the vultures might consume the very soul which, abject and base, had conceived so loathsome a crime."

There was dead silence after this; I could see Hugh, with clenched hands and lips tightly set, ready at any cost to prevent the terrible and awful deed, the consequences of which we had already witnessed in the lonely desert beyond the gates of Kamt. The Pharaoh had turned positively livid; amidst his white draperies he looked more ghostlike and dead than the corpses which had just now stood before us; Khefaran's face was still impassive.

Then the judges said solemnly—

"Take the gag off the woman's mouth; it is her turn to speak now."

I heaved a sigh of relief. There was a great sense of fairness in this proceeding, which, for the moment, relieved the tension on my overwrought nerves. I saw that Hugh too was prepared to wait and listen to what the woman would have to say.

The gag had been removed, and yet Kesh-ta did not speak; it seemed as if she had ceased to be conscious of her surroundings.

"Woman, thou hast heard the accusation pronounced against thee, what hast thou to say?"

She looked at the judges, and at the crowd of men, on whose faces she could see nothing but loathing and horror, then suddenly her wild and wandering gaze rested upon Hugh, and with a loud shriek she wrenched her arms from out her bonds, and stretched them toward him, crying—

"Thou, Beloved of the gods, hear me! I ask for no pardon, no mercy! Remember death, however horrible, is life to me; the arid wilderness, wherein the gods do not dwell, where bones of evil-doers lie rotting beneath the sun, will be to me an abode of bliss, for inaccessible mountains will lie between me and *her*. There, before grim and slowly-creeping death overtakes me, I shall have time to rejoice that I, with my own hands, saved Sem-no-tha, my son, my beloved, from the same terrible doom. He was a slave, abject at her feet, but he was tall and handsome, and she smiled on him. And dost know what happens when Neit-akrit smiles upon a man, be he freeborn or be he slave:—he loses his senses, he becomes intoxicated, a coward and a perjurer, and his reason goeth forth—a vagabond—out of his body. Hast heard of Amen-het, the architect, oh, Beloved of the gods? hast heard that for a smile from her, he perjured himself and committed such dire sacrilege that Osiris himself veiled his countenance for one whole day because of it, until Amen-het was cast out of

Kamt, to perish slowly and miserably body and soul. And I saw Sem-no-tha at the feet of Neit-akrit! I saw her smile on him, and knew that he was doomed; knew that to see her smile again he would lie and he would cheat, would sell his soul for her and die an eternal death, and I, his mother, who loved him above all, who had but him in all the world, preferred to see him dead at my feet, than damned before the judgment-seat of the Most High!

"Ay! I am guilty of murder," she continued more excitedly than ever. "I have nothing to say! I slew Sem-no-tha, the slave of Neit-akrit!—Her property!—Not mine!—I am only his mother—and am too old, too weary to smile! Beloved of the gods, they did not tell thee all my sins; they did not tell thee that when I saw Sem-no-tha lying dead at my feet, and Neit-akrit kneeling by his side, while a tear of pity for her handsome slave fell upon his white and rigid form, that, with the knife still warm with his blood, I tried to mar for ever the beauty of her face. I had no wish to kill her, only to make upon that ivory white flesh a hideous scar that would make her smile seem like the grimace of death. But Fano-tu stopped my arm ready to strike, and to punish me he, with his own hand, made upon my face this gaping wound, such as I had longed to make on that of Neit-akrit. You may condemn me—nay, you *must* cast me out of Kamt, for if you do not I tell you that were you to bury me beneath the tallest pyramid the proud Pharaohs have built for themselves, and set the entire population of Kamt to guard it and me, I yet would creep out and find my way to her, and I tell you Kesh-ta would not fail twice."

Exhausted, she sank back, half fainting on the ground, whilst deathlike silence reigned around; one by one every member of the jury dropped his lotus flower before him, and the judges, having taken count, pronounced solemnly the word "Guilty!"

Then Ur-tasen rose and delivered judgment.

"Kesh-ta! Kesh-ta! Kesh-ta! thou art accursed! Thy crime is heinous before the gods! Thy very thoughts pollute the land of Kamt.

"Kesh-ta! Kesh-ta! Kesh-ta! thou art accursed. Be thy name for ever erased from the land that bare thee. May the memory of thee be cast out of the land, for thou art trebly accursed.

"Kesh-ta! Kesh-ta! Kesh-ta! thou art accursed! The gods decree that thou be cast out for ever beyond the gates of Kamt, into the valley of death, where dwell neither bird nor beast, where neither fruit nor tree doth grow, and where thy soul and body, rotting in the arid sand, shall become a prey for ever to the loathsome carrion of the desert."

Kesh-ta's answer to this terrible fiat was one loud and prolonged laugh. I felt almost paralysed with the horror of the scene. My mind persistently conjured up before me the vision of the lonely desert strewn with whitening bones, the vultures and screeching jackals, and the loathsome cannibal who once had been just such a living, breathing, picturesque man as these now before me. The woman's crime was horrible, but she was human, and above all, she was a woman. Trouble seemed to have unhinged her mind, and the thought to me was loathsome that so irresponsible a being should suffer such appalling punishment.

Already Ur-tasen had handed up to the Pharaoh the document that confirmed the awful sentence, and the sick, almost dying, man prepared, with trembling hand, to give his royal assent to the monstrous deed, when, in a moment, Hugh was on his feet: he had shaken off the torpor, which, with grim horror, had also paralysed his nerves, and drawing his very tall British stature to its full height, he placed a restraining hand on that of the priest.

"Man!" he said in loud tones, which went echoing through the vastness of the building, "where is thy justice? Look at that woman whom thou hast just condemned to tortures so awful, which not even thou, learned as thou art, canst possibly conceive."

The judges and the jury had one and all risen from their seats and were staring awestruck at Hugh, who at this moment, tall and white amidst these dark sons of the black land, looked truly like some being of another world. The Pharaoh had, after the first moment of astonishment, quietly shrugged his shoulders, as if he cared little what the issue of this strange dispute might be between the stranger and the all-powerful high-priest. Ur-tasen alone had preserved perfect composure and dignified solemnity. Quietly he folded his arms across his chest and said—

"I, who am vowed to the service of Ra, am placed here upon earth that I might enforce obedience to his laws."

"Nay! not to the word, man, to the spirit," rejoined Hugh. "Remember Ra's decree transmitted to Mena, the founder of this great kingdom, through the mouth of Horus himself:—Be just, oh, man! but, above all, be merciful!"

"Remember too, oh, Well-beloved of the gods, that same decree which sayeth:—Let no man shed the blood of man, in quarrel, revenge, or any other cause, for he who sheddeth the blood of man, his blood too shall be shed."

"But Kesh-ta is irresponsible, half deprived of her reason by sorrow and the terrible mutilation which the hand of an inhuman slave-driver inflicted upon her. To throw a human creature in such a state in the midst of an arid wilderness without food or drink, as a punishment for a crime which her hand committed but not her mind, is barbarous, monstrous, cruel, unworthy the great people of Kamt."

"Let no man shed the blood of man," repeated the high-priest, solemnly, "in quarrel, revenge, or any other cause. Hast mission, oh, Beloved of Osiris, to upset the decrees of the gods?"

"Nay! I am here to follow the laws of the gods, as well as all the people of Kamt, but thou, oh, Pharaoh," he added, turning to the sick man, "knowest what physical ailments are, knowest how terrible they are to bear. Think of the moments of the worst pain thou hast ever endured, and think of them magnified a thousandfold, and then thou wilt fall far short of the slow and lingering torture, to which thou wouldst subject this half-crazed woman."

"Let no man shed the blood of man," repeated the high-priest for the third time, with more solemnity and emphasis, for he noticed, just as I did, that Hugh's powerful appeal, his picturesque—to them, mysterious—presence was strongly influencing the judges and the jury and all the spectators. One by one the pink lotus blossoms were lifted upwards, the judges whispered to one another, the men ceased to buffet and jostle the unfortunate woman.

"Oh, ye who are called upon to decide if a criminal be

guilty or not," adjured Ur-tasen, stretching his long gaunt arms towards the multitude, " pause, before you allow cowardly sentiment to mar your justice and your righteousness. Who is there among you here who hath not seen our beautiful Princess Neit-akrit? Who hath not gazed with love and reverence upon the young and exquisite face which Isis herself hath given her? And who is there among you who, remembering her beauty, doth not shudder with infinite loathing at the thought of that face disfigured by the sacrilegious hand of a low-born slave, of those eyes rendered sightless, of the young lips stilled by death? Oh, Well-beloved of Osiris," he added, turning again towards Hugh, " from the foot of the throne of the gods perchance thou didst not perceive how exquisitely fair is this greatest of the daughters of Kamt whom *thy* presence hath deprived of a throne. Is not thy god-like sire, whose emissary thou art, satisfied? And in addition to wrenching the double crown of Kamt from her queenly brow, wouldst take her life, her smile, her sweetness too?"

Ur-tasen, with wonderful cunning, had played a trump-card, and no doubt poor old Hugh was in a tight corner. His position towards the defrauded princess was at best a very ticklish one, and on the principle that the son of Ra could do no wrong, it was imperative that not the faintest suspicion should fasten on him that he bore any ill-will towards his future kinswoman. I wondered what Hugh would do. I knew my friend out and out, and there was that in his face which told me plainly that the unfortunate Kesh-ta would *not* be " cast out " from the gates of Kamt.

There must have been some subtle magic in the name of Neit-akrit, for Ur-tasen's appeal had quickly and completely done its work. One by one the lotus blossoms had again been dropped, and the judges simultaneously repeated—

" Death! Death! Death!"

The wretched woman alone among those present seemed not to take the slightest interest in the proceedings. She crouched in a heap in the centre of the hall, and the moonlight showed us at fitful intervals her great, wild eyes, her quivering mouth, and the hideous wound made by the cruel hand of Fano-tu.

" Death be it then," said Hugh, determinedly. " She has

killed, and dreams yet to kill. Sinful and dangerous, let her be removed from Kamt, but by a quick and sudden act of justice, not by the slow tortures of inhuman revenge."

"Let no man shed the blood of man," once again repeated the high-priest with obvious triumph, "in quarrel, revenge, *or any other cause*."

These last words he emphasised with cutting directness, then he added—

"Thou sayest, oh, Well-beloved of the gods, that thou dost honour the laws of thy sire; remember that he who sheddeth the blood of man, his blood too shall be shed."

And placing the document once again before the Pharaoh, he said commandingly, though with outward humility—

"Wilt deign to place thy seal, oh, holy Pharaoh, on this decree which shall expel from out the gates of Kamt the murdering vermin that even now crawls at thy feet?"

But with characteristic impulsiveness, and before I could restrain him, Hugh had snatched the paper from out the high-priest's hand, and tearing it across he threw it on the ground and placed his foot upon it.

"Not while I stand on the black soil of Kamt," he said quietly.

Breathless all had watched the stirring scene before them. Superstition, reverence, terror, all were depicted on the faces of the spectators. No one had dared to raise a voice or a finger, even when Hugh committed this daring act. The Pharaoh had turned, if possible, even more livid than before, and I could see a slight froth appearing at the corners of his mouth; he made no movement, however, and after a while took up his apes and began teasing them, laughing loudly and drily to himself. I fancied that he a little bit enjoyed Ur-tasen's subtle position. The high-priest still stood impassive, with folded arms, and repeated for the fourth time—

"The laws of Ra given unto Mena commandeth that he who sheds the blood of man, his blood too shall be shed. By no hand of man can the criminal's blood be shed. The vultures of the wilderness, the hyenas and the jackals that dwell in the valley of death must shed the blood of the murderess, that the decrees of Ra and Osiris and Horus be implicitly fulfilled."

Then he turned to the Pharaoh and added—

"Is it thy will, oh, holy Pharaoh, that the laws prescribed by the gods follow their course, as they have done since five times a thousand years? Is it thy will that the base and low vermin which crawleth at thy feet be allowed to go free and fulfil her murderous promises, and be a living danger to thy illustrious kinswoman, whom it is the duty of *all* the rulers of Kamt to cherish and protect? Or dost thou decree that in accordance with the will of Ra, who alloweth no man to shed the blood of man, she shall be cast out for ever from the land of Kamt, and her sinful blood feed the carrion birds and beasts of the arid valley of death?"

The Pharaoh gave an indifferent shrug of the shoulders, as if the matter had ceased to concern him at all. This Ur-tasen interpreted as a royal assent, for he commanded—

"Take the woman away and bind her with ropes. Let twenty men stand round to guard her, lest she fulfil her impious threat. Let her neither sleep, nor eat, nor drink. To-morrow, at break of day, when the first rays of Osiris peep behind the hills, she shall be led forth through the mysterious precincts of the temple of Ra and cast out through the gates of Kamt for ever into the wilderness."

"By all the gods of heaven, earth or hell," said Hugh, very quietly, "I declare unto you that she shall *not*."

And before I could stop him he had literally bounded forward, and slipping past the dumbfounded judge and jury had reached the centre of the hall and was stooping over the prostrate woman.

It was a terrible moment, an eternity of awful suspense to me. I did not know what Hugh would do, dared not think of what any rashness on his part might perhaps entail.

"Touch her not, oh, Beloved of the gods," shouted Ur-tasen, warningly; "she has been judged and found guilty, her touch is pollution. The gods by my mouth have decreed her fate."

"Her fate is beyond thy ken and thy decree, oh, man," said Hugh, with proud solemnity, as once again his tall stature towered above them all, "and she now stands before a throne, where all is mercy and there is no revenge."

The men round had stooped and tried to lift the prostrate

woman. She turned her face upwards to Hugh; the ashen shade over it was unmistakable, it was that of the dying, but in her eyes, as she looked at him, there came, as a last flicker of life, a spark of the deepest, the most touching, gratitude.

Then softly at first, but gradually more and more distinctly, the whisper was passed round—

"She is dead!"

And in the moonlight all of us there could see on the woman's dress a fast-spreading, large stain of blood.

"He who sheddeth the blood of man," came in thundering accents from the high-priest, "his blood shall be shed. People of Kamt, who stand here before the face of Isis, I command ye to tell me whose hand spilt the blood of that woman."

"Mine," said Hugh, quietly, throwing his knife far from him, which fell, with weird and metallic jingle upon the granite floor. "The hand of him whom Ra has sent among you all, the hand of him whom Osiris loveth, who has come to rule over you, bringing you a message from the foot of the throne of your god. Touch him, any of you, if you dare!"

Shuddering, awestruck, all gazed upon him, whilst I, blindly, impetuously, rushed to his side, to be near him, to ward off the blow which I felt convinced would fall upon his daring head, or share it with him if I were powerless to save. I don't think that I ever admired him so much as I did then—I who had often seen him recoil with horror at thought of killing a beast, who understood the extraordinary, almost superhuman sacrifice it must have cost him, to free with his own hand this wretched woman from her awful doom.

But with all his enthusiasm, scientific visionary as he was, Hugh Tankerville knew human nature well, knew that, awestruck with their own superstition, they no more would have dared to touch him then, than they would have desecrated one of their own gods. There was long and deathlike silence while Hugh stood before them all with hand raised upwards in a gesture of command and defiance; then, slowly, one by one, the judges and the jury and all the assembled multitude fell forward upon their faces and kissed the granite floor, while a low murmur went softly echoing through the pillars of the hall—

"Oh, envoy of Osiris! Beloved of the gods!"

Then I looked towards Ur-tasen and saw that the high-priest too had knelt down like the others. Hugh had conquered for the moment, through the superstition of these strange people and the magic of his personality, but I dared not think of what the consequences of his daring act might be.

Without another word he beckoned to me to follow him, and together we went out of the judgment-hall of Men-ne-fer.

CHAPTER XI

THE CROWN OF KAMT

HUGH needed much of my skill, when we got back to the palace that night and were rid of our attendants, safe in our own privacy. The strain must have been terrible for him to bear. His constitution was a veritable bundle of nerves; these had been strained almost to breaking, both in his fight with Ur-tasen and during the awful moment when, for the sake of a principle, he stained his hand with the blood of a fellow-creature.

As soon as we were alone I went up to him and grasped that hand with all the warmth and affection which my admiration for him commanded, and I felt strangely moved when, in response, I saw in his great dark eyes a soft look of tenderness and of gratitude. He knew I had understood him, and I think he was satisfied. Gently, as a sick child, he allowed me to attend to him; fortunately, through the many vicissitudes which ultimately brought us to this wondrous land, I had never discarded my small, compact, portable medicine-chest, and I soon found a remedy for the poor, tired-out, aching nerves.

"There now, that's better, isn't it, Girlie?" I said when he was at last lying, quietly and comfortably, on the couch, and there was less unnatural brilliancy in his eyes.

"You are awfully good to me, Mark, old chap," he said. "I am ashamed to have broken down so completely. You will think that I deserve more than ever my old schoolboy nickname."

"Yes! Sawnie Girlie you are," I said with a laugh, "and

Sawnie Girlie you have ever proved yourself—particularly lately. But now I forbid you to talk—most emphatically—and command you to go to sleep. I will not have you ill, remember. Where should I be without you?"

"Oh, I shall be all right. Don't worry about me, old chap, and I assure you that I have every intention of going to sleep, particularly if you will do ditto. But, Mark, is it not strange how the mysterious personality of Neit-akrit seems to haunt every corner of this land?"

"That old Ur-tasen seems to me, somehow, to play a double game, and I am positively shocked at so old and venerable a personage getting so enthusiastic over the beauty of a girl young enough to be his grand-daughter. I call him a regular old rip."

"She certainly seems to have the power to arouse what is basest in every woman, be she queen like my bride, or slave like poor Kesh-ta, to make fools of men and cowards of the Pharaoh and his priest."

"I think that after all your queen may have had the best idea: a woman who has so much power is best put out of harm's way. There are no nunneries in this pagan land, but you had best accede to Queen Maat-kha's wish, and command Princess Neit-akrit to become the priestess of some god."

"Then she would set to work to demoralise all the priests," said Hugh, with a laugh, "and finally upset the gravity of the high-priest. I must find her a husband, Mark; the cares of maternity will sober her soon enough. I wish you would take her off my hands."

The next day, at a solemn council, at which the Queen, Ur-tasen and ourselves were present, and which was held within the precincts of the temple of Ra, the high-priest seemed entirely to have forgotten the events of the night. He greeted Hugh with solemn and dignified respect, and it was impossible to read on his parchment-like face what his thoughts were with regard to the Beloved of the gods. I could not make up my mind whether he did or did not believe the story of Ra and of the soul of Khefren, and at times I would see his shrewd eyes fixed upon Hugh and myself with an expression I could not altogether define. Somehow I mistrusted him, in spite of the fact that his manner towards

Hugh, throughout the council, was deferential and respectful, even to obsequiousness. Hugh, I could see, was on his guard and spoke little. Affairs of finance were mostly discussed. It evidently was Ur-tasen's business to collect the reports of the governors and officials on matters agricultural, financial or religious, and to lay them before his sovereign. He seemed to be the " Bismarck " of this picturesque land, and to my mind it was unlikely that he meant to share the power which he had wielded for so long with any stranger, be he descended from the heavens above or not, and in the great trial of the unfortunate slave he had been publicly and absolutely discomfited.

At the same time, whatever might be the game he meant to play, he hid his cards well for the present, and neither made suggestion nor offered criticism, without referring both to Hugh.

Queen Maat-kha, attired in her sombre yet gorgeous black looked more radiant and beautiful than ever. She made no effort to hide the deep and passionate love she felt for her future lord; she had probably heard of the episode of the night, but, if she had, Hugh's daring action had but enhanced her pride in him.

Most of the day was again spent in visiting temples and public buildings, and in receiving various dignitaries of the city. The representatives of various crafts and trades came in turn to offer to the Beloved of the gods some exquisite piece of their workmanship, or object of art, fashioned by their hands: goldsmiths' and jewellers' work, smiths' or turners' treasures, which, I felt, would one day adorn the cases of the British Museum, and the barbarous splendours of which were a veritable feast to the eye.

We did not see the sick Pharaoh throughout the whole of that day. Once or twice we caught sight of his rose-coloured litter, with its gorgeous crown of gold, being borne along among the acacia alleys of the park, and we heard his harsh, sarcastic laugh echoing down the alabaster corridors; but he took no notice of either Hugh or myself, and did not appear at either council or reception. The mighty Pharaoh was sick unto death, and men with shaven crowns, in long green robes—the representatives of the medical profession of Kamt—were alone admitted to his presence.

Late that night we sat at table in the vast supper-hall. At the head of it, on a raised daïs covered with heavy folds of rich black tissue, Queen Maat-kha sat, with Hugh by her side. I was at her right, and behind each of us a tall, swarthy slave waved a gigantic ostrich feather fan of many colours, stirring the air gently over our heads. Through the massive alabaster columns there stretched out before us the bower of palms and acacias, among which the newly-risen moon threw dark and mysterious shadows. On the marble floor there stalked about majestic pink flamingoes, while around the columns fair musicians squatted, drawing forth from their quaint crescent-shaped harps, sweet and monotonous tones. Only one lamp, low and dim, in which burned sweet-scented oil, illumined with fitful light the hall in which we sat, together with the vessels of gold and exquisite fruit which littered the table, whilst around us dainty maidens flitted, filling and re-filling our goblets with aromatic wines from great stone jars, which they carried on their graceful heads: their smooth dark skins glittered at times like bits of old carved ivory. I confess that in the midst of this gorgeousness and plenty I was just thinking how delightful a good cigar would be, when, quite involuntarily—for I was gradually training myself to become a very efficient gooseberry—I caught a few words which Queen Maat-kha was whispering half-audibly to Hugh.

"Art thou not happy then with me?"

Hugh whispered something in reply, which I did not catch, but which evidently was not altogether satisfactory, for she shook her head and said—

"Then why dost thou wish to go? I would fain pray the gods to bid time stand still and Osiris to cease his daily wanderings on the vault of heaven. I but long that day should follow day in this same sweet, unvarying monotony."

"It is necessary that I should see my people, sweet," said Hugh, "and necessary I should pay my humble respects to the Princess Neit-akrit, whom my presence has deprived of a throne."

"Yes, I know. Ur-tasen has devised it. He nourishes in his heart a fond regret that he will not place the crown of Kamt on the head of Neit-akrit."

"I think thou dost him wrong; he is devoted to thee and to thy house."

"Because I load him with gifts," she said drily, "and because he fears the gods, whose Beloved thou art; but Neit-akrit is young, some call her fair . . . and . . ."

"Is she then so very fair, this mysterious Neit-akrit whom I have never seen, but who will be my kinswoman when thou art my wife? Tell me about her."

I thought that this was a false move on Hugh's part. It is never safe to express interest in one lady in the presence of another, and I was not surprised to see Queen Maat-kha's eyes flash with anger, and—I thought—jealous suspicion.

"What can I tell thee," she said indifferently, "save that some have called her fair?"

"Is she young?"

"She is little more than a child, her body is straight and angular; she has large eyes, but they are not dark, and her hair is of a peculiar colour. What can I tell thee of her?"

"Tell him that Neit-akrit is beautiful beyond what man born of woman can conceive," suddenly said a harsh and sarcastic voice immediately behind us, "that her eyes are blue and mysterious as is the light of Isis, when she rises silent and solitary in the night, that her hair is like the rays with which Osiris bathes the heavens when he himself has sunk to rest. Tell him that her body is tall and lithe as the graceful papyrus grass which sways gently in the wind, and that her feet are white and transparent like the polished tusks of the young elephant. Tell him that her voice is sweeter than the song of birds or chorus of goddesses around Ra's throne, and that her cheeks would shame the lotus blossom in their tints. Then, when thou hast described all this and more to him, who is Beloved of the gods, tell him that, though his soul be descended direct from the foot of the throne of Ra, and his heart was fashioned by the hand of Osiris himself, he cannot kindle one spark of life in the heart and soul of beautiful Neit-akrit, but that he will see his own, bruised and chilled unto death, trampled beneath the ivory white feet of the most exquisite daughter of this fair land of Kamt, while the very apes in the trees of her palace will laugh to scorn his lost manhood and the gnawing pain in his heart."

We had all turned towards the further end of the room, where stood the Pharaoh, supported on either side by two of his shorn physicians, his pale face emaciated by suffering, looking weirdly grotesque beneath the gigantic double crown of gold, studded with jewels, of Upper and Lower Kamt. Each side of him two torch-bearers stood, holding aloft a burning torch, the flickering light of which made his face appear strangely demoniacal in its expression of hatred and contempt, while with one long claw-like finger he pointed derisively at Hugh. It was the first time I had heard him speak, and his voice sounded strangely harsh and high-pitched. Suddenly he broke into loud and unnatural laughter.

"He! he! he! thou Beloved of the gods! what exquisite torments await thee! for thou wilt love her, I tell thee, and she will laugh and mock thee! Didst thou not know that Isis gave her a stone when she was born, instead of a heart? Ay! my lady mother! thou dost right to dread that thy beloved leave thy side to behold the fairness of Neit-akrit. I shall not live a year and a day, saith thy High Chancellor; well! perhaps not! but I shall live long enough to see the Beloved of the gods, the future king of Kamt, a weak and puling mortal rendered akin to the fools, and kicked at by the white feet of a woman. Thou desirest my crown, thou soul of Khefren?" now shrieked the unfortunate man, whilst he began to tremble from head to foot and tried to walk towards Hugh. "Thou wishest to wed a queen? and sit upon the throne of Kamt? I tell thee that before that time comes, thou wilt lie with thy pale head in the dust of the valley of death, and pray that thy sacrilegious foot had never dared to step upon the pedestal of Ra, since *thy* presence deprived *her* of a throne! Here! take thou my crown! My head has ached long enough with the weight of it! Take it, I say! and may every jewel it contains burn into thy flesh and make thy martyrdom doubly hideous to bear, since it will make of thee, who art Beloved of the gods, the abhorred and loathed usurper of the throne of Neit-akrit!"

He had with trembling hands torn the massive golden crown from off his head, and with a final shriek of execration and blasphemy hurled it at Hugh Tankerville's feet, where it fell with a loud clash, whilst some of the rubies, loosened from their settings by the vigour of the shock, rolled about on the floor like glittering drops of blood.

But the effort had been too much for the enfeebled frame; the physicians, completely paralysed by the frenzy of their patient, seemed unable to support him, for with a wild cry the mighty Pharaoh fell forward, prostrate before the man on whom he had hurled his malediction.

Hugh had jumped up, fortunately in good time to break the fall of the unfortunate man, and his vigorous chest received the main shock of the inanimate body. Then, lightly, as if the great Pharaoh had been a feather, he lifted him from the ground, and giving me a wink, he carried him across the hall in his arms, commanding the astonished physicians and torch-bearers to lead the way. As I followed him, and helped to support the inanimate body, I looked back and, in the dim light of the lamp, caught sight of the face of Queen Maat-kha. It was as pale as death, and in her large eyes, which rested on the inert form of her son, there was a look of bitter hatred, coupled with an eager and terrible hope, which made me almost shudder.

Gently we conveyed the fainting man to his own apartments, and imperiously Hugh ordered physicans and attendants out of the room. They were far too frightened not to obey, and together we set to work to undress the great Pharaoh and to lay him on his couch.

"I think now is your chance, Mark, or never, to examine the poor man and see what he really suffers from," said Hugh, when we had laid the bloodless, emaciated body on the gorgeous couch and rested the pale head on the rose silk cushion, which made the face appear more weird and livid than before.

"If those two bald idiots in yellow robes are a specimen of the medical profession in this highly-enlightened country, I, for one, must pray to be preserved from any ailment in which I cannot attend on myself," I said as I first of all endeavoured to administer such restoratives to the patient as I usually carried about me. I had examined the yellow, parchment-like skin, covered with pimples and blotches, the eyes circled with deep purple rings, the sunken temples and pinched nostrils, and, though I have no pretensions at vast experience in medical practice, yet I am an M.D. of

London, and had done some creditable work at St. Mary's, and I was not very long in coming to the conclusion what malady was undermining the very life of the young monarch.

"I should say he is suffering from advanced diabetes: though, of course, I cannot be sure till I have examined him more thoroughly. If my surmises are correct, then those shaven fools are doing their level best to kill him in the shortest possible period of time." And I pointed to the fine wheaten bread, the fruit and sweet cakes, which lay on a tray ready to the invalid's hand. "At the same time I think we should find it difficult to interfere with his medical entourage."

"Do you think you can save him?" asked Hugh, eagerly.

"Save him? No! Only stay the rapid course of the malady, perhaps. I cannot tell off-hand how far it has gone and, of course, I cannot thrust myself into the case without consulting the physicians who have charge of it."

"Does it not strike you, Mark, old chap," interrupted Hugh, with a smile, "that your *exposé* of professional etiquette as prescribed by the R.C.S., is a little out of place in this particular instance? Look here!" he added with his usual impulsive energy, "if your suppositions are correct, do you or do you not consider that this unfortunate man is being wrongly treated?"

"Yes! That I do most emphatically consider."

"Very well, then! From this moment you must look after him, and those bald niggers have got to do as *you* tell them."

"But . . ."

"There is no 'but,' Mark. We are not going to see this poor wretch die in agony, under our very eyes, if your skill can alleviate his sufferings. I appoint you my future son's physician-extraordinary; this shall be the first act of my autocratic rule."

"Hush!" I warned, "he is moving."

I hurriedly whispered to Hugh to go, for I was afraid the sight of him would upset the patient.

"Send his own attendants in, old man; they can see to him for the present, till we have decided what is to be done."

Shuffling and humble, the two yellow-robed personages obeyed Hugh's orders, to go and see to their illustrious patient.

The Pharaoh was slowly recovering consciousness, and I thought it prudent to leave him alone with faces that were familiar and more welcome to him than mine.

I think we were both heartily sorry for the unfortunate youth, so helpless in the midst of all his pomp and glory, and I was only too ready to devote myself to him, if the thing was feasible.

"Will you mention it to the Queen to-night?" I suggested.

"Not to-night," he replied, "but at the Cabinet Council to-morrow when Ur-tasen is present."

When we returned to the dining-hall the Queen had retired with her attendants, and we were left alone for the remainder of the evening, to stroll about under the acacia alleys of the park.

CHAPTER XII

THE IRIDESCENT SCARABAEUS

NEITHER of us felt like sleep. The night was peculiarly balmy and fragrant, even for this fair land where all flowers smelt doubly sweet, all bird song sounded more melodious than anywhere else in the world. There was only one flaw in this land of poetry and of art, but that was a serious flaw. The people did not grow tobacco, and on this beautiful evening, as we wandered aimlessly along the moonlit walks, we could not smoke a good cigar, and our delight did not reach supreme beatitude.

How far England seemed from us at that moment! London, Piccadilly, the Strand, hansom cabs—these were dreams, or rather nightmares I should say, for in these few brief days—so adaptable is the human creature—this gorgeous land, the shaven priests, the sickly Pharaoh, had somehow already become a part of our existence. I could no longer picture myself hailing an omnibus at Piccadilly Circus and getting out at Hammersmith Broadway; I could not think of myself sitting in a stall at His Majesty's Theatre and watching one of Mr. Beerbohm-Tree's beautiful scenic productions. The individual who used to sit opposite Aunt Charlotte at the breakfast-table in Harley Street, reading the *Daily Telegraph*, was not I myself; he was a sort of spook who still haunted me now and again, but who had really nothing to do with me, the counsellor of Osiris's son, the confidant of the Beloved of the gods.

I cannot attempt to explain this psychological phase of my sojourn in the land of Kamt. I can but record it, and do so chiefly because I know that Hugh experienced the same sensation as I did, only in a much more intense form.

He walked and looked as if he had never done anything all his life, but rule over strange and picturesque nations. He never found his robes uncomfortable, nor got entangled in the intricacies of the native tongue, and he met the great Pharaoh's sarcastic chuckles and the high-priest's hypocritical obsequiousness, with the same unruffled composure and truly regal dignity.

To-night, having dismissed our tiresome attendants, we gave ourselves over, heart and soul, to the beauty of the scene around us. To our right and left, in the dark shadows ghostly forms of birds or beasts fled frightened at our approach, and the white cows in the tall papyrus grass, disturbed by our tread, gave forth long and melancholy plaints, whilst overhead the crowd of monkeys in the branches of the acacia trees pelted us in wanton mischief with showers of white sweet-scented petals as we passed.

We had reached the edge of the canal and looked out across it on the majesty of the sleeping city, which with its alabaster steps, its roofs of copper and of gold, its mammoth temples and gigantic carvings, looked more than ever like a city of dreamland. Beyond, far away, stretched the line of mystic hills which divided this habitation of beauty from the vast graveyard in the wilderness. One by one we saw the lights of the city flicker and die out: on the canal one or two belated boats flitted ghostlike and swift, crescent-shaped, with a burning lamp at prow and poop; the boatmen, as they dipped their oars into the water, sang their monotonous barcarole, and beneath the gaily-striped awnings we could catch sight at times of young couples sitting with their dark heads close together—just the same as is customary in dear old England on the Thames. Soon the last light had gone out, the last boat flitted away in the distance, the dream city was at rest; only from the great temple of Ra came, faintly echoing, the sound of the midnight chant intoned by the blind priestesses of the god.

We had stretched ourselves out on the soft bed of velvety grass which sloped down to the water's edge, terminating with a low white marble parapet, and had each become silent, wrapped in our own thoughts and watching the mystic reflections cast by the moon into the canal when, suddenly, from the opposite side, we saw a dark head appearing in the water and approaching swiftly towards us. We watched with much interest, and soon by the light of the moon saw that the head was that of a young girl, with long dark hair streaming in two thick plaits behind her in the water; the thin girlish arms struck with much vigour against the current, and very soon the edge of the parapet hid her from our view. Very much interested, I was about to jump up, to further watch the graceful evolutions of the midnight swimmer, when Hugh's hand was placed upon my arm and a warning "Hush!" caused me to sit still.

Above the edge of the parapet, some fifty yards away from where we lay, the dark young head had appeared, and the same vigorous yet slender arms helped to hoist the girlish figure up onto the marble ledge. We hardly dared to breathe, wonder what was the purpose of this young and daring midnight prowler, as, for the space of a few seconds, she sat still, listening and peering into the shadows where we lay, silent and expectant, while the moon shone full upon her ivory-coloured skin, making the water on it glisten like a network of diamonds. One of her hands was tightly clutched, while with the other she wrapped more tightly round her the dripping and transparent folds of her white garment. After an instant's hesitation she jumped off the parapet onto the grass, and the next moment was running swiftly and noiselessly towards us, shaking the water out of her hair as she ran, and holding a warning finger to her mouth.

"Hush-sh-sh!" she whispered as soon as she was close enough and we could hear. Then she stood still straight before us, beneath the brilliant light of the moon, like an exquisite piece of delicately-carved ivory. She was looking at Hugh out of her great almond-shaped eyes, with a strange mixture of awe and pity.

"Hush-sh-sh!" she said again, as once more warningly she placed a finger to her mouth. "They must not hear . . . and I can but stay a moment. . . . I have watched since three times Isis rose and illumined the night . . . to see if thou, oh, Beloved of the gods, wouldst come, and wouldst come alone. For what I would say to thee none other must hear."

Hugh had jumped to his feet, but she immediately drew back a step or two, and put out both her arms with a pretty gesture of pride and of warning.

"Nay! I am not worthy that thou, oh, Beloved of the gods, shouldst step near to one so humble and poor as I. I have but a moment and the hours fly so fast. . . . See! Isis already turns towards the bed of clouds wherein she rests. . . . To-morrow, when Osiris is high in the heavens, thou wilt leave ancient Men-ne-fer, to shed the light of thy countenance on thy people who dwell far away. They will fall at thy feet and worship thee: for Ra and his high-priest have said it: thou art the messenger and Beloved of the gods. But lo! when once again Isis sheds her cold light on the waving papyrus and the crests of the tall sycamore, thou wilt look into a pair of eyes as blue, as impenetrable as the dark vault of heaven which cradles the goddess, thou wilt smell the perfume of tresses as golden as the rays of Osiris when he sinks to rest."

As once more the strange and poetic simile struck our ears—for the second time to-night, and spoken by two such different pairs of lips—Hugh and I both involuntarily murmured—

"Neit-akrit!"

"Nay! do not breathe it!" she entreated, and for the first time a shiver, as that of cold, shook her young figure, "for her very name is so sweet-sounding to the ear that every bird song after it sounds harsh and out of tune: and yet to-morrow, at this selfsame hour, Isis will watch from above, and will hear thee whisper it in her ear, while eagerly thine eyes, which have seen the majesty of the gods, will gaze into those deep blue eyes, fringed by heavy lashes, and read therein her strength and thine own weakness, her glory and thine abasement."

"I should be weak indeed," said Hugh at last, with a slight laugh, "if after such repeated warnings, from so many different quarters, I succumbed to the charms of the fair princess. I thank thee, pretty one, for thy concern in my welfare, but it is ill-timed and ill-advised, and my future happiness is not worth that thou shouldst dip thy pretty shoulders and arms in the cold waters of the canal, at this late hour of the night."

"Nay! I did not come to warn," she said reproachfully, whilst her hands wandered absently over her body, as if wondering to find it wet, "it is for the gods to warn and protect their beloved. I saw thee in the temple of Ra, the day when thou didst descend from the foot of the throne of Osiris to dwell amongst the people of Kamt, and as I saw thee I found thee beautiful beyond all sons of men. . . . Hush! do not speak! It was no sin to find thee fair! I had come to weep in the temple, for Amen-het, whom I had loved, was lost to me for ever."

I had already begun to think that the strange little person who had indulged in this rash swimming feat, in order to make pretty speeches to Hugh, was a little demented within that pretty, dripping head of hers. Her last words suggested to me that perhaps there was some cause for her strange frame of mind. She hid her face in her hands, and the drops, which escaped from between her fingers and trickled down upon her breasts, did not come from the waters of the canal. It was a very pathetic situation, and we did not quite know what to do. Here was a very pretty maiden, who had risked —to say the least—a very severe cold for the sake of speaking to us (or rather to Hugh, for as usual I was but a secondary personage). She was evidently in sad distress, and yet any attempt on our part at consolation by word or deed was promptly and coldly repelled. However, she soon looked up again, as if ashamed of her emotion, and spoke quickly and nervously.

"Wilt thou forgive me? I am weak, and Amen-het was very dear to me. We had loved one another from the days when my mother's foot rocked both our cradles side by side. He was motherless and fatherless, but he knew that I would be all in all to him : mother and sister, and wife and friend. We were happy, for we loved one another. He was a skilful artisan and carved exquisite images in the temples of the gods, and already his fame had spread far and wide, from Men-ne-fer to Se-ven-neh, and thence to Tanis. Then the princess, she whom they call Neit-akrit, built herself a palace more gorgeous and beautiful than aught the people of Kamt had ever seen, and hearing of the fame of Amen-het she bade him come and carve beautiful sculptures on the terraces of her garden, and upon the steps of her palace."

She paused, and in her eyes I saw that same look of deadly hatred which I had seen on the first day distorting the regal face of Maat-kha.

"Oh, Beloved of the gods! thou dost not know yet—how couldst thou? since thou art so fair—what it is to love and see thy love become a weariness to the beloved! Thou hast not craved for a look, a smile, a touch, and found nothing but an aching cold which chills the heart, and makes the brain dizzy with evil and jealous thoughts. Oh, Mother Isis! she has all that thou and the gods could give! She has beauty beyond the praise of song, she is great and rich above us all, while the land of Kamt lies prostrate at her feet. I had but him in all the world, but his love to me was more priceless than all the emeralds of Te-bu and all the rubies of Se-ven-neh, and yet, though Amen-het was humble and an artisan, she smiled on him and he forgot."

We were strangely impressed by this simple yet pathetic little story—so old and yet ever new—which the dainty little ivory carving with the dripping, childlike shoulders was whispering to us in the moonlight. She told it all in the peculiar, monotonous, sing-song way which is the characteristic of these people, and we both listened, for we both felt that there was something more to come, something that would explain why this demure little maiden stood half-naked before us in order to tell us her life's tragedy.

"Didst thou know that she is proud? and in her pride she wished that the hall, wherein she daily takes her perfumed bath, should be illumined by a lamp exactly like in design to the one which lights the inner sanctuary of the temple of Ra at Men-ne-fer. And Neit-akrit smiled on Amen-het until he was ready to sin for a look from her blue eyes, and would willingly have died for the sake of feeling her tiny naked foot rest for one instant upon his neck. Then she told him of her wish. The lamp—could he copy it?—ay! he could, if he but saw it. But 'tis sacrilege to dare to lift the veil which hides the sanctuary of Ra from all but his priests. Then she frowned and would not smile, refused to look on him again, vowed a more devoted artisan would in future receive her commands. And he, poor weak fool, swore an oath that he would do her bidding. After that she smiled again and Amen-het went to Men-ne-fer, and at dead of night his sacrilegious foot trod the inner sanctuary of Ra, the all-creating god, in order to find a graceful design for a lamp, for the bathroom of Princess Neit-akrit."

Again she paused, then added slowly, while her voice almost choked in her throat—

"Scarce twenty days had passed before I saw thy holy presence in the temple of Ra, oh, Beloved of the gods! and before the high-priest told us that thou hadst been sent by Osiris to be our king and ruler, I had seen Amen-het, pinioned and blinded, led forth towards the gates which mortal eyes have never seen, and beyond which lies the mysterious valley of death, where dwell neither birds nor beasts, and from whence no man can return."

She sank upon her knees, and her small round arms were raised upwards to the cold and silent moon, whilst we, with a shudder, looked at one another and remembered the awful tragedy we had witnessed in the vast and silent immensities of the wilderness, where the weird maniac gloated over his loathsome meal, where a half-human, wholly bestial creature was all that remained of him, who had once been Amen-het. Thank all the gods of ancient Egypt! the little maid who mourned her beloved dead had no conception of what he became, before we finally laid him beneath a few handfuls of sand and shingle.

"Canst wonder," she resumed, turning once more to Hugh, "that, seeing thee so fair, I have prayed to Isis that she may protect thee from the beauty of Neit-akrit's eyes? And see! the goddess did hear me, for as I wandered out in my mother's garden, I found at the very root of the sacred poppy, this precious treasure which I have brought for thee. It is a sacred scarabaeus, and thou knowest that he who beholds it, when Isis's face is turned towards the earth, and holds it tightly in the palm of his hand, sees no beauty save that of its exquisite body, sees naught that is blue save the iridescence of its wings. Then, when I had found it, I was happy. I waited, for I dared not approach thee while thy slaves were round thee, ready to drive me away, but to-night as I watched, again I saw thee and thy counsellor wander alone beneath the acacia trees, and I came across to lay my priceless offering in thy hands."

Graceful and exquisitely chaste, she now came towards Hugh and held out to him, in the palm of her small hand, a beautiful iridescent beetle of many hues of blue and green and gold. She looked so innocent, so confiding and trustful, and withal so pathetic in her grief, that, without a smile, and quite gently, Hugh took the simple offering, and, as he did so, respectfully kissed the tips of her trembling fingers.

Before we had time to realise what had happened, before we could say anything, or even stir, the little maiden had with one bound reached the marble parapet. We heard a splash, and the slow rhythmic movement of her strong young arms in the water, and through it all a faint and warning "hush-sh-sh" still lingering like the echo of a sigh in the sweet-scented air.

CHAPTER XIII

THE MAKING OF AN ENEMY

Is there such a thing as instinct, prescience? call it what you will. Nay! I know not. In my student days I had often dissected the human brain and studied its component parts, and wondered which of the numerous cells of fibrous tissue contained that inward feeling, which at times so plainly warns and foretells.

There *was* an instinct which told me that Neit-akrit, the beautiful and mysterious princess whom we, the usurpers, had deprived of the double crown of Kamt, was already a part of our very life. Her name haunted this place; it was whispered by the trees and murmured by the waters of the canal; it filled the air with its mystic and oppressive magnetism. Hugh felt it, I know. I think he is more impressionable than I am, and, of course, he is more enthusiastic, more inclined to poetry and visions. Even when wrapped in the most dry researches of science, he would clothe hard facts in picturesque guise.

To-night he talked a great deal of Neit-akrit. From a scientific point of view she interested him immensely, but, as a woman, she possessed no charm for him. *No* woman had ever done that. Above everything, he was a scientific enthusiast, and even in his own fair country he had never had so much as a schoolboy love. His friendship for me was, I think, his most tender emotion. He admired the picturesque, the poetic, above all, the mystic, and no woman, as yet, had embodied these three qualities in his eyes.

For the moment we discussed Neit-akrit as we would a coming foe. I refused to believe that a woman, young and fascinating, would without murmur or struggle resign her chances of a throne. Accustomed to rule by her beauty, she must love power, and surely would not resign herself patiently to a secondary position in the land.

We were looking forward to a preliminary battle on the morrow. Hugh was determined that the Pharaoh should be placed under my charge, and we both much wondered whether the arbitrary high-priest would allow himself to give way to the stranger upon every point.

"My one hold upon these people," argued Hugh, "is through their superstition. They look upon me as a being of another world, and any weakness would hopelessly endanger that position."

"Every conflict with that powerful and arbitrary high-priest might prove a fatal one, remember," I warned.

"I know that; but the Pharaoh is dying for want of proper medical treatment. It would be a sheer physical impossibility to me to watch him dying by inches and not raise a finger to help him. Having raised a finger, if it must mean hand and arm as well, then we shall see who is the stronger—Ur-tasen or I."

But whatever the feelings of the high-priest may have been,

he knew the art of concealing them to the full. The next morning, at the Cabinet Council, he was deferential, nay, obsequious to Hugh, and hardly spoke, but stood humbly with his tall gold wand in his hand, and only gave advice when directly spoken to.

Then, when it was almost time to go, and I had begun to think that Hugh, on the whole, had thought it wiser to make no mention for the present of the Pharaoh's sickness, the Queen suddenly said—

"My lord goes to-day to visit his future kinswoman, but the Pharaoh is sick, Ur-tasen, I know not if he will accompany us."

"I think he will," said the high-priest, with a sarcastic smile. "He will surely wish to be present in order to see the happy greeting of his young cousin to the future ruler of Kamt."

"He is too ill to bear the fatigue," said Hugh, peremptorily.

"Too ill, I fear," rejoined the high-priest, drily, "to bear the long days of impatience waiting for thy home-coming, oh, Beloved of the gods!"

"Ay! thou sayest truly, Ur-tasen; the holy Pharaoh is too ill to bear much, and my counsellor and I have consulted together, and together have decided that the hands which tend him are not sufficiently skilful to be entrusted with the care of so precious a life."

"A life, however precious, is always in the hands of the gods," retorted Ur-tasen. "None should know that better than thou, who hailest from the foot of their throne."

The duel had fairly begun. Hugh was determined to keep his temper, in spite of the high-priest's obvious sarcasm and mock deference.

"The gods," he said, "like to see such lives well looked after on this earth, and it will be my care in the future that wise counsels preside over the sick-bed of the Pharaoh."

I thought that the high-priest's parchment-like face had become a shade or two more sallow than before; the Queen, too, looked pale, but it might have been from fright at Hugh's audacity. She had been accustomed throughout her life to accept the dictates of the high-priest of Ra, as if they emanated from the gods themselves. Ur-tasen had raised his shorn head and, with slightly elevated eyebrows, was looking at Hugh.

"And how will the Beloved of the gods ensure this laudable aim?" he asked with the same mock deference.

"By appointing my counsellor to be the Pharaoh's physician and adviser; those who now fawn round him have no understanding of the terrible malady which is threatening to terminate his life, when he is yet scarcely out of boyhood. My counsellor is well versed in the science of drugs and herbs. He will advise the Pharaoh as to what he should eat and what he should avoid."

"The Pharaoh, though scarcely yet out of boyhood, is not one so easily counselled, oh, Beloved of the gods! and those who have now gained his confidence were appointed to the high honour by the will of Ra himself."

"As expressed by *thy* mouth, Ur-tasen, and though thy counsels may be wise in the administration of religion and the offering of sacrifice, I know not if they are worthy to be followed, where a serious malady threatens the descendant of kings."

"Such as they are they have been followed in this glorious land of Kamt, long before *thy* foot trod its soil, oh, Beloved of the gods!" said the high-priest, still trying to contain himself, though his voice shook with passion and his hand clutched the heavy wand of office, till the sinews of his gaunt arms creaked with the effort.

"Yet, nevertheless, in this matter *my* counsel shall prevail," said Hugh, with sublime calm, "and I solemnly declare that my counsellor here shall in future have constant access to the bedside of the Pharaoh, and that whatever he orders for the monarch's welfare shall be blindly and implicitly obeyed."

"And how dost thou propose to enforce this declaration, oh, Beloved of the gods?" asked the priest, with a contemptuous smile.

"By ruthlessly crushing beneath my heel him who should dare to disobey my orders," replied Hugh, slowly, as he rose from the litter and stood confronting the high-priest in all the glory of his youth and his powerful personality.

Ur-tasen had turned positively livid. He had been accustomed throughout his life to dictate his will to Queen Maat-kha and to the country. His commands had probably never been gainsaid, but at this moment he too felt, I think, that the next few minutes would decide as to who—he or the stranger—were to be master in the land.

"Beware," he said solemnly, his voice quaking with rage whilst he raised aloft the heavy wand of gold, emblem of his sacerdotal power, "lest thou thyself be crushed beneath the power, against which thou hast dared to raise thy sacrilegious voice."

But without a word Hugh turned and went up to the curtain which shut out the view of the city from the council chamber, and, pushing it aside, he pointed to where, lining the temple steps, thousands of men and women waited—as they did every morning—to catch sight of him who, until a few days ago, had sat at the very foot of the throne of Osiris. Some of the younger men and women were lying on the ground so that his foot might tread upon their bodies. Hugh waited a moment quietly while Ur-tasen, who had followed him, was also looking out upon the populace. Suddenly in the crowd there was a shriek, some one had caught sight of Hugh, and the next moment all had knelt, turning their dark faces with awe and reverence towards him, while the women began to chant a hymn of praise as they would to a god.

Hugh waited quietly while the flood of enthusiasm spread over the entire crowd, till the clamour became deafening, till the hymns sounded like an ode of triumph, then he calmly dropped the curtain and, smiling, turned to Ur-tasen.

"Didst *thou* speak of power, oh, mighty priest of Ra?" he asked.

"Wouldst thou defy the might that made thee?" thundered the high-priest, advancing threateningly towards Hugh and brandishing the massive wand over his head. "Beware, I tell thee, thou stranger in the land, lest the same hands which set thee above all the people of Kamt should hurl thee from that throne and send thee bruised and bleeding into the dark valley of death, a prey to the carrion of the wilderness from whence thou camest, followed by the maledictions of that same populace, which is now ready to proclaim thee akin to the gods!"

The old man was still vigorous, and I had jumped forward, seriously fearing that the next instant the heavy gold wand would descend on Hugh's skull, with a strength which might have silenced this dispute for mastery for ever. Queen Maat-kha, too, had put out both her arms imploringly towards the high-priest, who seemed to have lost all self-control; but it was evident that, with all his wisdom, the old gentleman knew nothing about the temperament of a son of prosy old England. Hugh looked down on him from his full altitude of six feet two inches, and with an impatient frown and a shrug of the shoulders, he quietly wrenched the massive wand of office from out Ur-tasen's nervous hands and, apparently without the slightest effort, bent it right across his knee till with a dull metallic sound the golden wand broke clean in half; then he threw the pieces on the marble floor at the astonished priest's feet and, smiling, shook the dust from off his hands.

"Thy age and thy weakness make thee sacred at my hands," he said as he calmly returned to his place beside the Queen, "but thou wouldst do well to remember that this broken wand might prove the future emblem of thyself and of thy power. The hour is late, my Queen," he added, turning to his *fiancée*, who was still speechless with terror and amazement, "and it is time we prepared ourselves for our journey. Pick up thy golden wand, Ur-tasen, and salute thy Queen!"

He gave a signal and the eight deaf-mute slaves hoisted up the litter ready to bear it away. The high-priest had silently picked up the golden wand as he was bid and silently had made humble obeisance before Hugh and the Queen. As I followed them out of the council chamber, I saw the high-priest still standing, gazing in amazement at the broken bar of gold and at Hugh's retreating figure with superstitious terror; then, as the first wild shouts of enthusiasm of the populace, at sight of the Beloved of the gods reached his ears, he fell upon his knees and stretched out his arms with a shriek, towards the sanctuary of Ra.

PART III

THE PALACE OF NEIT-AKRIT

CHAPTER XIV

NEIT-AKRIT, PRINCESS OF KAMT

"THERE is no doubt now, Girlie, but you have made an enemy of that man," I said, as soon as I had a chance of speaking to Hugh alone.

"It could not be helped, Mark. It was a choice between an enemy and a master. I see it clearly now, that after the first shock of surprise it was Ur-tasen's idea to use me as a puppet with which to further play upon the superstition of the people, and to consolidate his own power over Queen Maat-kha. I suppose that, with a woman at the head of affairs and a Pharaoh too ill to attend to anything seriously, the old fox has had it pretty much his own way."

"And when she asked him to allow her to marry again, he naturally did not cotton to the idea of a possible new master," I added thoughtfully, "or he never would have refused the cart-loads of gold dust or whatever other bribes the fair Queen offered for his consent. Then you appeared upon the scene . . ."

"And the old humbug was staggered for a moment, I daresay, but he knows well enough that we have come from somewhere on this earth, and not from heaven. I suppose that he suddenly saw possibilities of making me his tool and keeping the power in his own hands, whilst on the other hand the Queen might have rebelled against his wishes and married again in spite of him. Weighing one consideration with another, as W. S. Gilbert's policeman says, Ur-tasen thought he could make most capital out of me in my semi-divine capacity, and now I have taught him the salutary lesson that I have not come all this way, in order to become a priest-ridden tool for the furtherance of pagan superstitions, and of course he is not altogether pleased."

"You certainly have the people at your command, old man, but the priests, I should imagine, are treacherous."

"And that arch-humbug, Ur-tasen, the most treacherous of the lot," replied Hugh, with a laugh. "Of course he hates me now, and having found out that I simply will not dance to his piping, he will, no doubt, take the first possible opportunity of effectively getting rid of me."

"He dare not do that just at present."

"Of course not. But these picturesque and excitable people are only human after all. This enthusiasm is bound to cool down after a bit, and then 'ware of traps and plots."

"I cannot help thinking, Girlie," I added, "that Princess Neit-akrit will prove a source of great danger."

"To what, old croaker?—to our heads or to our hearts?" he said, with a laugh.

"I am inclined to think to both," I replied earnestly. "Do you feel at all impressionable just now?"

"I? Not the least bit in the world. Has not the dear little swimmer's talisman rendered me invulnerable? Besides, this land, fair as it is, is neither my home nor my country. At present it is a great and gorgeous prison, and I should not be such a fool as to court sorrow and misery within it."

"Do you know, old man, that if those are your sentiments your attitude towards your future wife is doubtful in its morality?"

"You don't understand what I mean, Mark. Marriage is a sacred tie, whether contracted in Christian or in pagan land. My word is pledged to Queen Maat-kha, and I will keep my word to her as much as I should, if I were pledged to a woman English-born like myself. And if ever I return to dusty old London, even if she did not choose to accompany me, I should still consider the tie which binds me to her indissoluble, as long as she chooses to hold me to it. But, believe me, she has no love for me; to her I merely represent the stranger—human or semi-divine—who has helped to keep the crown upon her head and prevented it from falling upon that of Neit-akrit, whom she hates. The Pharaoh is doomed, and by the curious constitution of this land, a woman can only sit upon the throne of Kamt if a husband or a son share that throne with her. That arbitrary old Ur-tasen would not allow her to wed one of her own subjects; he was surprised into accepting me. As soon as a son is born to her, she will release me from my word and see me depart without a pang."

"In the meanwhile, how are you going to induce the Pharaoh to accept me as his medical adviser?"

"I don't think it will be difficult, for I expect to-day he will be too ill to have much will of his own. Do you know that somehow I have had the feeling all along that neither Queen Maat-kha nor Ur-tasen *want* the unfortunate man to get well. He is no friend of mine, but I hope to goodness you can cure him, if only to annoy my arch enemy, the high-priest."

The difficult problem was unexpectedly and suddenly solved when, just as the sun was setting, our usual gorgeous retinue came to fetch us in order to escort us to the boats, which were ready for the journey. Gay-coloured sails, wrought in scarlet and blue designs, were attached to the crafts, which were manned by sixteen boatmen in scarlet leather skull caps, collars and belts, their naked bodies shining with some perfumed ointment with which they were smeared.

In the centre of each boat a pavilion was erected, with turquoise blue and green awnings, the gigantic double crown of Kamt glittering aloft at prow and poop. Queen Maat-kha, swathed in the clinging folds of her black kalasiris, wore the royal uraeus round her dark hair, which was thickly plaited with strings of emeralds and half hidden beneath a veil of dull blue and purple stripes. She looked very beautiful, though strangely excited and pale. As soon as she saw us she whispered for awhile eagerly to Hugh, then she came up to me and said—

"Will my lord's counsellor deign to step into the mighty Pharaoh's boat? He himself will be here anon."

"Is the Pharaoh well enough to travel?" I asked astonished.

"He has expressed the wish to see his royal kinswoman; and, as my lord desired, I have ordered that thou, oh, wise counsellor, shouldst be beside the mighty Pharaoh, to be a help to him in his sickness."

Hugh had triumphed; evidently the Queen, like Ur-tasen,

had thought it best to obey the Beloved of the gods, who had the whole of the population of Kamt grovelling at his feet. The Pharaoh himself, I think, felt too ill to care whether my insignificant self or his shaven, yellow-robed attendants sat opposite to him under the awning. He looked more cadaverous than ever amidst his rose silk cushions, as he was brought in his litter to the water's edge and lifted into the boat. He gave me an astonished look as I arranged his pillows more comfortably for him, and without a word took the heavy diadem from off his aching forehead and placed it by his side. He seemed like an automaton this morning and took no notice of anybody or anything round him. Complete apathy and drowsiness had succeeded his outburst of fury of the night before; even when he saw Hugh coming down the steps, looking positively regal in his mantle of shimmering green and gold, he turned his eyes listlessly away. On the alabaster steps the tiny musicians were playing upon harps and drums, whilst on the opposite shore the people had assembled in dense masses to watch the departure. Young athletes, among whom were many of the fair sex, had dived into the water, and were swimming about round the royal boats, peeping with bright, inquisitive eyes beneath the canopy, to catch sight of the Beloved of the gods. I remembered our pretty visitor of last night and wondered what Hugh had done with the iridescent beetle which was supposed to keep him from harm. Then, as the sun disappeared behind the hills in the west, slowly at first the boatmen dipped their scarlet oars into the water to the accompaniment of a low, monotonous barcarole, and gracefully the crescent-shaped boats glided down the stream, while a prolonged cry of farewell came from thousands of enthusiastic throats. Soon the wind swelled the sails, the boatmen plied their oars more vigorously, and the city of Men-ne-fer, with its rose-tinted palaces catching the last lingering rays of the setting sun, passed away before our eyes like a gigantic and gorgeous panorama.

It was long before the sound of sistrum and harp died away in the distance, long before the shouts of farewell ceased to echo from afar. One by one the sturdy swimmers dropped behind and returned to the city. I had given the Pharaoh a soothing draught, which, to my astonishment, he had taken obediently, and he was lying back against the pillows, with the gentle breeze fanning the matted hair on his forehead.

The city was soon far behind us; great fields stretched out on either side of the canal, covered with waving crops of barley and wheat, with groves of palms and fruit trees, and bowers of lilies, fuchsias and clematis. From time to time in the distance I caught sight of teams of white oxen walking leisurely homewards after the day's work was done; beside them the brown chest and back of a sturdy labourer of Kamt seemed to glisten in the evening light. Then at times, half-hidden among groves of palms and giant aloes, there peeped out the white or rose-tinted walls of some country mansion, or towering above the water there would rise, majestic and gorgeous, a temple dedicated to some protecting deity. As the royal procession sailed along the stream, from between the pillars would emerge a band of priests in flowing robes of white or yellow, and behind them a group of priestesses would intone a hymn as we passed.

I felt strangely anxious and excited, my mind dwelling persistently on the mysterious and poetic personality of the young princess, who seemed to create such unreasoning love in all male hearts of Kamt, and who had chosen this hour of night—mystic, poetic as she was herself—in which to receive him for the first time—*him* whose advent had deprived her of her throne.

The canal had considerably widened, and presently we drifted into a large inland lake. Night had entirely closed in, and I could not see the shore on either side, only the lights high aloft on the prow of the boats threw fantastic glints in the water. All was peaceful and silent, save for the rhythmic clap of the oars as they rose and fell in the water and the flapping of the sails in the breeze. Then gradually from the horizon in the west a blue radiance illumined the sky, and slow and majestic the silver moon rose above the fairy-like landscape; and as she rose the boatmen began to intone the hymn of greeting to rising Isis. Softly at first, and hardly discernible above the sighing of the reeds and papyrus grass in the wind, the chant rose louder and louder, as the silver disc appeared above the line of hills.

The Pharaoh had roused himself from his sleep, and impatiently he pushed aside the curtain which hid the distance from his view. I too looked out towards the west and saw that we were rapidly nearing an island, which rose like a veritable bower of flowers and palms from the middle of the lake, and the outline of which gradually detached itself from out the gloom. Then suddenly, in response to the chant of the boatmen, there came faintly echoing from that fairy island a flourish of silver trumpets.

The Pharaoh's face looked terribly set and hard; his dark eyes, framed by purple rings, appeared literally to glow as they gazed incessantly afar.

"Is it there!" he whispered.

Before us, above a gigantic flight of marble steps rising straight from out the water, there towered a massive building, its heavy pillars, covered in delicate sculpture, supporting the ponderous flat roof, which seemed to my strangely excited fancy to be made of massive gold. At the foot of the steps two mammoth sphinxes of white granite, mysterious and immense, frowned majestically across the lake.

As we approached, once again the silver trumpets sent a flourish through the evening air, and then I saw that the terraces high above us, the palm groves, and even the massive roof, were densely covered with people, while the whole gigantic flight of steps was lined with rows of slaves, dark and immovable as statues.

The Pharaoh's boat had scraped its side against the marble; his attendants had jumped out ready to help him to alight. But he pushed them almost brutally aside and stepped on shore, leaning heavily on my shoulder. He was trembling from head to foot, and I could see great beads of perspiration glistening on his forehead. I could not help feeling vaguely nervous too. This arrival by moonlight, the poetic fairy palace, the trembling man by my side, all helped to make my nerves tingle with the presentiment of something strange to come.

A song of welcome had greeted the arrival of the Pharaoh, and from above, a shower of lilies and iris fell like a sweet-scented carpet at his feet. He looked round to where Queen Maat-kha had just alighted, closely followed by Hugh; then I saw his trembling hand wander to the short metal dagger at his side, and clutch it with a nervous grin, while a hissing sound escaped his throat. But the next moment he had looked upwards and quietly he began to mount.

At sight of the Beloved of the gods a terrific shout of welcome had rent the air, and as I looked behind me for a moment, I could see that the whole length of the marble steps was—according to the strange custom of this land—literally carpeted with the bodies of young girls, eager that *his* foot should tread upon them. They crowded round him, kissing the tips of his sandals or the corner of his mantle, the more venturesome ones touching his foot or hand, as he walked with Queen Maat-kha by his side.

Then suddenly from above a strong and flickering light, from a hundred torches borne high aloft, changed the night into day. There was a moment of silence and expectancy, and then *she came*.

It would be an impossible task for me to attempt to put into words my first impression of Princess Neit-akrit, as she stood there on the edge of the marble terrace with a background of shadows behind her, the flickering light of the torches and the blue rays of the moon alternately playing upon the vivid gold of her hair.

Very tall and slender, almost a child, she embodied in her graceful person the highest conceived ideal of a *queen*.

She wore the quaint and picturesque garb of the country with unequalled grace. The great and heavy plaits of her hair hung on each side of her face down to her knees. The clinging folds of her straight and transparent kalasiris moulded every line of her figure; it was pure white and was held up over the shoulders by two silvery bands. It seemed to cling closely round her ankles and to slightly impede her movements, for she walked slowly and with halting steps. On her tiny feet she wore a pair of pointed sandals. In absolute contrast to Queen Maat-kha she had not a single jewel. Her arms, neck and bust were bare; on her head there was no diadem save that of her ardent hair, and in her hand she held the fitting sceptre to her kingdom of youth and beauty—a tall snow-white lily. Beside her there walked proudly a beautiful white panther, who fawned round her tiny hand and playfully rubbed himself against her knees.

She came close up to the Pharaoh, who seemed hardly able to stand, and held up her young face to his for the customary cousinly kiss. It was then that I saw how intensely blue were her eyes, and how deep the gold of her hair.

The next moment her voice, sweet and low, murmured, as Hugh reached the top of the steps—

"Welcome, oh, son of Ra! the Beloved of Osiris, to the humble abode of thy kinswoman."

And she too, like her slaves, knelt down to kiss the hem of Hugh Tankerville's garment.

"Then wilt thou not greet me as thy kinsman, princess?" he said as he raised her to her feet and waited for the cousinly kiss.

She stood before him and looked at him for fully ten seconds, while I could see that he was watching her with undisguised astonishment and admiration: then, resting her little hand very firmly on the head of her white panther, she said—

"If it is thy wish, oh, Messenger of Ra."

Fortunately I had a very tight hold of the mighty Pharaoh at that moment, for I doubt not that but for this and his own physical weakness, he would have made Hugh atone then and there for that cousinly kiss. His hand had once again clutched the dagger at his belt, and with a hoarse cry, like some wounded beast at bay, had tried to jump forward, but fell back panting in my arms.

Princess Neit-akrit had turned quietly to him.

"My kinsman is very sick. The journey must have been too fatiguing. Art thou his physician, oh, stranger?" she asked of me.

"I am deputed to alleviate the mighty Pharaoh's sufferings," I replied.

"Dost think thou wilt succeed?" she asked, looking at me with great wondering blue eyes.

"I can cure, I hope, the ailments of his body," I replied with a smile.

"Then I will kiss thee too," she said, with a merry girlish laugh, "for if thou restore my kinsman to health, thou wilt become very dear to me."

And I was given the top of a beautiful, smooth, young forehead to kiss—and I, prosy old Mark Emmett, was satisfied.

CHAPTER XV

DIVINELY FAIR

I HAD failed to notice, in my anxiety for the Pharaoh, how the two royal ladies had greeted one another; but now, at the gorgeous banquet, with which our young hostess made us welcome in her palace, I saw that the Princess sat beside the Queen, and that she had commanded her torch-bearers to stand close behind her, so as to throw a flood of light upon herself and her royal guest. The two women were a strange contrast—both beautiful beyond the average : one in all the pomp and magnificence of her regal attire, and the voluptuous charm of her mature beauty; the other in something white and clinging, with no crown save that of her ardent hair, no ornament save that of her own youth.

On luxurious couches, covered with white and silver hangings, we all reclined round the table, on which were spread the most wonderful and aromatic delicacies this lavish land could produce : peacocks' tongues and eggs of rare birds, petals of roses and lilies cooked in honey, and great crystal goblets filled with the rich wine of the soil—both red and white. All the while sweet little musicians crouched in various corners beside their tall crescent-shaped harps and sang us sweet songs while we supped, and pretty waitresses tempted us with dainty morsels.

The beautiful white panther lay at the feet of Neit-akrit, and she fed him with dates and figs, which she held for him between her teeth. The powerful creature would take the fruit from her lips, as gently as a bird. Hugh and I sat opposite to her. It was impossible not to admire the beautiful girl before us, the most exquisite product of this lovely, exotic land. There was a magnetic charm about every one of her movements, which recalled those of the panther beside her. After the first five minutes she had wrought hideous havoc in my dull old heart, and I was suddenly assailed with the wild temptation to make an egregious ass of myself. I was quite annoyed with Hugh that he did not seem very enthusiastic about her : he was surveying her as critically as he would have viewed a newly-unearthed mummy.

"Isn't she lovely, Girlie?" I contrived to whisper once during the banquet.

He did not reply, but with an inward smile, which made his eyes twinkle with merriment, he quietly slipped his hand beneath his cloak and drew out a tiny box which he handed over to me. It contained the iridescent scarabaeus, of which the little midnight swimmer had said that it would prove a subtle charm against Neit-akrit's beauty.

"Don't you want it?" I whispered again, astonished.

He shook his head, still smiling, and at that moment I looked up and saw Neit-akrit's eyes, more blue and iridescent than the beetle's wings, gazing across at Hugh with a strange, inquiring expression.

"What a beautiful jewel!" she said. Then, with the gesture of a spoilt child, "Wilt thou let me look at it?"

"Nay, Princess, it is no jewel," said Hugh, hiding the box again under his mantle, "and thou must forgive if I cannot allow even thy dainty fingers to touch it. It is a charm and its subtle virtue might vanish."

"A charm? Against what?"

"Against many serious evils and many grievous sins."

"I do not understand."

"I brought it with me from the foot of the throne of Ra, where a poor wandering soul, who had sinned deeply and suffered much, gave it to me when he knew that I was about to dwell among the fairest of the daughters of Kamt, so that it might preserve me from the same sin and the same suffering."

"But wilt thou not tell me what those sins and those sufferings are?"

"Nay! thou art too young to understand, but I will tell thee the name of the wandering soul who gave me the blue charm. He was a sculptor, far famed in ancient Kamt, and his name was Amen-het."

I gave Hugh a violent nudge, for I felt very much annoyed with him. To put it mildly, it was a singular want of good manners to rake up the terribly sad story of Amen-het, the sculptor, whilst partaking of the Princess's lavish hospitality. Amen-het had undoubtedly been a fool, and was punished for his folly according to the barbarous law of this beautiful country; but since time immemorial men have committed follies of the worst kind for women far less attractive and fascinating than was the Princess Neit-akrit.

To begin with, she was very young; she may, in a moment of thoughtlessness, have expressed a vague wish to possess some lamps similar in design to those which burnt in the sanctuary of Ra. The sculptor, like a fool, took her at her word and went there, where all the people of Kamt are strictly forbidden to go, within the inner sanctuary of the temple Surely she could not be blamed for his folly, and no doubt she had suffered horribly when . . .

But at this point my brief reflections were interrupted by Princess Neit-akrit's voice, truly the most melodious sound I had ever heard.

"How strange," she was saying, while her blue eyes gazed as innocently as before, as unconcernedly across at Hugh. "I knew a sculptor once whose name was Amen-het, but he offended the gods by his presumption, and I know not what punishment they meted out to him. Perhaps it was his soul which thou didst meet before the judgment-seat of Osiris, oh, thou who sittest at the foot of his throne!"

"Perhaps it was. In that case the blue charm will save me from Amen-het's presumption, and from the punishment meted out to him by the gods—for that was terrible!"

"Poor Amen-het," she said sweetly, "I spoke to him once or twice. He was a clever sculptor."

"But was too presumptuous, as thou sayest," said Hugh, who seemed suddenly to have grown irritable. "I saw him before he was quite ready to stand before Osiris. His flesh had withered on his bones, his voice was choked within his throat, burning hunger and thirst had made a beast of him, and the carrion had begun to gnaw his living flesh."

"Poor Amen-het," she repeated, and she selected a large juicy date from the dish and, holding it between her tiny sharp teeth, she called to her white panther, and the graceful, feline creature, as quiet as a kitten, took the ripe fruit from between her dainty lips.

I could see that Hugh was strangely irritated. He remained silent during the rest of the feast, in spite of the fact that the Queen made every effort to rouse him from his silence. As usual, the Pharaoh reclined, surly and silent, on his couch, which had been covered with a cloth of gold; obedient to my suggestion, he was taking only milk and left all the delicious fruit untasted. He avoided looking at the Princess or at Hugh; only when the story of Amen-het had been recounted, he laughed satirically to himself.

Long after everyone had retired and the fairy palace was wrapped in sleep, Hugh and I wandered beneath the gigantic overhanging fuchsia trees. It was a beautiful night and we were both singularly wakeful. The lake lay peaceful in the moonlight and, descending the great steps to the foot of the sphinxes, we found a small boat moored close to our hand. Though the crescent-shaped little crafts are very difficult to manage at first, we enjoyed a row all round the beautiful island, which seemed like the enchanted domain of a fairy princess. Beneath the trees large white peacocks slept, their tails shimmering like streams of diamonds, while in the branches myriads of birds had built their nests. We disturbed a troop of white gazelles from their sleep in the tall grass and a family of marmosets in the branches of the doum; golden tench and carp swam all round our boat, not the least frightened at the clap of the oars, and opening their mouths for a crumb.

We did not speak much, and then only about the beautiful dumb objects round us. I must confess that a strange love for this picturesque land was beginning to entwine itself round my heart, and as our boat glided so peacefully between the large clumps of lotus and water-lilies, I liked to feel that all this beauty, this peace, this poetry was truly my own. Busy Europe, with its politics, its squabbles, its socialism, its trades-unions and working-men's clubs, seemed altogether another world now, different and unreal; even the old Chestnuts was becoming a dream, beside the glorious visions of marble terraces and alabaster halls which had become so real.

For once in my life I was not in complete harmony with Hugh. I wanted to talk of our journey, our poetic arrival, of our fair young hostess, with her large innocent eyes and her pet white panther; but he seemed moody, and I felt that my enthusiasm for beautiful Neit-akrit would not find an echo in his heart.

The first streak of dawn was visible in the east when we

reached the palace steps again, tired yet refreshed with the midnight trip on the lake.

Our sandals made no noise on the white marble steps, and we kept in the shadow of the parapet, for we had no wish to be mistaken for midnight prowlers and rouse the slaves who guarded the palace.

All the lights had been put out, only the gilt roof glittered beneath the sinking rays of the moon. We skirted the palace, for the rooms which had been assigned to us opened out on to the broad terrace overlooking a garden of white roses. We were about to cross the garden, when suddenly Hugh put a hand on my arm and pointed to the terrace. Between the pillars which formed the entrance to our bedroom a figure stood holding back the heavy curtain. We could only see the graceful outline, clear and sharp against the bright light which burned within.

" Who is it ? " I whispered.

" The Princess," replied Hugh, as the figure detached itself from the gateway and glided slowly and cautiously across the terrace in the ghost-like, roseate light of dawn.

It was indeed Princess Neit-akrit, alone and unattended; she had wrapped a veil close round her figure, but her head was bare, and the colour of her hair was unmistakable.

She came straight towards us and presently caught sight of us both. She stopped, looking round her as if she wished to flee, then she put a finger to her mouth and came up quite close to Hugh.

" Hush ! " she whispered. " Dost wonder, I know, to see me here alone at this hour, without even Sen-tur by my side. And yet I came because I wished to speak to thee alone."

" Thou dost indeed honour me," said Hugh, quietly, whilst I made a discreet movement to retire.

" Tell thy counsellor he need not go," she said. " I know that thou and he are one, and I am not ashamed of that which I would say."

" Wilt go within then, Princess ? The morning is cold."

" Nay ! what I would say will not take long; yet I could not sleep till I had told it thee. The night seemed oppressive. I wandered into the garden, and Isis led my steps to thy couch. I thought thou wast asleep, and that I would sit beside thee, not waking thee, yet telling thee of this thing which lies so heavy on my heart. I thought to whisper it gently lest thou wake, to murmur it so that thou, half dreaming, shouldst hear my voice, and hearing it, dream on."

She certainly had that indefinable charm—an exquisite voice—and both Hugh and I listened to her strange words, charmed by its sweet-sounding melody.

"Nay, Princess," said Hugh, as she had paused; "sweet as the dream would have been then, I much prefer the reality, and as long as thou wilt speak I will listen."

"I came to tell thee . . . that . . ."

There was a little catch in her throat, but she tried to conquer her emotion and put out both her hands in a pretty, almost childlike appeal.

"Ah, I know! someone has told thee evil of me, and I longed to speak to thee . . . about . . . about Amenhet. . . . They told thee that I am vain and cruel . . . but . . . but . . . wilt believe me if I say . . . that I am beset with calumnies . . . and . . ."

Hugh came a little closer and took one of her tiny, trembling hands in his, and there was no doubt that in his voice, too, there was a slight catch.

"Sweet Princess," he said gently, "believe *me* when I say that I have heard no calumny about thee, which thy presence hath not by now dispelled."

She turned her face fully up to his and asked—

"Dost truly mean what thou sayest?"

"I swear it," he said earnestly.

"Nay! I will believe thee, for thou art great and good. I will believe thee if thou wilt look straight into mine eyes and if thou wilt kiss me between the brows, in token that thou art my friend."

She raised herself on tiptoe, for Hugh Tankerville is very tall, and British, and stiff-backed. There was a curious, half-dazed look in his eyes, as he looked down at the sweet face turned up to his. The veil had slipped down from her shoulders. The quaint Egyptian kalasiris, half transparent and clinging, gave her young figure the appearance of one of those precious idols which are preserved in European museums. A perfume of lotus blossom seemed to emanate from her, and about her whole being there was an exquisite savour of poetry and mysticism, mingled with truly human, charming womanhood.

For that brief moment I felt wildly, madly, stupidly jealous, and at the same time enraged with Hugh, who seemed to me so cold and impassive, when I would have given . . . well! . . . a great deal to stand in his place. At last he bent his tall six feet two inches and gave the kiss as she had begged.

The next instant she was gone and I had dragged Hugh away into our own room. A penetrating scent of lotus blossoms seemed entirely to fill it, and as we raised a lamp over our heads we saw that Hugh's couch was one vast bower of the sweet blooms, covering pillow and coverlet; but from the table where he had put it before we strolled out earlier in the evening, the iridescent scarabaeus, which was to guard him against the magic of Neit-akrit's beauty, had disappeared.

CHAPTER XVI

DANGER

All through my stay in the beautiful land of Kamt I never found that its balmy, fragrant air acted as a soporific, and it became really wonderful with how little sleep we both contrived to keep up our health. That night, or rather morning, after our quaint little adventure, I hardly managed to close an eye, and I am sure that Hugh, who had as usual a room opening out of mine, was as restless as myself. I found the scent of the lotus oppressive and penetrating, and the memories it brought back to me, very disturbing and harassing.

The sun was high in the heavens when I at last contrived to snatch a brief hour's sleep, and when I woke it was to find that Hugh had stolen a march on me, and had already gone out. The morning looked perfect, and after my delicious bath I felt thoroughly rested and at peace with this picturesque world and its fascinating women. It was one of those mornings when a book and a cigar on a verandah facing the sea would have been perfect bliss in the dear old country. But on this beautiful morning in Kamt, the scent of flowers, the songs of birds, the exotic beauty of the land gave mind and body so much to enjoy, that not even the cigar and the book were much missed.

I tried to pick my way through the labyrinth of alleys and walks, to the terrace that faced the lake, and just as I stepped on to it, I saw Hugh and Princess Neit-akrit there together.

She looked more lovely, I thought, by day than even she had been by moonlight. She was lying under a canopy of turquoise blue silk which vied in colour and brilliancy with the sky above it. Beneath it her hair looked like living copper, and her skin white and polished like the alabaster. Her beautiful panther lay at her feet, and Hugh stood on the steps which led up to the throne-like couch on which she reclined. Neither of them saw me, and I stood for a while looking at the dainty picture.

"I have oft wondered," she was saying, "what lies beyond those hills. Ur-tasen says that there is nought but the valley of death, where foot of man ne'er treads, but where carrion beasts prowl at night, and vultures fly screeching overhead. When he talks like that my flesh creeps with horror, and for days I cannot bear to look upon those hills; then, a lovely morning comes like to-day, Osiris emerges in his golden barge more radiant than ever from out that valley of death, and then all day I long to follow him in his course and disappear with him behind the hills in Ma-nu, so that I might see the glories that lie beyond."

I was debating with myself whether I should discreetly retire or interrupt this *tête-à-tête*, which my reason suggested was dangerous somehow to my friend.

"Thou who comest from the foot of the throne of Osiris," she resumed, turning eagerly towards Hugh, "thou must know whither he wanders every night, whilst Isis his bride reigneth in the heavens. Wilt tell me what lies beyond the hills of Kamt?"

"Ur-tasen has told thee: the valley of death; the desert wilderness, where no man can live, no bird sing, nor flower blossom."

"Ay! But beyond that?"

"Beyond it?"

"Yes! after death surely must come life again; after the darkness, light; after desolation, joy unspeakable. Oh! thou canst not know," she added, stretching out her arms longingly towards the distant horizon, "how I long to break the hideous fetters that bind me, and when Osiris shines so brightly, the flowers smell so sweet, and the birds' chorus of harmony fills the air, how I hate then the splendours of my palace, the marble halls and temples of Kamt, the very sight of the people almost worshipping at my feet, and long to run up those inaccessible hills and see what lies far away beyond this land, beyond the valley of death, beyond the pillars that support the vault of heaven. Wilt thou not tell me," she pleaded, "or, better still, wilt take me there one night when Kamt is wrapped in sleep?"

Hugh looked almost wildly down at her, and then round him with that curious dazed expression which had puzzled me already last night. Then he caught sight of me and seemed relieved, for he said very quietly—

"Nay, Princess, it is not for me to teach thee the secrets of this earth. But here comes my counsellor, he is wise, and if thou wilt he will tell thee all about Osiris and the vault of heaven, and even of the land which lies beyond the gates of Kamt."

She turned to me with a sweet smile, but I thought that there was a shade of disappointment in her eyes.

"It is always a joy to speak to the learned counsellor," she said evasively, "and soon, when he has leisure, when the holy Pharaoh is cured of his ailments, he will no doubt teach me much which I do not know; and in the meanwhile I will go roaming with Sen-tur, and perhaps if I sit on his back he will carry me there, where foot of man doth not tread."

She began playing with the panther, who seemed much disinclined for a game, and made sundry attempts at keeping his comfortable lazy position at her feet. But his mistress suddenly seemed in a teasing mood, for she tore a branch of roses from a great bush which stood in a vase close beside her, and began to playfully prick with it the kingly Sen-tur on the nose.

Soon his majesty's temper was up, and lazily at first, then

more and more viciously, he made great dabs at the branch and then at Neit-akrit's hand, with his ponderous paw.

"A dangerous game surely, Princess," said Hugh, after a while. "Sen-tur might lose control over his temper and might do thee an injury."

"An injury? Sen-tur?" she said, with a laugh. "Thou speakest in jest, or thou dost not know Sen-tur. At a word from me he becomes as furious as the maddest bull in Kamt, and his roar is like the thunder, and at a whisper from me he will again be as quiet as a lamb. But never would Sen-tur's wrath turn against his mistress."

"Thou holdest him in bondage," I said, with a somewhat clumsy attempt at gallantry, "as thou dost all men, high and low. Sen-tur is favoured indeed."

"Sen-tur loves me, and I love Sen-tur," she said drily; "he is the most precious treasure I possess, for he is wholly mine, and he has no cares, no affections, no thoughts save for me. He is dearer to me than the kingdom of Kamt."

"It is a merciful decree of Ra, then," said Hugh, with a smile, "that he sent me to take the kingdom of Kamt from thee and not Sen-tur."

"Believe me," she rejoined, looking steadfastly at him, "that all-powerful Ra showed his love for Neit-akrit the day that he decreed that the double crown of Kamt should never sit upon her brow."

Somehow, in spite of this earnest assurance, I did not think that she was sincere, and I did not altogether understand the look which she gave to Hugh as she spoke. She certainly began to tease Sen-tur more viciously than ever, till the great creature fairly roared and foamed at the mouth.

Suddenly we heard a sound of trumpets and of drums, and from beneath the terrace we heard the usual cry which always preceded the arrival of an important messenger.

"Make way for the messenger of the city of Net-amen, and of Hesh-ka, its governor!"

"What does he want?" asked the Princess, with a frown, as half a dozen slaves and a group of attendants began to emerge from everywhere, and stood waiting to receive the emissary of the great city, with the full complement of honours prescribed by the complicated ceremonial of this country.

A young Egyptian, dark and good-looking, had come forward, and after kissing the ground before Princess Neit-akrit, had turned straightway to Hugh.

"To the Beloved of the gods, to the son of Ra, do I bring greeting from the city of Net-amen."

There was absolutely no doubt in my mind at this moment that the fair Neit-akrit frowned very darkly: the red of her lips almost disappeared, so tightly were they set, and poor Sen-tur received an ugly blow with the prickly branch right upon his nose.

"Greeting, oh, Well-beloved," resumed the messenger. "The council of the city of Net-amen, and Hesh-ka, our noble governor, desire to lay their homage at thy feet. To-morrow, if thou wilt deign to set thy foot within its gates, one hundred thousand inhabitants will line its streets to bid thee welcome. The maids of Net-amen will draw thy barge along the canal; the youths and athletes will fight as to whom shall be the first to kiss the sole of thy sandals, and the city awaits thee with gifts of incense, gold and lapis-lazuli, for they will greet in thee the coming ruler of Kamt, the Well-beloved whose presence has blessed the land."

He began a long account of wonderful festivals and sacrifices which the important city was organising for the entertainment of the proposed guest. Hugh was barely listening to the messenger's words, he, as well as I, was watching, fascinated, yet horrified, Princess Neit-akrit's more and more dangerous game with her panther. She seemed to take a cruel delight now in pricking the beast with the thorn, for great drops of blood appeared on the snowy whiteness of his fur; and yet Sen-tur, apparently beside himself with rage, made no attempt to retaliate. I felt terribly helpless in case she did pursue her dangerous game too far, for I had no weapon about me, but looking up at Hugh I saw that underneath his cloak he was clutching his knife, ready to use it if emergency required.

The emissary had evidently finished his message, for now he knelt down with his head on the ground and said—

"Wilt deign to allow thy slave, oh, Beloved of the gods, to touch with his lips the sole of thy foot?"

At this moment I heard a short, sharp cry from Princess Neit-akrit, and a roar more ominous than before: the next, there was a bound and an agonised shriek which froze the blood in my veins. Sen-tur, goaded to madness at last by the merciless teasing, had turned and sprung upon the unfortunate messenger who was nearest to him, and before I or anyone else present had realised the full horror of the situation, the powerful beast was rolling the wretched man underneath him on the floor. I thought he was doomed, although after the first second of surprise Hugh and I had sprung to his rescue. But before we could reach the group where the powerful beast was, with mighty jaws, tearing bits of flesh from the shoulders and thighs of his victim, Neit-akrit was already by Sen-tur's side.

With utmost calm she placed her tiny hand upon his collar, and said, in a quiet, gentle voice—

"Sen-tur! Sen-tur! come!"

And, unresisting, suddenly as gentle as a kitten, with great jaws still covered in blood which he was licking with a smothered growl, the powerful creature allowed her to lead him away; and when she once more took her seat beneath the turquoise blue canopy, he lay down with a final snarl at her feet.

I was hastily examining the arms, shoulders and thighs of the injured man. They were terribly lacerated by the monstrous teeth of the brute, and I whispered to Hugh that I thought in one instance amputation would be necessary.

I had never seen so dark a scowl on Hugh Tankerville's face as I did then; he looked positively evil, and I was quite sorry for the poor little girl who, to my mind, was after all only guilty of thoughtlessness. Two shorn, yellow-robed medicoes had sprung up from somewhere: I directed them how to bandage the wounds, and ordered my patient to be removed to an airy room, where I could presently attend to him.

General gloom seemed to have settled on all those present; Neit-akrit was stroking Sen-tur's head with a defiant look at Hugh.

"Wilt allow me to speak to thee alone," he said abruptly.

To my astonishment she immediately ordered her slaves and attendants away, and when they had gone she said quite humbly—

"I know what thou wouldst say. Do not chide me; I

could not bear it. I . . . I . . ." and great tears gathered in her eyes.

Then with sudden impulse, from out the folds of her dress, she drew out a short dagger and held it towards Hugh.

"Do thou do it," she said, while great sobs choked her throat. "I know that that is what thou wouldst say. Sen-tur has sinned. Sen-tur must die! for perhaps now he might sin again. But *I* could not kill Sen-tur for he trusts me, and he would not expect a blow from me."

She was holding the dagger out towards Hugh, whilst he looked at her, astonished, as I was, by the quick and varying moods of this strange and fascinating girl.

"Do it quickly," she said, "lest I repent; for, believe me, it is not of my own free will that I have asked thee to kill Sen-tur. I would sooner see him kill every one of my slaves," she added naïvely, "than that harm should come to him."

Then, as Hugh would not take the dagger from her, she placed it quietly at his feet, then threw her arms passionately round the panther's neck, while great tears fell from her eyes on to his fur.

"Farewell, Sen-tur, my beauty, my loved one," she whispered. "I know that thou art not afraid to die, for thou, like Neit-akrit, dost long for that glorious land which lies beyond the valley of death. Come back, Sen-tur, to me at nights, and tell me what thou hast seen. Sen-tur is ready, oh, Beloved of the gods," she added; "thou needst not fear, he will not even struggle. Make haste. I wish it."

"Dost really wish me to kill Sen-tur?" asked Hugh at last.

"Yes, really! I wish it."

"Why?"

"Because Sen-tur has sinned grievously, and, sinning will surely sin again. He hath tasted the blood of a slave, he liked the taste and will wish to drink again."

"But will it not grieve thee to see Sen-tur die?"

"More than thou canst conceive," she replied earnestly. "Sen-tur is my only friend, but it would grieve me even more, if thou didst leave my presence now with evil thoughts of me in thy heart."

She looked divinely pretty, this exquisite product of a strange and mystic land: quaint as one of those images on ancient tombs, dainty as the lotus blossom and roses in her garden. She was—my reason told me—flirting outrageously, desperately, with Hugh, even to the extent of endangering the life of innocent Sen-tur. Had she but known him as I did—the scientific enthusiast, blind even to such beauty as hers—she would have realised how she was wasting her time. In spite of her pretty speech, her sweet, appealing look, Hugh was singularly unresponsive, and it was in a very matter-of-fact, prosy way that he picked up the small dagger and gave it back to her.

"Thou must punish Sen-tur in the way thou thinkest fit. I am no good hand at killing beasts."

"Thou dost confine thyself to killing women then," she retorted with one of those sudden changes in her mood, which to me were so puzzling.

"Thou art too young to understand the purport of thy words," rejoined Hugh, who had become very pale. "The motive which led me to kill Kesh-ta, thy slave, in the judgment-hall of Men-ne-fer, was one for which I have not to answer to any one, least of all to thee. But the hour is late, Princess; wilt deign to allow me to follow my counsellor? He will wish to visit the holy Pharaoh, and I would fain pay my respects to Queen Maat-kha."

And having bowed to her, Hugh took my arm and quickly led me away from the terrace.

I wished I had been a more subtle reader of feminine character, for then, perhaps, I could have interpreted the look with which Princess Neit-akrit followed Hugh's retreating figure.

CHAPTER XVII

LOVE OR HATE?

EH! you dull old Mark Emmett, what a difficult task you have set yourself! Do you really imagine that you can convey to the minds of strangers an adequate idea of a woman, young, exotic, voluptuous and divinely pretty, and with it all changeable, impenetrable as the waters of the lake?

I suppose if I had been born a woman I should have been

able to understand the various moods of Princess Neit-akrit. As a mere straightforward male creature, I must confess that I was completely at sea.

Of course, originally, she must have hated the idea of any man—be he beloved of all the gods or not—coming between her and the crown of Kamt, which already she must have looked upon as her own.

She was so absolutely queen of this land by her beauty, her fascination, her wonderful personality, that it must have been terribly galling to her suddenly to see a stranger placed, in virtue of his mystic descent, immeasurably above her in the hearts of the entire population of Kamt.

So much I understood and appreciated. Neit-akrit was a woman; she would have been more than human if she had not resented the intrusion of the Beloved of the gods. I suppose that she hated Hugh at first, hated his power over the people, hated the very messenger who knelt at his feet and brought homage to him from distant cities—homage which in future and in his presence were denied to her.

So, womanlike, seeing that a master was placed above her, she tried to make him her slave. Being superstitious, she had stolen the talisman which was destined to guard him against her fascination. Then she brought to her aid all the gifts which bountiful Nature had lavished upon her. Her exquisite voice became more melodious and more gentle as she whispered words of clinging, womanly humility into his ear; her blue eyes melted into tears when they met his. Alternately she tried to charm and to irritate him, to attract him by her tenderness and to repulse him by her cruelty.

Poor Hugh! I wondered how long he would be adamant. Inwardly I prayed that he might remain so always. If the beautiful Neit-akrit succeeded in her dangerous game of capturing his heart . . . well! . . . what could result but misery for him, since his word was pledged to Maat-kha?

Fortunately, so far, I had detected no sign of change in his frigid attitude towards her. She certainly seemed to have the power of irritating him and making him say—against his will I am sure—some very unkind words to her.

But there! how could I guess what went on in the minds of these two young people whom Nature in a freakish mood seemed to have fashioned for one another? Both ardent, passionate, poetic, mystic, both as beautiful specimens of Heaven's handiwork as it was ever granted to my eyes to see.

Princess Neit-akrit talked to me a great deal during the next few days, and I was fascinated with her strange questionings, the unaccountable and mystic longings she felt, in the midst of her ignorance.

"Tell me of that land beyond," she would beg, and I did not know what to say. Was it for my clumsy hands to roughly tear asunder the veil which fifty centuries of priestcraft had woven, thick and dark, before the eyes of all the children of Kamt?

There was no moonlight one evening. The sky was heavily overcast, and after the evening banquet, when we followed her on to the terrace, Neit-akrit leant against the marble balustrade and spoke as if to herself.

"How strange that Isis should veil her countenance when she might behold the Beloved of the gods!"

"It is a sight she has oft witnessed, Princess," said Hugh, with a laugh, "and therefore, probably, it has no overpowering charm!"

"Yes, of course! I know when thou didst dwell at the foot of the throne of the gods thou must have often seen the majesty of Isis herself, whose image up on the vault of heaven is all we poor mortals are allowed to see. Tell me about her."

"Nay, Princess, there is naught to tell thee which thou dost not know thyself. Her beauty is all before thee in those lovely nights of Kamt, when she shines upon sleeping Nature and throws diamond sparks upon the lake."

She shook her head.

"Ah, then I am wiser than thou art, for I know something more about the goddess than merely her cold image up there."

"Wilt tell me, Princess?"

Queen Maat-kha had remained within; she said that the night looked dark and cold, but personally I thought that she would have been wiser to look after her own property, which was being strangely and wilfully toyed with, and in grave danger of being stolen.

"I learnt it all in a dream," began Neit-akrit, looking dreamily out towards the hills. "It was just such a night as this, and I could not rest, for the wind was whistling through the fuchsia trees, making each bell-shaped blossom tinkle like innumerable, short sharp sighs. It was a dream remember! I rose from my couch and went out beneath the solitary alleys of the park; not even Sen-tur walked by my side. I felt unspeakably lonely and desolate, and the darkness weighed upon me like a pall. Suddenly I felt that someone . . . something took my hand, while a voice whispered, 'Come!' I followed, and the unseen hand guided me over the canals and cities of Kamt, above those hills yonder which mark the boundaries of the living world, and right across the valley of death, where, in the darkness, I heard the cry of the carrion and the moaning of the dying souls."

She stood—a quaint, rigid, infinitely graceful image—dimly outlined in the gloom, slightly bent forward as if her eyes were trying to meet through the darkness those of Hugh fixed upon her. I could see his tall figure, very straight, with arms crossed over his chest, and I longed to take him away, far from this strange and voluptuous girl whose every motion was poetry and every word an intoxicating charm.

"I knew that the valley of death lay at my feet," she resumed in the same monotonous, sing-song tone, dreamy and low. "I knew that all round me was desolation, sorrow and waste, but I did not see it, for my eyes sought the distance beyond, and what I saw there, far away, was so glorious and fair, that ever since my memory has dwelt upon that vision and my feet longed to wander there again."

"What didst thou see?"

"I saw a bower of tangled flowers drooping beneath the sun, whose rays I thought I had never seen so glorious and so hot, and between the roses and the lilies, the laurel and the mimosa, innumerable birds chirruped and sang. The ghostly hand still led me on, and presently I stood among the flowers and saw that each little bird had a nest, and each by his side a mate; and beneath the tangled trees of fuchsias and acacias, men and women wandered two by two. Their heads were close together, their arms were intertwined, even the trees above their heads mingled their branches and bent their trunks towards each other. The air was filled with sounds of whispers murmured low and sweet, of kisses exchanged, of fond sighs and endearing words. Then a great sorrow filled my heart, for I, whom men have called so fair, was all alone in this abode of love; no one stood near me to caress me, no one was whispering in my ear, and as I passed the young couples would pause a moment in their love-making and gaze at me with astonishment, whilst some of them would whisper, 'Behold! 'tis Neit-akrit, Princess of Kamt! Is she not fair?' And others would add, 'Yea! so fair, so high and so mighty, but she knoweth not the abode of Isis.' And all would sigh, 'Alas! poor Neit-akrit!' And I was so overwhelmed with sorrow, that I fell on the soft dewy grass and cried bitter tears."

I thought that Hugh must have felt very sure of himself to dare venture on such a subject of conversation with a woman who was beautiful and fascinating beyond words. He could not see her, for the night was very dark, only an outline and a warm glow round her head, as of living gold.

"Then," she began once more, "while I cried, suddenly I felt as if two arms encircled me, as if something undefinable and immeasurably sweet filled the air, and I was borne through the roses and the lilies, to a bower of blossoms, which smelt more sweet than anything on earth. And there in the deep shadows, peeped at only by tiny eyes of birds, there dwelt the majesty of Isis herself, and suddenly in the presence of the goddess, I ceased to be Neit-akrit, forgot all pomp and glitter, remembered only that I was young and fair, and when the arms which bore me had laid me down on the sweet-scented carpet, I and the owner of those arms knelt down and worshipped before the shrine of Isis."

She paused, and for a few moments there was deep silence in the darkness, only the splash of the water against the marble steps sounded at regular intervals like a faint murmur from below.

"Dost wonder that ever since I have longed to visit that spot again; that I have begged Sen-tur to guide me there, for I believe *he* knows that I have prayed sweet Death to lead me through that dark valley, so that I might behold Isis once again and worship at her feet . . . with someone else . . . who would be a part . . . nay! the whole of my life . . . who would love! and yet not worship . . . 'tis I who would worship, who would live for a smile, who would die for a kiss. I, who would be coward and weak, and prouder of that weakness than of the double crown of Kamt. But the throne of Isis is hidden from my view. It stands before the poor and lowly. The rich princess may not enter there."

Hugh said nothing, and presently we heard a footfall on the flooring, a frou-frou of silks and jewels, a last lingering sigh on the evening air and she was gone, leaving behind her an aroma of exotic flowers, of delicious young ripe fruit, of voluptuous womanly charm, which in this strange land spoke to us of country and of home.

During the next few days the changeable and capricious girl spoke not a single word to Hugh. She seemed altogether to ignore his very presence, and all her charms, her fascinations were lavished with a free hand upon the holy Pharaoh. I had become deeply interested in my illustrious patient, and had even begun to sympathise with him in his mental troubles. He hated Hugh, who was the person on earth to whom I was most attached, and yet how could I help acknowledging that he had a just cause for hatred? But now Neit-akrit seemed to have set herself the task of making him forget every one of his troubles, and succeeded fully by lavishing all her powers of fascination and sweetness upon him. Once more I fell into my *rôle* of gooseberry, and although the Pharaoh insisted on my presence near him at all hours of the day, and even night, there were many moments when I thought it more prudent to keep out of earshot. It was a curious kind of love-making, and throughout those few memorable days a strange feeling would now and then creep into my prosy old heart at sight of the beautiful girl radiant with youth and health, side by side with the sickly, emaciated man with one foot in the grave.

He was as silent as ever, but the ugly frown had almost disappeared from between his eyes and he too avoided being near Hugh or speaking to him.

Half that day and the next Neit-akrit sat beside him on the couch which overlooked the lake, and prattled to him in a merry way of a thousand nothings, which delighted him more than a chorus of nightingales; or she would take a harp and would let her slim young fingers glide gently along the chords, and sing to him sweet and quaint lullabies which soothed him into quiet, dreamless sleep.

Then when he slept she still remained by his side, softly humming her low monotonous tunes, ready to greet him with a sunny smile the moment he opened his eyes; if then I tried to speak to her she would place a warning finger to her mouth, and I sat and watched her while she watched the mighty Pharaoh, and once or twice I saw great tears rise to her eyes and trickle slowly down her cheeks. She puzzled me. I could not bring myself to believe that she was suddenly beginning to care for her ailing kinsman, who, but for his rank, must have been very unattractive to a young and beautiful girl: nor did I wish to admit to myself that I feared she was playing a cruel game, in order to arouse jealousy in Hugh.

As for Old Girlie, he was strangely reticent about the Princess, and once or twice when I mentioned her name he very abruptly changed the subject. I thought that the excitement, or perhaps the oppressive air of Kamt, was beginning to tell on him. He looked strangely pale and worn, and I knew he did not sleep at nights. His hand felt hot and feverish, as it had done during those terrible years when he took it upon himself to complete his father's work, and when I seemed anxious about him, he only laughed in a dry, sarcastic way quite unlike his usually bright and sunny laugh.

Late one afternoon I at last contrived to be alone with him. He had received many deputations, made speeches and heard others all the morning, no wonder that he felt tired and glad mentally to quit Egypt and wander in England for awhile with me.

"Maat-kha has expressed a wish," he said very suddenly, "that we should be married in a month. The town of Tanis sent a deputation to-day to say that already they are prepared to receive us. I understand that the temple of Isis, in which the royalties of this land are always married, is in Tanis, and I have no wish to postpone my marriage."

"Girlie, I wonder if you realise what a terribly earnest step you are taking. Though the rites may be pagan, marriage is always a sacred tie, and though you live away from your native land your home must always be beside your wife, whoever she may be."

"I know, old Mark, I know. I have thought more about the matter lately, but you must remember that there are things as sacred as marriage, and one of these is an Englishman's word."

"I don't like to hear you talk like this, Girlie. I am afraid that in this wild adventure you are risking some of your happiness."

"Oh, what tragedy, old Mark!" he said with a forced laugh. "My happiness? Why, it is complete! Have I not accomplished the aim of my life? Can I not now prove to the world that mad Tankerville and his fool of a son were neither visionaries nor liars? Am I not virtually king of the fairest land on earth? Why, old Mark, we came here for the sake of science, not for such paltry objects as my happiness."

"That is all very well, Girlie; but with all your scientific enthusiasm you have got a great and good heart somewhere about you, and that does not seem to me to be quite satisfied."

"It will be satisfied presently, old chap, when all these pageants, processions and welcomes are over and I can set to work to guide the destinies of these picturesque people, and gradually teach them the mysteries of an outer world. And when they have begun to understand, and my influence over them is absolutely established, then I can begin to destroy and pierce through those insurmountable barriers which divide them from Europe and modern civilisation. Then gradually we shall see my picturesque subjects take to wearing top hats and patent leather boots, and Queen Maat-kha look superb in a Paris gown. We shall build railways from Men-ne-fer to Tanis, and steamboats will ply the canals. There is plenty to dream of, old friend, never fear. My life will lack no excitement from now till its close, and there will be no room in it for sentiment or happiness."

We had reached one end of the terrace, and close to us we saw the daïs, where I had left the Pharaoh asleep an hour before, with his young cousin softly cooing to him like a pigeon, and fanning his forehead gently with a large palm leaf. They neither of them heard our footsteps, and we both stopped with the same instinct of curiosity watching the strangely ill-assorted pair. The Pharaoh was awake and speaking, but some inward emotion had made his deep-set eyes glow with unnatural, brilliancy and taken every drop of blood from out his cheeks and lips. His mouth seemed parched, and his throat half-choked as he spoke, whilst she, a radiant picture of youth and beauty, with fresh colour in her cheeks, a wondering look in her blue eyes, looked like a nymph beside a satyr.

"I do not often dream, Neit-akrit," the Pharaoh was saying, "when thou sittest by my side. I think Anubis chases dreams away and renders my sleep as refreshing as death. But just now I had a dream."

"Wilt tell me, cousin?"

"I dreamt, Neit-akrit, that I stood within the sacred temple of Isis, at Tanis. All round me the incense rose in great and dense clouds, so that I could not distinguish my people, but only dimly saw Ur-tasen, the high-priest, with his shaven crown, robed in his most gorgeous garments, standing before me, with arms outstretched, as if pronouncing a blessing."

"He blessed thee, Pharaoh, no doubt, for some great good thou hadst done to thy people, now that health is once again restored to thee."

"So I thought at first, Neit-akrit, in my dream," he replied, bending his head closer to her, "but soon Ur-tasen came up to me and whispered something which made my pulses thrill with a joy that almost made me faint. Ur-tasen had whispered that I should take thy hand."

She turned her head away from him, and from where I stood I could see that every vestige of colour had left her cheeks, and that her lips were trembling and absolutely bloodless. I thought that we had no right to stand where we did, or to listen any longer to a conversation which was evidently drifting into very intimate channels, and I had just turned to go, when something in Hugh's face made me stop. He, too, was gazing at the picture before us of the young girl and the sick, almost dying man, but in his eyes there was an expression I could not define.

"At first," resumed the Pharaoh, in the same harsh, trembling voice, "I hardly dared to obey Ur-tasen. That I should take thy hand, at the foot of the throne of Isis, before all my people assembled there, seemed to me a joy so great that death would be easier to bear than the agony of so wild a happiness. But Ur-tasen waited, and I turned my head, and thou, Neit-akrit, wert standing by my side. Thy head, with its ruddy tresses, was hidden beneath the diadem which belongs to the rulers of Kamt, and from it down to thy tiny feet thou wast covered with a golden veil, through which I, in my dream, could see gleaming visions of thy blue eyes, which made me swoon with delight. Then Ur-tasen whispered again, and I took thy hand in mine, at the foot of the throne of Isis, before all my people assembled there . . . for they had come to see the mighty Pharaoh take Neit-akrit . . . as his wife."

His voice broke almost into a sob, he had glided down from the couch on to his knees, and was lying half-fainting with the emotion which, weak as he was, was over-mastering him, while his arms tremblingly sought to clasp the young girl. She was as pale as death. Her blue eyes stared at him, strangely terrified, with a look which, to me, seemed almost like loathing. But he could not see. His eyes were half closed. I am sure he was not conscious of his acts : his hands, trembling and claw-like, wandered round her shoulders and her waist, while he murmured more and more inarticulately—

"Thou art beautiful, Neit-akrit . . . and at the throne of Isis thy hair gleamed red and hot, and made my eyes ache with its glow : thy veil but partly covered thee . . . and when I looked upon thee . . . it seemed to me that I would forfeit my double crown of Kamt to be allowed to look again, and perhaps see thee smile. And thou didst promise to be my wife . . . and Isis smiled down upon me. And she whispered that in the night . . . when she peeped through the fuchsia alleys . . . and looked on the lilies and lotus blossoms . . . thou and thy loveliness would be wholly mine."

He had fallen, half-fainting, upon the marble floor, and clung, still babbling inarticulate words, round her knees. Neit-akrit had stood up, rigid as a marble image : it were impossible to describe the look of horror and loathing with which she looked down on the unfortunate man at her feet.

"For God's sake take him away from her, Mark!"

It was Hugh Tankerville's voice whispering in my ear, but

I hardly recognised it, so hoarse and choked was it. Astonished, I looked up at him, and suddenly a strange presentiment of some terrible trouble ahead, which as yet I could not explain, cast a chill over my heart. On my friend's face there was such a look of acute mental and physical suffering, it was so deathly pale, that instinctively I put out my arm to help him, for I feared he would fall in a swoon; but he said quickly, with a forced laugh—

"Only a sudden dizziness, old chap. . . . The heat, I think. But have pity on her and take that moribund satyr away from her."

"It would be needless interference, old man," I replied, "and one for which she would not thank me."

And I pointed to the picture, which, to my own amazement, had changed as if with the magic touch of a fairy wand. Neitakrit, sweet and smiling, with tears of pity shining in her softened blue eyes, was bending towards the invalid, while her voice, soft and low, murmured—

"Hush, hush! cousin! remember thou art ill: thy health is precious and thy nerves are overstrained. Canst raise thyself and sit here beside me? See, thou canst pillow thy head upon my shoulder and I can brush away the hair from thy burning forehead with my fingers, which are soft and cool. Or, if thou wilt, I will play for thee upon the harp, and thou shalt watch Sen-tur chase the ibis along the terrace. Hush! do not speak now! Thou shalt tell me thy dream again some other time . . . but not now. . . . Now, thou must have rest."

And with wonderful strength and dexterity she half-lifted, half-supported the Pharaoh and placed him once more upon the couch. Then she sat down beside him and pillowed his head upon her shoulder, and soothingly, as if he were some sick and wayward child, she began to sing and coo to him a simple lullaby. I looked on amazed, not knowing what to do or what to think. Though I watched her closely, I never saw her eyes look anything but sweet, pitying and loving, even though his eyes were closed and his breathing became more and more regular, as if her song had at last rocked him to sleep. I began to think that I must have been mistaken: it seemed impossible to believe that the rigid statue, alive only by the look of horror and repulsion on the stony face, could be the same clinging, loving woman, full of tender pity and girlish compassion for the sick man lying happy and contented in her arms.

CHAPTER XVIII

A KISS

I SOMEHOW dared not look at Hugh. I felt his presence near me as rigid as a statue, and once my ears caught the sound of a sigh, which ended almost in a sob.

"Is it for the dying Pharaoh thou sighest, oh, my beloved," suddenly said a harsh voice close behind us, "or for her who deals death and sorrow with so free a hand?"

It was Queen Maat-kha, who had glided noiselessly near, and now stood beside Hugh, tall and imperious, with an ugly look of hatred directed towards the sleeping Pharaoh and his companion. Hugh started as from a dream. He passed his hand over his eyes, as if to dispel some haunting vision, and turned to his handsome *fiancée*, who returned his look, with a curious searching expression in her eyes.

"Thou dost not answer," she said. "Was the sigh for her?"

"Indeed, my Queen, it is sad to see so young a girl wooed by a man with one foot in the grave," replied Hugh at last, speaking with a mighty effort.

"Then thou dost not understand the girl before thee, and hast forgotten that the man, though he has one foot in the grave, has the other firmly planted on the throne of Kamt."

Princess Neit-akrit must have heard every one of Maat-kha's words, yet she took no notice of them, and remained quietly watching the sleeping Pharaoh.

"Thou hast also forgotten," added the Queen, "that thou and thy wise counsellor have decided to cure the mighty Pharaoh of his ailments, that, anon, he will once more hold with a firm hand the sceptre of ancient Kamt. Neit-akrit hath thought it worth her while to smile on him again, so that he may extend his other hand, and with it place upon her brow the diadem of a queen. Believe me, there is no sadness in that wooing, save perhaps for a deceived and befooled monarch."

"Thou speakest harsh words of a woman who hath done thee no wrong," said Hugh. "Art not satisfied that already by thy intended marriage thou dost threaten to deprive her of that which thou sayest she covets most? Wouldst add to the injustice by heaping calumny upon her?"

"No wrong?" exclaimed the Queen, impulsively. "Dost think that I am blind and cannot see? Dull-witted and cannot understand? Hath she done me no wrong? Ah! that I do not know as yet. Thy face is set and inscrutable; but the gods will open my eyes. That which they gave me, they will not take away. And if she come like a cunning jackal, prowling round my most precious treasure, then let her beware, for Maat-kha is powerful and will know how to hurl vengeance on the thief."

"What dost thou mean?" asked Hugh, very quietly. "Take care, oh, Queen! lest in thy blindness thou shouldst forget my dignity and thy self-respect."

"I forget everything," she said, coming quite close up to him, "save that I love thee and that thou art cold. I did not seek for thee, I did not even ask the gods to place thee across my path; thou didst come and didst stand before me and, with arm outstretched, didst claim me for thy wife. Now, that which thou didst give thou dost surely take away—thy word, thy fealty to me."

"My Queen," replied Hugh, gently taking her hand, "in that land from whence I come men have but one word, one pledge. Words such as thou dost speak, thoughts such as thou dost harbour, are an insult; look at me, Maat-kha, and tell me if I can lie."

She looked up at him, and I, who watched Neit-akrit, saw that she looked too. I did not know if these two strange, impulsive women could judge a man's character by gazing at his face, but Hugh's was not a difficult nature to understand; above everything he was upright and true, and whatever presentiments may have assailed me when first I guessed my friend's secret thoughts, I knew that whatever might happen, his promised bride need have no fear of his loyalty to her.

I thought that the Pharaoh had moved, and I was glad of

an excuse to go and attend upon him and leave Queen Maat-kha a moment alone with Hugh. Neit-akrit still looked very pale, and I could see in her eyes that she had been crying. I did not altogether understand her, but there was something strangely pathetic and appealing in the way in which she looked at me, eagerly waiting for some reassuring words concerning the sick man.

"I will send his slaves to him," I said, "he will need rest."

And I went within. When I returned I found that Queen Maat-kha had gone and that Hugh was standing beside Neit-akrit.

"I crave it of thee as a favour," I heard him say.

"So soon?" she replied. "Art already tired of Neit-akrit's hospitality? Has she forgot aught that would make thy sojourn here a happy one? Tell me, is not my palace beautiful? Are my gardens not fragrant with scent of flowers, the air not sweet with song of birds?"

"Thy dwelling is more beautiful than aught I have ever dreamed of."

"And yet thou wouldst leave it?"

"I crave of thee to forgive my seeming ingratitude, for though fair be thy palace and fragrant thy garden, I would fain leave them to-day."

"Leave them and me?" she said sadly.

"Ay! leave them and thee, Princess," said Hugh, with that same icy calm with which he responded to Neit-akrit's fascinating ways, "lest if I remained even one day longer, I might leave that behind me which is more precious to me than aught else on earth."

"What is that?" she asked. "Thou needest not fear, I will guard it for thee, wherever thou goest."

"Nay, a man is sole guardian of that most precious treasure; women often do not know its worth, and I fear I am proving but a sorry keeper myself, hence the reason why I would go."

"Wilt say farewell to me before thou goest?"

"I will do that now with thy permission. I have promised the inhabitants of Net-amen that I would visit them, and having gone I will not come back, but go straight to Tanis and await there the coming of Queen Maat-kha for our approaching marriage."

"So soon?" she asked very quietly.

"In seventy days, Princess."

"Farewell then, oh, Beloved of the gods; thou hast indeed graced the abode of thy kinswoman, by dwelling beneath its roof."

"Hast forgiven me then?"

"I to thee? What have I to forgive?"

"Everything. I came and the double crown of Kamt, which already hovered over thy brow, was ruthlessly snatched from thee. My presence deprived thee of a throne. It were meet that thou shouldst seek revenge upon the intruder, instead of which thou didst bid him welcome."

"Nay," she said sweetly, "I have naught to forgive, and revenge is in the hands of the gods." Then she added, "Farewell, oh, son of Ra!"

He bent his tall figure before her, then turned as if to go.

"Wilt thou not kiss me?" she said. "In Kamt a kiss denotes friendship, and if thou goest without a kiss, I shall fear that thou art my enemy."

"By all the gods of Kamt, I swear to thee that I am no enemy. But wilt pardon me if I do not give thee the kiss of friendship?"

"Why? A kiss is so soon given. It has so little meaning, for it is as swift as the flight of the bird through the air. Thou didst kiss me when thou camest, why wilt not kiss me now?"

"Because thou art beautiful above all things on earth," he said very quietly, "and because in my dazed mind there is still a glimmer of reason, which the perfume of thy hair would quickly dispel."

She blushed suddenly as if for the first time in her life she had been told that she was fair. How strange women are! When I told Neit-akrit that she was more beautiful than anything on earth, she smiled and looked pleased. When the Pharaoh fell half-fainting at her feet she became as white and as rigid as a statue carved in stone. And now when Hugh Tankerville told her, with frigid calm, and I thought with a singular want of conviction, that she was beautiful, she suddenly became a thousand times more so, for she blushed and the heightened colour became her well.

"Farewell, then, oh, thou who art of the gods beloved!" she said once more very gently.

The next moment Hugh had gone and Neit-akrit had thrown herself on the couch in a passionate fit of weeping.

CHAPTER XIX

A LETTER FROM HUGH

Hugh went away that same day. He was going to Net-amen, together with the gorgeous retinue which had, as it were, sprung up round him and escorted him everywhere. Queen Maat-kha did not accompany him this time: she was unprepared for the journey, she said. She would proceed to Tanis alone, there to meet him for the wedding ceremony.

Hugh took a very brief farewell from me. I could see that he dared not trust himself to speak, and, even before me, he shrank from breaking down. I could not go with him, for my patient demanded my immediate attention. He was undoubtedly worse since this morning: the strong emotion had done him an infinity of harm. Yet I was torn between affection for Hugh and my duty to the sick man. It seemed to me that Hugh needed my care as much as the sick Pharaoh. His sufferings were mental, but I felt that they were keen. And did I not love him as much as my prosy nature was capable of loving? and did I not know him, and his ardent, passionate nature, forcibly hardened by years of dry, scientific research, all the more ready to fall a prey to strong impressions, such as the strange and fascinating girl had undoubtedly made upon it?

Hugh had never been in love. During his early youth he had had no opportunity of meeting any woman who would appeal to his keen sense of the mystic and the picturesque. Such women are rare in Western Europe, and none had come across the recluse student's path. Then, suddenly, Fate and his own choosing threw him into this land of mysticism and beauty, where the atmosphere was fragrant and intoxicating with the scent of exotic flowers, where the air was filled with the twitter of birds, busy in making their nests. And, framed by these picturesque surroundings, which in themselves palpitated with youth and with life, there was the poetic, mystic, yet intensely-feminine vision of an exquisitely beautiful woman, who was irresistibly drawn towards him, and with the artless impulse of her own untrammelled nature showed to his enthusiastic mind visions of ardent and reciprocated love, such as he had never dreamed of. What wonder if for the moment Hugh forgot?—forgot that he had pledged himself to another woman, and only remembered when it was too late?

The first few days after his departure were terribly wearisome to me. My patient, fretful and irritable, would not allow me to leave his bedside, and, even at night, I was forced to take what rest I could, rolled in a rug, at the foot of his couch.

I saw little of Princess Neit-akrit, but, once or twice, when I caught sight of Queen Maat-kha in the gardens of the palace, I was shocked to see the change in her face. All its beauty had vanished to my mind: it looked hard and set, nay, worse, positively evil. On the night which followed Hugh's departure, when I strolled out to get a breath of fresh air, having at last soothed my patient to sleep, I saw Maat-kha in close conversation with Ur-tasen. To me this boded no good. I could not understand why the Queen and the high-priest should choose the hours of the night for their meeting. I could not get near enough to them to hear what they were saying—which I should most unblushingly have done—but in the shadows where they stood, I could see that Queen Maat-kha had buried her face in her hands, and that Ur-tasen seemed to tower over her as if he were dictating some commands.

My mind, filled with thoughts of my absent friend, dwelt persistently on fears for his safety. The high-priest was his enemy, of that I had no doubt, and I thought that he was trying to work upon the Queen's jealousy, for evil purposes of his own. I felt terribly helpless to be of any use to him, and vowed that when at last I could join him again, nothing would separate me from him. After all, the sick Pharaoh of this modern Egypt was but a secondary consideration to me.

Eight days after Hugh's departure a runner came in with a letter for me from him.

"DEAR OLD MARK,—Thank goodness that I can write to you and know that this letter will reach you safely. I am fagged to death bodily and long to have you near me, to talk over some of my wondrous experiences. The city of Net-amen is picturesque. It lies on the side of a hill and is a city of industry : the applied arts reign supreme, and I am looking forward to renewing my visit to it with you later on, and showing you the paintings and carvings on the walls and pillars of the houses, which to my mind are as beautiful as any we have seen. This is a wonderful country, Mark, and its people have lost none of the mysterious powers which have astonished Europe for so long. Will you believe me when I tell you that in the very heart of the city a palace has been built expressly for me?—yes! for me, the Beloved of the gods!—and I have only been in the land less than a month! And yet, there my palace stands, of rose-coloured granite with massive pillars and exquisite carvings, and a figure of my sire Ra, presiding in the courtyard. All built in less than a month by a hundred thousand workmen, who worked night and day in relays. The granite works are just outside the city, but still think of it, Mark, and remember how long it takes to put up a block of flats in London.

"Still, there is the sorrowful aspect of my palace : all the hard work was done by slaves, and these people use their slaves shockingly. This is the ugliest trait in their character. They are cruel, Mark, both to man and beast. The men are cruel! and the women more so. We have seen one or two instances of that already, but there is a thing I have learned which to me is horrible beyond words. You know of course that the Egyptians are monogamous—you have noticed in what high esteem they hold their women folk; as a consequence of this, their laws against adultery are barbarous beyond what words can describe, and in one respect hideously unjust, for it is invariably the woman who is punished—the man is allowed to go scot free.

"I saw a woman in the streets of Net-amen yesterday. She was blind, both her ears had been cut off, all her teeth drawn out, and her hair had been pulled out by the roots. Turned out from her home, she is obliged to live by the charity of the passers-by, and is driven from street to street as an example of sin and its punishment. She had been convicted of appropriating to herself the husband of a friend. Think of it, old

Mark! What about European society? And the man, who had allowed himself to be . . . appropriated, is one of the town councillors and much respected; he is a good-looking man, very pompous and self-satisfied. I gave myself the not very productive satisfaction of kicking him in the face when he grovelled before me, but I don't know if he guessed why he received that kick. Somehow it eased my conscience.

"The runner will bring back the message from you. Make it long, Mark, old fellow—I want plenty of words from you. I think I should feel better after I had read your letter. I admire these people, they are delightfully picturesque, but somehow I have no real sympathy with them—have you?—and at times I positively hate them. Especially when I learn some of their laws. I wonder now what devil framed them. No brain of man could conceive such horrors. Nous devons changer tout cela! You and I, eh? old chap.—Yours affectionately,

"HUGH TANKERVILLE."

The letter was hideously unsatisfactory. It told me nothing about himself, and I fancied that he had purposely avoided even telling me about his health. I did not carry out his wishes in the matter of writing him a long letter, but only scribbled a few words—

"MY DEAR GIRLIE,—Twenty-four hours after you have received this by messenger, you will see me in your new palace at Net-Amen.—Yours, etc.,

"MARK EMMETT."

Then I set to work to drill into the heads of two shaven medical idiots all that they were to do, and all they were to leave undone, with regard to my patient. They vowed by all their gods that the wise counsellor should be implicitly obeyed. I brought out every resource of my limited Egyptian vocabulary to impress upon them that he had better be, and then I sought an audience of my young hostess.

I found her in her favourite place, beneath the turquoise silk canopy, amidst a bower of cushions, overlooking the lake.

"I hope thou dost bring me good news of my kinsman, oh, wise counsellor," she said, turning to me with an anxious look in her eyes; "he hath seemed somewhat more cheerful of late."

"My news concerning the holy Pharaoh is no worse, Princess," I replied. "Thou knowest how serious is his illness, and 'no worse' with him hath become good news. It is not about him that I have sad tidings to-day."

I watched her very closely as I said this, but she seemed not the least moved, and she said indifferently—

"Hast had sad tidings? Of whom?"

"I am a lonely man, Princess; there is but one being in this world who is infinitely dear to me. It is of him that I have sad tidings."

"Dost speak of the son of Ra?"

"Even of him, Princess."

"How can aught that is sad come to him who is of the gods beloved?" she asked in astonishment.

"He is but mortal, and there are so many sorrows, even in this fair land. Suffering has overtaken him, I fear, and I have sought this audience of thee, Neit-akrit, to crave of thy goodness that thou wouldst allow me to depart and go to my friend, lest he have need of me and the comfort I alone can give him."

"Art so devoted then to thy friend that, if he call, thou must needs leave everything and go to him?"

"I have known and loved him ever since a tiny lad, we shared childish joys and sorrows together."

"Was that at the foot of the throne of Ra?" she asked with a touch of satire.

"In the land where first Ra whispered to his beloved to go forth and rule over the land of Kamt," I said, "and where the gods bade me follow him."

"And is he worthy of thy devotion, thinkest thou?"

"Nay, Princess, in that same land we do not pause to think if men and women be worthy, before we give them our love. The son of Ra is dearer to me than ever brother was to brother, or son to father. Therefore I crave of thee again to allow thy slaves to guide me to where he now is, for I feel that he has need of me."

"My slaves and my house are at thy command, oh, wise counsellor! Order what thou wilt. Fan-tu, who has charge of my slaves, will obey thy every word."

I thanked her, then as she was silent I turned to go, but she stopped me.

"Stay!" she said, "hast reflected that the holy Pharaoh can ill spare thee? He is very sick, and thou leavest him without regret."

"The holy Pharaoh is in no immediate bodily danger; and even if he were, Princess, my duty is to my friend."

"How strange," she said. "I have never heard of love and duty spoken of as between man and man. Is that love a product of that land where dwelleth Osiris, and whence thou and his emissary do come?"

"It is held as sacred there, as the love given by man to woman."

"Do men give love to women too, then, in that land?"

"Once only in their lives, Princess. Men have one love as they have one word, and part with their life sometimes because of either."

"I will not detain thee further, oh, wise counsellor!" she said with sudden coldness. "Deign to give thy orders to Fan-tu, and what boat or escort thou dost need shall await thy commands."

The Pharaoh took the news of my departure very quietly; nothing seemed ever to disturb his sullen, sarcastic equanimity. He listened quite patiently to my various recommendations concerning his health, and actually stretched out a hand to me, in token of a promise that he would follow them.

I asked for an audience of Queen Maat-kha, but she sent me a somewhat curt message that she was sick and could see no one.

In the late afternoon a boat and an escort had been prepared for me, and with a sigh of relief I saw the fairy palace of Princess Neit-akrit gradually fade away into the distance.

CHAPTER XX

A DEBT OF HONOUR

NET-AMEN is certainly the prettiest of the cities of this ancient land. It has been built on an undulating slope which rises upwards, with tier upon tier of palms and sycamores, mimosas and giant fuchsias. It is essentially an industrial city: the houses are not so imposing as those of Men-ne-fer, which is the royal residence and the abode of the wealthy. In Net-amen the houses are built of a species of burnt clay: there is less sculpture and very little marble: before each door-step the householders squat and ply their trade or craft. The goldsmith, with brazier and minute instruments, fashions necklaces of exquisite workmanship, pendants in imitation of birds and beetles, daintily chased and covered with enamel, the gorgeous colours of which these people alone know how to produce. Then the potters, who turn the soft clay jars, fashioning them into every kind of fanciful shapes, and then passing them on to the limner, who, with fine brush and colours, draws upon the vases those quaint figures which delight the antiquarian, and which—as I have learnt since I have caught a glimpse of Egypt as it was or is—are an exact rendering of the people of Kamt. Then there are the women, with their rough spinning-wheels and tall spindles made of rush, or sitting at the looms, weaving those gossamer tissues with which the noble ladies of the land only half hide their voluptuous charms.

The first aspect of Net-amen fascinated me. There was less grandeur but more of real humanity about it. The weavers, the potters, the goldsmiths seemed to me much more tangible, than the gorgeous and fantastic personages who in wondrous pageant had, in Men-ne-fer, moved before my eyes.

On the summit of the hills, surrounded by trees and flowers, stood the miracle palace, which one hundred thousand workmen had built in seventeen days for the Beloved of the gods.

Hugh did not expect to see me quite so soon, and I was told on landing that the son of Ra was in the palace, resting after the many festivities given in his honour. My advent had caused a stir, and from the houses along the quay people came rushing out to have a look at the wise counsellor, and hundreds of willing feet were ready to guide me to the palace, whilst others rushed forward to take the news of my arrival to the Beloved of the gods.

Tiny brightly-painted chariots, drawn by a couple of sturdy white donkeys, are the best means of locomotion in this hilly city. As soon as I could free myself from the chattering crowd I hailed one of these, and was soon pulled leisurely up the long steep road which led to the palace, the naked driver, hot and panting, pushing from behind.

It was a fearful shock to me to see Hugh. I could not conceive how any man could possibly have changed so terribly in so short a time. His eyes looked hollow and circled with dark purple rings, which told of sleepless nights, his mouth looked drawn and tightly set, without a vestige of that sunny smile which always used to brighten his dark, serious face.

When he saw me, however, a look of the deepest joy, and —I thought—gratitude, for a moment softened the hard set expression in his eyes, and my ears caught the faintly whispered "God bless you, old chap!"

The hand he gave me was hot and dry, and it needed no medical knowledge to guess that his pulse was quick and throbbing.

He soon dismissed the attendants, and when we were alone he said—

"I never knew how much I had missed you, old Mark, until the moment when I caught sight of you just now."

I did not say anything then, but quietly watched him for a moment, then, I put my hand on his shoulder, and forced him to look at me.

"What is the matter, old man?" I said.

"Matter? Oh, fever, malaria, I suppose. I can't sleep, and seem as weak as a rat. Is there such a thing as nostalgia, do you think?—stupid, foolish home-sickness?—because if there is, I have got a touch of it, I think."

"There is every kind of mental ailment, I am sorry to say, Girlie, and they can all be described to a fellow who has your welfare at heart more than his own."

"Fever, Mark, I tell you," he said with a frown. "Take out your watch and feel my pulse. It is fever, is it not? Malarial, do you think? or has the fashionable influenza travelled with us across the desert? I want a dose of quinine, I think."

"You want a dose of confidence, Girlie," I replied drily. "Your pulse is quick, your temperature is high, I can soon remedy that, if . . ."

"If what?" he asked abruptly, for I had paused, hesitating, strangely enough, for the first time in my life not daring to touch upon a point openly with Hugh.

"If you will tell me what you think of when you lie awake at night," I said at last, looking straight and searchingly in his eyes.

"Mostly of what a confounded fool your friend Hugh Tankerville is, old chap," he replied with a laugh.

"Is that all?"

"Yes! I think that is all. It embraces a very vast section of my life—its future. But I don't know why you should put me to such rigorous catechism, Mark. I am ever so glad that you came, and it will do me more good than all the medicines in the world."

"Nothing will do you good, Girlie," I said earnestly, "except one thing."

"What is that?"

"To talk to me—if only at random—of Princess Neit-akrit."

He did not say anything. His face became, if possible, even more pale, more careworn than before. I did not think that he was offended with my seeming importunity, and I continued—

"Girlie, you and I have gone through a great deal together: we nearly starved side by side in the desert, not so very long ago. We can therefore hardly measure our intercourse together by the same standard as other men. Besides being your friend, I am also a medical man, and . . ."

"And you would be interested to see before you, lying bare, as the dissected body underneath your scalpel, all the follies, the madness, the cowardice of which a fellow-man's brain is capable. It is not a pleasant sight, Mark, believe me; you are my friend—you had best not try to see."

"You misunderstand, Girlie; I have no wish to cause you needless pain by forcing a confidence which, I dare say, you do not care to give, but I have studied the nervous organisation of man long enough to know, that where there is an outlet for thoughts in speech, they become less injurious to bodily health."

"Yes, that's it, old Mark!" he said with quite an ugly, sneering laugh. "Confession, as the Catholics say, is good for the soul. You think I would ease my brain by telling you that I, Hugh Tankerville, lie awake at night like a cowardly fool, making loathsome compacts with my conscience and bargains with my honour; that, when at last a heavy dreamless sleep falls over me, I awake from it wondering whether I am not covered with some hideous leprosy, a fitting bodily ailment to clothe the cowardly vileness of my soul."

"Girlie," I said, for he had paused and was resting his burning forehead against the cool granite pillar, and was gazing out across the lovely flower garden with a wild, feverish almost mad gaze. I went up to him and placed my hand once more upon his shoulder.

"I ought never to have let you go away by yourself out of a mistaken sense of duty to a patient who, after all, is nothing to me. You have been brooding over your trouble and have worked yourself into a morbid state of self-analysis. I can assure you that I know you better than you know yourself, and know that you are absolutely incapable of any act of cowardliness or disloyalty."

"I think I was . . . at one time," he said dreamily. "I seem to have changed all of a sudden. Why, Mark! even temptation in this case is vile and base. We, Englishmen, who pride ourselves on our national honour—our inalienable characteristic, we proudly assert. Never was there a greater fallacy than man's belief in his own integrity. Here am I, the first Englishman who trod this foreign soil, and already my national honour is scattered to the four winds, since I have started a series of hideous compacts with it—at nights."

"Do you love her so much as all that?" I asked with a certain ill-defined feeling of jealousy and wrath. His hard, set expression relaxed, a look of infinite tenderness crept into his eyes, and it was with a softened voice, more like the voice I knew of old, that he said—

"Like a madman, Mark; like a base coward, if you will."

I shook my head.

"You would not look as you do, Girlie, if you did that. Compacts with one's honour are easy of making and do not bring fever and insomnia along with them. Tell me what you mean to do."

He shrugged his shoulders.

"Do?" he said with a forced laugh. "That is exactly what I have been wondering these last few days. I ran away from her like a coward, but I was a fool to think I could so easily escape—not in this land, at least, where everything speaks of her. Why, the very scent of the lotus flower which penetrates into my room at night . . ."

He stopped abruptly and bit his lip, as if determined to say no more—not even to me. I saw that he was making great efforts to contain himself, for his lips and hands were shaking as if with ague.

"You are killing yourself, Girlie," I said.

He laughed.

"And yet I don't want to die, old Mark. Not at any rate until I have made some arrangement for getting you safely out of this land."

"Not until you have gone back yourself, Girlie, and have shown to the world your discovery of this land, the truth of 'mad Tankerville's hobby,'" I said, trying to bring his mind back to its old enthusiasm.

"Yes!" he said with a weary sigh. "I came here for that purpose, didn't I? For that I toiled for years, studied, gave up home and country, everything—even dragged you away in my train. And now . . ."

"Well? and now that you have succeeded beyond your keenest hopes?"

"Now, Mark? Laugh at me if you like; I deserve it for the terrible fool that I am. Now I feel that I would gladly give up all that and more, toil again, slave again, find every glory the world can bestow, and lose it all again, in exchange for the certainty that one woman, out of all the millions who people this earth, loves me as I love her."

I shook my head.

"I know, I know, old fellow," he said. "I almost think that if I had the certainty that she merely made a fool of me, I should—perhaps—get over my folly."

I don't know if his talk to me had done him good. I felt like a cruel brute to have forced his confidence, and yet I think that it was for the best. I could not fancy Hugh Tankerville falling a prey to morbid pangs of conscience; I knew that he would never fail in deed. It was not in his power to keep temptation away. A word is easily broken, and I believe that Neit-akrit would have been willing, out of pride or ambition—perhaps out of love for Hugh: in either case she would not pause, I think, for the sake of any soft thoughts for Queen Maat-kha. Oh! that we could have got away—out of this country altogether—where, as he said—everything spoke of *her*. Was she not, as it were, the embodiment of everything that was fascinating, mysterious, poetic in this land? Somehow I believe that Hugh was as much in love with his own conception of what a daughter of Egypt would be. Though intensely enthusiastic, his nature was a sensuous one. The exotic beauty of Kamt, the scent of the flowers, the artistic charm of the life, all had prepared his mind for the strong impression to which an exquisitely beautiful woman gave the finishing touch How strange a thing is man! Why was it not Queen Maat-kha. —beautiful, picturesque, womanly—who had succeeded in arousing in Hugh that love, which might then have proved a happiness to him? whereas now, tied as he was by every tie of loyalty and honour, it was slowly killing him by inches. There was no doubt that he looked terribly ill, and that a kind of low fever, brought by brooding and insomnia, was already beginning to undermine his robust constitution.

I did not like to say anything more just now. We had been silent for some time, and Hugh gradually had conquered his emotion and seemed more like himself. He asked after the health of the Pharaoh and my first impression of the city of Net-amen. But it was my turn to be moody. I felt more anxious than I cared to admit. I knew that we were surrounded with enemies, and truly did not know whether among these we should count the beautiful woman over whom Hugh Tankerville was busy breaking his heart. But this was mere unreasoning instinct. It would have been worse than useless to give him a warning in that direction; though he might be blind as to her coquetry, he would probably not admit even the remotest possibility that she might be false. And I . . . well, though I admired them I quietly mistrusted the beautiful blue eyes and fascinating ways of Princess Neit-akrit.

PART IV

TANIS

CHAPTER XXI

THE BRIDAL CITY

HAPPY, beautiful Tanis! the city of love and romance and poetry. Even now, after all these years, as I write, the perfume of a bunch of gardenias and tuberoses placed on my writing-table brings back to my memory visions of the snow-white city, where the air is oppressive with the scent of exotic flowers, and Isis, clad in immaculate garments, silent and white, gives her blessing on those of her children who would worship at her shrine—the shrine of love, for Tanis is the bridal city.

All is white in Tanis: the houses of spotless stone or marble, the bowers of sweet-scented flowers, the barges on the canals, even the beasts of burden—cows and donkeys—all are white, and coquettishly throw that whiteness against a background of grey-green foliage or the dull, heavy leafage of palms. And in the midst of the city the temple of Isis, high aloft upon a hill, built of alabaster and silver, all white, with massive columns and gigantic steps, surrounded by groves of monster orange trees and tuberoses, amidst which the small apes—sacred to the moon—run chattering to and fro.

I loved Tanis. Men-ne-fer was gorgeous and rich. Net-amen was picturesque and bright, but Tanis was poetry, romance, and above all, living voluptuousness.

The penetrating scent of flowers rendered the temple gardens almost unbearable at nights, so overpowering was the odour of gardenia and orange blossom: that garden filled with the quaint and dainty forms of the priestesses vowed to the goddess and to love! I seem to see it before me now, in one vast tangle of palms and flowers, with shady nooks beneath showers of overhanging blossoms. Sensuous, voluptuous Tanis! where every refinement, which art and civilisation could devise, is brought to bear in order to throw a halo of romance and picturesqueness over the passion which makes gods or beasts of mankind. And Isis, silent, cold and immaculate, smiles from the sanctuary of her temple upon the loves which last a lifetime, the passions which live a day.

Men and women swear before her altar to cherish one another and be true, until the day when Anubis, the jackal-headed god, at last leads one or the other soul before the throne of Osiris: and all the while, outside, in the garden, under the same protection of the goddess, lithe young arms encircle the passer-by, and give freely of those kisses, which are forgotten on the morrow.

Sensuous Tanis! who dost place a crown of glory on the heads of thy courtesans, and makest a virtue of unchastity. Lovely, poetic Tanis! within whose sacred walls the holiest vows of truth and honour are spoken, in spite of all I love thee still. I shut my eyes and see thy snow-white walls, thy women clad in clinging folds of spotless white, hear the melancholy sound of sistrum and of harp, and above all smell the intoxicating odour of thy flower gardens and feel the delicious languor which thy heavy air doth give.

Strange people! Strange customs! Strange and sensuous Tanis! Within its walls is the temple of Isis, wherein bridegroom vows to bride honour, fealty and truth, as solemn, as binding, as the vows we swear in England unto those that we love; and within the self-same walls, surrounding the same hymeneal temple, are the gardens of Isis. Here he who would pronounce matrimonial vows must dwell for a day and a night before his wedding, alone and unattended, in a tiny pavilion, overgrown with climbing tuberoses, which stands in the middle of the garden. Here, at the evening, when the image of the goddess shines cold and pure upon the groves of cacti and orange blossoms, sweet music lures the would-be bridegroom without, and as he walks through the sweet-scented alleys, dreaming of future homely and legitimate bliss, the dainty forms of Isis's priestesses whisper of things he would fain not hear: white arms beckon to him, and red mouths, framed for kisses, sing with sweet voices quaint, licentious songs. It is the mission—honoured, respected, almost held sacred—of these priestesses, recruited among the fairest in the land, to dissuade the bridegroom from contracting indissoluble ties.

There is a subtle morality in this strange custom. None but the strong, the true, should wed in ancient Kamt; the marriage tie is a divine one, the oath an all-embracing one, and sweet voices whisper to the weak to pause and reflect, bidding him beware of bonds which later he cannot break.

When first we heard of this curious custom, expounded to us by a couple of solemn Egyptians dressed in snow-white robes, with a wreath of white roses over their funny shaven heads, for the first time, since many days, I saw Hugh's eyes twinkling with merriment, but he preserved perfect outward gravity and assured the people of Tanis that he would follow the ancient custom of the land and take possession of the lonely pavilion in the garden of Isis.

Then, when we were alone, we both burst into a fit of laughter, and Hugh's laugh sounded as infectious, as sunny as of yore. Of course he had to stand a good deal of chaff from me.

"For the credit of old England," I adjured him with mock solemnity as, late one evening, I accompanied him to the abode of temptation, "do not disgrace us both, Girlie."

"Well! I think I may safely promise not to do that, old chap," he said with a laugh.

Together we explored the pavilion and garden, which before moonrise was silent and deserted. The pavilion itself was built of alabaster and divided into two rooms—one room in which to eat, and one in which to sleep, when one could. Every drapery in it was white, the curtains, the couches, the seats; it was lighted from above, as well as from the sides, so that the rays of the moon could at all times penetrate within. Here the lonely and expectant bridegroom heard but little of the din and noise of the city, busy in preparations for the coming marriage festivities, and of course Hugh would see nothing of the deputations from every corner of the vast empire, which poured into Tanis, streams of people, men and women and children, who came to catch a glimpse of the most blessed in the land, the son of Ra, the Well-beloved of the gods.

Somehow I did not like parting from him. These twenty-four hours, the last before he took the irrevocable step, were sure to be trying for him; but we had all through our stay in this interesting land most solemnly decided to follow all its laws and customs, and after all, my wish to be with Hugh was mere sentimentality. He himself, I think, preferred to be alone. We never had spoken of *her* since the day when I forced Hugh's confidence. I don't think he could have borne it, and Sawnie Girlie was the last man in the world ever to break down, even before me. His word was a fetish to him. He had given it to a woman and demanded hers in return, and he meant to carry to the end the burden which his own hands had placed upon his life. There was no doubt that he was eating his heart out with longing and with love for the beautiful girl who could be nothing to him, and I could do nothing to help or save him. Outwardly he was cheerful, even enthusiastic at times, but to my ears and eyes, rendered acute by my affection for him, there was always a false ring in his laugh, a jarring discord in his enthusiasm.

He seemed to have aged all of a sudden, and on the temples, for the first time, to-day, I had noticed a few streaks of grey.

When the shades of evening began to draw in round the poetic retreat where Hugh was to spend the last night of his bachelorhood, I at last reluctantly decided to go.

"When do you suppose we shall meet again, Girlie?"

"Ah! that I don't know. The marriage ceremony is an hour after midnight to-morrow; I go straight to the temple from here, and it appears that it is against all etiquette that I should wander outside this garden of Eden until then. Perhaps you can find your way as far as my loneliness, some time during the day."

But I was doubtful.

"I can try. What happens after the wedding ceremony?"

"Another strange custom, Mark, old chap," replied Hugh, with a smile. "All those present in the temple during the ceremony, including the bride, retire, leaving the unfortunate bridegroom alone: he is supposed to pray and to worship Isis, until he sees the first streak of dawn through the marble gateway. Then he goes out to meet his bride. But these people, ever seeking for the poetic and the picturesque, ever sensuous and ever voluptuous, have a custom by which the royal bridegroom meets his bride in a special bower in the very middle of this garden."

"Under the vault of heaven?"

"At dawn, old Mark, and near a tiny waterfall which is sacred to Isis. You can hear the ripple of the water now."

"It is indeed poetic."

"This pretty spot is surrounded with walls and closed in by a gate which is never opened, save when a royal marriage has taken place. Then at dawn the bridegroom, having completed his vigil, goes into the garden, finds that gate open, and there he waits until . . ."

"I understand. How sensuous these people are. Even in their marriages, which I believe are as solemn, as earnest, though not as dull as our English weddings, they contrive to introduce a savour of romance and transfigure the bride, if only momentarily, into a courtesan."

"At anyrate, during the few hours before dawn, when I am all alone and supposed to be worshipping the pagan goddess, I am sure you can remain behind and bear me company. The day after my marriage we return to Men-ne-fer, and you and I, old Mark, can seriously set to work to govern our interesting subjects."

"Good-bye then, old Girlie!" I said, feeling a nasty, uncomfortable lump in my throat. "If I cannot get to you to-morrow, then I shall not see you again till after you are Queen Maat-kha's husband."

"In any case, Mark, in the temple, you will be somewhere near I know."

"Unless the holy Pharaoh claims me altogether. You know he is an arbitrary patient."

I shook him by the hand, and we parted. He still standing in the doorway of the snow-white pavilion, his dark head clearly silhouetted against the alabaster walls, and I hurrying quickly and regretfully through the tuberose-scented gardens of Isis, the voluptuous goddess.

The Pharaoh had entered Tanis earlier in the day with all the pomp and glitter of his gorgeous retinue. I went to meet him, and was shocked to see him looking much more ill than when I left him. I felt a little remorseful, and now feared that through my desertion of him I might have lost what influence I had gained over his irritable temper. However, to my astonishment he seemed quite pleased to see me, and as usual, once he had me by his side, refused to allow me to leave him even for an instant.

It was only during a brief interval while he was asleep that I had had the chance of accompanying Hugh to the pavilion of Isis.

Queen Maat-kha had accompanied the Pharaoh in his solemn entry into Tanis. She was closely veiled when she alighted from her boat, and vouchsafed no recognition of me, and quickly disappeared, followed by her women.

I believe that she had a special palace, close to the temple of Isis, where as a royal bride she would reside until her wedding day.

I saw nothing of Princess Neit-akrit, nor did I know if she meant to be present at the marriage ceremony. I sincerely hoped that she would not, and that Hugh would be spared the pain of seeing her until all was irrevocably over. Perhaps when finally wedded to another woman, in the midst of the many tasks which would naturally devolve upon him, he would begin to forget the poetic romance which threatened to destroy his future happiness.

CHAPTER XXII

THE CRIME

As I expected, the holy Pharaoh proved more exacting, more arbitrary than ever. He was really so weak and ill that I had not the heart to leave him. His mind seemed to wander at times, and he would babble of Neit-akrit, of the throne of Kamt, of his mother, and of the stranger who was usurping the crown. He seemed to have vowed special hatred against his mother, more so even than against Hugh; and his screams of rage, whenever he mentioned her name, were terrible to hear, and all day, with half-articulate words, he would make weird plans as to how best he could destroy her happiness.

Once he took my hand feverishly in both his own and asked with eagerness—

" Dost think she knows that the stranger hath no love for her ? "

I tried to soothe him, but he persisted—

" If she only knew how he loves Neit-akrit ! "

" Thou dost him wrong, oh, mighty Pharaoh : " I retorted. " The Beloved of the gods will plight his troth to Queen Maat-kha. And he never breaks his word."

The invalid laughed his nasty, sarcastic laugh, and muttered several times to himself—

" If she only knew how he loves Neit-akrit . . . she would suffer . . . ay ! and I think I would make him suffer too."

Late in the evening, at last, he dropped into a troubled sleep; and I, feeling momentary peace and freedom, went out upon the terrace. The Pharaoh's palace faced the temple of Isis, behind which lay the mysterious garden with the lonely, snow-white pavilion, and the sacred nook, beside the cataract, with beyond it the palace of the royal bride.

The night was exquisitely still, the moon was not yet up, and the shadows were not as yet very dark. It was a perfect evening, and my thoughts flew out across the poetic garden to the lonely spot where, in the midst of this picturesque and pagan land, an Englishman was preparing to sacrifice his happiness for the sake of his honour. An infinite sadness crept over me : I longed for dear old England and for peace, and above all I longed for sight of Hugh before the awful, the irrevocable had actually happened. Somehow I could not believe that the preposterous thing was really about to be accomplished; that, within the next few hours, a man so good, so true as Hugh Tankerville could be called upon to wreck his whole life without a protest. We were obviously doomed to remain in this exotic land for the whole term of our natural lives. I was willing enough to remain : I had no ties, save those which bound me to my friend, and if Hugh could but marry the woman he loved, I know he would have craved for nothing more. But we were amongst people as high-minded and more civilised than ourselves : a woman here was as sacred, as much worthy of respect as in our own distant homes, and conscience has an unhappy knack of following one wherever one may go. All this I knew and felt; and now, at the eleventh hour, I too in my inmost heart began to argue with my conscience, to bandy words with my friend's honour, and to try and find a loophole through which I could drag Hugh Tankerville away from the very foot of the hymeneal altar.

The longing to speak to Hugh, if only for a moment, became imperative. I was not sure whether I should find the way open through the temple gardens to his pavilion, but at anyrate I resolved to try. Wrapping a dark cloak round me, I found my way out of the Pharaoh's palace, and soon reached the outer precincts of the temple close.

The sacred edifice, in its severe imposing architecture, with massive columns, such as the Egyptians love, towered high above me, square and broad, upon a gigantic flight of marble steps. Hugh and I had visited it the day before, and I loved its simple magnificence, its gorgeous proportions, its great snow-white columns, the exquisite tracery, picked out in silver inlay, which gleamed in the gathering shadows of evening, looking singularly ethereal and ghostlike.

The evening sacrifice was just over, for I heard behind the temple the sound of sistrum and harp, dying away in the distance; and the song of Isis's sacred courtesans, as they took possession of their enchanted garden, sounded more and more remote. From the gardens an overpowering scent of flowers was wafted towards me, and I could see on my right the pavilion, where Hugh probably at this moment was pacing up and down the marble hall like some caged lion, nestling behind a clump of orange trees: and far beyond, the canals, like shimmering ribbons, wound in graceful curves towards Tanis and Net-amen, Men-ne-fer and Het-se-fent.

I had already turned towards the pavilion and was following a long path, which led away from the temple, when my ear caught the sound of stealthy footsteps upon the sandy walk, some distance behind me. Astonished, I turned to see who my companion was in this evening stroll, and to my amazement recognised my patient, the mighty Pharaoh, who, like myself, wrapped in a dark cloak, was softly walking at right angles from the path, which I myself was following, straight towards the temple, and the next moment had disappeared from my view behind a piece of sculpture.

An instinct, which I could not have accounted for at the time, prompted me not to run after him, nor to shout, but to follow him quietly and see what he would do.

Keeping him well within the shadows, I retraced my steps, and once more found myself at the foot of the temple, just in time to see the Pharaoh disappearing up above me somewhere among the pillars.

I could not imagine that he had chosen this evening hour in order to perform some tardy act of devotion, and a little anxious about his safety now, I followed up the massive stairs.

I had completely lost sight of the sick man, and having reached the last of the marble steps I peered round eagerly between the pillars. The façade of the temple was silent, dark and deserted. Immediately in front of me was the ponderous gateway, built of marble tracery, which opened into the sacred edifice. It was closed, but I went up to it, and through the tracery saw the interior of the building. The main body of the temple was dimly lighted by a single hanging lamp, which threw an uncertain, flickering light on floor and pillars; at the further end hung the usual heavy, semi-transparent curtain which hid the inner sanctuary of the goddess. This being brilliantly illuminated, the curtain formed a kind of shimmering wall, against which I saw suddenly silhouetted the figure of the Pharaoh not far from me, and that of a woman, Queen Maat-kha, by his side.

I could not see into the dark corners of the temple, but, as far as I could ascertain, the rest of the building was deserted and the royal bride-elect was unattended. The Pharaoh had evidently just finished speaking, for he was leaning exhausted against one of the pillars: he looked so very cadaverous and ill that I was seriously anxious for him, and at the risk of interrupting a private conclave between mother and son, I tried to get to him, but the marble gateway was closed. After the manner peculiar to Egyptian architects, it had been made to work with a secret spring, by which a child could set it in motion if he knew its working, but which the strongest man in the world, if he were ignorant, could not even shake; and I, of course, had no idea where and how that secret spring worked.

Suddenly I heard Queen Maat-kha's voice.

"Was it to tell me all this, oh, my son," she said, "that thou didst come, like a snake in the night, to pour thy poison into my ear, even while I worshipped at Isis's shrine?"

He laughed his usual sarcastic laugh.

"My poison?" he retorted. "Nay! sweet mother, that potion which thou must drink to the full is none of my mixing. Already thou didst taste a few of its bitter drops, I but add the last thought of deadly aconite to make it more unpalatable still."

"And art satisfied?" she asked quietly.

"Not quite," he replied with sudden vehemence, coming a step or two closer to her, "not quite, for that evil hand which, with arrogant pride, will snatch the kingdom of Kamt from my dying grasp, hath already taken from me the priceless treasure, which was the only joy of my life."

"I do not understand."

"He came," hissed the sick man close to her ear, "and with one look, one word, won that which I would have given my double crown, my life, my honour to possess."

"Dost mean the love of thy people?"

"No! the love of Neit-akrit."

Queen Maat-kha shrugged her shoulders and laughed a low, derisive laugh.

"'Twere better thou didst go back to thy sick-bed, oh, mighty Pharaoh! and didst take some of the soothing potions thy medicine men do order thee. Thy mind doth indeed begin to wander. Love! and Neit-akrit! . . . was there ever a more impossible union? Why, 'twere easier to credit the jackals of the wilderness with pity for the corpses they devour, than Neit-akrit with human love!"

"Were it easier too," sneered the Pharaoh, "to credit the son of Ra with love for Neit-akrit?"

But Maat-kha turned upon her son as if she had been stung.

"Beware, oh, most holy Pharaoh!" she whispered between her clenched teeth, "beware of the might of the gods, and rouse not the dormant passions in a woman's heart."

He laughed.

"Nay! it was to rouse these dormant passions that I came to-night, oh, mother mine! Didst think, perchance, that I meant to leave thee in peace and happiness, taking away from me all that the gods did give? I had a crown. Thy lover came, and with one blow struck it from off my head. Am I the Pharaoh? Ask my people whom it is they love, and whom they obey. Who sits upon the throne of Kamt? Not I, surely, for *his* hands deal favours and sign the decrees of justice. I am sick and of no account; my open enmity could but heighten thy lover's fame. But my hatred has been nurtured in the dark, and, like a foul snake, hath thriven well, the while thou didst rejoice and didst think of wedding the stranger, so as to oust thy son from the throne. But, I tell thee, thou didst rejoice too soon. I am not dead yet, and the Beloved of the gods is hated by many mortals: by those whose arrogance, *his* arrogance did curb, whose pride, *his* pride did humble, and amongst these thou must reckon the woman whom thou wilt defraud as thou didst defraud thy son."

"Thou talkest at random," she said with another shrug of the shoulders. "Just now thou didst say that she loved him, and now thou speakest of hate."

"And is not hate the twin of love, mother mine? And didst thou not feel hatred for him whom thou lovest so well, when thou didst see him standing beside Neit-akrit? his eyes devouring her young and ardent beauty, her eyes turned to him, moist and tender, ready to respond to the first word of passion? Didst see how he trembled when she asked him for a kiss?"

"Hold thy babbling tongue," she commanded. "I will not listen to the ravings of a lunatic."

"But thou wilt listen, for I will tell thee that, at nights, when Isis hid her face, and darkness threw a merciful pall over the garden of Neit-akrit's palace, she would creep out, and, her arms filled with masses of lotus blossoms, she would go to *thy* lover's couch. I have seen her on the terrace, at nights, standing like the carved image of voluptuous grace, with moist lips and shimmering eyes, and he . . ."

"Thou liest!" said Maat-kha in a hoarse whisper, raising

an imperious hand, as if ready to strike the son who with evil tongue hissed the cruel words into her ear, delighting with fiendish glee in goading her into jealous frenzy.

I could not understand what the man's object could be in the strange game he was playing. Was it revenge for his own wrongs, or merely the natural outburst of an evil mischief-making mind? I knew he hated his mother, but thought the game a dangerous one, for in this country passions run high, and a woman's love or hate is deadly and uncontrolled.

I could not tear myself away from my point of vantage; an unaccountable feeling or presentiment, which since then I have been so well able to explain, kept me rooted to the spot, with my face glued against the massive marble carving.

Maat-kha's face had become positively livid with rage; she was strong and muscular, and she tried with both her hands to smother the evil words in her son's mouth.

But this half-human creature repeated, with a truly demoniacal chuckle—

"I tell thee I saw them both. . . . Dost think perchance he cares for *thee*, beyond thy throne and thy riches? Look at Neit-akrit and then at thyself. Is she not made for love? young, ardent and exquisitely beautiful. She hath consumed my soul with wild passion, mad, unreasoning love, and he . . . hast seen him to-day? He is dying of the same complaint which has sapped *my* manhood, made a weak coward of the Pharaoh, the descendant of Ammoun-ra. . . . Hast seen his burning eyes, his hollow cheeks? He is dying, I tell thee! he will die in thy arms one day . . . soon . . . die of love for Neit-akrit."

"Thou liest! thou liest! thou liest!" she shouted. "I forbid thee to speak, thou liest!"

"He loves her, I tell thee, and thou wilt wed him to-morrow; but he will hate thee, for his heart belongs to Neit-akrit. Ay! mother mine, thou hast stolen my throne from me, but at least, in exchange for that throne, I think I have succeeded in stealing from thee the last shred of thy happiness."

But the semi-demented creature who ruled over the kingdom of Kamt had pursued his cruel game just a little too far. I was absolutely helpless to intervene, even had I thought of venturing to do so, for the heavy marble gates were between me and that mother and son, who were hissing words of hate in one another's ear.

"Thou liest!" repeated the Queen, but yet she listened, as if longing to drink to the last dregs of the poisonous cup, which her son was holding to her mouth.

"Thou art old, mother mine," added the creature, with truly Satanic fiendishness. "Of thee he will have but thy throne. I tell thee that as soon as he has wedded thee he will forget thy very existence: and Neit-akrit, the divine Neit-akrit, whom I, the Pharaoh, adore, will forget her rank, her maidenhood, and vow herself to Isis, that she may on moonlit nights put her white arms round his neck, and show him how well the women of Kamt have learnt how to kiss."

With a hoarse cry Maat-kha, whose whole body seemed to tremble with mad, uncontrolled rage, literally sprang upon her son. With both hands she gripped him round the neck, and she held him there tightly clutched, before her, until perforce his evil words died, choked within his throat. His head fell back, livid and ghastly, his arms beat the air once or twice, while his whole being shook in a violent convulsion.

Aghast, horror-struck, I shouted, with all the force of which my lungs were capable: I threw my body against the marble gate, only to fall back bruised, sore and helpless. The mad woman heeded me not, the wild mania of blind jealousy must have closed her ears. My voice went echoing amongst the massive pillars of the building, but nothing answered it save, far away, the song of the priestesses of Isis amidst the flowers and the balmy midnight air.

The Pharaoh's head had fallen back inert, and over him bent the woman—his mother—still furiously hissing at the livid face beneath her: "Thou liest! thou liest!" Then the body became rigid and still, there was a final convulsion, the head rolled from side to side: Maat-kha ceased her shouting, she still held the dying man by the neck, but her eyes, now large and terrified, were fastened upon him. Gradually a look of indescribable horror spread over her face, a look which almost froze the blood in my veins, so appalling was it. The momentary mania had disappeared and in its stead came the terrible realisation of what she had done.

Again I shouted to her to let me in, but she seemed not to hear, for she did not even turn towards me, though I screamed myself absolutely hoarse. For one moment I thought of turning towards the garden and shouting for help in that direction, then the idea of Hugh hearing my voice, of seeing what I had seen without warning or preparation, struck me with unspeakable horror, and stupidly, unreasoningly, I threw myself again with all my might against the stone gate hoping to attract some attention.

I must have done it very clumsily, for I caught my head a nasty blow which stunned me for a moment, and, half-unconscious, I fell down on my knees against the gate.

CHAPTER XXIII

THE ALTERNATIVE

WHEN I came to myself after a few minutes, the scene inside the temple had changed. The Pharaoh was lying rigid upon the marble floor and the hanging lamp overhead threw a weird, flickering light upon his livid, hideously-distorted face. Beside him, ghastly pale, with eyes staring full of horror upon the dead body of her son, Queen Maat-kha stood silent, with arms folded across her bosom, her lips tightly set. She was listening to the high-priest of Ra, who was speaking to her in slow and solemn tones, whilst he pointed upwards to the sanctuary of the goddess.

" Thy sin, Maat-kha, is beyond forgiveness. Thou knowest it; thy body and thy soul are doomed to eternal death. Thy very memory will be accursed in Kamt as the centuries roll slowly away."

She did not reply. I think she was absolutely dazed. No doubt that even a British jury would have found extenuating circumstances for her crime. She had been provoked beyond what her reason could stand. Momentarily it had fled, escaped her body, leaving her a prey to all the furious passions, which her maddened jealousy had aroused within her. Now reason had returned, and with it horror, repulsion and hideous, terrible remorse.

I was still very shaky on my legs, and somehow instinct kept me where I was, waiting to see the sequel to this awful and weird tragedy. There was dead silence after the high-priest had spoken, and the echo of his last solemn words still reverberated in the vast and mysterious temple. From afar the last sounds of life and bustle from the bridal city reached this lonely, poetic spot only as a murmur from dreamland.

Maat-kha stood as rigid and inert as her dead son, only from time to time a nervous shiver went right through her, and she gathered her veil close to her as if she felt cold.

"I am waiting for thy answer, Maat-kha," said the high-priest.

She looked up at him, half-appealing, half-defiant. There was no sorrow on her face for the dead son whom she had never loved, no fear of the punishment with which the high-priest threatened her. She said very quietly—

"What answer dost thou expect of me?"

"I wish to know if, after thy madness, thou dost understand the hideousness of thy crime, and dost fear the vengeance of the goddess whose temple thou didst desecrate?"

"My hands did act, but not my will. He taunted me and my reason fled. I had no wish to kill him, only to silence his poisonous tongue."

"Hold thy peace, woman! Do not slander the dead and heap more sorrow and humiliation upon thy doomed head."

"What wouldst thou have me do, Ur-tasen? Madness seized me. I am accursed. Wilt thou give me the boon of a dagger with which to send my sinful soul to the foot of the throne of Osiris? who perhaps will understand, and understanding, pardon."

"Thy soul is not worthy to appear before the gods. Judgment would decree that thy body be allowed to rot, lest so vile a soul find once more habitation upon earth and live to commit other most horrible crimes."

A shudder went through her; for the first time she seemed to realise that some awful punishment would inevitably follow her sin. She looked wildly round her as if in search of help or sympathy, then again appealingly at the high-priest before her.

"There is no help for thee, woman. Look not around. The very walls of the temple of Isis frown shuddering down upon thee. Nay! look not for help, for not even he, whom thou deemest all-powerful, could save thee if he would."

The words of Ur-tasen recalled me to myself. I realised that in a moment the whole aspect of Hugh's future had changed, and it was but just, that he should be apprised of the tragedy which had taken place, and of the awful doom which suddenly threatened Queen Maat-kha. There was no object in my staying here any longer to hear Ur-tasen's solemn invectives against the unfortunate woman, and I had almost turned to go, when it seemed to me that in the remote corner of the temple, behind Queen Maat-kha, there was someone standing and like myself watching the weird and terrible scene. I could only see a dim outline thrown darkly against the light curtain, but somehow that outline, the heavy hair, the quaint, straight attitude, forcibly reminded me of Princess Neit-akrit.

Surely I was mistaken. What could Neit-akrit be doing alone at night in the temple of Isis? and why should she have stood motionless and still while so awful a tragedy was being enacted before her? And yet, persistently I looked at the slight and upright figure and continued my *rôle* of eavesdropping, scenting vaguely danger hovering in the air.

At mention of Hugh's name, Maat-kha had closed her eyes. A look of infinite pain spread over her face, and slowly two heavy tears rolled down her cheeks.

But Ur-tasen was merciless.

"How he will loathe thee, Maat-kha," he said very quietly. "Hast thought of that? He never loved thee dearly: thy beauty had not even the power to ensnare his senses, but I think he honoured thee as a woman and as a queen: whereas now he will turn from thee as from a noisome reptile. With his own hand he will sign the decree which will cast thee out of Kamt, and as thy flesh begins to wither on thy bones, out there in the valley of death, thy dying soul can contemplate the picture of happy, prosperous Kamt, wherein the stranger, the Well-beloved of the gods, dispenses justice and wisdom beside Neit-akrit of the house of Usem-ra."

A prolonged moan of anguish escaped the unfortunate

woman's lips: she turned to the high-priest and very calmly she asked—

"Ur-tasen, why dost thou put this torture to my soul? Speak! What dost thou want of me?"

"I but want the salvation of thy soul, Maat-kha, seeing how grievously thou hast sinned. I but wish to adjure thee to think of the vengeance of the gods."

"I will think of that by-and-by," she said, "now . . ."

"Now thou dost think only of what thou hast lost and what Neit-akrit has gained."

"No, no, no, no! Ur-tasen, no! thou dost not know of what thou speakest. See! I will drag myself on my knees before thee. I will weep both my eyes out for repentance. I will go forth into the valley of death cheerfully and calmly, accepting thy decrees and blessing thy name. I will cause all my wealth, my jewels, my palaces to be left to thee, as thine own property, when I am gone, if thou wilt part my lover and Neit-akrit for ever."

She had sunk down upon her knees, and laying her pale forehead on the marble floor before the high-priest, she beat the ground with her head, and kissed the tip of his pointed sandals. I thought the high-priest's face suddenly assumed a satisfied, triumphant expression. He folded his arms across his chest and looked down upon the suppliant at his feet.

"Wilt come up before the image of the goddess, oh, Maat-kha! and at her very feet swear that thou wilt do my bidding, whatsoever I might command?"

She raised her head, and in the dim, flickering light I could see that she darted an inquiring, amazed look upwards at him.

"Dost believe that I am powerful?" he asked.

"I believe that thou dost hate him who is Beloved of the gods."

"Wilt swear to do my bidding?" he repeated.

"Dost wish to harm him?"

"Not unless thou also dost wish it."

"I love him, Ur-tasen," she said in truly heart-rending tones.

"Wouldst see him then in the arms of Neit-akrit?"

"I would sooner see him dead at my feet," she replied with

renewed passion, " slain by my hands, as was my son the Pharaoh."

" Swear to do my bidding, Maat-kha, and Neit-akrit will never wed the stranger king."

She rose slowly to her feet and turned towards the sanctuary of the goddess.

" Lead the way, Ur-tasen," she said with absolute calm. " I will swear to do thy bidding."

The sanctuary was at the further end of the building. Already the high-priest, followed by Maat-kha, was rapidly disappearing in the vastness of the temple. Helpless, I looked round me. The conviction had gradually forced itself upon my mind that Ur-tasen had concocted some evil plan against Hugh, for which he required the co-operation of the Queen. Her terrible, unpremeditated act had given him an enormous power over her, and, working upon her mad jealousy, he meant evidently to make her his ally in his nefarious scheme. At any cost I was bound to hear what that man and that woman would say to one another during the next few minutes, and there was the whole length of a vast temple and the thickness of marble gates between me and them. On the floor, beneath the lamp, the livid mask of the dead Pharaoh seemed to grin at my helplessness. It seemed as if, dead, he would be able to wreak that vengeance upon the man he hated which, living, he had never dared accomplish.

Already I could see Maat-kha prostrate before the goddess, with arms stretched upwards, swearing no doubt to add another deadly sin to her crime, and in Ur-tasen's attitude, standing erect and commanding by her side, there was an unmistakable air of exultant triumph.

There was no question that, from where I was, there could not be the slightest chance of my hearing what those two said. Certain of not being watched, determined to know the extent of the projected evil before I warned Hugh of his danger, I thought of rapidly skirting the temple walls, in the hope of finding some other gate or entrance nearer to the sanctuary, from whence I could watch and listen. The precincts of the temple were absolutely deserted, as far as I could see, and, in any case, my feet were shoeless, and the shadows between the pillars were long and dense. I had every chance of slipping round unperceived.

I made slow and very cautious progress. The temple was vast and it took me two or three minutes' measured creeping, before I reached its more distant side. As I had hoped, another gateway, also of marble tracery, led into this part of the temple, and to my delight I found that this gateway was opened sufficiently to allow me to slip inside, which I did.

I found myself, however, not in the temple itself, but in a kind of chamber or passage, I did not know which, for it was very dark. Some five feet from the ground a narrow opening, scarce the width of an arm, in the granite wall, showed beyond it the brilliantly-lighted sanctuary. At first, in looking through this aperture, I could scarcely see, for the dazzling brightness of the innumerable hanging lamps, and the thick fumes of burning herbs, shut everything out from my view. But gradually, as my anxious gaze travelled round, I saw Ur-tasen and Maat-kha not ten feet away from me to my left; but the gossamer curtain hung between the sanctuary and them, and I could only vaguely distinguish their forms. Beyond them I could see nothing but gloom; the dim shadow, which I had fancied to be Princess Neit-akrit, had apparently disappeared, if indeed it had ever been there, and the high-priest and the Queen evidently thought themselves alone.

"He often used to evade his attendants at night-time," Maat-kha was saying, apparently in answer to a query from the priest, "and wander about aimlessly in the gardens or the palace. I had come into the temple to pray, bidding my women go and leave me in peace for an hour, when suddenly I saw the Pharaoh before me."

"I know the rest, for I saw and heard all," replied the high-priest, quietly.

"And thou didst not move a finger to save him from death, and thy Queen from a crime ten thousand times worse than any torment?" she exclaimed with a smothered shriek.

"The will of the gods is inscrutable," he replied calmly. "I am but a servant of all-creating Ra. 'Tis he ordered me to be silent when the holy Pharaoh fell smitten by his mother's hand. His will must guide thee too. Thou hast sworn to do my bidding."

"I will obey," she said very meekly.

"Listen then to the commands of Ra, of Osiris, and of Horus, of Set, and of Anubis and all the gods in Kamt, whose wrath, if thou disobey, will fall heavily upon thy criminal head. I command thee to go anon, when thy women come to attend upon thee, back to thy palace peacefully and silently. The priests of Ra will guard the body of the Pharaoh, until such time as the soulless corpse will have helped to fulfil the deed of vengeance, which the gods of Kamt have decreed."

"I do not understand."

"Listen, Maat-kha," said Ur-tasen, more eagerly, as he bent his shaven crown close to her ear; "at the midnight hour, when Isis is high in the heavens, the stranger, who with sacrilegious arrogance doth style himself Beloved of the gods, will plight his troth to thee. Ignorant of thy terrible crime, he will swear that he will love and be true to thee, and reverence thee as men of Kamt do reverence the wife whom Isis places in their arms. Do thou be silent and at peace, none but I have seen the evil, midnight deed: do thou be silent and at peace, and place thy hand in that of the stranger."

There was a pause, while I pictured to myself the unfortunate Maat-kha listening to the priest's commands, not daring to cling to the thin thread of hope, which he was so enigmatically holding out to her.

"After the solemn marriage ceremony," resumed Ur-tasen, "by the custom of our beloved land, the royal bridegroom remains in the temple of Isis, waiting and alone. All those, who have come, bidden to the feast retire to their homes, to ponder of what they have seen, or to join the populace in their revelry in honour of the joyous night. But the royal bridegroom waits in solitude and prayer; waits until his bride is ready to receive him, at the first streak of dawn, when Isis herself sinks fainting into the arms of Osiris her beloved, and suffuses the vault of heaven with the roseate hue of her bridal blush. Then the royal bridegroom goes forth to meet his bride, and his footsteps lead him through the garden of Isis to that secluded nook, beside the sacred cataract, where stands the hallowed shrine of the goddess, and where foot of man ne'er treads, save if he be of royal blood, and hath not yet received the first kiss of his bride. Dost remember the spot, oh, Maat-kha?" he added. "There didst thou go twenty years ago, one summer night, beneath the light of sinking Isis; there didst thou hear the sound of the path crunch beneath the foot of Hor-tep-ra; there didst thou give the first bridal kiss to him whose son thou hast murdered, within the very temple of the goddess."

"I remember," she murmured dreamily, "and oh! how oft have I not thought of that solemn meeting within the sacred precincts, with him whom I love beyond all things earthly—with him who to me, to all Kamt, is sacred, nay! divine."

"It wilt not be thou, oh, Maat-kha! who wilt meet the bridegroom beneath the shrine of Isis."

"Who then, oh, mighty priest of Ra?" she asked with sudden terror.

"The dead body of thy murdered son."

"I do not understand."

"Nay! thy mind must be strangely over-clouded. The Pharaoh did oft in his life evade his attendants and wander about aimlessly in his palaces and his gardens. To-night, more sick than ever, he found his way to the precincts of the temple of Isis, but faintness overtook him—faintness so great that the priests of the goddess laid him on a couch within the sacred building and tended him with loving care. But he is too sick to attend the wedding festivities, and the priests of Isis will have charge of him while Tanis goes raving mad with joy. Tanis will forget the sick Pharaoh in her tumultuous happiness, and those few who will remember him will know that the holy monarch is well cared for by the most learned in the land."

I confess that not even then did I really understand the devilish plan which the high-priest of Ra had conceived. That it was in some way to encompass Hugh's ruin was of course evident, but what connection the dead Pharaoh was to have with it, or the mysterious and poetic retreat by the cataract, I could not as yet imagine. The Queen, too, was evidently as much at sea as I was, for she repeated mechanically—

"My mind is dull, Ur-tasen. Still I do not understand."

"During the joyous ceremony," continued the high-priest, "the sick Pharaoh again evades his thoughtful guardians, as he often has evaded his attendants, and his roaming footsteps lead him to the waters of the sacred cataract, the secluded spot wherein the royal scions of ancient Kamt whisper first of love and home. The shrine of the goddess is enclosed by high walls shut off by copper gates; these are never opened save on glorious nights—like to-night will be when the widow of Hor-tep-ra will await her stranger lord. But the holy Pharaoh, finding the sacred grove still deserted, doth lay himself there to rest . . ."

The high-priest paused, then added, in a whisper so low that I could hardly hear—

"He who calls himself Beloved of the gods hath no love for the sick Pharaoh, who stands between him and absolute power. . . . The night is lonely . . . the gardens silent . . . and the Pharaoh helpless. The stranger has the strength of a lion . . . the strength which breaks the golden wand of the high-priest of Ra with one touch of the hand . . . and which smothers the last cries of a dying man as easily as the carrion of the wilderness devour their prey . . ."

"Thou wouldst . . ."

"I would break the might of him who has ensnared the people of Kamt and broken their allegiance. . . . The priests of Isis will softly follow in the wake of the stranger, as he turns his footsteps within the hallowed nook. . . . Horror-struck, they will see the murderer standing beside his victim, then they will loudly call upon the people of Kamt to quit their rejoicings, to forget their songs and laughter and behold the hideous crime committed by him, who dared to call himself the son of Ra!"

"Ur-tasen!" shouted the Queen, appalled at the hideousness of so vile a plot.

But I did not wait to hear more—cared not to hear how the man of evil, that cowardly, treacherous priest, succeeded in forcing the unfortunate, criminal woman's will. My only thought was to fly to Hugh, to warn him of the base plots which threatened him, of the villainy of the woman to whom he had all but pledged his troth. Thank God! that monstrous oath had not yet been spoken, and my friend Hugh Tankerville had not, by any pagan ritual, sworn to love a murderess. Thank God !—*our* God—who led my footsteps to this idolatrous temple to-night, whereby I was allowed to see and hear, and warn Hugh in time.

"*If* thou refuse," I heard finally Ur-tasen saying in threatening accents; then he paused, and added with a touch of satire, "Thou art still at liberty to refuse, Maat-kha, to break the oath thou didst swear just now. The body of thy murdered son still lies there, and I, the high-priest, can yet summon the people of Tanis and show them their criminal Queen, she who then, to-morrow, will be for ever cast out of Kamt, a prey to the jackals and vultures, while in Tanis the wedding festivities will not even have been put off for so trifling a matter, seeing that the Beloved of the gods, the son of Ra, will still be there, ready to wed Neit-akrit of the house of Usem-ra. Ay ! thou canst still refuse, and think, when the gates of Kamt are shut for ever upon thee, of that same nook beside the sacred cataract, where the stranger will wait for the beautiful princess with the ardent hair and the eyes as blue as the waters of the lake; surely these will soon help him to forget the erstwhile Queen, the criminal, murderous Maat-kha."

I knew that she would give in, of course. Her love for Hugh was a barbaric, sensuous one, which would ten thousand times prefer to see the loved one dead than happy in another's arms. There was no object in my listening any further. The plot was hideously vile and treacherous, and perfectly well-conceived. I shuddered as I thought of what might have happened, had not divine Providence led me here.

It did not need much reflection as to what I should do. My first impulse had been to go to the top of the temple steps and there to shout until I had assembled the people of Tanis round me, and then to show them the dead body of the Pharaoh, its murderess and her accomplice. In any case I had not many minutes before me, as undoubtedly in the next few moments Maat-kha would give in and Ur-tasen would order the dead body to be removed.

I went back to the gateway through which I had slipped into this chamber not a quarter of an hour ago . . . it was shut.

That was strange! I tried to find the opening . . . impossible to move the gates. . . . I only succeeded in bruising my hands and smashing my nails. The gate was of solid marble, the tracery a foot thick. It was obviously childish to attempt to force it open. As for any sign of lock or hinge I certainly could see none. These Egyptians have secret springs to every door that leads to their temples. . . . Moreover, it was pitch dark all round me. Only between the carving the brilliant moonlight came weirdly creeping through.

CHAPTER XXIV

HELPLESS

It was obvious that from that side I was an absolute prisoner—temporarily, I hoped—but minutes, even seconds were valuable.

From the temple I could hear Ur-tasen's voice—

"For the third and last time I ask of thee, woman, wilt thou obey the decrees of the gods, or art thou ready to face the awful doom which thy loathsome crime has brought upon thee? Thy death and thy disgrace, or his? . . . which? . . . Dost love the stranger so dearly then, that thou wouldst see him happy in the arms of Neit-akrit with thy crown upon her head?"

And Maat-kha's voice, low and calm—

"I will obey, Ur-tasen!"

I returned to the aperture, from whence I had watched the two evil conspirators. It was no wider than my arm, and from there I could have done nothing but shout, which obviously would have been worse than foolish. I felt not unlike a caged beast, for although I had not as yet the slightest fear of not being able to warn Hugh in time, nevertheless there was no doubt that my position was, to say the least of it, a precarious one, and that I could in no case do anything summarily, to expose the murderous plotters.

From where I was I could not see the body of the Pharaoh, and now Queen Maat-kha, with head bent, was walking away towards the further end of the temple, whilst the high-priest remained standing before the sanctuary of his own pagan goddess, with arms outstretched, murmuring some heathen prayer.

There was long and deathlike silence in the great edifice. Maat-kha had probably gone, taking her conscience with her—if indeed she had any; the high-priest had finished muttering his prayers, and I watched—like a caged beast—Hugh's deadly enemy exulting over his anticipated triumph. I would not allow myself to reflect over the deadly peril of my position. My only thought was one of horror for the diabolical cunning of the plot, which apparently stood such a good chance of success. For the woman, I had more of pity than of loathing or contempt. The high-priest, with wonderful art, had known how to touch and play upon every sensitive and quivering chord of a highly passionate nature, had with sagacious dexterity roused every jealous instinct in her heart, until, blinded by her own passions, she had given herself over, body and soul, to his guidance.

No !—I don't think I reflected much upon my own danger. When thoughts of it rushed across my mind, I succeeded in speedily dismissing them. I could not do with such thoughts, for all must tend towards the future, upon how best I could save both my friend and myself. I cursed my own folly, my dilatoriness, the stupid way in which I had allowed myself to be trapped. How long I should remain merely a prisoner I could not of course conjecture, nor did I know whether my precarious position was the result of design or accident.

At the marriage ceremony Hugh would face the sanctuary, in the centre of the building, more than a hundred feet away from where I was, and probably with the gauze curtain between me and him, but I trusted to my lung power and to his presence of mind . . . if . . . I was left alive until then.

In the meanwhile I could do nothing but watch. Several attempts at pushing open the gateway had convinced me of their futility. Ur-tasen had been standing immovably for some time before the goddess, and I could see his shaven crown, which hid so many evil thoughts, shining behind the silvery curtain. Many absolutely British sentiments and desires with regard to the old beast made me gnash my teeth in my impotence, and even mutter several fine words, as with head erect he seemed to exult over his coming triumph. I supposed that as he stood there he was seeing visions of the stranger being comfortably cast out of Kamt, and of turning in the wilderness to human flesh and blood for final loathsome food and drink.

Suddenly, as I looked, it seemed to me that Ur-tasen was no longer alone, but that there stood beside him the same quaint and rigid form, which already before, in the gloom, I had thought that I recognised. It was but faintly outlined beyond the folds of the gauzy tissue, and I did not know if my tired eyes were not beginning to play me a few tricks, when Ur-tasen turned and spoke, in a humble and almost tender voice, so different to that in which he had addressed the unfortunate Maat-kha—

"I did it all for thee, Neit-akrit!"

Then I knew that I had not been mistaken. She was there, had probably seen and heard as much of the awful scene as I had, and had not made a movement to save her kinsman or to denounce his murderess. I recollected my old-standing distrust of her, and yet, remembering how young and beautiful she was, I could not admit to myself that she could approve, or in any way be accessory to the hideous treachery. She had not replied to the high-priest's words, and he continued eagerly—

"I bless the goddess, who led me to her temple to-night, who whispered to me that I should watch the sick Pharaoh, as he noiselessly crept up through the sacred building and disturbed his mother in her devotions. I praise the goddess, Neit-akrit, who with one terrible blow doth allow me to sweep from thy path all those, who dared to stand between thee and the throne of Kamt."

I don't know if Neit-akrit made any reply: certainly, if she did, it must have been in a whisper, for I did not hear. Then the high-priest repeated, with accents that were soft and pleading—

"I did it all for thee, Neit-akrit, that thou mightest wear the double crown of Kamt, and that thine enemy might be driven forth from the land, where, in his arrogance, he dared to lay hands upon thy throne."

"My enemy?"

Her voice came as a murmur, sweet and low: the words spoken half in astonishment, half in a strange and tender appeal.

"Ay!" said Ur-tasen, vehemently. "Thy throne is free now, Neit-akrit: I have cleared the way for thee. Maat-kha struck her dying son with wrathful arm; I did nought to save him, for by that blow thy kinswoman delivered herself and her stranger lover into my hands. At dawn, anon, when Isis has sunk to rest, he who has dared to call himself the son of Ra will go forth to his doom. Think of it, Neit-akrit! He, alone with the dead body of the Pharaoh! the opening of the gates! the call of the priests of Isis! the rushing of the mob! the shouts of joy transformed into cries of execration at the hideousness of the crime! Then, think of it, Neit-akrit! think of the judgment day, when thine enemy, he who had thought to place himself upon thy throne, is led forth bound hand and foot with ropes, humble—an abject criminal—within the great hall of Men-ne-fer, there, on the very spot, where thy slave Kesh-ta died, slain by his hand, so that she might escape the just and awful punishment of her crime, he—the son of Ra—will stand, and as the priests of Isis, one by one, with loud voice, will accuse him of the murder of the holy Pharaoh, one by one the lotus blossoms will drop out of the hands of the judges, and I, Ur-tasen, will pronounce judgment upon him. Then, after that—in the early morning . . ."

The bald old reprobate was evidently enjoying himself amazingly over the recapitulation of all he had prepared for Hugh, but here, suddenly, Neit-akrit interrupted him and her voice sounded curiously hard and calm.

"And hast no fear, Ur-tasen, that after that, in the early morning, the very gods will arise and kindle the flames of heaven and hurl down the mountains and the rocks over Kamt, in order to bury her and her shame?"

"I do not understand thee," said the high-priest, amazed. "Why speakest thou of shame?"

"Because already I see thy hands stained with his blood, and my very soul turneth in abhorrence from thee."

"Nay, Neit-akrit! his blood shall not stain the soil of Kamt: the vultures of the wilderness alone will see if it be red. Remember thy kinsman, the holy Pharaoh, died because his mother felt that he was the stranger's enemy. Remember that he set himself upon the throne of Kamt, which by right should be thine. Remember . . ."

"I remember," she interrupted again, speaking slowly and dreamily, "that he came to us and visited Kamt. He said he came from the foot of the throne of Osiris: well! that is as it may be; surely he is so good to look upon that some of the gods must have lent him their radiance. He came, and the people of Kamt were joyful, and in all the land, since he came, there has been one long and uninterrupted festival. He came, and put a check upon thy cruelty, when thou wouldst have sent a half-crazy woman to die of slow torture in the valley of death. He spoke to thee, and to all the judges of Kamt, of justice and of mercy. He came and we all found him fair, and we rejoiced and loved him, and kissed the ground before his feet. He made us all happy, and we waited all these days, then repaid him with treachery."

"Neit-akrit . . ." protested the high-priest.

"Nay! do not speak! I must have my say. I will not hear it again, that thou dost these evil things for me. I did not see Maat-kha's hand raised against her son: when I came into the temple, alone and unattended save by Sen-tur, the Pharaoh was lying livid upon the ground, and his mother had begun to feel the first pangs of remorse. This I swear by Isis herself, and thou knowest, Ur-tasen, that I never lie. But I saw thee, standing exultant in the gloom, and somehow I knew that thy thoughts were evil. I did not denounce the vile murderess, even while she bent red-handed over the body of her son, but I waited and listened: I heard thy treachery, thy cowardly plan, and that is why, Ur-tasen, I speak of shame to thee!"

She spoke very quietly, in that same monotonous, sing-song way which is the inalienable characteristic of this most ancient language. Ur-tasen, I think, was completely taken aback by her unexpected defence of Hugh, and probably the first inkling that she might prove *his* enemy instead of that of the stranger, penetrated into his scheming mind. I, from where I watched, felt a sudden wave of hope sweep over me, and of remorse for the wrong I had done the beautiful girl by suspecting her in my thoughts. I experienced an overwhelming desire to shout a triumphal shout at our enemy, for I felt that in Neit-akrit now I should have a powerful ally.

There had been a long pause after the Princess had finished speaking. I imagine that old brute was meditating as to what his next tactics should be. At last he said very calmly—

"Thou speakest with wondrous ardour, Neit-akrit. Hath the handsome presence of the stranger made thee forget that he has usurped thy crown? The gods commanded me to act as I did act, to hold my peace whilst Maat-kha and the holy Pharaoh fought out their last and deathly quarrel, and to speak their decrees to the murderess when tardy remorse had at last penetrated her soul."

"Nay, Ur-tasen!" she said, "blaspheme not, and take not the name of the gods of Kamt in so unholy a cause!"

"Who art thou, girl," thundered the high-priest in his most commanding accents, "who darest to upbraid the high-priest of the Creator?"

"I, Neit-akrit, Princess of Kamt," she replied proudly, "I, who dare to stand here and defy thee. Defy thee to do thy worst. . . . Ay! thou comest here in the temple of Isis, and in the guise of thy high and solemn priesthood thou lendest thy hand, thy mind, both of which thou hast vowed to the service of the gods, to a deed so base and dark that, methinks, Osiris will not rise to-morrow beyond the hills of Kamt, lest the very atmosphere, through which penetrate his golden rays, be polluted by thy treachery. Nay! prate not to me again thy thrice-told tale that thou didst so monstrous a thing for me! I tell thee, man, that Neit-akrit's foot would never ascend the steps of a throne rendered slippery with blood, but that her first act of justice in this land, since Maat-kha its Queen has forfeited life and crown by her unholy deed, will be to denounce thee and thy accomplice before the people, and for ever crush that power which thou darest to measure against the Beloved of the gods."

Thank God, and all his saints, the beautiful girl was proving true! It mattered not now whether I was free or a prisoner. Hugh, in any case, was out of danger, and my deliverance would follow in natural sequence; already I was sending up a prayer of heartfelt gratitude to Him who rules all our destinies and indulging in less Christian-like sentiment with regard to the discomfited foe, when his loud and derisive laughter suddenly dispelled these first glimpses of hope.

"Ha! ha! ha! Neit-akrit, Princess of Kamt! How strange and laughable are thy thoughts! Didst really think thou couldst pit thy woman's wit against that of him, who has for thirty years guided the destinies of Kamt? Wouldst denounce him, dost thou say? To whom, fair Princess? and for what? Hast strength to wield the mighty clapper which calls the people of Tanis to the temple, or might to shriek that those same people, mad, blind and deaf with joy, should hear, and, hearing, come rushing to the sanctuary of Isis to find—what? The dead body of a murdered Pharaoh? Where is it? . . . The holy Pharaoh is sick, and in the inner precincts of the temple, to which his footsteps led him, ailing and wandering . . . the priests of Isis are busy lavishing their skill and care upon him. There are twenty of these within my call now, who are ready to swear to the people of Kamt that, though sick, the Pharaoh lives. . . . And the people of Kamt, who left their rejoicings in answer to the wild shrieks of a woman, will return to their homes, their dancing and their music, with a puzzled and perhaps sad shake of the head, saying 'Princess Neit-akrit, of the house of Usem-ra, the beautiful, is no longer pure; madness has caused her tongue to lie, at the very foot of the throne of Isis, desecrating the temple of the goddess.' And some, no doubt, with a shrug will add: 'Madness which cometh of love for the stranger, unhappy love for him who will have none of her, since he will wed Maat-kha, anon.'"

"Hold thy peace, Ur-tasen, I forbid thee to speak of these things."

"Nay! I will not hold my peace, Neit-akrit, Princess of Kamt, thou who didst dare say that thou wouldst defy me! Didst think that it were so easy to circumvent the plans of Ur-tasen, the high-priest of Ra? Didst think I should allow thy girlish sentiments to upset what I have thought and dreamed of, ever since the stranger has usurped my power? Go and strike the metal gong, Neit-akrit, go and summon the people of Tanis. Derision and contempt await thee, and thou wilt not help the stranger withal."

Then, as she did not reply, but stood like an image of deep thought, with her golden head bent, he added—

"Hadst thou reflected, when thou didst venture to threaten and upbraid me, that thou wast within the precincts of a temple of Kamt, that in every nook, every corner of the gigantic building, the priests of Isis, and those of Ra, those of Horus and those of Osiris, are there lurking ready to answer the high-priest's beck and call. Go up the steps, Neit-akrit, which leads to the ponderous gong, take the mighty clapper in both thy hands, and I tell thee that before metal touches metal thou and thy soul will have fled to a land, whence thou canst not return to thwart the will of the high-priest of Ra, and a memory of something young and beautiful, the remembrance of a lock of golden hair will be all that will remain in the land, of Neit-akrit, Princess of Kamt."

I was glad that he had chosen to give this timely warning to the Princess, for I personally had been ready to shout to her, signifying my presence, and trusting to her wit and power to get me out of my difficult position. The mention of a host of shaven priests, hidden I knew not where, threw cold water upon my ardour, and I gnashed my teeth lest my British temper should get the better of me, and lest through the bars of my prison, I should be impelled to hurl an ineffectual, if to me convincing, malediction against the unscrupulous and treacherous blackguard, who was hemming us in all round.

"It was because I knew this, Ur-tasen, that I did not shout to the people of Kamt, the moment I saw the murderous deed and realised the blackness of thy treachery," said Neit-akrit, quietly. "I did not see the Pharaoh die. I came into the temple alone at the very moment when his body, after a final convulsion, rolled rigid upon the floor. Then I caught sight of thee; the flickering light of the lamp illumined thy face, and I knew that thy thoughts were evil. Silently I waited and listened; heard of thy villainy and Maat-kha's weakness, and trusted to the gods to give power to my words, to turn thee from the dark path, before it be too late."

I thought that she looked round her as if realising for the first time the loneliness of her position. Certainly these last few words showed decided signs of coming weakness, and my awakening hopes began to give way to a creeping feeling of disappointment. She was, of course, entirely at the mercy of an unscrupulous and daring man, whose sacred office gave him every power and opportunity of suppressing, temporarily or permanently, every inconvenient enemy. Personally I thought that his last threat had been a bluff; he would surely not have dared to put Princess Neit-akrit entirely out of the way at the time same as the Pharaoh. She was the idol of the male population of Kamt, and suspicion might perhaps fasten uncomfortably upon the high-priest and his deacons. At the same time, undoubtedly, Neit-akrit's life was doubly precious if she really meant to help Hugh. The question which agitated my mind was, Would she care to thwart the high-priest, at risk of some terrible retaliation on his part? Of course I did not understand her nature. How could I, a prosy Britisher, read the thoughts and feelings of so curious and ardent a temperament? Some time ago I had mistrusted her; then, a curious jealous feeling, of which I am heartily ashamed, made me turn against her, when I saw how completely she had taken possession of Hugh's heart. Both these feelings had in their turn overclouded my brain as to her real character, and I really was no judge as to whether she hated Hugh as a usurper, or if she cared for him. She was impulsive and capricious, sensuous and ardent, that I knew. Perhaps it had been mere impulse which had dictated to her to admonish, threaten and warn Ur-tasen, and to save Hugh if she could; that impulse had perhaps died out again, and visions of the throne rendered vacant for her by the Pharaoh's, Maat-kha's and ultimately Hugh's death, chased nobler thoughts away from her mind. She did not speak for a long time, and Ur-tasen stood and watched her with arms folded across his chest, his whole attitude one of scorn and command.

"The hours slip by, Neit-akrit, on the winged feet of time," he said with pronounced sarcasm. "Hast forgotten that within the next two hours the emissary of Osiris, the son of Ra, he who hath made us all happy and rejoicing, will wed Maat-kha our Queen, the widow of Hor-tep-ra? Hast forgotten that at the marriage ceremony, amidst all that are there, among all those who are fair in the land, there must be one who is fairer than all. Thy women await thee, no doubt, ready to deck thee with the snow-white robes which befit thy beauty and thy innocence. Nay!" he added with sudden softness, "thou art beautiful above all the daughters of Kamt, the perfume of thy hair sends delicious intoxication even through my shrivelled old body. Thou art fair, so fair that I would fain see the double crown of Kamt upon thine ardent hair. To accomplish this I plotted and I planned. Thou art a child and dost not understand. Leave thy destiny, the destinies of Kamt, in the hands of him whose firm will can guide them. Believe me, if in return thou wilt but smile on him and tell him thou art satisfied, he will be content."

She did not reply, and he added pleadingly—

"I did it for thee, Neit-akrit! In order that I with mine own hands might place the crown of Kamt upon thy golden hair, in order that none should rule over thee, that thou shouldst be queen indeed, as thou art queen only by thy beauty and by thy smiles. Tell me, art satisfied?"

And very quietly she answered—

"I am satisfied!"

I could scarcely believe my ears. Disappointment was so overwhelming, that I almost shrieked with the agony of it. Already she had thrown up the sponge. Ambition had quickly swept aside the noble impulse which had made her plead for Hugh. And again Ur-tasen was triumphant, and I, helpless, left once more, after a brief ray of hope, in an uncertainty which was now still harder to bear.

"Before thou goest, Neit-akrit," said Ur-tasen, "I would have thee swear to me, that neither by look nor word wilt thou betray to any one the plans of the high-priest of Ra."

But Neit-akrit was silent; and Ur-tasen added quietly—

"Nay! perhaps thou needest not swear. An oath can so easily be broken, in the spirit if not in the letter. I think I can trust thee best when I say that, shouldst thou before dawn anon, think of warning the stranger of what awaits him in the nook beside the sacred cataract, and his footsteps should not in consequence lead him thither, then, of course, no obstacle will stand between the Beloved of the gods and Maat-kha, his bride. The priests of Isis, after the first hour of dawn, will take the body of the holy Pharaoh back into his palace, and swear that he died of sickness in his bed. Then the happy union can be consummated, and thou Neit-akrit, the defrauded Princess of Kamt, canst in thy unselfish joy watch the happiness of Maat-kha, the murderess, in the arms of her beloved, the son of Ra, loved of all the gods : and I can swear to thee that he shall not know that the wife of his bosom is the murderess of her first-born, until she hath borne him a son, the heir to all her vices. Farewell, Neit-akrit, future queen of Kamt ! "

Oh ! he was a cunning brute was old Ur-tasen : again he had put his finger upon the most vulnerable spot in any female armour. Death to the loved one or his happiness in another woman's arms : the great problem which has torn passionate women's hearts in every country and beneath every clime, since the world began. Oh ! that I could have read in Neit-akrit's heart and known what she would do ! How far and in what way did she care for Hugh ? The alternatives seemed to me equally hopeless. If she had no love for him then, no doubt, ambition would seal her lips : she would remember the throne of Kamt, the glorious double crown, the homage of the people, and in the pomp and glitter forget the awful doom which alone could drive the usurping stranger from her path. But if she loved him, then what . . . ? then the great and subtle puzzle of the eternally feminine, the mysterious workings of a woman's heart, of a woman who, in spite of the high culture, the civilisation, the artistic refinement of this land, was pre-eminently exotic, passionate, semi-barbarous in her love and her hate. Nay ! I knew not. How could I guess how she would act ? Can man read the uncut pages of that romance, of which a woman only shows him the title leaf ?

But, in the meanwhile, the dangers round my friend seemed to close in tightly. Ur-tasen with subtle cunning had worked upon the loves, the jealousies of the two women who alone could save him, whilst I was still a caged prisoner, and the hours were swiftly speeding on.

Neit-akrit had disappeared, and Ur-tasen alone remained, quietly standing before the altar of the goddess, with arms outstretched, murmuring one of his pagan prayers, but as I still continued my weary watch, it seemed to me that newly awakened though still hidden life began to pervade the great and mystic temple. Within the main aisle the hanging lamps were lighted one after the other by—to me—unseen hands, and in the distance fresh young voices were rehearsing a bridal chant. Behind me in the outer precincts I could hear the muffled sounds of shuffling footsteps passing swiftly to and fro, and although from where I was I could see nothing save the brilliantly lighted and lonely sanctuary, yet I felt that around me there was bustle and animation : the preparations for the coming festivity.

I was carefully maturing my plans. Determined to keep well within the shadow of my prison, I would wait quietly for the best moment in which to attract Hugh's attention. I was in no sense of the word nervous or agitated, even I began to feel strangely drowsy and had much difficulty in accomplishing my numerous yawns noiselessly. The atmosphere became insufferably hot and heavy; clouds of smoke from the incense and burning herbs were continually wafted in through the window of my prison, and this no doubt was beginning to make me stupid and sleepy.

Not knowing how time was going on, I had squatted into the angle of the wall, with my knees drawn up to my chin, in an irresistible desire for sleep.

Suddenly I heard heavy footsteps outside, slow and halting; trying to shake off my drowsiness, I raised my head and listened. Through the marble tracery of the gateway I could see the vague forms of a group of men, who seemed to be carrying something heavy between them. A great cloud of some peculiarly scented burning herb came in a great wave right through the window, and seemed literally to strike me in the face, blinding me and making me gasp for breath. Drowsiness became intolerable, and yet when I sleepily reopened my eyes, I saw the gigantic marble gateway slowly moving on its hinges. . . . This sight roused me from my lethargy for the moment. . . . My senses fully alive, I watched and waited. . . . It was pitch dark in the further end of my cell, but I heard the footsteps within three feet of me, still shuffling and halting. . . . Through the open gateway the shadows appeared less dense : noiselessly on my hands and knees, keeping my shoulder close to the wall, I crawled towards the opening.

The men had put their heavy burden on the floor : they did not speak, hardly did I hear them breathing. My fear was lest they should detect me, before I had reached the gate, but they seemed not to have noticed me, and now, one by one, they turned and filed out. I was close to the opening, leaning against the wall, ready to crawl out in the last man's wake. . . . From the inside of my prison the same unknown scent of some highly aromatic herb was wafted in great clouds towards my nostrils . . . the fumes were overpowering, and I was tired and sleepy from my long, anxious wait. . . . The men had all slipped noiselessly through the opening . . . the cloak of the last one had caught in a projecting bit of carving . . . he stooped quietly to disentangle it . . . I could see his outline very clearly against the lighted corridor beyond. . . . My lids fell heavily over my eyes . . . I tried to shake off my torpor, for the last effort for freedom . . . but I was too sleepy. . . . I could not move. A great whiff of that enervating, burning herb made me long for rest and sleep! . . . I was too tired . . . I would slip out by-and-bye. . . . Now I must have sleep.

The man with the cloak had slipped out . . . I think the gate swung to, and I crouched once more with my chin between my knees. . . . I wondered what the herb was. . . . I must find out . . . it would do instead of ether in cases of minor operations . . . it was sweet and pleasant, but overpowering.

From the sanctuary a sudden brilliant ray of light struck for an instant through the aperture . . . someone must have gone past carrying a lamp or torch. It lit up the centre of my prison, and forced me to open my eyes for a second. . . . During that second I saw that, on the floor, sharing my captivity with me, was the body of the murdered Pharaoh. . . .

Then I remember nothing more. . . .

CHAPTER XXV

THE MARRIAGE

"AND thou, oh stranger, who dost hail from the foot of the throne of Osiris, who art the son of Ra, the emissary of Horus, the Beloved of all the gods, tell Isis, the mysterious goddess, why thou art here."

"I am here to crave of Isis the pure, Isis the beloved, Isis the most holy, that she deign to pour the fruits of her blessing upon me, for I would take this woman to be my wife."

It was Hugh's voice which spoke slowly and solemnly, and which was the first sound that penetrated to my brain, still wandering in the realms of cloudland.

Through the window of my prison an intense flood of light filtered brilliantly, illuminating the granite floor and walls. A strong scent of incense and myrrh had driven away the stupefying fumes of that burning herb which had lulled me to sleep. I tried to collect my scattered senses, but a terrible pain in my head and eyes still kept me half-stupefied. And yet I heard Hugh's voice speaking strange and momentous words, and a dull instinct whispered to me, that I must get to him, somehow, for a reason, of which I was not as yet, fully conscious. A raging thirst had made my tongue swell and parched my throat: the events of the last few hours danced before my clouded brain, like some weird phantasmagoria.

The Pharaoh . . . dead! murdered! his body lying close to me, when last I had opened my eyes, but now, carried away, whilst I had been asleep. . . . Maat-kha! . . . the murderess! . . . Hugh's promised bride! Ur-tasen, the evil plotter! . . . who had done . . . I knew not what . . . something that would wreck Hugh's life as well as his honour. . . . Neit-akrit! . . . who might be a friend, and yet was a foe! . . . and I . . . a helpless prisoner, stupid, senseless, half-drowsy still, after a drugged and heavy sleep!

"And thou, Maat-kha, who art daughter of Uah-ab-ra, the son of Ach-mes, the son of Ne-ku, tell Isis the mysterious goddess, why thou art here."

I did not know that voice, some priest probably . . . no concern of mine . . . I could perhaps get another half-hour's sleep . . . I was still so tired.

"I came here to crave of Isis the pure, Isis the beloved, Isis the most holy, that she deign to pour upon me the fruits of her blessing, for I would swear fealty to this man, and be his wife."

That was Queen Maat-kha's voice, and just now I had heard that of Hugh . . . the pain in my head was intolerable . . . my limbs felt weak and stiff; there was the whole length of my prison between me and the aperture, through which probably I should be able to see those who had spoken. I began to drag myself along, but I was only half awake, my limbs only just managed to bear me along, and I did not know if I should ever reach that aperture.

" Art awake, oh Isis, who art daughter of Ra ?

" Art awake, oh Isis, who art sister and bride of Osiris ?

" Art awake, oh Isis, who art mother of Horus ?

" Oh Isis, give life to this man and to this woman, who have sought the sanctity of thy temple !

" The gods above do rejoice ! the glorious company is full of joy, giving praise to thee, oh Isis, who art pure !

" Isis who art beloved !

" Isis who art most holy ! "

I had at last, after terrible difficulties, succeeded in reaching the window; with infinite pain, I struggled to my feet, but I could not stand ; my head was heavy and my knees shook under me. Twice I fell down, but at the third struggle my hands convulsively fastened on the marble ledge, and steadying myself, as best I could, I looked out, dazed, before me.

The sanctuary and the temple beyond it were one dazzling mass of lighted lamps and torches. The gossamer curtain had been drawn aside, and I could see the interminable vista of snow-white columns, on which the silver inlay glistened with a thousand sparks. Between the pillars, a sea of dark heads, adorned with gaily-coloured caps and kerchiefs, amongst which, occasionally, I caught sight of the glitter of a golden uraeus, or elaborately jewelled belt. . . . I could distinguish no details : my eyes were blurred, my brain overclouded. I remember that gorgeous picture, only as one remembers a dream.

Immediately before me Isis towered, wrapped in her sacred mantle, which hand of man has never dared to touch. On her head a gigantic pair of snow-white horns, between which glittered the silver disk of a huge full moon. Immediately at her feet a group of priests, with shaven crowns and long flowing robes of white, stood in a semi-circle, in the middle of which the high-priest of the goddess stood with arms outstretched, reciting the invocations.

Beneath the many hanging lamps, wherein burnt lights of

different colours, the other priests of the gods of Kamt were massed in imposing groups: the priests of Ra with yellow robes and leopard skins round their bodies: those of Phtah, with monstrous scarabaeus of iridescent blue and green enamel on the top of their heads: those of Thot, with masks of apes, entirely covering their faces, and those of Hor, with masks of sparrow-hawks, whilst the jackal's head hid the features of the priests of Anubis. Immediately to the right of the officiating high-priest, stood Ur-tasen, the high-priest of Ra.

"*Isis is strong!*

"*Isis is great!*

"*Isis is living and mighty!*"

The various attributes of the goddess reached my dull ears only as the sound of muffled drums.

At the foot of the sanctuary steps, against a background of men and woman in gorgeous raiments, and beneath a canopy of white lilies, stood Hugh Tankerville and his promised wife. His face was even paler than when I had seen it last: his eyes gleamed darkly and with an unnatural fire. He held his arms tightly crossed over his chest, and in his whole attitude there was the expression of an indomitable will triumphing over an overwhelming passion.

I saw him, as I had seen the sanctuary, the goddess, the crowds of people, only as one sees a vivid dream. It seemed to me as if he were not really there, but that slowly, very slowly, I was waking from that sleep which had held me enthralled for months, and that when I was fully awake I should look round me, and see myself sitting in the dear old Museum, at The Chestnuts, with Mr. Tankerville sitting beside me, telling me of beautiful, mysterious, legendary Neit-akrit.

I tried to speak to Hugh, for he was not far from me, but my tongue seemed rooted to my palate, and, as in a dream not a sound escaped my throat. Clouds of incense rose all around, and when the high-priest had ceased to laud the magnificence of his goddess, the priestesses, clad all in white, with their huge disfiguring wigs over their heads, began a sweet and monotonous chant, accompanying themselves upon their crescent-shaped harps, and beating upon the sistrum and the drum.

Beside Hugh, underneath that same canopy of lilies, and with her hand holding his, was Queen Maat-kha. She had discarded her gorgeous funereal draperies, and was standing clad all in white, her regal crown over her low, square brow, her great black tresses descending each side of her pale face, almost to her knees, and intertwined with ropes of pearls. And I, in my dream, thought that I could see, clinging to her finger tips, the last drops of her murdered son's blood.

Again I tried to scream, but my throat seemed paralysed. Gradually memory, as a vague, still indistinct shadow, began to creep back into my mind. Hugh was before me, clad in sumptuous robes, his dark head uncovered, his tall figure erect, ready to plight his troth, to pledge that word, which he worshipped as a divinity, to the vile murderess by his side. Twice a murderess, since having slain her son, she would ruthlessly sacrifice her lover to save herself from the tortures of jealousy. Yes, I did remember! It was imperative that I should warn Hugh of some terrible danger, which the woman beside him and the high-priest of Ra had placed across his path.

"Oh, thou who art Beloved of the gods, and thou who art Queen of Kamt, behold! Isis the goddess is awakened!

"Ra, all-creating, all-powerful and mighty, doth descend to earth!

"Phtah, the mysterious, and Osiris, the bounty-giver, do hover invisibly over your heads!

"But Hapi who proceedeth from Ra, who, in his divine person, is the living representative of Isis, of Osiris and of Phtah, Hapi himself will pass before your eyes!

"With the finger of your right hand ye may touch the sacred star upon his brow!

"With both your eyes ye may gaze upon him!

"But, ye all, children of Kamt! veil ye your countenance! the god will pass amongst you, and the sight of him gives blindness to those who are not wholly pure!"

A terrific cloud of incense rose from every corner of the edifice. Hugh and the Queen mounted two of the steps which led up to the sanctuary and behind them the silver tissue of the veil fell together with a prolonged and softly-sighing sound. Immediately underneath the window where I was a bowl full of incense must have been burning, for a cloud rose like a curtain between me and the sanctuary.

Through it I could see Hugh, not twenty yards away from me, and I tried to scream . . . and my throat was absolutely paralysed.

Now, there was great tramping of feet, and opposite to me a brilliant *cortège* came slowly towards the bridal pair. Adorned with bunches of gardenias and tuberoses, but with heavy chains round his feet and head, a gigantic ox was being dragged along. He was black, save for a white spot upon his forehead, and a patch upon his back : his horns were silvered, and he was led by ten priests of Isis, who held him by heavy silver chains. The great beast, snorting and puffing and evidently much annoyed at having been dragged from his stable, allowed himself to be taken fairly peacefully along, until he was brought to a standstill in the middle of the sanctuary, immediately at the foot of the throne of Isis. All the priests had prostrated themselves face downwards on the ground. Hugh and Maat-kha alone remained standing. At a sign from the high-priest they both placed their hand upon the forehead of the beast, while the priestesses intoned a triumphal march. Then, as stolidly as he had come, the god Hapi retired from the gaze of his worshippers.

" Oh thou, the son of Ra ! the emissary of Osiris ! the Beloved of the gods ! art ready to take the oath which will bind thee, thy body and thy soul, the breath within thy body and the blood beneath thy flesh, to the woman who is to be thy wife ? "

And I, in this strange and vivid dream, which was so real, and which I could not grasp, heard Hugh's voice clear and distinct—

" I am ready."

And I, his friend, his chum, his schoolfellow, I, Mark Emmett, who would have given at any time my life for his, could not succeed in giving one warning shout to stop this monstrous deed.

The poison—whatever it was—was still in my viens . . . my limbs felt like lead . . . I could not keep my head erect. . . . I could see all, hear every word, and smell the incense . . . but I could not utter a sound.

" Oh ! son of Ra, Beloved of the gods, at dawn when anon, Isis, the pure, sinks fainting into the arms of Osiris, her beloved and glorious spouse, thou wilt stand beside the sacred cataract, where since five times a thousand years the kings of Kamt have given the first kiss to their bride!

"Oh then! oh, son of Ra, wilt swear to give thy bride that kiss and to take her for wife?"

"I swear!" said Hugh, earnestly.

"Oh, son of Ra, Beloved of the gods, having taken unto thee a wife, wilt swear to be true to her with thy soul and with thy body?"

"I swear!"

"Oh, son of Ra, Beloved of the gods, dost swear before all men that thou wilt be true to her, whom thou wilt take to thyself as wife?"

"I swear!"

"Wilt swear it on the names of the gods of Kamt, of Ra, of Osiris and of Horus? of Anubis and Set? Wilt swear it upon thy manhood and upon thy honour?"

"I swear it!"

Hugh Tankerville, calm and impassive, had pledged his honour to be true to her who even now was plotting his death and his shame.

I seemed to remember all now as in a flash. The sight of Ur-tasen's face as he watched the high-priest of Isis administering this oath to my friend, for the space of a second, illumined a corner of my dulled intellect. I saw it all with the vividness of reality: the murdered Pharaoh lying beside the cataract; Hugh wandering unsuspectingly thither, with the shaven priests of Isis creeping on his trail, like jackals after their prey: then the mob yelling and cursing: Hugh, helpless in the face of the terrible accusations; the hall of justice: the doom from which probably even his own personality could not save him: and all the while I tried to shriek. I opened my parched lips, and but a few dull, guttural sounds escaped my throat, and Hugh could not hear. He was there within a few yards of me, pledging his manhood, his honour, to a pagan murderess, and I could do nothing, for I was in a dream, which gripped my throat and numbed my limbs. Once it seemed to me as if Hugh held up his head suddenly, while a look of surprise came into his eyes: encouraged, I tried again; my head fell back as if weighted with lead, the lids closed over my aching eyes, the vision of the snow-white temple, the brilliant crowd, the gorgeous and motley group of priests became more and more dim. With a feeble effort I tried to raise my hand, and beat childishly, impotently, against the immovable and cold stone walls of my prison; but even that effort proved too great: my grip on the marble relaxed, my knees absolutely gave way under me, and stupefied, drowsy, sleepy still under the potency of the mysterious drug, I sank again into heavy, dreamless sleep. . . .

CHAPTER XXVI

WHITE ROSEMARY

THE cloud was being slowly lifted from round my brain: the dream was gradually being dispelled; reality—terrible, appalling—forced itself before my enfeebled mind. My head still felt like lead, my eyes burnt like pieces of charcoal in their sockets, my limbs still were paralysed and stiff—but my brain was clear and I remembered.

Through the window of my prison a very faint glimmer only was creeping in from the sanctuary, throwing a dim band of light upon the floor. In the air there hovered the heavy odour of burnt incense and myrrh, but everything around was silent and at peace.

Had it all been a dream? or had the brilliant marriage ceremony taken place? Had I seen Hugh standing before the altar of the goddess swearing to wed the murderess of her son?

Slowly I raised myself upon my knees, then another mighty effort brought me to my feet, but I could not stand alone, I had to lean against the wall; an intolerable feeling of nausea overcame me, and I feared that I would again lose consciousness. At last I managed to look through the window. In strange contrast to the last picture which I had seen, the snow-white temple of Isis now was dark and deserted. The guests had gone, as had the priests with their grotesque masks, the priestesses with their harps and lutes—the canopy of lilies hung from above, but from beneath it bride and bridegroom had disappeared. The sacred edifice with its interminable vista of white and silver columns stretched out before me in all its imposing and majestic vastness. Suddenly it seemed to me that in the gloom my tired, aching eyes perceived a tall and solitary figure leaning against one of the pillars not very far from me. The curtain had been drawn aside to enable the lonely watcher to see the great goddess in her sanctuary, during his long and lonely vigil. My eyes ached and burned so, I could scarcely see, and was forced to close them from sheer pain, but tired as they were they had not failed even in the gloom to recognise in the lonely watcher Hugh Tankerville, my friend.

I could not see his features, for the temple itself was not lighted up; only through the distant gateway beyond, the rays of the moon sinking towards the west threw weird patches of blue light upon the pillars and the floor. I tried to call him, but the same terrible grip seemed still to hold my throat; what poison was it, I wonder, with which the treacherous high-priest had succeeded in silencing my warning voice? The memory of the past few hours became intolerable torture, the feeling of utter helplessness, coupled with the comparative clearness of my brain, was harder to bear than the physical ailments which still paralysed my throat and limbs. Longingly I looked at Hugh; it seemed to me as if some subtle magnetism in my gaze must ultimately succeed in drawing his. O God! was I then presently destined to see him walk forth from this accursed temple right into the hideous trap which had been set for him? I tried to use what little power I had to make as much noise as I could, vaguely hoping that Hugh would hear: I scratched the marble wall with my nails, I beat it with the palm of my hand, but the temple was very vast, my efforts weak, and Hugh did not hear. Then I tried to stretch out my arm and perhaps wave my handkerchief through the narrow window: I tried to fumble for it, but the effort was too great, my arms were almost inert, and I literally could not stretch them out far enough. Dizzy with the feeble attempt, I leant back against the wall tired out.

Yet the danger grew every moment more terrible. If I

remained too feeble to call out, if I could not succeed in attracting Hugh's attention, if I did not in fact warn him of the damnable plot that had been hatched against him, he would presently go forth from the temple to the sacred grove of Isis, thinking to meet his bride; there he would find himself alone with the dead body of the Pharaoh, placed there by Ur-tasen's commands.

I remembered all the details of that awful, treacherous plan quite clearly: nay, more, I saw the whole thing realised before my mind's eye, as clearly as if I were gazing on a picture. I could see the high-priest of Ra creeping in the wake of Hugh, I heard his hypocritical voice loudly denouncing the man I loved best on earth, and accusing him of the foul murder . . . and after that what would happen? . . . I dared not think. Would the crowd who had worshipped Hugh turn worship into execration? Would they believe that the son of Ra, he who was Beloved of the gods, was nothing but a vile criminal who would strike a feeble enemy in the dark?

Who knows? A crowd is as wayward as a child, as fickle as the most capricious flirt. . . . And I could not warn Hugh, for I was a prisoner, and the hour of dawn was nigh.

And Neit-akrit, the beautiful Princess? . . . Vainly I tried to cling to that last ray of hope. Surely a girl, so young, so beautiful, could not allow such vile treachery to be committed against the man whom she loved. Yes, she loved him, I knew that, I felt it: when she spoke of him to Ur-tasen, her voice almost broke in a sob. Oh! for the knowledge of that mysterious thing called a woman's heart! Loving him, what would she do? Give him a word of warning, ere it was too late, thereby sending him into the arms of Maat-kha, his wife, or let him go to disgrace and death sooner than see him happy with another.

These thoughts chased one another in my poor aching head, until the physical pain of it all became more than I could bear. I closed my eyes, the sight of that great temple, of Hugh standing there, alone and unsuspecting, was positive torture to me.

When I looked again Hugh was still there, leaning against the pillar, but it suddenly seemed to me as if something was moving close to him. Gradually the moving form took a more definite shape, and in the shadow my burning eyes had recognised a quaint and dainty outline, and an aureole of golden hair. It was she ! silent, mysterious, walking towards him with that undulating grace which was peculiarly her own. Absorbed in thought, he evidently had not heard the sound of her tiny bare feet upon the smooth floor. She was wrapped in a white kalasiris, without jewels or ornaments of any kind, and Sen-tur was not by her side.

She came quite close to him, and then he raised his head and saw her. She looked exquisitely beautiful, graceful and tall as the white lilies of Kamt; she placed a warning finger to her mouth, but he took the tiny hand in both his own, and murmured, as if in a dream—

" Neit-akrit ! "

" Hush ! " she warned, " the very air is filled with potent dangers, and thine enemies lurk hidden all around."

" But thou art here," he said. " Do not speak ! stand still for a moment, for I would look at thee ! How beautiful thou art ! and how thy presence doth fill the temple of Isis with a radiance which is almost divine ! "

Obedient to his wish, she stood quite still, her dainty form against the ghostlike whiteness of the marble pillars, on which the rapidly sinking moon threw its last brilliant rays. Something in his look, however, must have made her move, for she turned away.

" Dost wonder why I am here ? " she asked.

" No ! I hardly dare believe that thou art real, that thou art not an enchanting dream, with which Isis thought to soothe my aching senses. Wilt speak to me again ? "

" I would tell thee why I came," she said.

" Nay ! not that," he pleaded. " What care I, so long as thou art here, and I can look at thee."

" Nay ! but thou must know," she said, with a half merry, half nervous little laugh. " Hast heard, oh son of Ra, that in Kamt we, who are maidens, deem it the luckiest thing on earth to pluck the flowers from out the canopy which sheltered the heads of the bride and bridegroom, if they come of royal blood. The posy thus made brings to the owner lasting happiness. And so, to-night; while Tanis is mad with joy, I crept out of my palace, and came to the temple of Isis, to twine the nosegay, and having twined it, give it thee."

I gazed and wondered; little did I understand what the strange girl intended when she came alone to see Hugh in his solitude. A wild hope was in my heart that she had come to warn, and an earnest prayer that he might listen. He did not speak. I fancy he would not trust himself to say much, but when she so daintily expressed her desire for his happiness, he raised both her small hands to his lips. She withdrew them quickly, and said—

"Nay! we have no time to lose, for the posy must be large. There are many flowers needed to make the bunch of happiness complete. Thou must help me to pick them, for some of them are too high for me to reach. But thou art tall! See . . ." she said, pointing eagerly up to the great floral canopy, whence masses of blossoms hung in fragrant shower, "that perfect lily up there, would it not make a lovely centre for the bunch? Thou art so tall," she repeated with a pretty gesture of entreaty, "wilt reach it down for me?"

And Hugh obediently stretched his long limbs and with much difficulty succeeded in disentangling the coveted lily.

"Is it not beautiful?" she said admiringly, "so chaste! but oh! so cold. Dost know, oh Beloved of the gods, what the white lily of Kamt means?"

He shook his head.

"All flowers have a meaning, of course, and the lily means duty," she said with a sigh, "that is why it seems so cold, even cruel, in its waxy, spotless whiteness, but it must form the centre of the bunch, for I think thou dost love duty dearly, too dearly methinks, and perhaps wouldst not be happy without it. But," she added more gaily, "we will soften her waxy coldness: dost see that graceful bunch of white acacia? that means homely happiness. It would look well in graceful clusters round the stern centre of duty."

He was listening to her merry talk, I fancied, with a slightly puzzled air sometimes. Still less than I could he guess why she had come; but her presence made him happy for the moment, and it was quite gaily that he said—"But I cannot reach the homely happiness."

"Oh, what a pity!" she said earnestly. "Duty will look so ugly without home to soften it."

She paused perplexed, then added with an odd look at Hugh—

"Canst jump, oh Beloved of the gods?"

He laughed gaily, merrily, as I had heard him laugh of old.

"Can I?" he asserted triumphantly, and with gesture and action hardly befitting the solemn majesty of the temple of Isis, Hugh made a sudden grab for the drooping acacia, and brought down a perfect shower of white petals, as the floral canopy trembled with the shock.

"Homely happiness is hard to get," he said with a laugh, "but it well repays the effort; the scent of the acacia is very sweet."

She was laughingly shaking her golden tresses, to which the white petals persistently clung.

"It was hard," she said, "but see! how pretty it looks; now, I wonder, what would look well beside it."

"These orange blossoms are pretty."

"Yes! . . . they are pretty. . . . Wouldst like a cluster? . . . In Kamt we call them wedded bliss. . . . Dost want it in the posy?" she asked with a quaint anxious tone in her voice.

"No!" he said abruptly.

The moon must have sunk down very low behind the distant hills of Kamt, and the temple of Isis was dark, only the fitful glow of one of the sanctuary lamps lit up the dainty scene before me. Hugh, I could see, still had himself in absolute control. How long that would last I could not say. I considered that he owed no allegiance to the woman who had planned his murder; the sacrilegious marriage had not been completed, and I, feeble, half-paralysed as I was, had yet the strength to pray that beautiful Neit-akrit would make my friend forget the fateful hour of dawn.

There had been long silence between them while she, a trifle nervously, was fumbling with the flowers, and he was looking tenderly, longingly, at her.

"Ah, I know!" she said at last, "I must give thee white roses; they will look lovely beside the homely happiness. See! a beautiful cluster hangs just above thy head. Thou canst reach it quite easily and needst but to stretch out thy hand."

" A lovely cluster indeed, and the scent is delightfully sweet. Wilt tell me what white roses mean in Kamt ? "

He was handing the drooping cluster of roses to her, and she stretched out her small hand for it; the other was already loaded with flowers.

" In Kamt white roses mean love," she whispered, as she took the flowers from him.

I could see that his fingers fastened upon hers, that his whole body trembled as if with a mighty effort. It was a cruel position for any man deeply in love with a very beautiful woman, to be alone with her in this vast and silent temple, with myriads of flowers round him, making the air fragrant and heavy. She did not try to disengage her hand, but stood a little while, with her great eyes meeting his, boldly and fearlessly.

It was only when, with sudden impulse he tried to draw her closer to him, that she gently withdrew her hands and said lightly—

" Now we must have white rosemary. Wilt thou not gather it for me ? " she added, as Hugh, inert and dazed, was looking at her with that weary longing, that infinite tenderness, which always made my heart ache for his pain. " Dost know that white rosemary spells remembrance ? "

" Rosemary, for remembrance ! " he repeated, as quietly he turned and with loving care picked the humble blossom from out the crowd of its more gorgeous sisters. He looked at it, and as the light flickered, I could see two great tears glistening in his eyes. " Rosemary, for remembrance ! "—the very words spoke of England and of home, and brought to his weary heart probably, more strongly than anything else could do, the thought of what he had lost.

" Rosemary, for remembrance ! "—we, in England, thousands of miles away, speak of the little plant as meaning remembrance : before me, in one moment, with those words, the gorgeousness of mystic Kamt had disappeared, and I saw its loveliest daughter filling the old Chestnuts with the radiance of her beauty, the melody of her voice. She became the incarnation of womanhood, of her who alone knows how to combine the tender friend, the wife, the mistress. There was dead silence in the temple. Neit-akrit had taken the bunch of rosemary and was fastening it to her posy, while Hugh watched her silently.

Then, suddenly, from the further end of the sacred edifice, there where the great gateway faced directly towards the east, it seemed to me that a dull yet rosy light began to creep gently through.

" Neit-akrit," said Hugh after a long while, " if thou didst wish to give me that posy as an emblem of happiness, it was wrong to add remembrance to it."

" Why? "

" Because since I have smelt that sprig of rosemary my memory has come back to me. Remembrance, like duty, is at times cold and cruel, and her figure now stands beside that gate and points towards the east."

" Nay, not yet! " she pleaded; " 'tis but the lights of the city of Tanis gone crazy with joy."

" Remembrance whispers, Neit-akrit, that I have plighted my troth, and that if I stay beside thee and chase remembrance away, I break the pledge which I gave to another."

" Nay! the heralds of dawn have not yet sounded the trumpets. Osiris is still well hidden behind the hills, and my nosegay is not ready. I have no tuberose which means passion, and no white pansy which means forgetfulness."

" It is not in thy power, Neit-akrit, to put white pansy into thy bunch, and I . . ."

" And thou? "

" I would not put them there if I could."

" Then, thou hast no wish to forget? "

" Rosemary, which is for remembrance, will be my most cherished flower. Give me that one, Neit-akrit, out of the bunch . . . touch it once with thy lips and then let the poor fool go his way."

Ill, paralysed, numbed as I was, all my hopes tended towards the beautiful girl who alone could keep Hugh away from the terrible danger. I longed to give her courage to tell Hugh all, yet feared every moment that she would, and that he would not believe, that his loyalty to his bride should not allow him to listen to terrible accusations framed against her by another woman. The moments were precious; already through the distant gate the light of dawn grew stronger and more clear.

"Nay! what is the use?" she said as she drew a step back from him; "thou dost seem to remember all that thou dost wish—thy duty, thy word; the white rosemary should not come from me."

"Sweet Neit-akrit, thou art a child," he said with almost rough earnestness. "Thou dost not understand—how couldst thou? I am a senseless fool. . . . Give me thy hands to kiss . . . place them both upon my mouth . . . for I dare not take them in mine . . . lest their touch should indeed make me forget . . ."

Quietly she pulled out from out the canopy of flowers a bunch of white pansies, and stretching out both her hands up to him she murmured—

"White pansies for forgetfulness!"

He had fallen on his knees, and his arms encircled her dainty figure. She turned towards the statue of the goddess as if to beg of the cold, immovable image inspiration and perhaps strength. Aye! she needed all her woman's wits; there were a hundred unseen enemies to fight, and one whom she feared more than any—the other woman to whom he had plighted his troth. I suppose she found it hard to say to him, "Beware, that woman has murdered her son; she even now has planned thy ruin." Supposing his loyalty forbade him to listen! Her accusations to him might sound like the words of a woman mad with jealousy . . . and she thought that she could not prove them; she did not know I, too, had seen and heard, that I was here, close by, a caged and useless log, a dumb beast, whilst twenty priests—a hundred, if need be—were ready to swear that she lied.

And I was helpless—a caged, helpless, dumb creature—and the minutes were speeding so fast.

Suddenly from afar the sacred heralds of Osiris rang out upon their golden trumpets the announcement of the sun-god's approach.

In a moment Hugh had sprung to his feet, but Neit-akrit now would not let him go; she clung to his garments, dragged at his cloak.

"Thou must not go," she entreated. "The temple is dark and lonely—I am frightened; for pity's sake do not leave me!"

"Nay, sweet! thou art safe enough here . . . for the love of heaven take thy dear hands from off my cloak!"

"Thou wilt not leave me?"

"I must go, sweet. Remember I have sworn! wouldst make a coward of me? . . . Nay! thou hast all but succeeded . . . be satisfied and let me go!"

She took her hands from off his cloak, but came up close to him and whispered—

"See! I do not hold thee, and yet thou wilt not go . . . thou art free! and yet thou wilt stay . . . thou hast smelt the perfume of the white pansy, and thou wilt forget all . . . save that thou dost love me. . . ."

"Neit-akrit!"

"Nay! thou dost entreat in vain. . . . Sweet, I would not have thee go! What is duty? what is the meaning of oath or pledge? Wouldst know why I came to-night? . . . I came because I knew that danger doth await thee outside this sacred temple. . . . I came because I knew that thou dost love me . . . and I trusted that that love would make thee forget the dawn, thy duty, thy pledged word, forget all, in order to remain beside Neit-akrit."

"Forget? Aye! I have forgotten but too long already. Neit-akrit, thou speakest of danger; to me there is but one, and that is that I might forget all—my manhood, my honour, my pledge, my word, might forget thy innocence, and remember only that thou art fair."

"But that is all I would have thee remember," she whispered so softly that her voice hardly sounded above the murmur of the flower, which some stray current of air began gently to fan. "If I am fair it is because Isis hath made me so in order that *thou* shouldst love me! I am young, and I have waited for thee all these years because, although I knew it not, I wished that my beauty should gladden *thine* eyes. Nay! at first I longed for thy love out of sheer pride and revenge. Dost remember the iridescent scarabaeus, which should have guarded thee from the peril of giving thy love to Neit-akrit? Sweet! 'twas I stole the scarabaeus. I would not have thee turn coldly from me; thou hadst taken from me my crown and my throne; I wished to steal thy heart from thee, and then to break it in wanton cruelty, and I threw the charmed scarabaeus into the lake. . . . Then thou didst speak to me . . . I looked into thine eyes . . . I knew thy soul was mine . . . but . . . I guessed even then, my sweet, that Isis had made me doubly fair, had placed radiance over my body and my soul, for that day I learnt . . . that I loved thee!"

"Neit-akrit, for pity's sake," he pleaded.

But her arms were round his neck, her sweet face quite close to his, her eyes looked ardently into his own.

"I love thee!" she whispered.

"Wouldst make me mad, Neit-akrit?"

"I love thee!"

And far, very far away, the sacred heralds of Osiris rang out upon their golden trumpets the announcement that the sun-god was emerging behind the hills of Kamt, which hid the valley of death.

"I love thee, oh thou who art Beloved of all the gods!"

Hugh had clasped her in his arms, and as I closed my burning eyes and fell back fainting in my prison, I knew that he was safe, that Neit-akrit had succeeded in making him forget.

CHAPTER XXVII

THE THREAT

SHUFFLING footsteps, muffled whispers and hard breathing were the first sounds which greeted my dulled senses, when once again I woke from one of those strange and fitful sleeps in which the mysterious poison held me periodically enthralled.

Through the marble tracery brilliant daylight came peeping

in, making the sanctuary lamps appear pale and ghostlike. My head felt less heavy, and my eyes were less painful. It seemed to me that the shuffling steps drew nearer, and as they approached, the whispers ceased. I was still a prisoner, but my brain was fully alert, and soon I perceived the two forms, swathed in white, had paused a moment beside the gateway.

I made an earnest appeal to all my wits, and, holding my breath, crouching against the wall, I waited. Soon a refreshing current of outer air told me that the gateway had been opened, that if I kept my wits about me, my one chance of deliverance had come.

Like the flash of a sudden instinct, the thought came to me that perhaps some one was coming to see whether the deadly narcotic had thoroughly accomplished its work? or perhaps, after all, Hugh had fallen into the awful trap, and it mattered nothing if I were prisoner or free. With my mind filled with terrible doubts and presentiments, I yet had the strength to remain perfectly still: I guessed what I ought to look like, if indeed I were still under the influence of the drug, and crouching, with my head buried between my knees, I waited.

The shuffling footsteps came quite close to me, a cold bony hand forced my head back, then allowed it to fall again; a muffled voice murmured—

"Some more?"

"Aye! perhaps, for safety," replied another.

This was the crucial moment. Weak as I was, another whiff of the poison would perhaps render me helpless for ever. I heard a click like the opening of a metal box, which then was placed on the floor close beside me. I had been a good diver and swimmer once. I could hold my breath for a good sixty seconds, and already the shuffling footsteps were hastily retreating away from the poisoned atmosphere. I crawled upon the floor, flat as a serpent; I had need of my breath now—and the stupefying odour reached my nostrils in one terrible whiff. The white-robed figures were in the doorway: my deadly peril gave me one last flicker of strength: with a sudden movement I stretched out my hands, and caught hold of one of the sandalled feet before me: the priest tripped and measured his length upon the floor, at the very moment that I was trying the same schoolboy trick upon his companion. Whilst, stunned and bruised, they sprawled upon the ground, and frightened by the sudden shock, tried to struggle to their feet, I had crept past them out by the marble gateway. The fresh air from without put renewed strength into me, whilst my enemies were probably tasting the noisome odour, with which they had sought to render my sleep an eternal one.

My knees shook under me and I felt hideously sick and stiff; but I struggled on from pillar to pillar, skirting the gigantic temple which had never seemed so vast to me. I wished to reach the further gateway, find Hugh if he was still there . . . if not . . . well! if he had gone, I would still find him, somehow, now that I was free.

The great gateway was open—exhausted I leaned against it: my legs would carry me no further.

"Girlie!" I gasped.

He must have been standing quite close to the entrance, for he heard me, and the next moment, had half dragged, half carried me within the temple and laid me down on the floor, with my head resting against his shoulder.

"Mark! in heaven's name, what is the matter?"

"Nothing is the matter now," I said, as audibly as I could, "now that I have found you and that you are safe."

"What in the world do you mean? You can hardly talk! you are ill! Let me take you to the pavilion. . . . I can look after you there and you can try to tell me. . . ."

I shook my head vigorously.

"No, Girlie! the moments are precious. . . . I have been drugged, stupefied and caged up, so that I might not get to you, and tell you. Listen, Girlie . . ."

And as best I could, in jerky half-choked sentences, I told him all. He listened without a word, then said quietly—

"Ur-tasen shall pay for this. She came, Mark . . . you knew it; saw her perhaps . . . she put her arms round me, and kept me a prisoner. . . . A little while ago she slipped away . . . and left me alone with my dream."

" Ur-tasen will not rest content in the midst of failure," I said. " Pray to God he does not play us some terribly cruel trick yet."

" Dost speak words of wisdom to thy friend, oh! wisest of counsellors," said a loud sarcastic voice close behind us, " or dost adjure him to pray to his God, to watch protectingly over his head? Whatever else thou sayest, tell him one thing, in that language which comes from beyond the valley of death, and that is, that Ur-tasen will not rest content in the midst of a failure. In the language which *he* speaks there is no such word as fail."

Hugh had jumped to his feet, and confronted the high-priest of Ra, who from some remote corner of the temple had crept noiselessly close to us.

" What dost thou mean? Why art thou here?" demanded Hugh. " Art bold indeed, Ur-tasen, that thou darest stand before me and my wrath."

" Bold indeed, oh! son of Ra!" replied the high-priest, making a mock obeisance. " Ur-tasen now hath no cause for fear . . . he is an old man, and thy hands are mighty and strong, and yet the old man, with one foot in the grave, hath struck a blow at thee which will crush thy life, and wither thy manhood, and throw thee, a weak and puling coward, at the foot of him whose power thou hast defied."

" What dost thou mean? Speak! Thou hast not many moments of peace before thee, for I will make thee answer for thy treachery against my friend."

" Aye! I am willing to bear the full brunt of thy wrath, oh! stranger who hailest from the foot of the throne of Osiris. . . . Thy counsellor hath no doubt told thee that I and Maat-kha did plot against thee. He says so, and thou dost believe. . . . I care not to deny; we failed, she and I . . . and whatever crime she hath committed she must atone for, according to the laws of the land. But thinkest thou perchance that Ur-tasen did rest content? didst think that a weak and passionate woman could throw herself across his plans? Fools were ye both! oh! thou who dost style thyself the son of Ra, and she . . . who once was called Princess of Kamt."

"Name her not, thou infamous priest," said Hugh, raising his hand, as if ready to strike the miscreant; "I forbid thee to speak her name!"

But Ur-tasen shrugged his shoulders, with a low sarcastic chuckle.

"Nay! I will not name her, since it rouses thine anger; but, anon it will not only be I, but all Tanis who will shriek out her name in loathing and execration."

I had struggled to my feet and was clinging with all my might to Hugh, for I could see that he could scarcely restrain himself from strangling the old man, then and there. But I felt that at any cost we ought to know what nefarious schemes he had concocted, and my heart filled with awful forebodings, I whispered to Hugh—

"Girlie! . . . for her sake . . . find out first what he means. Then, I will help you to murder him, if you like."

"Doth thy counsellor whisper prudent advice in thine ear, oh! Beloved of the gods? Nay, then! do thou follow it. Thou wilt need to be calm . . . if thou canst. Thou hast played a losing game, oh! son of Ra, and now, wilt find that it was not good to defy the might of the priests of Kamt. I could not destroy thee and thy fame, the evil power of Set protects thee; I know not, perhaps thy body is invulnerable . . . thou art strong, and the people love thee. A hundred priests are at my command, yet not one of them would dare to lay hands on thee. But thou hast a soul, oh! mighty son of Ra! a soul which I—thine enemy, have known how to torture, with a torture so exquisite that anon it will unman thee. Thy soul," he added, with a loud triumphant laugh, which sounded weird and demoniacal, as it went echoing through the vastness of the temple, "thou didst give it to one who was beautiful and great, and praised above all. Dost know where she is now, oh! Beloved of the gods? A prisoner in the hands of the priests of Isis, who seized her, even within the precincts of the temple of the goddess, while thy kisses were still warm upon her lips."

"Thou liest," hissed Hugh with smothered rage. And he raised his hand and struck the evil-mouthed priest an ugly blow upon the face, so that a few drops of blood began to trickle down his gaunt cheeks.

"Thou liest!"

"Nay! Thou knowest well that I do not lie," replied Ur-tasen, who literally had not turned a hair under the terrible insult. "The priests of Isis had noticed the women of Princess Neit-akrit standing about outside the temple at dawn. They warned me and I ordered them to watch. Osiris had not made a long journey in the heavens when from out the gates of the sacred edifice they saw a woman glide. The priests of Isis waited . . . she parted from her lover at the gate. . . . They saw it all . . . the laws of Kamt are severe upon the sin of unchastity, and a sin committed within the temple is doubly heinous . . . that woman was Neit-akrit, Princess of Kamt. Before her women could reach her, she was a prisoner, and now awaits her doom, for the crime she hath committed."

But like a madman Hugh was upon him, and his powerful hands had clutched the old priest by the throat.

"Man, thou art bold indeed," he whispered in his ear, "to stand with such a tale before me and my wrath! Dost know that if that tale is true, that if thou or thy priests do harm but to one hair of Princess Neit-akrit's head, I will kill thee, even where thou dost stand."

Ur-tasen made not a movement, only his eyes started out of their sockets, and his lips parted, for the grip round his throat must have been very tight. At last he began in a choked voice which gradually grew stronger and firmer as Hugh relaxed his hold.

"Kill, oh! son of Ra! . . . Kill! if it is thy will! Dost think I would make the faintest struggle? or call my priests to my aid? There are a hundred well within my call, and yet, see! I do not even raise my voice. Kill me! Aye! how gladly would I die, knowing that my death had at last encompassed thy ruin, after I had succeeded in wrecking thy soul. Ay, I think we are quits, oh, Beloved of the gods, who with thy mighty hand didst break the wand of office of the high-priest of Ra. In exchange for that wand I have broken thy heart, and I will die happy, knowing that that which thou lovest best in all the world will become more abject, more pitiable than Kesh-ta, the slave, whom thou didst snatch from out the clutches of the inexorable justice of Kamt. . . . Nay, why dost thou hesitate? In the name of Ra, thy sire, and Osiris, whose Beloved thou art, strike, oh, emissary of the gods! strike! and with the blow which sheds the blood of the high-priest even within the temple which it will desecrate, perhaps the people of Kamt and the priests of their gods will waken from the spell which thou hast cast over them with thy magic. Strike! for beyond that one act of brutish force, thou art powerless! Neit-akrit is a prisoner in the hands of the priests of Kamt. Hidden from all eyes, none can know where she is. Her sin, in this land, is not judged in open court, nor doth any one hear judgment pronounced upon her. . . . But, to-morrow, a being—blind, maimed, bruised, who once was the fairest in ancient Kamt, will beg in the streets of Tanis for the charity of the passer-by, and scornful fingers will point pityingly at her and say, ''Tis Neit-akrit, once Princess of Kamt, who sinned even within the temple of the goddess!' Ay, thou mayest strike, oh, Beloved of the gods, for within the grave where my body will quietly await the return of my soul, there will be joy and happiness in the thought that thou, mighty as thou art, Beloved of the gods and worshipped of all Kamt, canst do nothing to save her from that doom."

Gradually Hugh's hands had dropped from off the priest's throat. I could see that all his furious rage was outwardly gone; he was as pale as death, only his eyes glowed with a weird fire, and his arms were crossed tightly over his chest.

He waited with seeming patience until the high-priest had finished speaking, then he said very calmly—

"And didst thou really think, oh, mighty priest of Ra, that events would shape themselves, even as thou hadst cunningly devised? Didst really think to find it so easy to pit thy power against mine, and remain the conqueror? Truly, I pity thee! thee and thy blind folly. Thou comest here before me, calm and triumphant, to tell me that she whom I worship is a prisoner in thy hands; that she, who to me is akin to a divinity, is to be vilified and slandered by impious priests, is to be disgraced, nay, worse, tortured, and then calmly dost say that *I* can do nothing to save her from her doom. *I*, the stranger who did break the impassable barriers which since five thousand years have hidden the secrets of Kamt, *I* can do nothing to save my most cherished treasure? Well, perhaps not! perhaps, fearing that some terrible doom might overtake thee, before thou hadst time to accomplish thy criminal resolve, thou hast already dared to lay hands on my divinity! Then, indeed, thou art right. Even *I* cannot undo the past, I cannot save her from her doom! But hast thought of afterwards, oh, mighty priest of Ra?"

"Afterwards?" he asked, with a quiet shrug of the shoulders.

"Ay! Afterwards! Didst think, perchance, that, having in my wrath sent thee and thy vile body, broken into a thousand atoms, into the darkest corner of the valley of death, I would suffer the extreme penalty of the laws of Kamt, and give thy wandering soul the happiness of seeing my shrivelled body withering by starvation, and rotting beneath the claws of the vultures in the desert? or didst think that, shuddering from a crime, I would wander about the cities of Kamt, a broken-hearted and miserable coward? Hast forgotten who and what I am, oh, mighty priest of Ra, when thou didst think *I* would ask aught of *thee?* Hast forgotten that I hold the hearts of Kamt and of its priests in the palm of my hand, and its allegiance at my feet; that from the inaccessible heights of my throne, built upon the love or superstition of the people, I do not ask, but I *command* thee never to dare lay one of thy fingers upon the person of Princess Neit-akrit, not to allow one breath of slander to touch the purity of her name; and if thou, in thy presumption, shouldst perchance dream of disobeying my commands, shouldst think that within the hallowed precincts of thy temples thou canst defy me, then, for the first and last time, Ur-tasen, I bid thee beware! for not upon thy puny body alone will fall the weight of my wrath, not my hand alone shall descend upon thy enfeebled shoulders, but my voice, which now maketh Kamt half-mad with joy, will then be raised to kindle into its people thoughts of evil and of blood; the spell of my magic will hover over their heads, whispering of murder, of incest and of sacrilege; a mist of blood will swim before their eyes, and from Tanis to Net-amen, from Men-ne-fer to Khe-me-nu, I, as the new prophet of evil, will carry before me the burning torch of a bloody revolution. And, ye who are mighty, ye who are rich, and, above all, ye who deem yourselves sacred, pale and tremble! for I will speak unto the people who follow me of desecration and of sacrilege! Ay, even I, who but yesterday spoke of mercy and of justice! And the people of Kamt will follow me, Ur-tasen," he added, as, drawing himself up to his full height, he seemed already to tower above the terror-stricken man as some inspired prophet of evil. "Man is ever ready to listen to the voice which would beckon him back to his original level of savage beast. They will follow me, and become mad with fury, thirsting for carnage, for murder and for bloodshed; they will hurl the rulers from their thrones, destroy their temples and desecrate their tombs! And thou, Ur-tasen, who art the embodiment of that priesthood which hath kept the people of Kamt in superstitious ignorance, against thee and thy priests will the scorn, the loathing, the outrage tend. Buffeted and scorned, thou wilt stand at the very foot of the throne of thy god, as within a pillory of shame; men, women and children will howl and hoot at thee, will point to thee with scornful fingers still reeking with blood, and thou wilt see in that land which thou hadst hoped to rule, man murder his brother, woman her child, child its parent; thou wilt see rape and theft and sacrilege rife, thou wilt see famine and pestilence. And when every foot of the land of wheat and barley hath been polluted by crime, and every temple been desecrated, when the people of Kamt have sunk to the level of the wild beast, then, at a final word from me, they will, with superhuman effort, wage war against Nature herself, and tear down bit by bit every shred of that barrier which thou and thy priests did build around their land; they will tear down palaces and temples, hurl down marble pillars and alabaster steps, set fire to the four corners of the mighty kingdom, till stone does not remain upon stone, and in one vast and burning ruin bury at last their rulers and their priests, their glorious history and their ignoble shame."

Superstition and terror had gripped the high-priest by the

throat more firmly than Hugh's fingers had done before. He grew gradually more livid and more pale; his lips, from which a few drops of blood still slowly trickled, began to twitch and tremble, and once or twice he stretched out his arms towards Hugh as if appealing for mercy.

Hugh was playing a bold game. The woman he loved was in a terrible plight, and his hold upon the people of this land was entirely one of superstition and mysticism. It seemed to me as if from the distance, in the temple, I could hear terrified groans, and I thought that I saw white and ghostlike shadows rush frightened hither and thither.

Hugh had finished speaking, and still the powerful echo of his voice lingered amongst the pillars: the high-priest had buried his face in his hands. He was silent for a while, struggling against his own fears, then we heard his voice, hoarse and trembling, whisper softly—

"Who and what art thou?"

"One who has but one word, one pledge," replied Hugh; "who never speaks but of that which he can accomplish."

"Thou art the soul of Set, the power of evil, descended upon earth to bring sorrow in thy trail."

"I brought joy and happiness when I came; upon thy head rest the burden of desolation and of sorrow."

"I have not sinned," he said, almost in entreaty; "Neit-akrit is still safe . . . a precious hostage in my hands," he added, noting Hugh's sudden look of infinite relief, "that which thou dost hold most dear, and yet hast overwhelmed with sorrow."

"Name her not, Ur-tasen," interrupted Hugh, "she is as pure and holy as the goddess whose image thou dost worship."

"Nay, I had no evil thoughts of her," replied Ur-tasen, quite humbly; "I was speaking of sorrow; thou canst not command so intangible a thing to keep clear of her path. Thou hast sworn to wed Maat-kha: as long as she lives, thy love for another can but give sorrow and shame. And Maat-kha will live! None saw her do the evil deed save thy counsellor! . . . will *he* accuse her before the awful judgment-seat of Kamt?

"Thou hast conquered, oh, Beloved of the gods," added the

high-priest, with sudden strange eagerness. "See! I, who had defied thee and thy might, am the humblest of thy slaves; and yet, mighty as thou art, thou canst not, whilst thou art in the land of Kamt, change thy destiny and hers! Thou art wedded to a murderess, and Neit-akrit cannot sit upon the throne of Kamt. For thoughts of thee she will not wed another; sorrowing she will turn to the gods for comfort, and seek refuge against a guilty love in the vows of a priestess of Ra. Nay! . . . What canst thou do? . . . thou art mighty! . . . but it will only be when all the gods of Kamt are dethroned, and all their temples desecrated, that thou canst break the bonds which bind thee to Maat-kha, or place in Neit-akrit's hand the sceptre of a queen."

The high-priest paused again, and once more his keen eyes searched those of Hugh. We held one another tightly grasped by the hand: I think we both felt that we were nearing the final crisis in our strange and weird adventure.

"Thou art mighty, oh, Beloved of the gods," whispered Ur-tasen, so low that we could scarcely hear; "thou art great, and the people of Kamt do worship thee . . . and I, the most powerful in the land, more powerful than any Pharaoh—for I rule over the dead as well as over the living—I do grovel at thy feet. Call forth the people of Kamt! . . . let them come in hundreds and in thousands, and in tens of thousands! let them come to Men-ne-fer . . . to see the high-priest of Ra kneeling humbly before the emissary of the gods, and with his hands tying the sandals upon the stranger's feet. . . .

"It is a great and glorious festival," he added with growing eagerness, seeing that Hugh and I had, in a flash, realised what was passing in his mind. "The most exquisite products of the land will decorate the temple of the god. . . . In the middle of the sanctuary, upon a throne of gold, surrounded by the priests of Ra, there will stand he who is Beloved of the gods . . . the festival shall be great and glorious, but sorrow will be in the hearts of all the people of Kamt . . . for the son of Ra, the emissary of the Most High . . . will return to the heavenly land . . . from whence he came."

Hugh did not speak; in his eyes I read the awakening of a great hope—an infinite peace and relief; he had guessed that the high-priest, terrified and humbled, was, of his own accord, begging for that which Hugh even would never have had the power to force him to grant.

"But in the hearts of the people of Kamt," added Ur-tasen, finally, "there will for ever dwell the memory of him who first in the judgment-hall of Men-ne-fer spoke to them of mercy and of truth; and at even, when Isis is high in the heavens, and ties of home and love bring men and women together, they will talk of him, who was Beloved of the gods, who left the land, beyond the blue vault of heaven, to dwell for a while upon Kamt. Then Maat-kha, twice a widow, will weep shuddering over her sin, and Neit-akrit, Queen of Upper and Lower Kamt, will dispense truth and justice to her people, while dwelling on the fond memory as upon a happy dream—the memory to which will be attached neither sorrow nor shame."

He had sunk down upon his knees—a humble, cringing suppliant, and his shaven crown rested upon the floor, at Hugh's feet, which he was kissing like any abject slave.

"Mark, old fellow, this is happy deliverance, is it not?"

"Do you wish to go, Girlie?" I asked.

"How can I stay? This man has said it truly, I am wedded to Maat-kha; my love can only bring sorrow on her whom I worship, shame perhaps . . . and I . . ." he added with a sigh, "I could not live now here, without her, while I am a prisoner in this land. . . . When I am gone . . . I think . . . we should both forget."

"Listen, Ur-tasen," he said after a little while, "I still have much to say to thee. See that the Princess, whom thou hast outraged, is respectfully conveyed to her palace. The priests who have dared to lay hands upon her must grovel humbly at her feet until she hath deigned to forgive; if she chooses to mete out a punishment to them, then see that it is carried out, whatever it may be. . . . When that is done, do thou go back to Men-ne-fer . . . I and my counsellor will follow later on. . . . Within thy temple I will speak to thee again."

"Then . . . thou dost consent, oh, Beloved of the gods?" whispered Ur-tasen, without daring to look up.

"Nay, I know not! Remember . . . I make no compact. . . . I cannot say. . . . But I fain would see what reparation thou canst offer to Princess Neit-akrit, and I must speak with my counsellor."

"Wilt deign to allow the servants of the temple to accompany thee to the palace? The Pharaoh is dead . . . Maat-kha is Queen, and thou art the holy Pharaoh, since thou art her lord."

"Nay, I would be alone with my counsellor. Go, Ur-tasen! 'Twere best that thou who wast witness to her crime shouldst tell Maat-kha that I know all."

"I am ever ready to obey thy commands, oh, Beloved of the gods, and in all Kamt thou dost not own a more humble slave than Ur-tasen, the high-priest of the Most High."

Painfully he struggled to his feet: he seemed a broken-down old man now. When, after another deep obeisance, he turned to go, we remarked that he did no longer walk erect, that his humiliation had bent his tall figure, and placed the full weight of his years upon his shoulders.

CHAPTER XXVIII

THE DEPARTURE FROM TANIS

THAT same afternoon we left for Men-ne-fer. Tanis perforce had to put aside her bridal finery and plunge herself into mourning. All day the scribes of the temple ran up and down the streets, shouting at the top of their voices that the holy Pharaoh was dead; that he had succumbed to his many ailments, in the arms of the priests of Isis, who had helped to soothe his dying moments. His mother, broken down with grief, could not be persuaded to leave his lifeless body, and would remain in Tanis until such time as, the elaborate process of embalming being completed, the dead Pharaoh would be ready to be conveyed to Men-ne-fer, for the solemn obsequies.

Hugh had tacitly allowed this version of the Pharaoh's death to be spread among the people. He had no wish to publicly accuse her who already was his wife in name, and hand her over to the cruel justice of her country. No doubt she suffered enough. Hugh would not see her, and she had been told that he knew of her crime.

When, having taken farewell of lovely Tanis, our boat began to glide slowly along the canal, it seemed to both of us that on the height where stood the royal palace we saw a figure swathed in black, sharply defined against the white background, stretching out its arms entreatingly towards our fast disappearing boat.

Tanis in sorrow had not dared to speed our departure with shouts of farewell, nor did the snow-white city, coquettish in her perpetual bridal attire, know that the son of Ra was leaving her never to return.

Hugh had not hesitated a moment. He longed to get away, and I confess that I viewed the prospect of leaving this strange exotic land for ever without the slightest pang.

" We will make our own terms with Ur-tasen," said Hugh; " and I promise you our return journey will not be attended with any privations."

" You are glad to go ? " I asked.

" Very glad," he replied earnestly. " She will be happy . . . and we shall both forget."

As long as we could, we watched the white city gradually growing more hazy and dim, until at last a turn in the canal, a thick clump of papyrus grass hid it entirely from our view; even then it seemed to me that the echo from sistrum and harp, the strange songs of the priestesses of Isis hovered for some time in the air.

The journey from Tanis to Men-ne-fer direct was a long one. We spent two nights beneath the canopy of our boat, lulled to sleep by the rhythmic clap of the oars and the monotonous lullabies sung by the boatmen. The third night we passed before the palace of Neit-akrit.

There was no moon, and it was very dark all around; the marble palace hardly appeared as an outline against the heavy sky, only the gigantic Sphinxes seemed to frown down upon us in the gloom. A warm breeze was in the air, and as the boat glided swiftly past the great fuchsia trees gave forth a long and melancholy sigh. We neither of us spoke; but by the dim light of the lamp at the poop I could see that, for a long time, Hugh watched that ghostlike palace, those fuchsia trees, those snow-white walls, within which he had buried his earthly paradise.

We neared Men-ne-fer towards the early morning and, after a rest in the palace, we went to meet Ur-tasen in the temple of Ra.

He looked to me very much aged, and anxiety had traced many more lines on his face. He met Hugh very eagerly, but knelt humbly on the floor, waiting for him to speak.

"Where is Princess Neit-akrit?" asked Hugh.

"To-night her boat will have reached her palace, where she has decided to remian until the obsequies of the dead Pharaoh, when she will come to Men-ne-fer," replied the high-priest, humbly, and almost in a whisper.

"And those priests who dared lay hands upon her person?"

"They await her pardon in the vault beneath the temple of Isis. But I do not doubt that Neit-akrit will grant it."

Hugh breathed a sigh of relief. There was no doubt that Ur-tasen had not even thought of defiance; moreover, we gathered from this that, though he feared and hated the Beloved of the gods, he did not distrust him.

"What dost thou know of the land which lies beyond the gates of Kamt?" asked Hugh, abruptly, after a slight pause, during which he had scanned with a scornful frown the figure of the high-priest kneeling at his feet.

"Nay, I know nothing, oh, Beloved of the gods. I care not to know, whatever in my dreams I may at times have guessed. Never hath foot of man crossed the valley of death and lived."

"Yet I came. Dost know from whence?"

"Thou saidst it: from the foot of the throne of the gods."

"Ay. And thither will I return, taking with me the hearts of the people of Kamt. Now listen to my commands, and 'twere well for thee that thou seest that they are implicitly obeyed. From among thy priests choose those whom thou wouldst trust, as thou dost trust thyself, who, like thee, know that beyond the valley of death there lies some other land, and do thou tell them that I would visit it. Then bid them secure eight sturdy oxen and two light but roomy carts, to each of which four oxen should be yoked. These beasts and carts must be lowered through the gate of Kamt into the valley of death. The priests whom thou wilt have chosen as being silent and discreet shall load the carts. In one they shall place sixty gourds, each containing two measures of water, and two gourds, each containing three measures of wine; two sacks of dried dates and figs, and five jars of dried fish and goose's flesh; the other cart must be heaped with oil cakes, barley and dried grass, in as great a quantity as the four oxen can bear quite easily. When the carts are ready and loaded and the oxen put to, bid thy priests choose a healthy cow and tether her to one of the carts. At dawn thou shalt accompany me and my counseller to the gates of Kamt, and thou shalt cause thyself to be lowered into the valley of death, before I myself do follow thee. Thou shalt come with me across the wilderness as far as the Rock of Anubis, against which, if thou hast in any way disobeyed me, or played me false, I will chain thee and bind thee, and leave thee to starve slowly amidst the carrion. But, if thou hast punctually obeyed my commands, thou canst then return : thy priests, in the meanwhile, can keep a watch for thee."

The high-priest made no comment, but merely asked quietly—

"Are these all thy commands, oh, Beloved of the gods?"

"All, as regards my journey hence. Before I leave thou shalt proclaim from the foot of the altar of thy god that I, their emissary, have returned from whence I came, that my mission among the people of Kamt is fulfilled, for I came by the will of Ra himself to infuse mercy into their laws. No man or woman shall in future be cast out living from Kamt, to die of starvation in the wilderness; no man or woman shall, for any sin or crime, suffer torture or mutilation. This thou shalt proclaim from the inner sanctuary of Ra, even while I, ready to go upon my journey, will listen from the outer precincts, which lead to the gates of Kamt, and hear that thou dost do my bidding. Then, when thou hast done that, thou shalt tell the people that I enjoin them, as a parting wish, to honour and reverence Neit-akrit, their Queen, whom Ra himself, by my mouth, hath decreed shall rule over them as long as she lives, whether she take a husband or no. She shall be the sole and mighty Pharaoh, and on her head alone shall rest the double crown of Kamt."

Ur-tasen's face brightened up. It was obvious that Hugh need have no fear that this parting injunction of his should not be implicitly obeyed. The high-priest of Ra, in spite of all, was still under the magic spell of beautiful Neit-akrit.

There was nothing more to be said, and we left the temple of Ra to have a final look at the land which we had found so fair.

I was glad to leave it; the gilded cage had somehow become an intolerable prison, but . . . it was a parting, and all partings are sad. The people of Men-ne-fer did not know that their idol was leaving them; though the death of the Pharaoh had thrown outward gloom over the city, they made no attempt to restrain their enthusiasm, their delight in having him in their midst again, who was Beloved of the gods.

The picture of that day in Kamt is one of the most vivid in my memory. The sun was dazzlingly bright, and Men-ne-fer —gorgeous Men-ne-fer with its rose-tinted palaces, its temples and gardens and market squares—displayed before our saddened eyes all the splendours of its beauty. The royal palace, on the steps of which the pale pink flamingoes stalked lazily in the heat of the mid-day sun, the broad canal, each side of which the marble palaces rose in a gorgeous line, the market, where gigantic piles of pomegranates threw a brilliant note of vivid orange and red against the blue and the green of water and foliage, and above all the silent and immense judgment-hall, with its great marble throne, from whence it seemed to me that I could still hear the harsh, sarcastic laughter of the dead Pharaoh and the screeching of his apes.

Once or twice during that day I saw Hugh's eyes turned with unutterable longing towards the East, beyond the great canal where, in the midst of fuchsia groves, stood that white palace, the terrace with its turquoise blue canopy and its marble floors, on which Sen-tur lazily chased the ibis up and down.

He had made up his mind that he would not see her again. . . . The parting perhaps would be easier to bear. . . . There was no doubt that it was all for the best. . . . She would be happy again when she knew that he had gone away for ever into the land of dreams.

CHAPTER XXIX

ROSEMARY FOR REMEMBRANCE

One more picture—the last—in the gorgeous panorama which had so uninterruptedly passed before our eyes ever since we had as it were taken possession of this beautiful land—the picture of Kamt in mourning, bidding farewell to him who was Beloved of the gods.

Hugh had made hard conditions with the high-priest of Ra. He had demanded beasts, provisions for the journey across the desert, and Ur-tasen's own person as hostage for his good faith. The high-priest, humbly, without question, had agreed to all, and now two days later at even, while we, wrapped in our dark mantles ready for our great homeward journey across the desert, stood behind that heavy black curtain on the very spot at the rear of the sanctuary of Ra, from whence we had first caught a glimpse of the glories of Kamt, Ur-tasen prepared himself to obey Hugh's final commands.

The oxen had been chosen, we had inspected the carts and provisions, all of which stood ready in the vast corridors which led to the great copper gate, and now, from where we stood, we watched the high-priest as he went up to the mighty gong, and taking the clapper, beat the metal, so that its volume of sound went echoing far beyond the gateway of the temple. Thrice he struck the gong, then there was silence in the sacred edifice; but only for a while, for, very soon, from the city which was preparing for its evening rest, after the toil of day, sounds of fast-approaching footsteps, of hurried whispers, penetrated to our ears. The people of Men-ne-fer heard the summons which bade them come to the temple of Ra, and obedient, half-frightened, lest they were being called to hear some tidings of evil, they hurriedly left their homes and flocked to the sanctuary of the god.

Ur-tasen had withdrawn to the foot of the statue of Ra; there he waited until the vast edifice was full of people; the lights glimmered low, only bringing out here and there into brilliant relief some blue or green iridescent enamel upon a pillar. Men, women, and children were lying prostrate upon the floor waiting for the high-priest to speak. The gossamer veil had been drawn aside so that all might look upon the majesty of the god, and at the foot of the sanctuary steps the blind priestesses intoned their monotonous, lugubrious chant.

Then, when from end to end the gigantic building was filled with prostrate figures, Ur-tasen began to speak—

"Oh, people of Kamt, behold the majesty of the gods!

"They who have filled you hearts with joy, have now shed sorrow upon the land!

"Thou art mighty, oh, Ra, and mighty is thy son!

"Thou art great Osiris, and great is thy beloved!

"Oh, people of Kamt, look upwards to the vault of heaven, and there, amidst the innumerable lamps, which the hand of Phtah doth kindle in the skies, seek for the face of him who was the emissary of the gods!

"People of Kamt, look upwards to the skies! and at night, when Isis doth shine, pure and bounty-giving from above, then remember him who is Beloved of the gods!

"Oh, people of Kamt, look within your hearts, for there alone shall in future dwell the image of him who is the son of Ra!"

Awestruck, not understanding, one by one, the dark heads were raised aloft, and thousands of anxious eyes peered upwards in the gloom.

"Oh, people of Kamt, do not mourn! He who is Beloved of the gods hath dwelt amidst you all! He gave you joy and happiness, he spoke to you of mercy and of love! but the gods up above have need of him, they called to him, and he hath gone!"

There was a long and universal shriek: the sorrow and disappointment it expressed was quite unmistakable. I felt strangely impressed and sad, as if I were assisting at my own funeral. Hugh's face too was white and set. It is hard to leave those who love one dearly, hard to go in the very summit of one's popularity.

The high-priest had waited for a while, until the demonstration of sorrow had somewhat subsided, then he added—

"Oh, people of Kamt! the Beloved of the gods has gone!

"Remember, his spirit still hovers round you!

" Remember the joy he gave you and obey his behests.

" Before he left, he spoke his wishes to me, the humble servant of Ra, our god, his sire, and bade me transmit these wishes unto you, his people. He, as your ruler and your king, has appointed as his successor upon the throne, Neit-akrit, the well-beloved of the house of Usem-ra, and he hath ordained that since Maat-kha, now twice a widow, hath decided to vow herself to the service of Ra, that you do obey Neit-akrit as you would himself. She will rule over you, she, the holy Pharaoh, entrusted by him with the fullest powers, and on her head alone shall rest the double crown of Kamt, which I, the high-priest of the Most High, all-creating Ra, will place upon her brow."

Ur-tasen had done his duty. Hugh could rest satisfied. Neit-akrit would be Queen indeed, and after the proclamation issued at the very foot of their most cherished god, the people of Kamt would truly reverence and honour her.

After this Ur-tasen read a short proclamation embodying the other promises he had made to Hugh; the abolition of the " casting out " form of punishment, the complete cessation of all description of mutilation. The blind priestesses began to sing again, and from the four corners of the temple clouds of incense rose : the priests of Ra had crowded round the steps of the sanctuary; they were offering up a final sacrifice in honour of him who had gone.

Then suddenly, from amidst a distant group, one solitary figure detached itself. I did not recognise it at first, but Hugh gave a start, and then I knew who it was.

She came slowly forward, while on each side of her the people knelt, in order to kiss the ground on which she walked. I don't think that I had ever seen her look more beautiful; she was draped from below the bust, down to her ankles, in a long kalasiris of dull black, against which her ruddy tresses fell in strands of living gold, each side of her, right down to her knees. She had neither jewel nor ornament of any kind; her tiny feet were bare, as were her arms and shoulders. Beside her Sen-tur walked slowly and majestically, as if conscious of the solemnity of the sacred building. She stared straight before her, at the figure of the god; the blind priestesses were softly chanting a hymn, and she—Neit-akrit—almost as in a dream, began to mount the sanctuary steps.

Instinctively my hand grasped that of Hugh: it was cold as a piece of marble. He did not move, but watched her with a yearning look which brought the tears into my eyes.

I think that Ur-tasen had not expected to see her, and I saw him glance furtively in our direction. The group of priests parted when she came near, to allow her to pass; none dared to stop her, though the sanctuary of Ra is sacred, and no profane foot should ever stand upon its steps. But she seemed almost ethereal, as if she had left her body away somewhere, it was only the exquisite spirit of love, beauty and womanhood which stepped towards the god.

At last she reached the foot of the great marble throne—she and Sen-tur, for the panther had not left her side—her tall figure looked strangely small and childlike standing alone in the vast sanctuary, at the foot of the mammoth statue. She was very pale, and her large blue eyes looked upwards searchingly in the gloom above. Then she raised her hand, and I saw that in it she held a sprig of white rosemary; she raised it to her lips, and placed it at the foot of the god.

"Rosemary for remembrance," she whispered softly, so softly that I felt sure none behind her could hear, and as slowly, as automatically as she had come, she turned and went, the group of priests parting respectfully in order to let her pass.

And the vision of the quaint, straight figure, draped in black so like an Egyptian idol, standing as in a dream at the foot of the marble statue of the god, was the last which Hugh had of the beautiful girl whom he loved so passionately, and the word "remembrance" was the last which would for ever linger in his ear.

After that we allowed the heavy curtain to drop; we neither of us wished to look again. Let that vision be the last which we should carry away in our hearts of the beauties of ancient Kamt. Poor old Hugh, I think he suffered terribly. But he was a man of iron determination; he had decided that it was right, for her sake and his own, that he should go, and at this moment even I do not think that any temptation assailed him to change his resolution. About an hour later, Ur-tasen joined us; he preceded us up the great staircase of black granite, which was so peopled with memories of our first arrival. The sleek and poisonous guardians of the gates of Kamt were lying caged under the baskets of rush, to enable those who had charge of the preparations for our journey to pass to and fro.

How strange it was to see that great copper slab lowered from within, and to look out from the gloom of the temple precincts on to the illimitable desert beyond. Far ahead the rock of Anubis towered against the sky, and all along we could see the long road, made white by innumerable bones of the dead criminals of Kamt.

One by one, on the ponderous grapnel, oxen and carts and provisions were lowered into the desert. Three priests of Ra were already below, and were busy loading the waggons and harnessing the oxen. Then, when all was ready, they were hauled up, and Ur-tasen, without a word, allowed the belt to be slipped round his waist. The three priests stood above, placid and silent, doing their work, obeying Hugh's directions without a comment. They were to remain here, ready to re-open the gates for the returning high-priest.

I followed Ur-tasen, and finally Hugh also descended.

Everything was in order. I took charge of one team of oxen, Hugh of the other. And we started on our way.

Above us, without a sound, silently, drawn by unseen hands, the gates of Kamt were shut against us for ever.

CHAPTER XXX

THE END

BESIDE the Rock of Anubis, Ur-tasen parted from us. He had not spoken one word since we started, but here he asked if Hugh was satisfied.

"Quite satisfied," he replied.

"Then farewell, oh, son of Ra!" said the high-priest,

solemnly. He knelt down and kissed the sand of the desert, then quietly he rose and started to walk back towards the gates of Kamt. We watched his gaunt figure across the desert until a boulder hid it from our view: it looked bent with age and disappointment. I think he felt that the youthful ruler of Kamt would not place much power in his hands, and that the stranger, though absent, had conquered after all.

The journey across the desert was terribly wearisome at first, but gradually Hugh's taciturnity fled and we spent many happy hours in remembering our golden visions and looking over the many treasures which lay at the bottom of our carts. The oxen, however, stood the journey very badly; one by one they dropped upon the road, and the last six days of our voyage we did on foot, carrying as little water as we dared, and we were very close on starvation point when, late one evening, we reached the grave of the Greek priest, which faced the setting sun. We rested here that night, and weak, tired out as we were, we spent half the night in watching . . . watching an imaginary point on the horizon, which is more fair, more gorgeous and grand than aught which Western civilisation has ever dreamed of.

And now we are back at The Chestnuts, and Hugh and I are not as young as we were. Dear old Janet welcomed us, much shocked at our terrible appearance; but the day after our arrival there was no trace outwardly on either of us of the strange adventures we had just gone through. We resumed our quiet, English, bachelor life, as if the last few months had been all a dream; and at times now, when I sit beside the great log fire and watch the dying embers in the hearth, I wonder whether the vision of the ancient hordes of Egypt, the glories of Men-ne-fer and Tanis, are not all a product of my excited fancy, and, above all, I wonder whether the vision of a tall, girlish figure, whose hair is like the rays of Osiris when he sinks to rest, and whose very name breathes romance and mystery, is not one of those dreams with which the remembrance of dear old Mr. Tankerville was always wont to lull me to sleep.

Then I look up lazily from the fire in which my aching eyes

had seen vast temples and mammoth carvings, and I see close to me Sawnie Girlie sitting at his desk.

He is writing one of those learned books which have spread his fame from one corner of Europe to the other, and before him there is a tiny gold casket with a glass lid, within which lies a faded and dried sprig of rosemary.

"White rosemary for remembrance!"

THE END